Doña Gracia's Gold Pendant

Michal Aharoni Regev

Doña Gracia's Gold Pendant
Michal Aharoni Regev

Copyright © 2018 Michal Aharoni Regev

Translated by Yael Schonfeld Abel
Contact: michalregev11@gmail.com

ISBN 9781983168598

DOÑA GRACIA'S
GOLD PENDANT

Michal Aharoni Regev

Dedicated to the memory of Doña Gracia Nasi, the lady who changed the course of history.

To the ascension of the soul of Rabbi Abba, my ancestor, who died a hero's death for the sanctification of God when he refused to convert.

To the memory of my dear husband, Shmuel Regev. May he rest in peace.

To my children; Orel Yehuda and Orit, Omer and Oshrat, Shira and Avi, Daniel and Mor, and my beloved grandchildren.

To Zvika Goldberger, my life partner.

Gracia La Chica—Gracia Nasi

Lisbon

March 21, 1497
Nissan 9, 5,257 Years from Creation

Prologue

Thousands of people were gathered under the scorching sun in the stone plaza next to the Port of Lisbon, surrounded by a wall comprised of Royal Guard soldiers. Elegant ladies, merchants wearing their best finery, rabbis wrapped in their prayer shawls, hugging their Torah books, craftsmen and their wives in their humble garments, in supplication, some of them laid out in exhaustion upon their bundles and the travel chests enclosing the trappings of their lives.

Brawny farmers and women in dresses of coarse fabric came down the twisting alleys leading to the plaza, joining the peddlers from the market in the port, the fishermen and drunken seamen to huddle around them. Young men whose eyes sparked in anger crowded into the plaza. "*Judeus*," they cursed, spitting in contempt.

"Have mercy on the wretched ones!" The call of a nobleman looking down from the balcony of the municipal hall was swallowed up by the shouting of the Royal Guard soldiers, the screeching of the seagulls on the pier, the prayers rising to the heavens and the hushed weeping. A hot gust of wind carried the stench of the Tagus River.

On the searing stone tiles, a dehydrated mother sat, attempting to breastfeed her wailing infant.

"Please, a little water and a slice of bread," she begged.

A noblewoman waving an ivory fan in order to ease the heat murmured quietly, "Queen Esther, save us as you saved your people," as the tears streamed from her eyes.

"Joseph, where are you? Bring me back my son!" a father's cry tore through the bustling plaza.

"*Yea, though I walk through the valley of the shadow of death, I will fear no evil, for Thou art with me,"* the young Rabbi Zemach commenced praying.

"*Señor, por favor,* can you tell me when we can expect the ships that our king, Dom Manuel, promised would take us far from Portugal?" the head of the community addressed the commander of the Royal Guard. The commander surveyed him with a cold gaze from the heights of his perch atop his noble steed and ignored his question.

A blacksmith, embracing his wife with his coal-blackened hands, whispered in her ear, "I've heard that his betrothed, Isabella, Princess of Asturias, does not want us. She's as evil as her parents, Ferdinand and Isabella."

"Shush… have you lost your mind? Do you want us to be burned?" his wife attempted to silence him.

Four white sails were gradually revealed in the curve of the river.

"A ship! Here's a ship!" the cry rang out, and thousands of people began to storm the pier, shoving and yelling.

"I have tickets!" the head of a family waved the tickets in his hand desperately, attempting to forge a path for his wife, his daughters and himself.

"Let the *señora* pass," a servant woman tried in vain to convey her mistress through the thick crowd amassing on the pier.

The ship approached slowly. The captain dropped the anchor and brawny sailors tossed the ropes, tying the ship's stern to the bollard.

"Stop, immediately!" the head of the guard commanded, raising his sword. A riot broke out as the soldiers viciously pushed men and women, young and old, with their bayonets back toward the plaza.

"Block the passage to the ship's gangway!" the head of the guard decreed.

"No! Let us board!" a flushed old woman thrust herself forward, her one hand waving a walking cane while the other held on to her husband's arm.

"Listen!" the head of the Guard declared, unfurling the royal writ he held in his hand. The plaza grew silent. "Our beloved king, Dom Manuel the First, has forbidden the captains of the ships from allowing passengers to board the decks."

A stunned silence engulfed the Jewish crowd.

The sky began to redden, the sun about to set. Severe-looking priests and nuns, holding lit torches that cast bewitching shadows upon their faces, stood before the Jews huddled in the plaza, crammed tightly against each other.

Bishop Afonso de Costa, clad in a black robe with a crimson hem and holding a 'warp and weft' a cross embedded with diamonds, turned his lined visage to the panicked people.

"Our brethren, dear people of Portugal," he commenced in his soft voice, raising his hands over their heads. "Our beloved brothers, join us as well. Come into the fold of the Christian religion and accept the true faith. Our Messiah yearns for your arrival. Kiss our holy symbol. Your soul will be redeemed and your sin forgiven!"

An oppressive silence filled the plaza. No one advanced toward the bishop.

A parade comprising hundreds of boys and girls, youths with priests and nuns beside them, strode with downcast eyes toward the assembly of Jews, which grew increasingly agitated.

"My Estherika, where are you?" a mother ran toward them, her hands thrown out before her.

"Halt!" a soldier commanded, blocking her with his bayonet,

A pretty adolescent girl looked up. "Mother!" she called out.

"Estherika!" The mother tried to force her way between the soldiers bedecked in armor and helmets.

"Back!" a soldier yelled, stabbing her arm with his lance. Bloodstains spread across her dress, reddening the stone tiles. The mother held on to her arm, attempting to stop the flow of blood and growing silent.

Bishop Afonso watched the woman. "People of Portugal!" he called out. "These dear children have taken on the religion of grace. As you have chosen to remain Jews, the children have been declared to be orphans. Know that godfathers and godmothers have volunteered to lovingly accept them into their families. If you wish to see them, you must be baptized." The bishop paused briefly, then added ceremoniously, "Father Paulus is with us today. He has chosen the religion of truth and mercy."

"My beloved Jewish brethren!" Paulus the convert addressed the crowd. "I, too, was like you. The Church took me in with open arms. Be baptized into Christianity, and your children will return to you."

"Anchors aweigh!" a cry tore through the stillness. "Hoist the sails!"

Three long blares of the horn rang out. The agile sailors undid the ropes securing the ship to the pier. The ship raised anchor, slowly turned its bow and began to sail toward the great sea.

A moan of pain and terrible despair rose from the crowd, echoing through the city.

"Oh, beloved sons of the Kingdom of Portugal!" Bishop Afonso called out loudly. "In his immense benevolence and kindness, our king, Dom Manuel the First, is allowing you to choose the religion of mercy and truth. However, you have maintained your rebellion for three days now. In an hour or so, the royal decree will expire. From that moment on, no Jew will be allowed to tread upon Portuguese soil. Those who do not accept the Christian faith will be conveyed to the king as slaves, with our symbol branded on their arms." The bishop cast a threatening look upon the horrified crowd.

"The preservation of life supersedes blasphemy," one of the fathers said, beginning to advance toward the priests.

"Welcome, my son!" The bishop sprinkled him with water from a large bucket standing next to him.

"*Moshe emet vetorato emet...!* Moses is a true prophet and his Torah remains true!" A man's cry rang out as he began running swiftly toward the Tagus River.

"Yitzhaki, no!" Rabbi Zemach grabbed onto his coat, but the man shook off his hand. "*Shema Yisrael, Hashem e-loheynu, Hashem ehad.* Hear O Israel, the Lord is our God, the Lord is one!" His cry pierced the heavens a moment before his body plummeted into the depths of the Tagus.

The bells of the cathedrals and the churches rang out firmly as priests and nuns poured buckets of water over the stunned assembly.

"The time has come. The decree is now in effect," the bishop declared, raising the 'warp and weft.' "In the name of the Father, the Son and the Holy Spirit, I declare you to be Christians."

"By authority of the Court on high, and by authority of the court on earth, with the knowledge of All-Present, and with the knowledge of this congregation,[1]" the rabbi cried out.

"You must get to church immediately," Bishop Alfonso commanded.

Clad in armor and helmets with their bayonets drawn, the soldiers of the Royal Guard burst into the crowd of men and women still frozen in their spots. The soldiers stabbed anyone who dared to resist with their weapons. They tossed off hats, grabbed at the kerchiefs covering the women's heads, pulled cruelly on the men's beards, grabbed their arms roughly, and with cruel smiles, dragged them to the nearby churches. The cries of pain from women and men whose dignity had been violated pierced the heavens. Rabbi Zemach tore the hem of his clothing in the traditional gesture of mourning, weeping copiously.

Hundreds of burning candles illuminated the dozens of effigies in the Santa Maria Cathedral in pale yellow light as thousands of forced converts crowded inside, their legs faltering beneath them.

Trembling, their fingers entwined, a tall man of forty or so and his pretty wife, her eyes dim and her brown hair loose, sat before the bishop. The bishop picked up a quill, immersed the nib in his inkwell and looked up from the thick journal open upon his desk. His eyes glanced at the effigy in the nook across from him before returning to the couple sitting before him.

"Welcome to the true religion!" he greeted them. "Would you like me to choose a name for you?"

The man tightened his hand around his wife's. "Thank you, we've already chosen," he replied faintly. "Philippa and Alvaro de Luna."

---

1   This line is taken from the introduction of the Kol Nidre prayer, traditionally recited on Yom Kippur, which pre-emptively annuls any personal or religious oaths or prohibitions made to God during the next year, so as to avoid the sin of breaking vows made to God that cannot be or are not upheld.

PART ONE

Lisbon
1522-1537

Lisbon, 1522

"Beatricci, get away from the window immediately!" Mama called out. She closed the window forcefully and pulled the curtains shut. "It's dangerous outside, we mustn't be seen!" she said as she left the room. Sounds of singing, shouting and beating drums echoed from the street, infiltrating the library through the closed window. I couldn't hold myself back and peeked toward the street.

Franciscan monks in brown robes, carrying 'warp and wefts' in their hands, marched down the narrow, twisting alley, singing hymns. The enflamed masses held up banners adorned with skulls, hurtling toward the cathedral in the central square, as they kicked mud everywhere, knocking down vases of flowers and pushing aside slaves with the 'warp and weft' branded on their arms, carrying burdens upon their backs.

"New Christians!" a monk screamed, pointing at the 'warp and weft' engraved on the wall surrounding our house. A skinny, awkward boy was running by his side, beating a blue drum with sticks and further agitating the crowd.

"*Conversos*—forced converts!" a laundress with a wicker basket on her head screeched out. She pursed her meaty lips and spit in the direction of the house.

"New Christians, you're the ones who caused the drought. Get out of our homeland!" a young man who was running barefoot called out.

"*Marranos*[2]—you pigs, you took our wheat!" a shout rang out, and a barrage of stones hit the house gate, which began to sway.

---

2   *Marranos*, like *conversos*, is a derogatory term for Jews who had converted to Christianity.

Stray dogs and squawking chickens fled between the yards of the crowded houses. Dogs barked, while the horses in the house stables neighed in fright. Clouds of dust and heavy odors rose from the street.

"Beatricci, what are you doing?" Mama grew pale. She gently drew me away from the window, her eyes brimming with tears. My heart trembled within me.

Papa hurried to the library, holding my little sister Brianda in his arms, with a frightened Grandma Reyna in his wake. "The Lord save me and deliver me from mine enemies," Grandma whispered, bursting into tears.

"Papa, why are Mama and Grandma crying?" I asked.

Papa surveyed me with his sharp gaze, reserved for occasions in which he did not like my questions.

"Antonio, proper rest upon the wings of the Divine Presence." Mama wiped away a tear.

"Who's Antonio?" I asked. "Why are they throwing stones at us?"

"*Conversos!*" the angry cries rang out from the street once more. A rock hit the wall surrounding the house, causing the window to shake.

Grandma undid the gilded buckle of her red velvet reticule, took out a tiny vial and sprayed a few drops on her embroidered handkerchief. She inhaled them off the kerchief, and a sharp mint scent spread through the library.

I wanted to ask Papa again, but before I could, he looked at me and said, "Mama and Grandma are crying because of Antonio."

Brianda opened her eyes in fright and burst out in tears. Mama pulled her close and sang to her quietly.

"Sleep, oh, sleep, my darling dear,
May sorrow and pain never come near."

The yelling gradually drifted away from us. Papa, Mama and Grandma huddled in the corner of the room, whispering.

"We have to…"

"We can't hide…"

"She'll find out…"

"…Secret."

"Philippa, enough with the tears." Papa stroked Mama's hand. "Brianda has fallen asleep. Tell her."

Mama took a deep breath and began her tale.

"On that terrible day, in the year of the drought sixteen years ago, a week before Easter, a rabble, some drunken sailors, were squabbling and arguing among themselves who would contribute more money to buying kindle in order to build a giant bonfire at the entrance to the church next to our home. We closed the windows and the blinds tight and waited for the riot to move on. Suddenly, we heard shouting: 'Catch those converts, grab those *marranos* pigs!'

"'You took our food!'

"'Break down the gate!'

"'Inside, inside!'

"The heavy tread of feet climbing up the house steps terrified us. Quickly, we fled to the hidden stairs and escaped through a tunnel to Grandma's house, but my brother Antonio tripped, and the mob that had broken into our home caught him.

"'Toss him to the dogs!' we heard the screaming of the mob. The flames illuminated Antonio. A monk and a seaman had grabbed onto his feet and his head was dangling beyond the balcony, over the teeming square. 'New Christians!' 'Throw him down!'

"Cries of joy rose from the rabble when those lowlifes threw my brother on the cold stone pavement."

Eek! I smothered the exclamation that had almost escaped my mouth with my palm.

"Why did they kill him?" I asked.

"*El mazal no se merka kon paras.* Luck is not bought with money. It's a decree from heaven," Mama said.

"What does fate have in store for us?" Grandma wrung her hands.

"Beatricci, the time has come to tell you the secret," Papa said.

"The secret?"

Shrouded Secrets

Papa shifted aside the books of the New Testament lined up on the shelf and pressed his hand against the wooden board behind them. Slowly, the bookcase began to move, revealing a hidden door. Papa produced a ring of keys from his pocket, chose a small key, inserted it in a lock just above the floor, and opened the door. I stared in wonder at the narrow staircase revealed.

Mama lit a candle in the lantern. "Come on," she reached out to me.

The heavy wooden door closed behind us. I heard my heart beating wildly and Papa's footfall as he quickly descended the stairs. Grandma went down slowly, leaning on a sculpted wooden cane. At the bottom of the staircase, I found myself in a small hall. A faint odor of mildew hovered in the air. Next to the high ceiling was a narrow window, letting in a little light. Dark shadows passed before the aperture.

"Don't worry," Mama quickly told me, her voice quiet. "They can't see or hear us from the street."

Wooden chairs stood next to the white walls.

"Beatricci, sit down, please," Papa said, his black eyes fixed upon me.

I sat erect upon the hard seat. Mama sat down beside me, and her soft palm stroked my cheek.

"Beatricci," Papa said, "soon, you'll be twelve years old. It's time to reveal the family's secret to you."

"Beatricci," Mama said softly, "your name is not Beatrice, or Beatricci, your pet name. Your real name is Hannah-Gracia."

"Hannah? Gracia?"

"Beatrice or Beatricci is your outside name, in society outside our home. Your real name, here among us, is Gracia Hannah Nasi." Mama rolled the words gently upon her tongue. "You're Jewish."

"*Jewish?*" The room spun around me. "Who are we?" I asked.

"We're Jews," Papa said, stroking my hair.

"Jews?"

A sigh escaped Mama. "We're Jews in secret and Christians ostensibly."

"But I always wear the warp and weft," I stammered.

"My daughter, we call it 'the warp and weft' and you only wear it outside the house. We hide our faith, although there is no forgiveness for those who conceal their faith," Papa explained sadly.

"Their messiah was Jewish, too," I heard Grandma whispering to herself.

Her hands trembling, Mama poured a glass of water from the pitcher standing on the table at the corner of the dim room. She passed her hand over her hair, held back in a knot, and her brown eyes grew solemn.

"Our family, the Nasi and Benveniste family, is part of the People of Israel, 'those belonging to the letter Yod,' which is short for the word 'Israel.' That's how we refer in our secret language to our people who were exiled from Spain and forced to convert to Christianity, so that strangers will not understand us.

"Your ancestors, who lived in Spain for hundreds of years, were advisors and physicians to the royal family, and heads of the Jewish community, until the Spanish monarchs, Isabella and Ferdinand, may their names be cursed eternally, exiled us from our homeland. Only those who converted to Christianity were allowed to remain in Hispania.

"Our family insisted on retaining our forefathers' faith, and on the ninth of Av, 1492, we left our memories behind, along with our loved ones forced to convert to Christianity and plenty of property, and migrated to Portugal," Mama sighed.

"But five years after we had gotten settled in Portugal, King Dom Manuel the First prohibited us from living as Jews. We were shuttled into a large plaza close to the port, the priests sprinkled water on us, and we were declared to be Christians, dragged to the Santa Maria Cathedral and given Christian names." Mama paused briefly.

"Philippa and Alvaro de Luna are our new names. My daughter, we are *annusim*, forced converts," Papa said.

"From now on, Gracia, you are a mature girl. It is your obligation to protect the secrets concealed in your heart, even if it puts your life at risk," Mama warned me.

From the moment the truth was revealed to me, I understood that lies would envelop me like a scarf, and that my life would change forever.

Mama gently opened an oval jewelry box made of silver and produced a gold pendant inlaid with precious stones. At its center was a pale blue sapphire shaped like an icicle, surrounded by six shiny gems.

"I bought it on Gold Street from Enrico, the old goldsmith." Her fingers fluttered across the pendant. "The sapphire symbolizes the Hebrew letter Yod, short for 'Israel,' the gems represent our people, while the links on the chain are the daughters of Israel. Gracia, when the time comes, you will pass on the secret and the gold pendant to your daughter, who will pass it on to her own daughter. Thanks to *Señor*, the Eternal Lord, the chain remains unbroken." Mama gently clasped the chain around my neck.

"The chain remains unbroken..." I murmured after her.

"Look how pretty you are." Grandma handed me a sliver mirror. I liked the reflection I saw in the mirror.

"The pendant emphasizes your almond eyes and your hair, which is shiny like cherry liqueur." Grandma kissed my forehead and added, "And your high, intelligent forehead."

"Thank you," I replied, but in my heart of hearts, I knew very well that I was not beautiful like Giomar, my sister who had passed away, or like my two-year-old sister Brianda.

Grandma closed her eyes and covered them with three of the fingers of her right hand.

"Repeat after me," she said. "*Shema Yisrael, Hashem e-lhoeynu, Hashem ehad*. Hear O Israel, the Lord is our God, the Lord is one." Ever since then, every night, before covering my eyes with my palm and whispering Shema Yisrael, I would kiss the blue sapphire and imagine that every link on the chain was a secretly Jewish woman, holding on with all her might to her friend, protecting her from evil hands threatening to grab her.

Blessed Candles

Up the street, the tambourine man was playing a melody for people with a yearning heart. His black, melancholy face stood out against the red cloak he wore.

Three brief knocks were heard.

Thomas, the butler, walked through the rooms, lit a fire in the hearth, ignited the lanterns scattered through the room, then went out to the street and lit the torch at the entrance to the house. Grandma went out to the colonnade, opened a hatch at the top part of the door, peered through it, nodded and opened the door. One by one, our relatives snuck into the house. The first to enter was my uncle Francisco Mendes, about forty years old, tall and impressive. His face was tan, his graying beard short and sleek. Thick black eyebrows shaded his green eyes.

"Welcome!" my parents greeted him.

"Greetings to those present! Hello, Grandma Reyna." My uncle kissed her withered cheeks.

Mama asked my brother Leo to hang Francisco's velvet cape and hat in the closet. Leo shrugged. Unfortunately for him, Mama had sent the servants away for a day off and he had to pitch in. However, he did not dare refuse.

"How are you, Beatricci? You're radiant today." Francisco's eyes examined me.

"I'm well, thank you," I replied, curling a strand of hair around my finger.

"The pendant you're wearing suits you well," he said.

I wrapped my hand around the pendant, feeling how flushed my face was.

"Where's Brianda?" Francisco asked.

"Sleeping." Mama pointed at Brianda, who was slumbering peacefully on the small sofa, her golden curls cascading down her shoulder.

The next to enter were Mama's brother, Dr. Samuel Migois, who had been the personal physician to Dom Manuel the first, and currently served as physician to our king, Dom Joao the Third, his wife, the lovely Doña Rosa, and their son, the four-month-old Bernardo. I loved my gracious physician uncle, who was always interested in my science studies.

I saw that my aunt and uncle were whispering to each other and furtively glancing at me.

"Welcome!" Mama hugged them.

"Sweetie, come to me," Mama extended her arms to Bernardo, but he burst out in tears and held on to his mother tightly.

"Don't cry, honey. You'll have plenty of reasons to cry in your life…" Mama stroked his cheek, which only made him cry harder.

"Rosa, lay him down in the crib, next to Brianda," Grandma requested. "*La ninya durmiendo, el mazal despierto.* The girl is sleeping, and her good fortune is awake."

"Philippa, your daughter is beautiful. May God protect her." Aunt Rosa kissed Brianda's golden curls.

The tambourine man passed by the house, beating on the taut skin of the drum held under his armpit. A sad tune drifted in from the street. Three more knocks were heard. Grandma looked out through the hatch and edged the door open.

Amatus Lusitanus, the young doctor with the pleasant visage and the winning smile, who had come to Lisbon from Castello Branco, entered the house with a vigorous stride.

"Hello, Señora Philippa, Señor Alvaro, I apologize for being late."

"Welcome!" Papa shook his hand.

The last to arrive was Papa's sister, Aunt Elvira, whose quick, chubby hands had birthed Brianda and Bernardo. From the day Yitzhaki, her husband, had drowned in the Tagus River, she wore only black. Her son, Gabriel, was an altar boy at the church.

"Hello, darlings!" she called out. "Isn't Beatricci already supposed to be in bed?"

"Beatricci is joining us," Papa announced.

Francisco's green eyes alighted upon me. "Welcome."

"At last, it's time. *Carida*, my dear!" Uncle Samuel and Aunt Rosa embraced me.

Aunt Elvira extracted some crystal sugar from a muslin bag wrapped in a ribbon and handed it to me as she pinched my cheek. "*El ke buen mazal tiene, nunka lo piedre*. She who is lucky never loses."

I'm too old for candy, I thought, but didn't say a thing. When my aunt's back was turned, I placed the sugar next to my sweet sister.

Amatus Lusitanus' gray eyes were smiling.

"It's time!" Papa said.

"I'll stay with Bernardo and Brianda," Aunt Rosa said, sitting beside them.

Quietly, we descended the stairs to the cellar.

"It's too bad they told you. It's better not to know," my brother Leo whispered to me, running past me.

Papa extracted a tiny wooden box from his pocket. I looked at him in query.

"This is a mezuzah[3]. It protects us," Francisco explained.

Mama, Grandma Reyna and Aunt Elvira covered their hair with white silk shawls, to which Grandma affixed a red rose.

"The white kerchiefs commemorate the tallit, the prayer shawl once worn by Jewish men," Francisco whispered to me.

"Blessed wicks," Mama intoned as she arranged linseed wicks in the lantern and gently poured in olive oil. She lit the wicks, and soft light and a pleasant scent filled the room. Mama closed her eyes and covered them with her palms. "Gracia, repeat the blessing after me:

"Blessed are You, the Lord our God, Lord of the universe,
Who has sanctified us with His commandments,
and commanded us to light the blessed wicks.
So the Lord illuminates our souls and saves us from offenses,
transgressions and sins. Amen."

---

3   A *mezuzah* is a piece of parchment enclosed in a decorative case and inscribed with specific Hebrew verses from the Torah.

A sensation of holiness engulfed me as I repeated the words after Mama.

"My daughter, the candle will never be extinguished!" Mama kissed me.

Papa laid his hands on my head. "Gracia, may our God and *Señor* of the universe grant you the standing of Sarah, Rebecca, Rachel and Leah. I am blessed to have been privileged to see you light the holy wicks." His eyes filled with tears.

"Zemach, *Rabbi Annus*[4], respectfully," Papa addressed Francisco.

Francisco glanced at me. "Gracia, please repeat after me, even if you don't understand the meaning of the words."

I mulled a strand of hair between my fingers, overcome with excitement. My uncle swayed in place and began praying.

"In the holy Sabbath, we will cease from all occupations
And pray to the God of Israel
He is one, and his unity is incomparable."

"Amen," everyone replied.

Deeply touched, I watched the men and women praying passionately, their voices trembling as they repeated the prayer which was utterly incomprehensible to me. Grandma placed her right hand over her heart, while her left hand was extended heavenward in prayer. At the end of the prayer, Papa placed his hands on Leo's head: "May the Lord lead you to the path of success, my son."

"Shabbat Shalom! Have a peaceful Sabbath!" we wished each other, climbing the stairs back to the house.

In the dining room, the table was covered with an immaculate tablecloth, set with blue china plates with a sliver trim, shiny crystal goblets and napkins folded into birds in accordance with the latest fashion.

We whispered the traditional blessing over the bread, drank a bit of sweet port wine, and Mama served fish in pepper sauce, salads and warm pastels filled with cheese.

While the men were immersed in eating, the women chatted cheerfully. Doña Rosa reported that the royal court was abuzz over the anticipated betrothal of our King Dom Joao, the Third to Princess Catherine,

---

4   "Coerced rabbi" in Hebrew.

the sister of Dom Carlos, King Charles of Spain, as well as Charles's engagement to Princess Isabella, Joao the Third's sister.

"Beatrice, please pass me the bowl of pastels," requested Francisco, who was sitting beside me.

"With pleasure." I placed the bowl next to him.

"Thank you. The pastels are wonderful. You should try them."

"King of Spices, when will we be allowed to attend your wedding?" Aunt Elvira shook her head. "*Ombre sin mujer, komo kavayo sin montura.* A man without a wife is like a horse without a saddle. A man needs a wife by his side."

Francisco's brow furrowed briefly. I felt angry at my aunt for inserting herself into others' private lives.

"Please, I have something important to tell you." Aunt Elvira raised her wine goblet, silencing everyone. "My son Gabriel, may the Lord have mercy on his soul…"

Mama stroked her arm. "Elvira, you did the right thing sending your son to serve in the church. It's important that someone can tell us what's going on there."

Aunt Elvira sipped her wine and continued. "Gabriel said that Bishop Afonso was complaining that some families among the New Christians don't pay their proper respects to the Church, and don't attend Sunday prayers. The bishop promised a handful of coins to anyone who informs him of the names of any *conversos* who don't praise the Holy Trinity at the end of the prayer." Her voice shook.

"Those louses!" Leo pursed his lips in anger.

"The priests know that this Monday is 'Santo Puro,' the holy Yom Kippur. Last week, I went to church and heard the bishop enflaming the congregation with his sermon. He demanded that they spy on their New Christian neighbors and asked that on Monday, they check whether the New Christians are hanging up laundry and cleaning their homes, and whether smoke was rising from their chimneys," Aunt Elvira recounted.

The room grew quiet.

Papa was the first to recover. "On Monday, we'll behave normally," he said. "Don't wear white clothes or cloth shoes[5]."

"We'll fast on Thursday," Francisco said.

"*Rabbi Annus* is correct," Papa agreed.

"Don't forget to wear their 'warp and weft' outside the house," Grandma quietly reminded.

"On Sunday, we have to get to church on time. Once they finish reading the Psalms, we'll mumble a few words, so they think we're praising the Trinity," Francisco whispered.

"That's it. I'm sick of living in this damn country!" Leo blurted out a curse.

"Leo, watch your tongue!" Papa grew angry, turning a harsh gaze upon him.

"I should have gotten out of here with Giomar's husband. May she rest in peace." Leo pushed his chair back, preparing to leave the table.

"Leo, sit down!" Papa commanded.

Mama noticed that I was clutching my belly and asked, "Gracia, what's wrong? Are you all right?"

"My stomach hurts suddenly," I said in a low voice.

"Honey, I'm making you a glass of hot water mixed with rosewater," Grandma said, departing for the kitchen.

The young doctor, Amatus Lusitanus, handed Mama a little vial.

"Señora Philippa, this is a new type of medicine. Seven drops in a glass of water will ease your daughter's pain."

My uncle, Doctor Samuel, examined the label on the flask.

"This is good medicine, Amatus my student—you're an excellent physician! Give her the drops," he instructed Mama.

Mama drizzled the drops into the rosewater infusion that Grandma had brought me, and invited everyone to partake in her famous fried rose cookies and the cherry preserves.

After the meal, the guests departed at intervals of several minutes from each other so that our neighbors would not note the gathering. Mother informed me that tomorrow, *Rabbi Annus* would come to teach me. A brief thrill of excitement rushed through me.

---

5   On the holy fast of Yom Kippur, Jews traditionally deny themselves certain luxuries, including leather footwear.

Rabbi Annus, 1522

On the afternoon of the Sabbath, I debated what to wear to my first lesson with Francisco. Usually, I would come to a decision quickly. Teresa, my beloved governess who had raised me, and whose steel eyes knew how to read me, would lay out the dress I had chosen for the next day on the bed in the evening. We would choose matching shoes, a small purse, hair ornaments, earrings and a necklace, in addition to their 'weave and weft,' which I always wore outside the house. But yesterday, I had been too tired and excited, and had postponed the choice till the next day.

In the morning, after much deliberation, I chose a light blue dress with no adornments and small earrings and put on my gold pendant.

I entered the library with Mama and Papa. Francisco was waiting there for us. "Hello, my sister Philippa and Señor Alvaro, and hello Miss Gracia. It's a nice day for a lesson," he greeted us.

I noticed the creases in his brow, his solemn eyes and his elegant attire. "Hello, Uncle Francisco."

"Shall we go down?" Papa asked, opening the hidden door for us. Mama lit a candle in the oil lamp and handed it to Francisco. "I'll wait for you here," Papa said, leaving the door slightly open.

It felt strange to study with my Uncle Francisco in the dim cellar. I asked him why he was called *Rabbi Annus*. Francisco told me he had been born under the name Zemach Nasi in Hispania, Spain, which he still missed, and that Grandfather had taught him the Torah.

"They call me *Rabbi Annus*—'Coerced Rabbi'—because when the holy books were confiscated, many grew unfamiliar with the prayers and the Torah. I remembered the prayers by heart, and agreed to secretly teach the Torah to the children of the *annusim* when asked to do so." Francisco produced a thick tome from a tiny hidden door in a discreet nook.

A slight cloud of dust dispersed in the room as he leafed through the yellowing pages. "This is a holy Torah and prayer book that I brought with me from the old country," he told me. I ran my finger along the odd letters, written in black ink from right to left. "*Bereshit bara...* In the beginning, God created..." he read to me.

"Gracia, this is Hebrew. With these sacred letters, the world was created." His long fingers caressed the book. "Yom Kippur is the holiest day for Jews. We fast and ask forgiveness and absolution for our sins," he explained, and to my great embarrassment, began to sing softly.

"By authority of the Court on high,

and by authority of the court on earth:

With the knowledge of All-Present,

and with the knowledge of this congregation,

we give leave to pray

with them that have transgressed."

I trembled as Francisco told me that this hymn, "Kol Nidrei", was composed by the forced convert de Silva, the minister of finance for the Spanish monarchs Isabella and Ferdinand. De Silva was caught singing the hymn with his fellow *annusim* on Yom Kippur, in a secret cellar. Queen Isabella tried to save him so long as he would swear allegiance to the 'weave and weft,' but de Silva refused and was burned at the stake in an auto-de-fé.

***

At the end of the lesson, I went out to the patio and sat next to Mama and Grandma, who were waiting for me expectantly next to the fountain. A small bird was there, sipping water. The sun had set, and shadows covered the sky.

"My daughter, how was the lesson?" Mama asked.

I thought to myself that Francisco had kind eyes, but he was too serious. He wasn't funny like Papa, who amused us with his impressions of the dandy Italians, the arrogant French and the severe Poles, whom he met on his trips to deal in silverware throughout the world; and he wasn't jolly like my dance and lute instructor, or fascinating like my drawing instructor, or like Professor Augustino Henricks, my history and government teacher.

"Uncle is a good teacher," I answered just as Francisco entered the patio. Apparently, he heard me, as the corners of his mouth rose in a smile.

"Philippa, I'm honored to teach Beatricci. She grasps everything quickly," he said.

Grandma Reyna straightened in her seat. "*La pera no kaye leshano del peral*. The pear doesn't fall far from the tree." She and Mama exchanged looks.

I wanted to point at the handful of stars twinkling far above in the graying sky, but stopped myself. I remembered that once, when I was little and pointed at the stars, Grandma pulled roughly on my arm and lightly slapped the back of my hand.

"Anyone who points at the stars will have pustules and scars on his face, and who would want to marry an ugly girl?" she berated me.

Francisco suggested that we occasionally conduct a short lesson.

On the next Sabbath, Francisco tried to teach me the Hebrew alphabet, and was patient even when I couldn't manage to copy the letters or pronounce them properly. I made mistakes with every letter and every word. The language sounded distant and foreign to me, and I was ashamed of my errors. At the end of the lesson, Francisco seemed discouraged, and I thought this might be the end of our shared lessons.

But on the next Saturday, Francisco arrived looking energetic and cheerful.

"Miss Beatricci," he addressed me, "today we'll move on from the Hebrew letters. I have an idea." He opened the Torah and told me about our forefather Abraham, who shattered his father's idols, and our forefather Jacob, who fought an angel and won.

On the next Sabbath, he continued on to tell me about the touching meeting between Isaac and Rebecca, who fell off her camel when she saw him praying in the field. I had tears in my eyes as he told me about Jacob's love for Rachel, and the envy between Rachel and Leah.

Over the next few Saturdays, Francisco continued relaying his wondrous stories. I prayed along with Hannah who begged for a son, and was full of admiration for Deborah who fought for her people, for Yael who killed the general Sisera, and for Judith who beheaded Holofernes.

On one of the Sabbaths, Francisco informed me, "I'm opening branches of the Mendes Company in Evora and Porto. I'll be leaving in a month or so."

I thanked Francisco for the lovely stories he'd told me, but he looked at me with an amused expression and pointed out that the stories were not his, but taken from the Torah, and that they would help me better understand life.

"My loved ones are leaving me, one after the other. Giomar passed away, my son-in-law and his daughter Lisbona left for Flanders, Diogo is in Antwerp, and Alvaro is preparing for a business trip to Italy…" Mama sighed.

It was a good thing she hadn't heard what Leo had told me—that at the first opportunity he got, he would be leaving Portugal.

"Philippa, my sister, don't worry, I'll be back soon," Francisco said, smiling at me.

Those Belonging to the Letter Yod, Lisbon, 1527

"I shall enter this house, though I shall not worship wood and stone, but only the God of Israel, who rules all," I said to myself. I entered Santa Maria Cathedral and sat in one of the front rows on the hard wood pew.

A quiet murmur passed through the worshippers. I turned back.

Distinguished men and women in gold-embroidered dresses whispered among themselves, sending curious, respectful glances toward a tall, impressive man with a square face, a firm jaw and gray hair. He strode in with vigorous steps, elegantly dressed, with a green velvet cape tossed across his broad shoulders.

"The King of Spices…"

"The wealthiest among contemporary merchants…"

"A bachelor…"

The whispers echoed everywhere.

Francisco! For a split second, I had not recognized him.

As he walked by me, Francisco slowed down, curled his graying mustache, and the pupils of his eyes dove into my own.

Brianda giggled through the kerchief she had laid over her mouth, and elbowed my waist.

"Did you see how he looked at you?" she asked.

"No… Not at all." My face was ablaze.

Brianda continued giggling.

"Don't deny it. I could see."

"Welcome!" Papa shook Francisco's hand.

"Francisco, I missed you, what a surprise!" Mama hugged her brother warmly.

"Philippa, good to see you! You've remained as young as you were four years ago!"

Mama laughed and glanced at his little potbelly. "Thank you. You haven't changed much, either."

"Hello to the pretty maiden," Francisco smiled at me.

"Hello, Uncle," I answered, mulling a strand of hair with my fingers.

"Beatricci, please, call me by my first name," he asked, a mischievous spark igniting in his eyes.

I looked down.

Mama looked at me. "*Kon buen komportamiento alkansas buen kazamiento.* With proper behavior, you'll find a proper match."

"This beauty must be Brianda," Francisco chuckled.

Brianda, whose golden, honeyed curls, brown eyes and endearing dimpled chin enchanted all who encountered her, curtsied swiftly before him, her laughter ringing out.

A moment before the prayer began, a stranger with a round face, a black beard and a thin mustache entered the cathedral. As he walked down the aisle next to Papa, he pulled his cloak up his shoulder and quickly ran his hand over his scalp as if combing through his thin dark hair.

Papa swiftly ran his own hand over his graying hair in a nearly imperceptible gesture. I realized that the stranger was one of us, "those belonging to the letter Yod."

Dressed in a red cape, Bishop Afonso strode toward the pulpit imperiously, but paused next to us. The church grew silent.

"Greetings, Señor Alvaro de Luna." The bishop stared fixedly at Papa.

Papa wiped away the drops of perspiration upon his forehead.

"It's been quite a while since I've seen you. The Church is glad that you've honored us with your presence," the bishop proclaimed, hastening his steps.

When we stood to sing the hymns, I sensed, through my lowered lashes, that Francisco was furtively glancing at me.

***

"Come on, before the priests leave," Mama spurred me on when the prayer ended. Usually, I would be instructed to pace slowly and politely, as behooved a young maiden who would soon be of age.

In the cathedral's paved front courtyard, between the two tall bell towers, Francisco stood surrounded by families of the nobility, city dwellers and merchants who were excited to see him and inquired what he had been up to. A genteel *señora* proudly introduced him to her daughter, a girl of eighteen or so with a delicate face surrounded by shiny black hair, wearing a silk dress with gold embroidery.

Aunt Rosa hurried out of the church, trying to catch up with Juan, my cousin. Juan was enjoying the chase and tried to disappear among the worshippers gathered outside the church. My uncle, Doctor Samuel, and five-year-old Bernardo ran after him and snagged him by the sleeve of his blue coat. "Stay next to me," my uncle instructed him and embraced Francisco. Two-year-old Juan made his way determinedly through the crowd, stationing himself next to Francisco.

"Hello, little man! What's your name?" Francisco addressed him.

"My name is Juan Migois Mendes. Mama calls me Mick, and my friends call me Mickas, and I'm two years old." Juan shook his hand.

"Young man, you have a bright future!" Francisco's eyes filled with laughter.

The cathedral courtyard emptied gradually of worshippers. Uniformed servants extended glove-clad hands and assisted the noble families in boarding lavish horse-drawn carriages.

Francisco looked around. "I don't see Leo."

"Alvaro took Leo along on his latest journey to the silver mines in Europe, and he stayed behind," Mama began to recount.

Papa signaled Mama with his eyes and she grew silent immediately.

Bishop Afonso approached us with leisurely steps. His small eyes surveyed our family.

"Hello, Father Afonso," Papa greeted him.

"Señor Alvaro de Luna, the professor of theology from Salamanca University is awaiting your answer regarding his excellent proposal to wed your daughter," the bishop said.

I grew pale. Mama held on to my arm.

"Father Afonso, we're honored by your grace's proposal for a match. If you please, we'll provide our answer in a few days," Papa replied, his voice hoarse.

"Señor." Annoyance was evident on the bishop's face. "The professor is very much in demand among the daughters of nobility. Your daughter," his eyes examined me from head to toe, "is already seventeen."

Papa adjusted his wide-brimmed hat. "Please, Father Afonso." A slight hesitation was apparent in his voice.

"Señor Alvaro," the bishop interrupted him. "The professor comes from a well-established family, among the oldest Christian families in Portugal." He raised his voice. "To marry into an old Christian family is a great privilege of which not everyone is worthy."

Francisco cleared his throat.

"Hello, Father Afonso."

"Dom Francisco Mendes, it's good to see you at the cathedral. I've heard you're working in the service of our dear King Joao the Third."

"Father Afonso, I returned to Lisbon on a mission from our king. The Royal Perfume Fleet has returned from its journey to the new colonies in the countries of the East, and the royal galleons are docked in the Port of Lisbon."

Francisco reached into his pocket and produced a bundle of velvet tied with thick twine. "I'd be happy to contribute a sizable donation to the church in honor of the successful journey." Francisco handed the bundle over to the bishop.

"Señor, our wise king provides your wages in this world, and the Holy Trinity will provide your wages in the next world. Fare thee well!" the bishop chuckled, bidding us goodbye.

"Please meet my assistant and faithful accountant, Jacob Morro," Francisco introduced the stranger who had accompanied him.

"It's a pleasure to meet you," Jacob replied.

"How do you know each other?" Papa inquired.

"I studied Talmud and astronomy with Jacob Morro at Salamanca University, with Rabbi Professor Avraham Zacuto," Francisco explained.

"If you'll excuse me, I have to go over to the port," Jacob Morro apologized, shook my father's hand and departed.

"Come on," Papa instructed us.

The worshippers left in the courtyard stared in amazement at a white carriage, etched with gold adornments, which had stopped next to us. A uniformed servant opened the carriage door, bowing politely to Francisco.

"Señor, the king sent the carriage to bring your honor to his palace, to dine at his table."

The cathedral was close to our house, and we preferred to enjoy the warm sunshine and return on foot. We made our way up the narrow allies, passing by a group of old men who were playing cards on a small table in the square. Under the large fig tree, old women clad in black, sat and chatted.

"Careful, water!" a heavyset woman screeched out. She leaned out of the window with a full chamber pot in her hand, pouring its contents out onto the alley. Malodorous fluid splattered everywhere. I jumped aside, careful not to stain my dress or my delicate shoes.

When we got home, Thomas opened the house gate before us. I looked up at the round balcony, adorned with black lace etchings, and counted three potted plants. No guests were present.

"Francisco is back. He'll come to dinner!" Mama informed Grandma joyfully.

"Francisco is in Lisbon? Every night, I pray I'll be allowed to see my boy before I die!" Grandma was thrilled, casting a glance in my direction.

"Grandma, he's forty-seven years old," I heard Papa's laughter.

***

The house was filled with the bewitching aromas of frying and baking. Mama walked over to the kitchen to make sure the cook was frying the fresh, pink sardines only briefly and preparing the tasty garlic sauce in which they would be served. She checked whether the fish and rice paella was properly cooked, and whether the *bomallos*, the tiny potato pancakes that were my favorites, had come out golden. She supervised the cook to make sure she was thinly rolling out the dough for the *pastilla*, which she would prepare as a dessert on special occasions, and that she filled it with almonds, nuts and rosewater.

After the cook took the *pastilla* out of the blazing oven, I volunteered to scatter the fine sugar over it. Brianda, who had come into the kitchen, could not hold back and plucked one hot *pastilla* for herself. Grandma separated the lettuce leaves, raised them to the sunlight one by one, let them soak in a bowl of vinegar, washed them carefully in water and laid them out on a china plate with a golden trim. Mama sent the servants off on their usual Sunday afternoon time off, and I, who was feeling tired, went up to rest in my room.

I was awoken by the stirring of doves. Two cooing doves were resting on the window of my room. A cool breeze had begun to blow, and the sky turned gray. From the living room, I heard fractured sentences.

My curiosity got the best of me. My feet carried me to the living room, and the conviction that something important was about to happen echoed within me. Through the open door, I could see Mama and Papa huddling.

"We have to marry her off."

"Under no circumstances…"

"Francisco…"

"Our daughter won't marry an Old Christian."

Mama looked up in fright, saw me and grew silent.

"Let's go dine," she said at last.

Black Peppercorns
& Cinnamon Sticks

We sat down at the table. Laid out upon the festive tablecloth were white porcelain plates, gleaming goblets, silverware and napkins folded into the shape of swans. Papa poured cherry liqueur, kept in our cellar for special occasions, into the crystal goblets. A sweet aroma spread through the room.

"*L'Chaim!* To life! "

"To your return, Francisco!"

"May we be blessed with a good life and happy occasions!"

Francisco handed Mama an ivory box engraved with flowers and elephants.

"A gift from India for you," he said.

Mama undid the ribbon and opened the box, whose interior was coated with bright gold. Dozens of tiny black pellets were densely laid out inside it, emitting a sharp, intoxicating scent. I began to sneeze. I counted five consecutive sneezes and after a brief pause, two more.

"'Black gold,' that's what they call the black peppercorns. You add them to the dish you're cooking, whole or ground. Mainly, they're used to preserve meat and fish," Francisco explained.

I took a peppercorn and bit into it. My face grew flushed.

"Be careful, the peppercorns are very hot!" Francisco handed me a slice of bread. "Eat this. The bread will ease the spicy taste, as if by magic."

Juan reached out to touch the black pellets. Aunt Rosa pulled his hand away.

"Sit quietly for a moment, like your brother Bernardo!"

"I've never seen black grains like these. What country do they come from?" I asked.

"From the new colonies that Prince Henry the Navigator, the son of Joao the First, discovered. Thanks to him, the sailor Vasco de Gama found the shortest sea route from Portugal to India and China. In one of my journeys to India, I visited the black pepper plantations, and saw from up close the fruit of this wondrous plant, which the natives credit with medicinal qualities. But our king has a monopoly on dealing in spices, and is the only one entitled to trade in them. Luckily for me, the royal fleet doesn't have enough galleons to sail to the colonies and meet the immense demand for spices in Europe. The company I established in the year you were born," Francisco turned to me, "the House of Mendes Company, which deals in trade and monetary loans, has received a concession to import and export black pepper from the king," Francisco paused briefly, "in return for an advance payment of a million cruzados a year."

"A million cruzados a year, paid in advance?" I sputtered.

"The king needs cash in order to pay the natives in the colonies for spices and gems, as well as for the immense dowry of eight hundred thousand cruzados he had committed to pay his brother-in-law, King Charles, when he married his sister."

"Francisco, what happens if you pay the king for the spices at the beginning of the year and the galleon is lost at sea, or pirates rob the crates? Don't you lose money?"

"I purchase the spices from the natives at low prices and sell them at a 'hot' price to the noblemen of Antwerp, Venice and Paris, who are willing to pay any price for black pepper, cloves, nutmeg, tamarind, ginger and cinnamon I import from Mozambique, India and China.

"I've leased light, swift galleons and equipped them with maps and the innovative navigation device, the metal astrolabe, designed by astronomer Abraham Zacuto, which was used by Christopher Columbus, as well."

Papa raised another glass of liqueur.

"To your business success!" he called out.

"*Ombre sin mujer, komo barka sin timon.* A man without a wife is like a boat without a rudder," Grandma nodded.

"What, you don't have a wife?" Brianda asked.

"Brianda, that's not a polite question!" Mama chided her.

Francisco coughed lightly. "I've rented a residential palace on the most prestigious street in Lisbon, close to the king's palace." He produced a small, yellow, silk sachet from his coat and presented it to me.

I opened the sachet and extracted a few brown sticks with a sweet aroma.

"Beatricci, do you remember when we read in the Song of Solomon, '*A garden enclosed is my sister... Spikenard and saffron, calamus and cinnamon, with all trees of frankincense*'? This is cinnamon," Francisco twirled his mustache.

I tentatively sniffed the sticks, breathing in their wondrous aroma. The handsome doctor who had been invited to dine with us, Amatus Lusitanus, smiled at me.

"Beatricci, I recommend warm water to go with the cinnamon stick," he said.

I played with my pendant absent-mindedly.

"Doña Philippa, the *bomallos* are wonderful," Amatus complimented my mother.

"Thank you," Mama replied and turned to my uncle. "Francisco, how is our brother Diogo?"

"Diogo is a financial genius. Two years after founding the company, I appointed him as the manager of House of Mendes in Antwerp. The nobility of Antwerp and its merchants call him 'the King of Pepper.'"

"How did you manage to arrange a travel permit for him?" Papa asked.

"Diogo dedicated the astronomy and astrology book he had written to King Manuel. As a token of gratitude, the king granted him a travel permit to Antwerp to continue his research, and ordered a personal astrological map from him."

"What's astrology?" Brianda asked sweetly.

"Astrology is the map of the stars when a person is born, which reveals his future."

"I wish I could meet Diogo as well. He would tell me about my luck," Brianda said, her eyes dreamy.

Mama caressed her curls. "My daughter, your luck is beautiful."

"Do you only import spices?" I asked curiously.

"I also deal in silk, perfume and gems," Francisco replied. "My accountant, Jacob Morro, is sailing to Antwerp tomorrow to convey a cargo of rare pearls I imported from China to Diogo. Diogo will personally hand over the pearls to Mary, Regent of Hungary, the sister of King Ferdinand of Hungary and King Charles of Spain."

Three loud knocks on the door interrupted the flow of Francisco's speech.

Papa looked at Brianda and pointed at the door.

"Why can't I stay? I'm big!" Brianda shrugged and walked slowly to her room.

Grandma went out to the colonnade to see who was at the door. Aunt Rosa rose from the table, calling Juan and Bernardo to come with her.

None of the household members made a sound.

Aunt Elvira, whose face looked jaundiced, entered the room and sank heavily into a chair. "I'm sorry I'm late," she said. "I got held up with Gabriel. Francisco, welcome back."

Grandma handed her a glass of cold water.

"Calm down. What's going on?"

"Gabriel, my son, heard that the king was sending Bishop Afonso to Spain for a month so the Church there can teach him the interrogation methods the Council of the Suprema uses on the heretics denying Christianity." Elvira pounded her chest in anguish.

"May God protect and defend us!" Grandma called out.

"It's true, King Joao insists on establishing the terrible Council. He sent emissaries to the Vatican to bribe the cardinals and influence the Pope to grant his consent for the establishment of the Council," Francisco confirmed.

A tense silence reigned around the table.

"I've appointed Duarte de Paz," Francisco continued, "in cooperation with Diogo, as a special emissary to the Vatican in Rome. Duarte's role is to act against the establishment of the Inquisition and to bribe the cardinals to sway the Pope not to sign the writ to establish an Inquisition."

Sighs of relief filled the room.

"In addition, I loaned King Joao tens of thousands of crozados."

"Praise the Lord Above," Grandma sighed.

"Happily, our battle was successful. The Pope agreed to postpone signing on to establish the Inquisition in Portugal. Who knows how long we can persist," Francisco said.

"What is the Inquisition?" I asked.

"Shush... shush... Be careful, you can't say it out loud. Anyone who falls into its hands is in dire straits." Mama wrung her hands.

"The Christian fanatics believe in *limpieza de sangre*—purity of blood—possessed only by the Old Christians. The king wants to ruin and tear apart the unity of our brothers 'belonging to the letter Yod' who have achieved prominent status in the state. The Inquisition interrogates the *annusim*, the forcefully converted accused of heresy against Christianity. It requires them to confess their sins and inform on acquaintances who practice Judaism. The Inquisition also confiscates their property for the monarchy's treasury," Francisco explained.

"Excuse me, what you're saying is just words. Beatricci, let me tell you what the Inquisition does. In the name of the 'religion of mercy,' they hang the poor wretch they've captured by his arms, spin him on a wheel of torture and tear out his fingernails, and when he faints, they spray cold water on him. He doesn't always wake from his swoon," Aunt Elvira sighed.

"Elvira, that's enough," Mama tried to stop her, but no one could stop my aunt.

"My friend Shoshana, who willingly converted to Christianity and chose the name Flora, was summoned by the Inquisition. The interrogators tied her to the stocks by her wrists and feet and poured water into her mouth.

"The Lord help us!"

"When she insisted that she hadn't sinned, they pulled the poor woman's body by her hands and feet until her feet broke and she confessed that she had bathed and changed her linens in honor of the Sabbath. After she was released, she had to pay a fortune from her own funds to finance the interrogation, and since undergoing torture, she's been limping. After a year, she passed away."

I felt dizzy, as if I was about to vomit.

Francisco poured me some water. "Drink, please." I took a small sip and thanked him.

Amatus Lusitanus produced a small vial and drizzled a few drops into my cup. "Drink this. You'll feel much better."

I ran out to the inner courtyard, where I stroked my gold pendant and tried to shake off the fear. A few minutes later, Francisco followed me out, coming to stand next to me.

"Miss Beatricci," he turned to me. "I have a request for you. I've received your parents' permission, and would be happy to invite you for a short ride. The air is good outside."

***

The cracks of Thomas the butler's whip cut through the air and the horses cantered more quickly. The numerous passersby cleared the way for the elegant carriage. Noblemen doffed their hats gallantly and greeted Francisco. Fishermen loudly declared their catches as they fried cod in boiling oil. Francisco signaled Thomas to stop the carriage. Apron-clad peddlers, both men and women, approached us, offering fragrant sweets. Francisco produced a small coin and gave it to a young peddler girl. She curtsied deeply and presented us a bag of sweets with both hands.

"My deepest thanks, Señor," she said, polishing the coin with the hem of her sleeve.

"Beatricci, look how pretty the galleon is," Francisco enthused as the galleon, flying the flag of the kingdom high on its mast, approached the harbor and joined the vessels docked at the pier.

"The elongated body and the rounded stern endow the galleon with the ability to maneuver, as well as with speed and stability in choppy waters." Francisco's tone had changed. He was speaking passionately, a look of determination in his eyes.

Jacob Morro was standing on the dock, supervising the seamen and porters who were busy unloading barrels and crates, rolling them to the House of Mendes storehouses on the other end of the port.

Servants, bearing a covered litter passed by us, slowing their steps.

A noblewoman and her daughter were sitting upon the litter. Francisco doffed his hat and greeted them through the windows of the carriage. The noblewoman and her daughter nodded their heads and directed a welcoming smile at him.

"Who are these ladies?" I asked.

"Doña Affaitati, the wife of my partner, Joao Affaitati, who is on a trip to Venice, and his daughter. I'll introduce you as soon as I get the chance."

We continued on our way to Gold Street, where a series of jewelry stores and counters dealing in gold bars had opened. Thomas stopped the carriage next to the store belonging to Enrico, the old goldsmith who could create magic using gold and precious stones. Enrico came out to greet us and handed Francisco a package.

The horses neighed when the carriage stopped before the gate to our home. Francisco reached out and helped me disembark.

"*Carida*, my dear, I'll always be here for you," he said quietly.

Strands of Light

An autumnal wind blew reddish-orange fall leaves with a hushed susurration into the garden of the house. The limbs of the grapevine were heavy with bunches of ripe red grapes. A flock of birds began to twirl under the canopy of the cloudy sky in the interval between the golden day and the grayness of the evening.

"My daughter, you know you're precious to us, and that we want to see you happy," Papa said.

"I know."

"Francisco praised you to us. I told him we would summon the girl and consult her," Papa said.

"I'm still young," I said quietly.

"My daughter, Francisco is a dear man. He'll treat you like a queen. He'll be a good husband to you, and a good father to your children," Mama said gently.

"Mama, Francisco is almost thirty years older than me."

"*Kuando la fortuna te espande un dedo, espandele la mano.* When fortune extends a finger to you, extend your hand to it," Mama said.

"How many unmarried men from our people and in our station do you know?" Papa asked.

I hesitated whether to answer, my eyes downcast.

"Gracia, you know that we only marry within the family," Mama decreed.

"You two are well suited. Francisco's business spans the world, and you, Gracia, can help him. *La mujer sevia fragua la kaza.* Woman, in her wisdom, manages the home," Mama smiled.

Papa grasped both my hands and Mama hugged my shoulders. "My daughter, we want you to be happy. You know Queen Catherine sent a messenger to us with an urgent proposal to marry you to one of her cousins, and the bishop is coercing us to accept the proposal of the theology professor from Salamanca University. We have to give them an answer."

I looked up at the misty sky.

"We'll explain to them that you were destined for Francisco ever since you were a child." Papa kissed my forehead and walked into the house with Mama.

The sun drifted away and evening crept in. The leaves fell slowly, covering the garden with a tapestry of golden fronds. I felt small and fragile beside the tall, handsome, dignified man who had entered the garden. I snuck a glance at him. The small furrows at the corners of his eyes had deepened, and his hair had grown white.

"Sit down, please." Francisco gallantly shifted a chair for me.

"Gracia." I looked up and met his kind eyes, which enveloped my face with their gaze. "My dear, your beauty and your grace have captured my heart," he addressed me gently.

The gurgle of water in the fountain, covered by a pallet of leaves, muffled my silence. Francisco took off his cloak and wrapped it around my shoulders.

"Thank you," I whispered.

"Gracia," he said. "I have waited many years for you to grow up. My lovely girl, I can't stop thinking about you. You have won over my soul."

I turned my head toward him as my thoughts roiled within me. Francisco may have been older, but *Rabbi Annus* was well educated as well as a fascinating conversationalist.

Francisco drew his chair nearer to me.

"Marry me, my dear."

I remained silent, watching the red sun set and disappear.

"Beatricci, you don't have to answer me now. Consider my offer."

Francisco pushed his chair back and stood behind my own to help me up.

"Come on, let's go in. It's chilly out here."

"Francisco…"

"Yes, dear?"

Drops of perspiration emerged on my palms. "Francisco, yes," I replied softly.

***

A week later, we sat down at the ceremonial table. Mama served Francisco and me a silver bowl full of sweet sugar crystals. "A charm for a happy, sweet marriage."

Papa produced the prenuptial writ, written in Hebrew, although using Hebrew was a violation of the law. This was the financial agreement my father and Francisco had conducted, as was the custom among the wealthy families of Portugal.

Papa promised me a substantial dowry in gold and silver coins, as well as valuable possessions for our home.

I peeked at the agreement and read the words out loud slowly:

"And I will betroth thee unto me forever; yea, I will betroth thee unto me in righteousness, and in judgment, and in loving kindness, and in mercy.

"Señora Gracia de Luna Nasi and Senor Zemach Mendes Benveniste have agreed that after their marriage, in the event that Senor Benveniste dies during her lifetime, Señora Gracia will share the assets with their sons and daughters equally, half for her, and half for their sons and daughters."

"Gracia, don't worry, we'll raise our grandchildren together," Francisco laughed.

He opened an ivory box and slipped a diamond ring on my hand and a gold bracelet on my wrist. I presented Francisco with a silk scarf on which I'd embroidered his initials with a gold thread, praying that strands of light would bind our hearts.

The cries of joy, the hugs and the kisses eclipsed Brianda's whisper, which stabbed at my heart.

"My sister, he… he's old."

The Tambourine
& The Toll of Bells, 1528

The wedding at the cathedral was set for Sunday. The Jewish wedding was held ten days earlier, a day after the fast of Holy Reyna Esther[6].

The preparations for the ceremony lasted a month. My hair was washed in rosewater and anointed in olive oil, my brows plucked, and a honey, egg white and lemon juice mask placed upon my freshly washed face. My body was massaged with oil infused with jasmine flowers and pomegranate peels. I felt like Queen Esther, whose body was bathed in perfume for six months.

A week before the secret wedding ceremony in the afternoon, when Mama, Brianda and I sipped an apple drink spiced with rosewater and accompanied by cookies, Teresa entered my room, bearing a gift wrapped in red silk ribbons.

"Beatricci, for you," she declared joyfully.

I undid the silk ribbons, and was left breathless. In an ivory jewelry box laid a necklace of red rubies, next to a parchment that read: "For Beatricci, my beloved fiancée. Francisco."

"I want one of those too!" Brianda declared enthusiastically, trying on the necklace in front of the mirror, but Mama took it away from her.

The next day, Teresa entered bearing a box wrapped in silk. A pair of

---

6   The Fast of Esther is a dawn-to-nightfall fast held on the day before the Jewish holiday of Purim, commemorating the fasting of the Jewish people in response to the mortal threat experienced by the Jews during their exile in the Persian Empire and described in the biblical Book of Esther.

ruby earrings twinkled at me from the box.

"For the most beautiful of women. Francisco," I quietly read the inscription and blushed.

On the third day I received a leather pouch containing a gold bracelet inlaid with rubies, emeralds and amber. "Awaiting our wedding day. Francisco."

And so, during the week, the gifts piled up in my room. Every day, I received a piece of jewelry more breathtaking than the item that had preceded it.

The dowry chests, engraved in shiny copper and embedded with gems, grew swollen with immaculate cotton linens, dresses, nightgowns, fur coats, silk fabrics and wallpaper, dinnerware, jewelry, gold coins, shawls, shoes and decorative items prepared for me since the day I was born in anticipation of my wedding day.

On the evening of the secret wedding, as the stars shone in the sky, I followed Mama down into the cellar. Behind a small cabinet, Mama opened a hidden door I had never seen before. We walked for several minutes down a dark, wet, twisty corridor until we reached a dead end.

Mama knocked three times. The door opened. I was surprised to find myself among shelves on which jars of jam, carafes of wine, clay jars, aging cheeses, pots and pans were all arranged in straight lines. It was the cellar of Aunt Elvira's house, where my grandmother and my aunt Doña Rosa were waiting for me.

"Congratulations!" My aunt gathered me in her arms and kissed me. Elvira moved a few crates aside, lifted four boards from the floor, and much to my surprise, revealed a waterhole that had been carved out, at the bottom of five narrow stairs.

"What is this?" I asked, amazed.

"The *baño—mikve*—in which the bride bathes on her wedding night, and every month after she counts out seven clean days."

"It only enhances the love..." Aunt Rosa chuckled.

Mama handed me an elegant white silk satchel.

"*Bogo de baño*, a gift from Francisco," she said. From the satchel, I extracted a white bathrobe on which my name was embroidered in gold thread, inhaling its pleasant scent. The satchel also contained a mirror, a silver hairbrush adorned with gems, embroidered slippers, jars of perfume and fragrant soaps.

"You're very lucky, you've found yourself a charming, rich groom," Aunt Elvira pinched my cheek.

"He's found himself a charming bride as well," Grandma Reyna said.

"Gracia, in the pure water of the *mikve*, the ritual bath, the bride's sins are forgiven." My mother kissed my cheek.

I immersed myself in the cool water, and a sensation of purity and warmth enveloped me.

"My daughter, just as you dwelled in pure water in the womb, so shall the living water, the cleansing rainwater gathered in this hollow, endow you with a sanctified marital life," Mama blessed me, placing her hands on my head.

When I rose from the water, Mama wrapped me in the absorbent bathrobe. My aunts offered me cookies and sweets and directed significant looks in my direction.

The next morning, Mama told me that according to Jewish custom, the bride fasted on the day of her wedding, but I felt dizzy and only fasted until noon. The servants were told I was not feeling well.

My hands and feet were shaking. I was eager to see Francisco, and be with him under the *chuppah*, the wedding canopy. In my excitement, I could not manage to clasp the gold bracelet Francisco had sent me that morning. I asked Mama to help me. Suddenly, a tear dropped down on my hand.

"Mama, why are you crying? Be happy, I'm getting married!" I said.

"My daughter, you're a part of me, a part of my body, of my soul. I'm happy for you, but you're leaving home..." Mama clasped the bracelet around my wrist.

"Our house is close to yours," I said, trying to calm both her and myself.

∗∗∗

Evening came. The tambourine man was playing a happy, rhythmic melody up the street.

Relatives and their wives gathered in the cellar, illuminated by dozens of lanterns and decorated with flowers. The women of the family quietly played cheery wedding tunes with an undertone of yearning on tambourines, mandolins and small flutes.

The table, covered with an embroidered tablecloth, displayed an array of bowls containing red apples, purple grapes and fragrant pears, plates with sweet cookies, silver pitchers full of fruit punch and bottles of wine.

The tambourine man played on.

Papa drummed his fingers on the table. "There are only nine men. We're missing one for the *minyan*[7]."

Luckily for us, Mama entered with Enrico, the elderly goldsmith. "Hello to you all, congratulations!"

"Greetings," Papa happily received him.

Jacob Morro, Professor Augustino Henricks, Amatus Lusitanus and my uncle Samuel Migois held wooden poles, with my father's tallit, which he had brought with him from the old country, stretched out between them.

I looked at my Francisco, wrapped in his own tallit.

"Gracia, you look wonderful," he whispered to me, his expression thrilled. "I chose a wise, beautiful woman. I'm so fortunate that you're marrying me."

I blushed to the very roots of my hair.

My mother, whose face was radiant with joy, entwined her arm with mine and escorted me under the *chuppah*. With great gentleness, Francisco covered my face with a silk veil embroidered with gold and pearls, which I had been lovingly working on since our engagement, and the pace of my heartbeats increased.

Grandma Reyna displayed the scroll of the *ketubah*, the prenuptial agreement, which I had decorated with a pair of doves in shades of gold, red and green. Papa poured wine into a silver goblet. "We will begin the wedding ceremony," he declared quietly.

The goblet shook in his hand, drops of perspiration appeared on his forehead, and he let out a heavy sigh.

Seeing that Papa was emotional, Mama offered him a cup of water, but

---

7   The *minyan* is the quorum of ten Jewish men required for certain religious obligations.

he declined.

After several long moments, Papa recovered, wiped away the drops of sweat from his forehead and the ceremony began.

"In the name of our God and the God of our forefathers,

Abraham, Isaac and Jacob, I join you,

Zemach Mendes of the house of Benveniste

and Hannah Gracia de Luna of the house of Nasi

May you maintain the traditions of Israel

And be endowed with boys and girls

who will maintain the Torah of Israel."

"Amen," we replied.

Francisco placed a gold ring on my finger and bent down to kiss my lips. My heart was beating with excitement.

We were shocked by the sound of loud knocking and dim crying. Papa clutched his heart.

"Alvaro." Mama placed her hand on his, which was covered with gooseflesh. "Do you feel well?"

The knocks grew more insistent.

"Shhhhh…" Grandma called out.

Papa hastily placed the goblet on the table. Drops of wine stained his white shirt. He leaped toward the staircase. "Stay here! Philippa, if you hear five knocks, go immediately to Elvira's house!"

Francisco held me close and hugged me tightly. "My wife, I'm watching over you."

"May the Lord save us and protect us from our enemies," Grandma prayed.

The men swiftly removed the tallit from the poles and hid it in a hidden nook. Grandma Reyna hastened to conceal the scroll of the ketubah among the layers of her dress.

I quickly took off the veil, shoving it in a drawer.

We remained in the cellar with the guests and the dark shadows cast by the flames of the candles on the walls of our trembling hearts. After a few minutes that seemed to last an eternity, Papa entered, his face pale.

A collective sigh of relief rang out.

Mama brought over a chair for Papa, wiping the drops of perspiration emerging on his forehead with a kerchief. We all crowded around him.

"Bishop Afonso…" Papa's voice was shaking.

"The bishop?"

"Why did he come?"

"He said he was passing by the house, and came to inquire about the preparations for the wedding at the cathedral," Papa recounted softly.

"The bishop was surprised that I was wearing fine clothing. I explained to him that I was trying on my wedding outfit," Papa continued, while Mama wiped the sweat from his forehead again.

"Are you feeling well, Alvaro?" Mama waved a fan in front of his face.

"Ahh, it's nothing, I'm having some chest pains, probably due to the fear."

"Come on, let's go up to the house. You can lie down and rest."

"I'm fine. We have to keep going…"

"How did you manage to send him away so quickly?"

"Luckily for us, Brianda woke up and started crying. I apologized that the other members of the household were asleep, and that I had to put her to bed. The bishop waved goodbye with a weak gesture and hurried to leave the house."

"May the Lord be forever praised." Mama's eyes filled with tears.

"Philippa, I beg you, smile. We're marrying our daughter!" Papa implored her.

Suddenly, he clutched his chest and collapsed.

Francisco leapt from his place, caught Papa in his arms and laid him down on the floor.

"Alvaro!" Mama cried.

Samuel Migois kneeled down immediately beside Papa and placed a hand on his chest. "Señor Alvaro?"

Papa did not answer. We crowded around him in a panic. Stunned, I stared at Papa, his eyes gaped wide open and his face white.

"Amatus, quick, let's drain the bad blood," my uncle Samuel Migois rallied.

Amatus handed my uncle a thin needle he had extracted from his doctor's bag. Francisco held Papa's arm and Doctor Samuel brought the needle to it.

I hugged Mama, helping her into a chair.

"May the Eternal Lord have mercy upon him," Grandma Reyna prayed.

"A feather!" Samuel requested.

Francisco plucked a feather from his hat and handed it to him. My Uncle Samuel brought it to my father's nostrils.

Shivers wracked through me. The strands of the feather did not move at all.

"Papa, wake up!" I begged.

Mama knelt down across from Papa and stroked his face. "My darling, don't go," she cried.

"Blessed be the True Judge," Samuel sighed, closing Papa's eyes.

"No! No! My Alvaro!" Mama called out, ripping her dress in a gesture of mourning and bursting out in tears.

"Shush… Don't let them hear you," the men tried to silence her.

Grandma wept silently and opened the secret door. She took the pitchers of water from the table and poured the water out into the corridor.

"Elvira, walk the guests to your house. Make sure they leave one by one."

"We have to bring him up to the house quickly. Migois, hold his legs," Francisco said.

"We'll lay him down in his bed so that the priest thinks he died in his sleep," Samuel suggested.

With a massive effort, my husband and my uncle managed to hoist Papa to his room, laid him out in bed, dressed him in a nightshirt and covered his cold body, while Mama lit candles.

"We'll wait till the morning to call a priest," Francisco said.

In the morning, Mama tearfully told the priest that when she had woken up, she found Papa lifeless in his bed. The priest expressed his great sorrow over the fact that Señor Alvaro de Luna had not been allowed to confess to him before his death.

After the priest departed, Francisco made sure that Papa was washed with warm water and that his body was wrapped in a shroud. Mama briefly placed a gold coin in his mouth. "A commemoration of the Israelites crossing the River Jordan," she whispered in his ear, and bestowed the coin upon the impoverished seamstress.

Francisco quietly conducted the necessary arrangement for organizing Papa's lavish funeral.

Father's coffin was buried in the ground at the cemetery.

I kept hoping that at any minute, he would awaken, and everything would be as it was before. But Papa did not return.

My day of joy had become a day of grief.

The Wedding

The bells of the cathedral rang cheerfully. Esteemed guests wearing elegant clothes arrived in luxurious carriages and litters at the sumptuous Santa Maria Cathedral. Dozens of candles were lit in tall sconces lined up beside the pulpit, in the aisle, in the nooks and chapels.

The trumpeters of the Royal Guard blasted their horns. The king's archers were stationed before the cathedral.

"Long live the king!"

"Long live the queen!"

The guests cheered and bowed deeply. King Joao the Third, in a gold embroidered cloak and wearing a gold crown upon his head, and little Queen Catherine, in a purple, velvet dress and bedecked with jewels, paced regally to their seats at the front of the cathedral.

I strode beside Francisco, my head held high. My silk dress, pale blue and embroidered with gold threads, my wavy collar made of hardened silk, my puffed sleeves, in the style of the Medicis, my pink silk shoes and the pearls adorning my hair all masked the terrible pain I was experiencing over my father's death.

The king sat with a serious expression, while the pretty queen smiled at me.

The respected guests craned their necks to see the daughter of the late Señor Alvaro and Doña Philippa, the eighteen-year-old bride, who was about to marry one of the wealthiest men in Portugal, the forty-eight-year-old, Francisco.

"A princess…"

"Look how much gold!"

"A lavish dress!"

"Such jewelry!"

"Did you see her diamond ring?"

"Orphaned…"

"Swimming in riches!"

"The King of Spices!"

Whispers were heard. One whisper, "*Conversos*, New Christians," sounded louder than the others to me.

Brianda, in a turquoise silk dress with a white collar, her hair pulled back in a braid interwoven with gems, walked behind me in exhilaration, holding on to the hem of my dress. I was overcome by weakness. God help me! If the bishop only knew that we were already married, that we had wed secretly in a Jewish wedding ceremony! The king would throw us into Morus Largos, the big prison. I was shaking like a leaf. Mama blew me a kiss, tears in her eyes.

Bishop Afonso raised his hand. "Please repeat the words of the vow after me," he ceremoniously instructed. "In the name…" I mentally blocked my ears, "…and in the name of all the saints, I, Dom Francisco Mendes, agree to accept Señora Beatrice de Luna, daughter of the late Señor Alvaro and Señora Philippa de Luna, as my bride and my lawfully wedded wife."

I laced my fingers and quietly repeated the marriage vow, while in my heart, I intoned, *Moshe emet vetorato emet. Moses is a true prophet and his Torah remains true.*

Francisco, my love, placed a wide, heavy gold band on my finger, as befitting our station.

Along with the pain and the loss, I was also happy, the kind of happiness that filters down slowly from the top of the head, tickles the belly and sends an exhilaration of sorts into the arms and the legs. Brianda laughed at me later, saying there was a radiance of light in my eyes that she called "a happy, laughing light."

In my heart, I prayed, *Dear Queen Esther, holy Queen Esther, watch over us.*

An Arrow of Pain, 1531

I leaned out from the balcony of our home, looking over the masses of cheering children who had come to watch, along with their parents, the parade of strange animals and black-skinned natives brought over from the new colonies.

A tot with black curls, riding on his father's shoulders, observed, bright-eyed, as a tiger paced back and forth in a metal cage borne by dark-skinned natives.

His sister's small, chubby fingers grasped the hem of her mother's wide dress, thrust forward by the curve of her pregnant belly, while an elephant bedecked in shiny gold trundled heavily in the opulent street. The dimples in the child's cheeks deepened as she cheered enthusiastically at the sight of natives clad in skins and feathers, stomping their feet to the rhythm of the tune played by the trumpeters and drummers.

"Ow, that hurts!" the girl cried after inadvertently biting her finger instead of into the apple her mother had peeled for her.

The mother looked at the small finger, brought it to her mouth and kissed it.

A sharp arrow of pain and envy shot through my empty womb. *Oh Lord, remember me, and give me sons*, I prayed. A feeling of sadness and loneliness engulfed me. I was barren. Why couldn't I be a mother?

Despite the sorrow I witnessed in his eyes, Francisco consoled me, asking me to ignore the pointed looks of the women directed at my belly, to stop crying and blaming myself. He promised me that if we prayed, like Hannah and like our foremother Rachel, God would answer our prayers.

The city is celebrating, and my Francisco is not with me, I thought. I decided to call him and descended to the office floor.

***

"Mr. Silva, I leased the ship from you!" I heard his furious voice.

"I'm sorry, Señor Mendes, but…" The voice of the brawny ship owner was shaking.

"Señor Silva," Francisco interjected, "I leased the ship from you to import sacks of ginger from India. The ship *will* sail there!"

"But, Señor Mendes, the Venetian is paying me more."

"Señor Silva, a gentleman does not renege on his signature."

The ship owner's face grew flushed. "I implore you, that is impossible. I've leased it to the Venetian."

Francisco's eyes opened wide, his gaze unrelenting.

"Silva, in two days, the ship will be ready to sail to India," he said, his voice razor-sharp.

"Señora," the merchant doffed his hat to me as he passed by me, rushing out of the office.

"My wife, it's good to see you." Francisco's expression softened.

I placed my hand on his. "Francisco, why don't you build ships that you would own? That way, you're not dependent on the ship owners."

"An interesting idea, but I always saw myself as a merchant, rather than a shipbuilder."

"Francisco, the city is celebrating. I'd be happy if you joined me to watch the parade."

"I'm sorry, darling, but I have to prepare for a meeting with the minister of finance. King Joao is asking me for a contribution to the kingdom's treasury."

"Please, Francisco…"

Francisco rang the crystal bell and the serving girl showed up immediately.

"Please set a table for lunch for Señora Mendes and the *señor* on the balcony."

His fingers drummed on the accounting book lying on the antique escritoire.

"Darling, Jacob Morro has departed for Porto. Can you go over the accounts?"

A stab of pain tore through my belly. I knew my husband was proposing that I go over the accounts hoping that tracking buyer debts, sup-
plier payments and inventory would help ease the pain and tension that
dogged me month after month—would my monthlies be late? Would my
body acquiesce to my pleading? Would a baby develop in my womb?

***

White snowflakes fell all week, blocking the entrance to our home. I
sat with Francisco next to the hearth, which was emanating a pleasant
warmth.

"Francisco, I've been going over the accounts and noticed that 'the
Merchant King' Joao still hasn't returned the loan he took from the
company, and is asking to postpone payment of the debt."

"Darling, write to the king that we cannot postpone the payment. I'll
sign. If we agree, it will never end."

I blushed. Francisco was asking me to write a letter to the king.

The snow was piling up on the windowsill. Francisco stroked his beard
and gazed at me at length.

"Gracia, I believe I can trust you and tell you," he said.

A shiver passed through me. "Tell me what?"

Francisco walked over to the door, opened it and looked around to
make sure none of the servants were eavesdropping. He then closed the
door, brought his armchair closer to mine and held my hand.

"Gracia, the ships transporting merchandise for my company don't
transport only spices, fabric and gems to Europe," he whispered.

I had a feeling that something mysterious and unexplained was taking
place right under my nose.

"What do you mean? What else do they transport?"

Francisco leaned in toward me. "Gracia, do you remember visiting
Porto after the wedding? You wanted to see your friend Ermilanda
Ferreira, but her husband let us know she would not be home all week."

"That's right," I recalled.

"Father Gabriel told me that someone had informed on your friend
Ermilanda to the priest, telling him that she had swept the rooms of

her house on Friday evening, and prepared the wicks for the lighting of candles."

"Oh, no!" I cried out. "Was she imprisoned in Morus Largos?"

"No, no, we managed to save her from the Big Prison."

I looked at him in surprise. "Who's 'we'?"

"This is a joint endeavor by me, Diogo, Jacob Morro and the company's agents." Francisco looked deep into my eyes. "The Mendes Company is acting to save our forcefully converted brothers who wish to escape the persecution of the Christian Church and live openly as Jews."

I gripped the armrests of the chair until my knuckles turned white.

"What do you mean? How? Where?" I stammered.

"We smuggle them out of Portugal. Diogo risks his life and helps them cross the border into the lands of the Turkish sultan, who has opened the gates of his country to them. We concealed your friend Ermilanda and her children in an isolated monastery. During the night, my faithful agents took them to a fishing boat that sailed off to a desolate port. The agents made sure there were no members of the Church Guard patrolling the shores, equipped them with food and blankets, and brought them on board a waiting ship. The captain did not include the stop at the port in his log."

I listened to him with bated breath. "Why didn't you tell me?"

"Gracia, smuggling the New Christians involves an actual risk of death. You are obligated to keep the secret."

I placed my hand on his arm. "I'm your full partner."

"You should know our lives are in danger! My brother Diogo, who invests his fortune and his energy in saving our brethren, has been detained twice for interrogation."

I grew pale.

"Several different people have informed on him to the authorities on multiple occasions. About ten years ago, merchants who envied his success complained to the emperor that Señor Diogo Mendes, one of the New Christians, has a monopoly on black pepper, and was responsible for its high price. At the emperor's instruction, an arrest warrant was issued against Diogo, and he was imprisoned in a jail in Brussels. The arrest caused massive unrest among the gentry of Antwerp, who were afraid that commerce in Antwerp would come to a halt. They appealed to Queen Mary, who agreed to their request, and thanks to the writ of protection that Diogo received from the emperor several years ago, he was released from his confinement that same day. His friend Daniel de Negro, also the subject of an arrest warrant, managed to escape, leaving all his property and assets behind.

"Lately, due to another denouncement, my brother was arrested again, and all House of Mendes merchandise in the company's warehouses and aboard ships docked in the port was confiscated for the kingdom's treasury. Diogo was accused of heresy, practicing Judaism and encouraging immigration by New Christians to Constantinople. He was also accused of abusing his monopoly to fix the price of spices. He underwent an intense, prolonged interrogation at the bureau of the Inquisition. In his defense, he claimed that he was born Jewish, but lived as a good Christian, and that the aid he extended to New Christians was part of his regular commerce activity.

"I met with the king and asked him to intervene. Joao and his wife Catherine were afraid that confiscating the merchandise would cripple commerce with Portugal, and they appealed to the emperor."

Francisco produced two letters from the desk.

"The king's secretary gave me copies of the two letters they composed," he said. "Read them, please."

August 26, 1532
Lisbon

My esteemed brother, King of Spain and Emperor of the Holy Roman Empire,

Diogo Mendes, the brother of Francisco Mendes Benveniste, one of the most prominent merchants in Portugal, has been arrested and his property seized. Diogo is the company's business manager in Antwerp, while the confiscated merchandise belongs to Francisco, the owner of the Mendes Company, as well as other merchants.

Francisco Mendes, whom I value as a loyal servant of the crown, is begging and imploring Your Majesty to look into the incident, in your infinite kindness.

I will thank the emperor to open an urgent inquiry into the reason for these accusations, and ask that Diogo's rights be respected, that he be released from imprisonment, and that the merchandise be returned to him.

Your sister,
The Queen

***

August 28, 1532
Lisbon

To the beloved, excellent and powerful prince, Emperor Charles the Fifth of the Roman Empire, King of Germany, Spain and Jerusalem

My dear, honorable brother!

Francisco Mendes Benveniste has been living in my kingdom for forty years, and thus far, has accumulated a vast fortune. Francisco is a man with a stellar reputation, acclaimed as one of the most important and popular merchants and suppliers in the state, who deals with the colonies honestly and faithfully as a representative of the royal treasury.

His brother, Diogo Mendes, lives in Flanders. He acts as Francisco's representative, and respected Portuguese merchants who have deposited their merchandise under his management owe him an immense sum of money according to the agreements with India regrading commerce in pepper and spice.

Francisco Mendes has informed me that his brother Diogo was arrested under the instructions of the parliament and the council of the Flanders government and all his assets have been seized and confiscated.

If the confiscated merchandise is not released immediately, Diogo Mendes will be unable to pay the sum of two hundred thousand in gold coins that he owes the state, and Portugal will be facing a financial crisis and bankruptcy.

I would ask the emperor to release Diogo from internment, to return the confiscated merchandise and to dismiss the accusations against him.

It is highly essential that this matter be completed, and I will view it as a personal, distinct favor.

Esteemed sir, may the Lord preserve and safeguard you and your majesty under his protection.

King of Portugal
Joao the Third

I looked up from the letters. "They hold him in high regard."

"The king of England, Henry the Eighth, wrote to the emperor as well. He claimed that to the best of his knowledge, Francisco Mendes, the proprietor of House of Mendes, was a devout Christian, and as part of the seized merchandise and funds belonged to English merchants, he was asking the emperor to dismiss the accusations against Diogo," Francisco told me.

"All this pressure proved effective. After several difficult months, the emperor released Diogo from his confinement, with a financial guarantee of fifty thousand ducats, signed by his friend, the merchant Erasmos Shitz."

"But who informed on Diogo?" I asked.

Francisco drummed his fingers on his knees nervously, rose from his seat and opened the window. Snowflakes swirled into the room. Francisco breathed in the fresh air and closed the window.

"The Inquisition keeps the names of informers confidential, and they are listed in a separate file, rather than in the interrogation file. I made use of my connections among the heads of the Church and obtained the file."

Francisco struck the table with his hand. "The person who informed on Diogo was the son of a woman forced to convert. Diogo had helped her family escape from Antwerp."

"Do you know who he is?"

"Emilio, the son of Ermilanda Ferreira."

1534

The sky was clear and bright and a hot summer wind was blowing. I was wearing a light silk dress as I looked for Francisco on the office floor. Thomas said that early in the morning, the servants had carried Señor Mendes in a litter to the company's offices at the port.

Throughout the day, I walked around impatiently, waiting for my husband to return home.

"Good afternoon, dear," I heard his voice. "You look radiant!" Francisco entered our room and kissed my cheek.

"Francisco, please, I have something important to tell you," I whispered.

"Gracia, what is it?"

"Francisco, I have some news…" My fingers played with the pendant. "I think that… My monthlies are late by two months… I believe I'm pregnant…" I whispered.

"My darling, that's wonderful news! What happiness!" Francisco rose and held me close to his heart.

The months of the pregnancy were difficult, but I accepted the morning nausea and the vomiting with love. My feet swelled up and I could barely walk. I blessed every day in which the baby resided in my body.

About a week from the day I told Francisco the news, my body was beset by pain and bleeding. I was afraid I would lose the baby.

Francisco summoned my uncle, Doctor Samuel Migois, who taught medicine at the University of Coimbra, to take care of me. My uncle and his wife Rosa arrived to visit us along with their sons. Samuel gave me medicine to strengthen the womb and eased my anxiety.

It was a good opportunity to gather the family and reveal our secret to my thirteen-year-old sister Brianda, who had grown up into a beautiful, genteel adolescent, very elegantly dressed, as well as to twelve-year-old Bernardo, who was introverted, shy, and silent by nature, and to mischievous ten-year-old Juan with his abundant mane of black hair, whose two blazing black eyes missed nothing.

***

On the eve of Passover, "the holy holiday," I was in the midst of my eighth month of pregnancy, with a small belly and swollen feet. My heart contracted with a sharp pain due to the absence of my father, may he rest in peace. My mother, whose sorrow and loneliness were reflected in her eyes, gave all the servants some time off.

We wore white undergarments and over-garments that the seamstress had sewed for us particularly for the holiday, as well as white cloth shoes, donning white hats on our heads. Brianda, Juan and Bernardo, who were all celebrating Passover for the first time, chattered excitedly when we went down to the cellar of the house to prepare the sacred Passover bread[8].

The men placed new shingles on clay urns in which the fire used for baking burned. The women laid out white cloths on the floor, placing bowls with flour and water upon them. They got down on their knees, vigorously kneading the dough.

I sat in a chair, plucked a piece of the batter and threw it into the fire burning in the urn along with the other women. I listened to the sound of the dough crackling in the fire.

"For the offering of the challah," I explained quietly to Brianda, whose eyes were devouring these new sights.

I made sure that Grandma's matzah cookies, which she had placed on the blazing shingles, would not swell and round like my belly.

A murmur of excitement was heard as the hot, flat matzah cookies were placed on a white plate and handed out to everyone. We hugged and

---

8   Passover commemorates the liberation of the Israelites from slavery in ancient Egypt. It is observed by avoiding leavened bread, substituting special, unleavened bread called matzah instead.

kissed. The men picked up fresh branches and we began singing softly.

"I will sing unto the Lord
For He hath triumphed gloriously
The horse and his rider hath He thrown into the sea
The God of Israel, I will exalt Him."

***

On the Friday after Passover, early in the morning, I began experiencing strong contractions. Francisco sent the worried Teresa to fetch the midwife.

Aunt Elvira examined me and said the contractions were weak. The hours went by, the contractions increased, and my back was aching. Elvira examined me again, her face growing solemn.

"Sweetheart," she said gently, "the birth is complicated. The baby is lying horizontally. I have to turn him around."

I was weak and beset with pain, and prayed to God to have mercy on the baby in my womb, preserve and save him.

Teresa's kind hands massaged my aching back with warm olive oil, easing my pain.

Mama let Francisco into the room briefly.

"Please, I want the birth to end successfully," I whispered to him.

Francisco caressed my face. "My darling, I'm praying for you and for our child." He kissed me and departed.

Aunt Elvira rolled up her sleeves, crossed her chubby arms and laid them horizontally against my belly. Slowly and gently, she began to push at the embryo, turning him around while she talked to him.

"Dear baby, don't you worry, these old hands have already flipped over a few babies. Help me bring you into the world. Beatricci, one last effort."

The pain tore at my body. I bit my lips."

Elvira continued to push and turn the baby around "for just another moment." I bit my lips and suppressed a shout.

"We've done it. The head is facing down… Push hard! Harder!…

There, I can see the head… welcome," Elvira lifted the baby in her arms. "Congratulations! You have a sweet daughter." She placed the baby on my stomach.

My girl, my beauty, I love you. My heart expanded with happiness.

Francisco's eyes were full of tears when the midwife placed our baby in his lap. He gently stroked the strands of her black hair, peeking out from under the white wool blanket that swaddled her tiny body.

"You're so delicate! I've been waiting for you, my sweet."

I had no energy to breastfeed, and Teresa put a snatch of cloth dipped in boiled sugar water in the baby's mouth.

Francisco walked over to me. "Thank you, my dear," he said. "She's wonderful! Don't worry, she'll have brothers, as well."

True, I confirmed with a nod. But I knew that we would not have a son or another daughter.

A week later, Brianda and my cousins Bernardo and Juan decorated the crib with pink ribbons, the cooks and the bakers made sweets, baked cakes and cookies and stewed jam. On the Sabbath, during the secret prayer, Francisco wrapped himself in a tallit, recited *Shema Yisrael*, and bestowed two names upon our daughter: the secret name Reyna-Malka, after my grandmother Reyna and Queen (*Malka*) Esther, and the name Ana. Mother laid both her hands on Ana and blessed her:

"The Merciful One will bless the child's father and mother
and allow them the privilege of raising
and educating her to wisdom, honor,
and to be a pride and joy to her entire people.
May the Creator of the World be with her."

I kissed my daughter. "My Ana, I wish you had gotten to know your grandfather," I said.

Ana-Reyna was a quiet, calm baby. My cousin, the wet nurse Allegra, who had given birth a month earlier, breastfed her on a regular schedule. I asked Brianda to tell her stories and sing her songs, but she was always busy.

Juan and Bernardo did not conceal their curiosity, and occasionally sent her furtive smiles, gently stroked her, and made strange sounds and funny faces at her. All of the aunts discussed the crucial question—who did the baby resemble, her father or me?

Every few hours, Francisco would cease from his work and go into her room. Gently, he would lift her from her crib, kiss her and talk to her.

"She's a baby," I would laugh.

"Ana understands everything I tell her," Francisco protested, tickling Ana, who responded with a joyful smile.

As a birth present, Francisco gave me a bracelet and necklace made of gold and inlaid with rubies and jade. They were admired by everyone, particularly Brianda, who asked for permission to try on the bracelet. Francisco promised her that for her birthday, she would receive a bracelet with gems that would fit her wrist.

About two months after the birth, once I had recovered, we left for the cathedral for the baptism ceremony. As godparents, we chose my beloved uncle and aunt, Samuel and Rosa Migois, who arrived especially for the ceremony.

Bishop Afonso drizzled water three times on Ana's forehead and declared, "Welcome, Ana Mendes, to the bosom of the Church."

Null and void, null and void, null and void, I whispered in my heart.

The Palm Reveals the Soul's Destiny, 1535

I clearly remember that day at the beginning of June. In the morning, the sky was clear and blue, while in the afternoon, a gale of warm winds broke out.

Francisco felt ill. His face grew pale and his temperature rose. My strong husband canceled all his appointments for that day. Teresa, who was growing older, served him warm water with a cinnamon stick. Francisco only took a small sip. I dipped a kerchief in water and placed it on his head to ease his fever.

I wanted my uncle, Doctor Migois, to tend to my husband, but the king had invited him to his palace in Evora to see to Queen Catherine, who had come down with a cold.

I asked Teresa to summon our friend the physician, Amatus Lusitanus.

In the meantime, Juan strode in, tall and vigorous, as he buttoned the ivory cuffs of his white lace shirt. He walked over to me and kissed my hand.

Francisco opened his eyes, rose slowly and sat up in bed, leaning heavily against the pillows.

"How are you, dear uncle?"

"Thank you," Francisco replied. "Young man, did you do as I asked?"

"Uncle, immediately when the ship *Isabella* arrived from Antwerp and docked at the port, I gave the captain the package you sent for him, and he gave me an envelope to pass on to you."

"Well done, young man, I see you can be trusted."

"Uncle Francisco, Juan is always at your service."

"I'm proud of you," Francisco handed him two silver coins. "One for you and one for your brother Bernardo, wages for your good deed. Go over to Ana. She'll be happy to see you."

"Thank you," Juan smiled and left the room.

I opened the envelope with a knife made of carved ivory, a present from the king of Sri Lanka, from whom we purchased clove and cinnamon groves. I smoothed the missive, written in the secret alphabet.

June 23, 1535
Flanders, Antwerp
Francisco my brother,

I was hoping that this time, as well, we would succeed, as we did four years ago, when we recruited funds for Pope Clement the Seventh, thanks to which the Pope canceled the establishment of the Inquisition, claiming that anyone who was forcefully baptized could not be considered a Christian.

I did manage to reach an agreement with the papal legate, Bishop Marco della Rovere, according to which we will convey a sum of thirty thousand gold ducats to Pope Paul the Third, as a condition for halting the Inquisition's activity in Portugal.

I placed a very high sum in the fund of the New Christian congregation, but an argument broke out between the heads of the congregation and its wealthy members. Those opposing the proposal said we should not pay the entire sum in advance, and that conveying twenty thousand gold ducats in cash was enough. Those supporting it tried to convince them to pay the required sum, but were unsuccessful. To my immense sorrow, the battle has been lost this time. The decree is out, and an Inquisition will be established in Portugal.

Pray, leave everything behind and flee to Antwerp.

"Inquisition!" I let out a scream.

My head began to spin and fear ran through me. The anxiety was always there, but I didn't know I could feel terrified to the very depths of my soul. My legs were trembling. Francisco's fingers, once powerful and thick, now pale and wrinkled, caressed my cheek. "Darling, we're in danger, but the king can't refuse Henry the Eighth's request to allow us to leave for a visit in England, and will provide us with a writ of protection."

"I'll ask Teresa to start packing," I said, envisioning the tablecloths made of damask silk, the delicate embroidered linens, the dresses, the shoes and all the jewelry I must try to smuggle out of the country where I was born, and which was now becoming my enemy.

I took a deep breath and read on:

Francisco, I have asked my friend Thomas Cromwell, principal secretary for Henry the Eighth, king of England, to send King Joao the Third a letter recommending that he allow you to leave the country under the excuse that you wish to conduct a short visit to the bank subsidary I've opened in London, as well as provide you a writ of protection for the journey.

My friend Cromwell has influence over the king. He had advised him to sever connections with the Catholic Church, which opposed his divorce from Catherine, the daughter of Ferdinand and Isabella, so he could marry his mistress, Anne Boleyn.

Unfortunately, I have not managed to purchase the central building next to the cathedral in Rome for the company's offices.

With love,
Your brother, Diogo

Amatus Lusitanus, dapper and elegantly dressed, as was his custom, came in, placing his physician's bag on a chair.

"My friend..." Francisco sighed. "The 'devout' king dismissed the promise made by his father, Manuel the First, that we would not be accused of heresy until the end of 1537. The pope has signed the papal bull, and an Inquisition will be established in Portugal."

Amatus sat down in the chair, stunned, without saying a word.

"It looks as if Diogo de Silva, the king's brother, will be appointed as head of the Inquisition," Francisco added.

"Francisco, please, I want to examine you," Amatus said at last, inspecting the color of Francisco's tongue. He then looked into his pupils and listened to his breathing.

"Your heart is a bit weak. You must rest, and cannot become agitated."

Amatso Lusitanus opened his bag and took out several jars of medicine, which Francisco was to take twice a day along with food.

"I'll come by in the evening to see how you're doing," Amatus promised.

Mama, Grandma, Brianda, Juan and Bernardo came to visit Francisco. They were informed of the terrible news, and Mama said that trouble always came in bundles.

Suddenly, frightened voices rang out.

Thomas entered the room, looking stunned and battered, a blood-soaked shirt wrapped around his forehead.

"Señor and Señora Samuel and Rosa Migois," Thomas trembled, "have been killed in a horrifying accident on their way back from the king's palace in Evora."

Thomas leaned back against the wall. "The coachman of the carriage coming at us had been drinking wine. He lost control of the carriage and ran into us. The horses were going wild and the carriage flipped over..."

"You desire the best by your side..." Mama called out in agony and began to weep in a heartbreaking manner.

"It was a miracle I survived..." Thomas mumbled while the servants wiped the blood from his face. Amatus quickly applied a concoction to stop the bleeding and bandaged Thomas's head.

"*Escrito en la palma lo que va a passar la alma.* The palm reveals the soul's destiny..." Mama sighed. "Such is life. A man's fate is determined in advance."

I hugged Bernardo, who curled up in his chair, pursed his lips and refused to talk. He appeared to be in shock. Brianda sat next to him and cried along with him.

There were tears in Juan's eyes, as well. He interrogated Thomas, wanting to know what had happened down to the smallest detail and whether his parents had suffered.

"The *señor* and *señora* did not suffer. The doctor and his wife were tired and fell asleep when we left the king's palace," Thomas soothed Juan.

Despite his infirmity, Francisco began to handle the details of the funeral, sending a carriage with our servants to fetch the bodies of our loved ones.

After two days of pain and sadness, hundreds of esteemed attendants from Coimbra, Porta, the king's court in Evora and Lisbon arrived for the funeral at the cathedral. The stunned Bernardo wept next to the wooden caskets in which his parents were buried. Juan kissed his mother's coffin, hugged his father's and refused to part from him.

I turned my eyes to heaven. "Papa Alvaro, our dear Samuel and Rosa Migois are joining you. Take care of them," I whispered.

Let Our Prayer Come Before Thee, 1535

Summer had passed. A gale of wind and rain was raging outside. The servants added logs to the hearth.

I hadn't slept a wink all night. As morning neared, I fell into an unquiet sleep, full of terrible dreams, but the true nightmare began in the morning, when I saw Francisco in his bed.

His head, laid on a silk pillow, was tilted sideways, his thin hair stretched upon his face like pale parchment, and his breath grew increasingly labored, his chest rising and falling. He emitted a deep, heavy sigh, his speech fading away.

"Gracia, my darling," I read his lips. "My days are numbered. Ana-Reyna, my daughter..."

I poured a little water from the pitcher next to his bed into a cup, moistening his dry lips.

"Please, bring Ana," I asked Teresa.

Ana reached out and clung to me. I sat her in Francisco's lap. He embraced her with a loving gaze infused with deep sadness, gently caressing her face.

"Ana... My daughter..." he murmured sorrowfully.

Little Ana's face grew solemn, and her lips began to tremble. I hugged her and took her out of the room. "Gracia, the papal writ of protections is in the secret drawer... Flee to Antwerp," Francisco said, with much effort.

I'm losing my husband. The impossible thought filtered gradually into my mind.

I kissed his face, which had assumed a jaundiced hue. "My Francisco, forgive me if I've hurt you."

Francisco stroked my face. "Do you remember how we dreamed of leaving Lisbon and reaching the Promised Land...?" His black eyelashes lowered and his lids closed. "Promise me you'll bury me on the Mount of Olives in the Holy Land," he whispered.

He's saying goodbye to me, the realization hit me. I looked up to the heavens. *No, please, don't take him, he's still young... We have a two-year-old child!*

"Francisco, don't go. Stay with us," I begged.

The shutters of his eyes opened and closed, hooded with a murky whiteness.

"Señora, Doctor Amatus Lositans," Thomas said meaningfully.

"Let him in."

Amatus stood at Francisco's head, leaning in toward him.

"Zemach Benveniste, my friend, forgive me... Do you want to recite the confession with me?" he whispered in his ear.

Francisco blinked.

"Lord of the Universe, let our prayer and supplication come before Thee, and may my sins be atoned for," Amatus whispered.

Francisco made an effort to repeat the sentence, while a large tear rolled down his cheek.

"Amen," I replied with a heavy heart.

"'If there is anyone sick among you, let him call for the elders of the church, and let them pray over him,'" I heard the voice of Bishop Afonso behind the closed door.

Immense pain was reflected in Thomas's face. "Señora, Father Afonso, the confessor priest, wishes to conduct the confession with Francisco," he said.

How do they already know? I wondered bitterly.

Francisco's hand touched my own, and with a massive effort, he shook his head.

"Tell the bishop that Señor Francisco is sleeping," I told Thomas.

Francisco's breathing grew gradually heavier. I saw his lips moving. I brought my ear down to his mouth while he turned his head toward the wall.

"*Shema Yisrael, Hashem e-lhoeynu, Hashem ehad.* Hear, O Israel, the Lord is our God, the Lord is One," were his last words.

Francisco passed away as a Jew. I closed his eyes and kissed his forehead. "Farewell to your soul, which has departed from this world."

With trembling hands, I poured the water in the pitcher into the potted plant on the windowsill next to Francisco's bed. I passed a gold coin through his mouth and hid it in a drawer for charity. I opened the door and invited the bishop to enter.

***

On a cold winter day, I dressed in black and left to bury my Francisco in the cemetery.

King Joao, Queen Catherine, the Pope's legate, ambassadors from the kings of Spain, England, France, Antwerp and the Holy Roman Empire, his partner Señor Affaitati, noblemen, company agents, merchants and commoners—all of them escorted Francisco on his final path. Overwhelmed with sorrow, my mother, Brianda, Bernardo, Juan and Aunt Elvira all walked beside me. At the end of the lavish funeral parade were Thomas, Teresa and the staff of servants.

Bishop Afonso sprinkled water on Francisco's opulent casket and said a prayer. Slowly, my darling's coffin was lowered into the open grave as the tears fell from my eyes.

***

The house filled with guests. I maintained a reserved expression. I did not want to share my heartache with anyone, but at night, I wet the pillow with my tears.

The many people consoling me looked at Ana with pity.

"Ana, your father is in heaven," I tried to explain to my daughter, but Ana wouldn't stop calling out, "Papa, Papa!" and when no answer came, she lay down on the sofa beside me and cried.

***

A week after the funeral, the company solicitor entered the study where

I was waiting with my mother. Puffed with self-importance, he read the will to us:

> I, Francisco Mendes, bequeath half of my assets to my wife, Beatrice Mendes. I bequeath the other half of my assets to my brother and business partner, Diogo Mendes, who resides in Flanders. I request that my brother Diogo be merciful, and if he dies without children, shall bequeath the assets to my daughter, Ana Mendes.
>
> Of the half of my assets inherited by my wife, two-thirds are intended for my daughter, Ana Mendes, who will receive her inheritance at the age of eighteen or on the day she is married.
>
> The remaining third is intended for expenses related to the will and for charity. The sum left over is intended for my wife, Beatrice Mendes.
>
> I appoint my dear wife, Beatrice de Luna Mendes Nasi, as sole guardian to our daughter, and financial and business manager in charge of the perfume trade. I have full faith and trust in my wife's wisdom in managing the property. In case my wife Beatrice passes away before our daughter Ana turns eighteen, the property will pass in trust to my brother Diogo, who will convey the entire inheritance to my daughter Ana once she turns eighteen.

I froze in place. The will Francisco had left behind contradicted our prenuptial agreement. I was supposed to inherit half the family fortune.

The solicitor left a copy of the will on the desk. "Señora, I'm at your service," he said and left the house.

"Mama, why? Why did Francisco cancel the agreement between us in his will?"

"Listen," Mama said, "Francisco was a wonderful man, and I loved him very much, but what has taken place cannot be undone. With all the sorrow and the pain about his passing, listen to my advice: it's better to be a widow than a married woman."

"Mama, I can't believe you're saying that it's better to be a widow!"

"Gracia, you are a twenty-five-year-old widow, mother to a daughter. As a widow, this is the only time in your life when you can make independent decisions. Until you got married, you were under the control of your father. After your marriage, you were dependent upon your husband. Now you have equal rights to any man." Mama clutched both my hands.

"Think about it. Even if Francisco didn't leave you half of the property, you are Ana's guardian and the trustee for her inheritance. In fact, you are the sole manager of the House of Mendes company. As of today, you are entitled to sign letters on behalf of the company, make deals, buy houses and merchandise, lend money… Gracia, from now on, you are in charge of your destiny."

A Royal Invitation, 1536

I looked out the window. The king's soldiers, clad in armor and helmets and bearing bayonets in their hands, stood taut and erect outside our home, making sure no one would remove the contents of the house.

Thomas knocked on the door of the parlor. "The royal messenger is waiting in the colonnade."

My eyes met those of my mother. *What do they want this time?* I wondered. After all, the king had agreed to my request and ordered to postpone the execution of the writ given to his clerks, to conduct an inventory of all the property left by Francisco, for four months.

"Let him in, please."

The messenger swept back the hem of his lavish blue velvet cape, grasping the hilt of the long sword dangling from his waist. He strode toward the damask silk sofa on which I was sitting, bowed to me slightly, handed me a gilded missive signed with the royal seal, and departed.

May 1536
Evora

For Señora Beatrice Mendes

Their Royal Highnesses King Joao the Third and Queen Catherine are happy to inform you that the daughter of our dear Dom Francisco Mendes Benveniste, who has departed from us, and of Señora Beatrice Mendes, Señorita Ana Mendes, is invited to the royal palace to be educated under the patronage of Queen Catherine, the granddaughter of the monarchs of Spain, Ferdinand and Isabella, and learn the manners, the genteel customs and the arts of the nobility and the Church. When the time comes, she will enjoy the privilege of having us marry her to a worthy man from a noble family.

The King and Queen will send a royal carriage to bring Señorita Ana Mendes to their palace in ten months from today.

Their Royal Highnesses
Joao the Third and Queen Catherine
Monarchs of Portugal

I felt the clutches of the Catholic Church grasping me by the neck and slowly, in a long, vicious act of torture, suffocating me. My breath became short and rapid.

The king and queen weren't wasting any time! Those cads wanted to distance my daughter from me and use her to take over Francisco's inheritance.

"Mama, I'm frightened." My voice was trembling. "The king is planning to take Ana from me and marry her off to one of his lords."

Mama hugged my shoulders. "You mustn't lose hope. No one believed you would manage to defer their intention of taking inventory of Francisco's property and of House of Mendes assets."

I paced back and forth in the room in agitation. "But if Ana becomes their protégé, we'll never be able to leave Portugal for the Ottoman State, as Francisco and I had planned."

The door opened. It appeared as if Thomas, his brow deeply furrowed, had been listening in on our conversation. He handed me a missive. "Señora, the captain of the perfume boat returning from Flanders has brought a letter from Diogo with him."

The lovely words written on silk paper flickered before my eyes:

Señora Beatrice, waiting for you in Antwerp. I promised Francisco I would take care of both of you. Leave as soon as possible! The emperor is planning to forbid New Christians from settling in his country.

"Gracia, your brother-in-law is right. You have to leave," Mama said softly.

What would Francisco do? I asked myself. I remembered that Francisco would write down lists for himself, planning his next steps in writing. I sat down at the desk and took a sheet of paper.

Final destination: the Ottoman State, I wrote down in capital letters, which I underlined.

Request a certificate of transit to Flanders from the king.

The problem: how to get the inheritance money out of Lisbon?

Sail through London. Secure lodging.

Preparations: sell assets to family members, collect debts, pack, book passage on the ship and purchase tickets.

Important to show that business is going on as usual, order merchandise, offer loans.

My lips curved in a subtle smile. It was true that the king had posted a decree prohibiting New Christians from leaving Portugal, but I had two valuable documents. I extracted the key to the secret drawer from my dress, opened it, and took out the two documents enclosed in a red leather file.

The first was a writ of protection and security that the Pope had granted to Señor Francisco Mendes, his wife, the members of his family and their servants, four years before his death.

The second document was a royal writ of protection as well as a certificate of transit to visit London. This important certificate had been given to Francisco by King Joao at the recommendation of Thomas Cromwell, principal secretary to Henry the Eighth, king of England.

The problem was that Joao's writ of protection permitted me to go to London, and not to Antwerp, and I did not want the king to send his soldiers after us.

Another problem was that the king had forbidden New Christians from removing chests of gold and silver from the country.

I dipped my quill in the inkwell, but could not write even a single letter. I did not know what excuse I should use to ask the king for permission to leave for Flanders. I wondered what Francisco would have written.

"Make use of your femininity… appeal to their emotions," Mama suggested.

I put down my quill. Sipping a bit of the water perfumed with rosewater that Mama had poured for me, I gazed out the window at the bustling city I was planning to escape.

"The only way..." I lowered my voice, "...to get to Antwerp safely and get my money out of Lisbon would be to use the excuse of a wedding. I'll write to the king and queen that Brianda was promised to Diogo at birth. Now she's turning sixteen, and Diogo is requesting that they wed. Since Brianda is an orphan, I'll ask the king for permission to escort her to her wedding, which will take place in Antwerp, taking the chests of gold that will serve as her dowry with us."

Mama's eyes ignited. "An interesting idea, although—" Subtle wrinkles appeared at the corners of her eyes. "I thought that..." Her fingers drummed on the arm of the chair.

I rose from my seat. "Mama, I don't have another solution."

"Gracia, do you think the king will believe you?" Her fingers began tapping again.

"I have to try."

I unrolled a map of the world and pointed at Lisbon. "If the plan succeeds, we'll sail from here." I outlined the path to London with my finger. "I'll explain that I want to visit the branch of the House of Mendes Bank, and get to know the company's agents," I continued to draw the imaginary line. "From London, we'll sail to France, and from there to Flanders. Mama, start getting ready; you and Grandma are coming with me."

I promised Mama that Juan and Bernardo, who had joined my household after their parents were killed, would come along on the journey as well.

Since appealing to King Joao the Third and Queen Catherine and requesting their permission to escort Brianda to her wedding in Flanders, I had been experiencing tense days and sleepless nights. I went over mountains of House of Mendes documents as well as the accounting books, asking the agents to collect debts from the merchants.

After about three weeks, the permission I'd been longing for was received at last, but only on the condition that Mama and Grandma stayed in Lisbon.

"Gracia, I'm staying with Grandma. You know she's very sick," Mama said, her voice choked. She knew that after we left, it was possible that we might never see each other again.

Brianda was hesitant. She was afraid to leave home for the unknown and wanted to stay with Mama. But Mama convinced her that she would have a better life in Antwerp.

The house submerged in a chaos of sorting and packing of clothes, valuables and documents.

There was only one thing I still had to do. I wanted to ask dear Thomas, my household manager, to come with us. Even as a child, I had formed a deep bond with him after my mother told me that his entire family had been murdered in the terrible riots in Porto. Thomas's family had lived in the village of Belmonte, two days' drive away from Porto, but the murderous rioters had reached it, as well.

On that day, the ten-year-old Thomas had been sent up to the attic to fetch a wooden crate as part of the preparations for fleeing the village. Suddenly, he heard the gallop of horses, followed by shouting: "*Marranos*—pigs! *Christo Judeus*—Jewish Christians!" The yelling mingled with cries for help, sounds of struggle and the lashes of a whip, coming from the ground floor. The marauders had blocked the doors and were not letting anyone in.

Thomas hid under the boxes and the old clothes. He heard his family members begging for their lives. Peeking down through the wooden boards, he saw the enflamed rioters heft an ax and murder his parents and eight brothers and sisters.

Only after twenty-four hours without food or water, with the silence of death inhabiting the house, did Thomas, whose secret Jewish name was Eliezer Hacohen, dare to come down from the attic. His kind neighbors buried the members of his family.

When rumors of the tragedy reached us, Papa sent emissaries to bring the child to us. Thomas arrived suffering from a high fever, chills and nightmares. The only things he had brought with him was a white tallit with blue stripes, which his mother had knitted him and made him secretly swear to pass on to his sons, and the proclamation of "*Shema Yisrael, Hashem e-lhoeynu, Hashem ehad*, which he remembered.

Our dear Thomas never managed to overcome the horrific sights he had witnessed, and did not get married or start a family. Sometimes, at night, shouts of anxiety were heard from his room.

"Thomas," I addressed him now, "we're going to London. Please join us."

A bashful smile of gratitude surfaced on his kind, lined face.

"I want to thank the *señora* for inviting me," he said. "The *señora* and her family are my only family on earth. There is no doubt that I will take care of the *señora* and her family."

PART TWO

Flanders
1537-1545

Antwerp, 1537

The wind beat at my face as I stood on the deck of the *Elizabeth*, sailing from gray and cloudy London to Flanders. Drops of water masked my tears of loneliness and the emotional turmoil that had taken over me.

Five weeks ago, I had left my loved ones behind in Lisbon, the city of my birth, and sailed to chilly London. We stayed with our relative Antonio de la Ronja, who had managed to flee Portugal with his family and was running the House of Mendes Bank. He told us that the Jews had been exiled from England in 1290, but a few wealthy families had been permitted to return. He introduced me to these families, as well as to the city's nobility. I visited the bank's offices, met the company's agents and got acquainted with their activity, and managed to get five chests full of gold coins out of London.

I wondered how our life would look in this new country. Would Ana, Brianda and my cousins grow used to the foreign language, people and customs?

Ana tugged at my dress. "Mama, when will we get there? I want to go home. Is Papa waiting for us?"

I stroked her hair. "Sweetie, Papa… passed away."

"I want Papa," Ana begged.

Brianda, the freckles on her cheeks bright in the sunlight that had emerged between the clouds, caressed Ana's face and told her, "Papa is watching over you from heaven. Let's go for a walk." She gave Ana her hand and they strolled toward the stern of the ship.

Juan was running around on the deck, warmly saying goodbye to the many friends he had made. Bernardo was leaning over the ship's banister, wrapped up in his own thoughts.

The ship maneuvered between the various vessels docked at the busy port, stopping near a large, impressive stone fortress. The captain cast the anchor, the sailors tossed the ropes and tied the ship's stern to the bollard on the dock, and a young seaman swiftly climbed the ship's mast and began to unrig the sails.

I thanked the captain. The ship's ramp was lowered. I held Ana close to me as her eyes devoured the new sights around her.

"My daughter, we've found safe harbor."

We were greeted by elegant buildings, their spires towering skyward, fish stands, spices in a variety of bright colors and intoxicating aromas, breathtaking fabrics and lace, people wearing colorful, sumptuous outfits, and a mixture of languages and nationalities.

A party of distinguished gentlemen was waiting on the bustling pier. At its center was a tall nobleman of fifty or so with a strong face, thick eyebrows, a short, graying beard and brown hair peppered with white peeking out from under his elegant hat, sporting a blue feather. The vitality in his brown eyes won me over. He looks like Francisco! I realized suddenly.

The esteemed nobleman approached us with a vigorous stride, gallantly doffed his hat and gave me a small bow. "Hello, Señora Beatrice, I'm delighted to see you all. Welcome!"

"Hello, my brother-in-law, Señor Diogo Mendes."

"Señora Beatrice, I'm sorry that my brother Francisco did not live to make it to Antwerp, and that my sister Philippa and Grandma were not allowed to leave Lisbon."

"Señor Diogo, the important thing is that we managed to carry out Francisco's wishes and escape to Antwerp. Mama and Grandma send you their love."

Diogo's gaze surveyed the excited family members.

"*Chapeau*," he doffed his hat to me again. "Señora Beatrice, you are certainly worthy of respect. A young widow with a small daughter taking responsibility for her sister and cousins and sailing by herself to England, and from there to Flanders…" The gentlemen surrounding us nodded, appraising me with approval.

"Thank you, I was just doing my duty. Anyone else would have done the same under the circumstances."

"This lovely girl must be your sister, Mademoiselle Brianda." Diogo turned to look at her.

"Señor Diogo, hello!" Brianda laughed melodiously, favoring him with a flattering smile. "Antwerp is pretty!"

"Act politely and appropriately for a sixteen-year-old girl," I whispered to Brianda, who had not taken her eyes off Diogo.

"Hello, sweetie," Diogo stroked three-year-old Ana's cheek while I held her tiny hand.

"Papa?" Ana tilted her head up, tentatively examining Diogo, who resembled his brother.

"What a beauty. It's sad that her father won't enjoy the privilege of raising her," Diogo said.

"Dear boys, you must be the sons of Samuel and Rosa," Diogo addressed Juan, who was a head taller than Bernardo.

"Hello, Uncle Diogo, my name is Juan Migois and I'm thirteen years old. We're so happy that Aunt Beatricci, the best aunt in the world, has taken us with her," Juan smiled, bowing.

"Good morning, sir, my name is Bernardo and I'm fifteen," Bernardo introduced himself.

"Juan and Bernardo, in Antwerp your last name will be 'Mickas' and not 'Migois,' in accordance with the custom here."

Thomas, whom I'd put in charge of the luggage and the servants, came down the ship's ramp, supervising the porters who were unloading the forty crates and ten chests containing the family treasures.

"Señora, please, you're my guest. Raphael del Vino, my major-domo, will take care of the servants and of conveying the merchandise to your new home, accompanied by a guard of armed soldiers who will replace the English soldiers."

"At your service, señora," said Raphael del Vino, a strand of his black hair falling across his forehead, and turned to Thomas.

A chubby man, his gray beard wafting in the breeze, approached the pier at a brisk run. "Hello, Señora Beatrice! Mademoiselle Brianda!"

"Hello, Jacob Morro." I was happy to see a familiar face.

"Dear señora, welcome," Jacob Morro kissed my hand, clad in a white glove.

"Gentlemen, you may approach," Diogo addressed the party of dignitaries waiting patiently.

"Dear Señora Beatrice, it's good to see you," said Professor Augustino Henricks, whose ruddy face was now lined with wrinkles.

"Madame, Gabriel Enriquez, House of Mendes's Paris agent, at your service," a tall, handsome man, elegantly dressed, raised his hat. "It's an honor to meet you. I've heard a lot about your cleverness and knowledge from your husband, Francisco."

"Thank you," I replied, touched. I hadn't known that Francisco talked about me.

"Señora, welcome. Emanuel de Orte, the accountant," a short gentleman of fifty or so, with shaggy hair and a broad nose, introduced himself.

"Señor Diogo, with your permission, I'd like to invite the esteemed gentlemen to a meeting," I said. Diogo's eyes sparked with rage. The House of Mendes agents stared at me in amazement.

"I'm sorry, the *señora* is inviting us to a meeting? For what purpose? Señor Diogo, do you consent to this assembly?" Emanuel de Orte asked.

Diogo tried to maintain an inscrutable expression.

"Gentlemen, the *señora* is the heir to and manager of Casa Mendes," Jacob Morro said.

My brother-in-law Diogo raised an eyebrow.

"Mama, I'm tired," Ana tugged at my dress.

"Gentlemen, excuse us. Madam, I can see that you're all tired from your journey. Come on, I'll take you to your home," Diogo said.

House of Mendes

A procession of lavish carriages awaited us beside the pier. Servants in livery opened the door of the white carriage for me and my family. Diogo extended his hand and helped me climb on board the coach, which was hitched to four white horses. He sat down across from me and the carriage began to move slowly.

"Señora Beatrice, I was surprised by the invitation you extended to the House of Mendes agents without asking my opinion." His nostrils were quivering.

"Forgive me," I said softly, looking into his eyes. "Francisco, may he rest in peace, appointed me as trustee to Ana's inheritance and as manager of House of Mendes," I replied leisurely.

"Beatrice, the agents of the House of Mendes receives instructions solely from me!" His voice creaked out.

"At the beginning of the year, House of Mendes must convey 1,200,000 gold ducats to Joao the Third, king of Portugal, in return for the concession to deal in black pepper." I emphasized the immense sum. "I have to ascertain that the money is at our disposal."

"Señora, in Flanders, it is not considered acceptable or proper for a woman to summon the heads of a company and its agents to a meeting. Even if there is a problem, since I am the head of the company and your elder, the managers will only accept instructions from me."

"To my immense sorrow, I was widowed." I sighed, holding back the tears that wanted to force their way out. Diogo averted his eyes and offered me an embroidered handkerchief.

"A widow is entitled to conduct business." I wiped the tears away. "Queen Mary was widowed by her husband, Lajos—Louis the Second, king of Hungary and Bohemia. Her brother Ferdinand, crowned as king of Hungary, appointed her as Queen Regent."

Diogo looked down at his shoes, adorned with silver buckles. "Señora Beatrice, please don't cry. We'll postpone this conversation for another day. Right now, I'll be happy to introduce you to our lovely city."

The carriage drove us along the Schledt River, to bustling Grote Market Square, with a fountain at its center.

"The Cathedral of Our Lady," Diogo pointed out the tall spire of the cathedral.

"We'll join you for Mass on Sunday," I said.

"Good idea. The bishop and the city's gentry will be waiting to meet you.

"These are the guildhalls for the merchants and the craftsmen. That lavish palace with the tall façade and the statuettes on its roof pediments belongs to the diamond merchants," he continued to provide me a tour of the city.

"For the use of all merchants, of all nations and tongues," he read out the declaration embossed on an impressive marble building. "The stock exchange building," Diogo said. "This is where commerce in perfume takes place, and where I spend many hours."

"I would be happy to visit the stock exchange," I said. Diogo looked out the window, ignoring my request.

"This is City Hall, the Stadhuis. It was designed by the architect Cornelius Floris, who also designed my estate," Diogo boasted.

The carriage swept through congested streets which housed workshops and studios for goldsmiths and silversmiths, bookbinders, printers, painters, sculptors, tailors, silk weavers and lacemakers. Diogo asked the coachman to stop next to a crowd of people.

A man of fifty or so was standing on an upside-down wooden crate and sermonizing against the Catholic Church, preaching passionately in favor of Luther's reformation. The crowd was protesting loudly against the speech, pelting him with various objects.

"The Reformation movement is spreading like wildfire, and many of the New Christians are joining the Protestants," Diogo explained.

The coach continued on its way, circled between the squares and the

narrow allies, departed the city for the Kipdorp region, full of gardens
and verdant estates, crossed the bridge over the quiet river, with a grove
of tall trees beside it, passed a wrought iron gate and turned onto a
twisting dirt road. Beside the path was a copse of trees whose leaves were
glowing in golden-red, like a guard of honor. We approached the most
beautiful estate I had ever seen, including a central building and nine
wooden houses, with a forest stretching out beyond them.

"We're here!" Welcome to your residence," Diogo said. "My home is
your home. I purchased the estate from Jacob Marsilas, a Jew who converted to Christianity after the riots and the expulsion of the Jews from
the city in 1370. To this day, I'm still paying the Jewish Tax on the land,"
he told me quietly, examining my face.

"At the end of the night comes daybreak," I replied softly, my hands
fluttering at the gold pendant I wore.

Diogo nodded.

The procession of servants continued driving to the back entrance of
the servants' quarters and the stables.

At the entrance to the estate, stood a marble sculpture in all its glory.
A rider upon a horse, which was rearing back on its hind legs, its front
legs thrust powerfully in the air. We entered an inner courtyard with a
gilded fountain at its center, cheerfully spraying water into a goldfish
pool. Liveried servants opened the carriage doors for us.

A line of curious servants, men and women, stood at the entrance to
the main building, bowing and curtsying before us. Ana held on tightly
to my hand when an elderly servant opened the palace's two heavy doors.

Stunned by the opulence, we walked around in a parlor whose ceiling
was adorned with gold illustrations of flowers and leaves, its floor made
of reddish marble and its high walls covered with Flemish tapestries and
with a magnificent collection of paintings.

Diogo strolled among the paintings like a proud father. "Raphael's
Ezekiel's Vision. I purchased it in Milan, when I opened a branch of House
of Mendes, our company, in Milan."

Why is he saying 'our company'? I wondered. After all, Francisco had
been the one who had founded the company, as well as owning it!

Brianda paused next to an ancient harp standing on a wooden cabinet adorned with gold etchings. "That's a beautiful harp," she said.

"Thank you." Diogo placed his hand on the harp. "Leonardo da Vinci himself played this harp. He built it with his own two hands and won a harp-playing competition held in Milan. Later, he put the harp up for sale and Lorenzo de' Medici bought it. At a literary reading in the palace of his son Giovanni de' Medici, his sister, Queen Catherine, who married Henri the Second, played it. Its wondrous sound won me over, and I decided I had to have it in my possession."

"You must have paid a fortune for it…" Juan commented.

"Juan!" I raised my finger in front of his eyes in warning.

Diogo twirled his mustache. "I was willing to pay a lot for it, and after sustained negotiation, Giovanni agreed to part from it."

"Señor Diogo, does anyone play the harp?" Brianda queried.

"Sometimes, at receptions for ambassadors or princes that I hold at the palace, I strum it," Diogo replied.

"Brianda and I learned to play the lute. A troubadour passing through our town taught Brianda to play the harp," I told him.

Brianda's fingers fluttered lightly over the strings of the harp. "Please, can I play?" she asked.

"I would be honored to hear you play," Diogo doffed his hat.

"Thank you!" My sister directed a heart-melting smile at him.

"Señor Diogo, why don't we get settled in our rooms first? We can hear the performance later," I said.

Brianda caressed the dark brown wooden chest. "Please…"

"Señora Beatrice, please stay for a few more minutes. Sit down, please. Some refreshments for our honored guests."

Serving girls in aprons and immaculate white kerchiefs passed among us, bearing gold plates with warm, airy wafers and cups of lemonade.

When Brianda's long fingers gently plucked the strings, tender sounds filled the room, imbuing me with yearning.

Diogo clapped enthusiastically. "Señorita Brianda plays so beautifully! I'd be happy if you played for us again."

"I'd love to, any time the *señor* asks," Brianda replied, blushing slightly. "It's a shame I left my lute at home. I was afraid it would be damaged during the journey."

"I'll order you a lute," Diogo promised.

"Can I play it too?" Bernardo asked.

"Bernardo, I'd be happy to order a lute for you, as well." Diogo mussed his hair.

A sharp stomachache cut through my body. I was caught by surprise. Brianda had instantly become a star around which Diogo orbited. While I, who had always been at the center of society, was hardly getting any attention at all.

***

I dove into the canopy bed. The conversation with Diogo had exhausted me more than the trip from Lisbon to London, and from there to France, and finally to Flanders.

The ringing of the cathedral bells woke me from the slumber that had taken over me. I peeked at the silver watch I had received as a gift from Amatus Lusitanus. It was now noon. I heard a light knock on the door.

Teresa and a Flemish serving girl in a white lace kerchief, holding a pitcher of water and a thick towel, entered the room.

"Señora Mendes." The maid curtsied deeply. "My name is Valera. Señor Diogo has appointed me as your personal handmaid," she addressed me in Portuguese.

"Ahmm…" Teresa cleared her throat, took a hairbrush lying on the dresser and began to brush my hair with vigorous motions.

"Teresa is my personal handmaid. I'll be happy if you serve me together," I replied.

"Teresa, are the rooms you were assigned handsome? Did you drink? Eat?" I asked.

"Thank you, Señora Beatrice, we were given nice rooms. The crates and chests are in the rooms. The major-domo made sure Thomas and the *señora*'s servants will eat in the house servants' dining room," Teresa said, binding my hair into a knot.

"The *señora* is invited to lunch. I'll help the *señora* get dressed." Valera handed me a warm towel and poured water from the pitcher into the bowl. I washed my face in the cool water.

Teresa hastened to open the wooden chest with the silver etchings, taking out a pink gown embroidered with a pattern of green leaves, orange velvet shoes, hair ornaments and kidskin gloves.

Valera stretched the pink silk cover with the rose pattern over the white canopy bed, straightened the various creams and unguents on the dresser, and wiped an invisible speck of dust.

"Señorita Ana is waiting for the *señora* in her room," Teresa said once she had finished dressing me.

"Mama, mama!" Ana hugged me when I entered her room, while Allegra gently gathered back her hair.

With a sense of relief tempered with tension, I went down to the dining hall. Diogo sat at the head of a table set with gold dinnerware. "Hello, ladies," he rose from his seat for us.

A white-haired servant pulled back the velvet armchair on Diogo's right for me, and seated Ana next to me. Brianda was sitting across from Diogo. She had changed her travel dress for a mint-colored gown with a square neckline. At her throat was an emerald necklace and on her wrist was a bracelet that Francisco had given her as a birthday present. Bernardo was next to her. Juan, who ran into the room, was seated to Diogo's left.

We said the blessing over the food. I tasted a bit of what was laid out in front of me: rice with saffron, baked fish and dumplings filled with mushrooms.

Diogo told us about the lively trade in black pepper and other spices going on at the perfume exchange, describing the competition between the merchants over the sacks of spices sold in advance even before they had been picked at the colonies.

"Uncle Diogo, please, I want to see the trade at the stock exchange," Juan grew enthused.

"Juan, Señor Diogo Mendes and I will be happy to have you join us at the stock exchange and learn the secrets of trade." My heart was roiling within me, but my speech sounded calm. I had learned from Francisco that a good merchant was a combination of a gentleman and a sharpshooter, who never hesitated and hit his target straight on.

Diogo looked at me, surprised, but a slight smile played at the corners of his mouth.

After the meal, Brianda asked to go for a drive in the city. I explained to her that much work still awaited me, and that we would put off the tour till tomorrow.

Diogo asked me to accompany him to the study, whose walls were covered with tapestries and landscape paintings of farmers plowing green fields and boats sailing on the river. He poured plum liqueur into crystal cups and said, "Señora Beatrice, call me by my first name. Here's to family!" He drank all of the liqueur in one gulp.

"Well, then, please call me by my family pet name, Beatricci."

Diogo poured himself another glass of liqueur. "Beatricci, I understand that you've decided to continue my brother's business."

"Francisco instructed me in his will to continue managing the company's business, both overt and covert," I said quietly.

Diogo's thick brows rose sharply. He signaled me to stop talking and opened a secret door. We entered a beautiful room where the chests I had brought with me from Lisbon were stacked up. Diogo locked the door after us.

"Beatricci, these days, you can't tell whom to trust. What do you mean by 'covert business'?"

"Francisco told me his goal in life was not just to make money but to save the *annusim*, the forced converts. I know about the Carmelite monasteries, about the ships and about the promissory note, the *lettres de change*, that the escapees receive in return for their property."

"Francisco must have had great appreciation for the *señora* if he shared his business with her." He stroked his beard.

I smiled and placed my hand on a silver chest engraved with roses. From a leather pouch tied to the lock securing the box, I retrieved a scroll stating, "Dowry for Brianda de Luna." I extracted a small key from my reticule and opened the chest's golden lock. As I lifted the lid, thousands of gold coins glimmered at us. I gathered a few coins in my hand and let them fall, illuminated by sunlight, the jangle of the coins rubbing against each other ringing out in the room.

"It's unclear to me how King Joao allowed you to leave Lisbon and take money out of the country," Diogo said.

"I appealed to Joao and Catherine and asked them for permission to depart for the wedding of my sister, Brianda, intended for Don Diogo Mendes, Francisco's brother, which will take place in Antwerp. I promised that after the wedding, Ana would move to the palace to be educated under the patronage of Queen Catherine. I asked their permission to take my sister's dowry with me. The king agreed to my request and allowed me to leave with my family for the wedding and to remove crates of diamonds, gems and gold coins from Lisbon."

"Beatricci, you're daring. You matched me up with your sister... Who taught you to be so spicy?" Diogo burst out in laughter.

"Your brother Francisco was a good teacher. I brought some of the boxes from England. They contain thousands of ducats of gold!"

"Unbelievable!" He shook his head and gazed at me appreciatively.

***

My head was spinning with ideas on how to expand the fortune I had inherited.

"Diogo, could we call a meeting for the House of Mendes agents next week?" I fixed my eyes upon him in anticipation.

"Beatricci, I'll think about it," he replied quietly.

The Meeting

A week later, the managers of House of Mendes were gathered around the oval mahogany table, waiting for Diogo's arrival. I was amused by the managers' startled expression as they rose for me when I entered the conference room and sat at the head of the table.

"I'm very surprised that Señor Diogo invited the *señora* to the meeting," Emanuel de Orte whispered to Gabriel Enriquez. Apparently, they thought that I couldn't understand French at all.

"Very odd," Gabriel Enriquez nodded.

"Gentlemen, these sorts of comments are not befitting of you," Jacob Morro noted in French.

"Señora Beatrice Mendes, I'm happy to see you," I was greeted by Antonio de la Ronja, who had arrived especially for the meeting from London. Ever since he had been our host in London, I had grown quite fond of him, although his right eye, covered with a black eyepatch, frightened Brianda, as he looked like a pirate.

"Welcome, Antonio de la Ronja, I replied, continuing immediately: "Greetings, esteemed gentlemen. I'm glad you've honored us with your presence at this meeting." The dignitaries' expressions reflected their embarrassment when I addressed them in French.

"My lady and gentlemen," Diogo said as he sat down on the other side of the table, "as of today, Señora Beatrice Mendes is a full partner to the management of the company, in every regard."

"Don Diogo, are you whole-hearted about this decision?" asked Emanuel de Orte.

Diogo struck the marble desk forcefully. "Your role is to ensure the smooth administration of the company's accounts, rather than interfere in its management!"

"I'm sorry!" Emanuel de Orte apologized.

Diogo surveyed the company's commerce and lending activity, as well as its connections with royal houses, the Vatican and the ambassadors of various countries.

Augustino Henricks briefly reported on the attempts to help the New Christians.

"We'll be happy to hear from Señora Beatrice, if the respected lady has any suggestions," said Emanuel de Orte.

From my reticule, I produced a parchment on which I had written several notes before the meeting.

"Gentlemen, the scope of activity you have presented is very impressive. In my humble opinion, we should take action to increase the company's autonomy."

"Señora Mendes, what do you mean? After all, the House of Mendes is a private company," Diogo said.

"According to my understanding, we should lease groves, and not just purchase spices from the growers. That way, we can decrease expenses and increase profits. As you know, in the near future, the House of Mendes will have to make an annual payment to the king of Portugal for the concession to lease the black pepper."

The room grew quiet. Some of the agents brought their chairs closer to the table.

"In addition, the lack of ships available to transport the merchandise is hurting the company. Francisco would say, 'Stagnant money is a loss, like a man standing in place, rather than moving forward.' I suggest we purchase ships that will be under company ownership, and therefore we will not be dependent upon the ship owners."

The agents looked at me as if they were seeing me for the first time and nodded.

"Your proposal is accepted," Diogo said.

"I'm sorry, one more little thing," I said. "From Emanuel de Orte's review, I understood that the scope of debts to the company is extensive. I believe collection should be enhanced, and that we should not permit extension of the debts beyond the time specified in the promissory notes."

"The *señora* was my most talented pupil," Professor Augustino Henricks boasted to the agents, who mumbled their agreement.

Diogo stood up. "Señora Beatrice, I must admit you have surprised me with the sharpness of your mind."

A feeling of exhilaration spread through me. Diogo appreciated me. I surveyed the agents.

"One more thing." I lowered my voice. "As the company needs cash to finance the covert activity…" A murmur passed through the agents, interrupting me.

"What? The *señora* knows?"

"The information has been shared with her?"

"She's putting us at risk!"

Diogo struck the table with his hand. "Señora Beatrice is one of us! We shall grant her proposal serious consideration." He gathered his papers and closed the meeting.

***

Since the meeting with the agents, Diogo and I took care to conduct almost daily work meetings at his office, in which princes, noblemen, merchants, and his competitors, the Fuger family, also converged. I accompanied him to meetings at the stock exchange and the port, where he was respectfully greeted by the nickname "King of Spices." I got to know the activity of the House of Mendes's branch in Antwerp, consisting mainly of concessions to deal in perfumes, managing marine commerce, and granting loans and credit.

After a short time, I began to initiate ventures. I proposed expanding our marketing of perfume, pepper and ginger, to which doctors attributed medicinal and life-extending qualities, to additional central port towns in Europe. I also suggested increasing our commerce in frankincense, cinnamon, nutmeg and its flowers, cloves, myrtle, tarragon, and gems and ivory, whose prices were soaring from day to day.

In addition, I suggested expanding our fleet of ships and purchasing a shipyard to repair the vessels.

I studied the map of Europe and thought it would be wise to open another branch in France, in the city of Lyon, ideally situated in the confluence of two rivers. The city was known for its Merino sheep and its excellent wool, and I thought we should expand our business and start marketing wool.

The king of Poland agreed to my request, and in return for a handsome sum, granted the House of Mendes concessions to mine salt and silver ore.

Antwerp's merchants and its nobility initially treated me with suspicion. They were not used to a woman taking part in their usual masculine club, in which they were used to treating themselves to shots of cognac and smoking cigars. However, gradually, they learned to respect me and appreciate my contribution to the company. Thanks to my ideas and initiatives, the company profits soared.

I enjoyed Diogo's company. For the first time since Francisco's death, I felt I might manage to fill the void that had formed in my life.

A New Life

During the first few weeks after our move to Antwerp, Ana spent many hours by my side. She had a hard time adjusting to her new home. When I left for meetings, Allegra took her for walks in the estate's garden.

Brianda roamed the sprawling palace in excitement, charming the members of the household with her beauty, her enchanting smile and her pleasant manner. However, she did not help much with supervising the servants who unpacked our travel chests and placed the clothes, the linens and the kitchenware we had brought with us in the heavy wooden cabinets.

She also did not watch over curious Juan, who ran through the palace opening the doors of rooms, cabinets and drawers, and suddenly left the house, disappearing in the garden or visiting the horses in the stables, examining the swords and bayonets in the arsenal. Juan immediately picked up the Flemish language and chatted with every guest, proud to show off his knowledge. Bernardo liked to shutter himself in the immense library, dedicating the majority of his time to reading books.

In the first few days, my conversations with Diogo were very practical, focusing on getting settled in the palace, room arrangements, furniture and household purchases.

One morning, Bernardo and Juan accompanied us for a visit to the stock exchange building. In the arched vestibules in the large courtyard, the merchants heaped the long tables with chests of gems and hundreds of bags of spices with exotic scents. Juan did not take his eyes off the barker who rang the bell and loudly declared the opening of commerce, vigilantly tracking the vocal trade of buyers huddling around the long tables.

Diogo introduced the boys to his faithful solicitor, Johan von Frederick, who tested their knowledge in mathematics. Bernardo asked to see the painters and sculptors working on their creations in the well-lighted workshops on the second floor.

***

Fashion in Antwerp was more colorful and cheerful than Lisbon's solemn styles. Brianda, dizzy with the variety of innovations, accompanied Teresa and I when we set out to buy fabrics and accessories. I endowed her with a large sum of money to buy fabrics, hairpins, shoes, furs, coats and bags.

On one occasion, Brianda joined Diogo for a purchase spree at the trade shops. When she returned from her shopping, the serving girls' arms were overflowing with packages. I assumed the sum she had spent was higher than the one she had been allotted.

Brianda burst out in laughter when she saw my face. "Sister, don't be angry. Diogo bought me these pretty textiles," she said as she undid the ribbons around the wrapped packages. "Feel the softness and delicacy of these colorful fabrics." She spread out the vibrant rolls of cloth on the table. "Sister, I allowed myself to pamper you and buy you fabric for a dress. You're so busy managing the household and unpacking the cargo we brought that you don't even have time to buy anything for yourself." Brianda brought a sky-blue silk to my face and handed me a mirror. "Look at the mirror, that color is lovely on you!"

"Thank you," I said, folding the cloth.

"Look at this amazing fabric that Diogo and I chose for sweet Ana." She opened a small package with a yellow velvet ribbon, took out some red-and-blue checkered fabric, and mulled it against her cheek. "I added ribbons to decorate it," she said.

A knock was heard on the door. Diogo strode in vigorously, a smile illuminating his face. Brianda blushed when she saw him.

"Señora Beatricci, I had a wonderful morning with your younger sister. It's too bad you didn't come with us! It was such a pretty day. To stroll with two beautiful women would have made it a perfect day…"

"Señor Diogo, you know there's so much to do here. We have to watch over the servants when they're unpacking the crates, and compare the inventory to the lists of belongings with which we left Lisbon. I have to make a list of the items being stored in the closets, the number of sheets, pillow covers, tablecloths, dresses and accessories, otherwise we won't know where everything is…" I felt that I was babbling, talking uncontrollably.

"Beatricci, you're right, but it could have been nice for you too if you'd gone out and gotten to know the city a bit."

"First I'll finish the organizing and the arranging. Next time, I promise to come along," I said, adding, "Señor Diogo, you shouldn't have paid for the fabrics."

"It's a pleasure for me to buy you things. Don't deprive me of the joy of buying a variety of Antwerp fabrics for two such beautiful women. We buy merchandise from all over the world. The cloth I chose for your beautiful daughter is from England." He gestured at the beautiful plaid fabric.

"Thank you," I whispered, my voice somewhat hoarse.

I noticed that Brianda was too quiet while Diogo was speaking. She had told me that she had been the one to choose the fabric for Ana.

"Please, Señor Diogo, can we go shopping tomorrow as well?" she addressed him in her ingratiating, somewhat oversweet voice.

"Brianda, there's a lot of work to do here. You've bought enough fabric," I said quietly.

"Ladies, I have a surprise for you. Tomorrow, after breakfast, which will be served in the sunroom, Estella, the illustrious and most accomplished seamstress in town, will arrive for fittings. Please clear your schedules," Diogo said.

"Thank you so much, Uncle! It's nice of you to take care of us." Brianda clapped in delight and gazed at him in admiration, opening her eyes wide and tilting her head slightly like a little girl.

Diogo flushed, looking embarrassed. Was something taking place here, right under my nose? My instincts usually did not lead me astray, and if something was indeed going on, I was not sure what my reaction should be.

In the next few weeks, Brianda did her best to ignore me. She spent money on new purchases of luxury items, boots, belts and jewelry. I tried to limit her excessive spending, but she was cunning enough to ask me to increase her allowance over dinner, and when I did not agree, Diogo would appeal to me in his gentle manner. "Beatricci, please, let her. Your younger sister is excited by the fashion in Antwerp."

I had no choice but to agree, although Brianda knew very well that I was not at all pleased. I made sure they purchased the finest fabrics for Juan and Bernardo as well, and that the clothes they deserved in accordance with their elevated social status would be sewn for them. I hoped their parents, Samuel and Rosa, were watching from heaven and would be happy to know their children were in good hands.

My affection for my brother-in-law increased daily, thanks to his gentleness and the pleasant smile on his face, as well as the endless patience he exhibited in regard to Brianda and his warm treatment of his young nephews.

The company's agents, arriving for urgent discussions from the countries in which the House of Mendes had branches, were constantly in and out of the house. Also present were merchants, sea captains, city dignitaries, guests, ambassadors from foreign countries and emissaries of Sultan Suleiman the Magnificent, in their red uniforms and turbans with a trailing scarf covering the back of their neck.

Five weeks later, after the clothes and the delicate lace linens had been meticulously counted and folded away in the closets, after the many pieces of jewelry Brianda had purchased had been stored in jewelry boxes embedded with conch and ivory, Diogo turned to me at breakfast and suggested we "go to the study to discuss family finances."

"Can I join the conversation as well?" Brianda inquired gently.

"Brianda, have you forgotten you have a couples' dancing lesson? I'm sure you wouldn't want to give it up," I replied immediately.

"I actually don't mind giving it up. The dance instructor isn't nice to me. He's tough," she replied.

"Brianda, I'm sure you'll be happy to hear that the *señoras* are invited to a ball at the palace of Jonathan Fuger. The dancer Don Monteleto, who recently arrived from Venice, is considered the best teacher of the volta dance," Diogo smiled at her.

"That's great, we're invited to the ball!" Brianda laughed and began to twirl in small steps around the dining room. Diogo extended his arm to her and danced with her as Ana, Bernardo and Juan applauded enthusiastically and the serving girls smiled.

"Señor Diogo, please dance with me at the ball." Brianda fluttered her eyelashes at him. As far as I knew, I thought, it was the gentleman's role to invite a maiden to dance, and not the other way around.

"It would be my pleasure." Diogo bowed at her ceremoniously.

"Excuse me, I'm going to my dance lesson." Brianda flitted out of the room like an enchanting butterfly.

I thought my brother-in-law was looking after Brianda because she was young and fragile, but I felt uncomfortable. Diogo was cool towards me, while enthusing like a little boy over my younger, mischievous sister's follies.

"Beatricci, your dress is pretty," he complimented me.

A sour sensation rose within me. "Thank you," I replied politely. I did not want to hear that my outfit was pretty; I wanted him to tell me that I was pretty.

My head began to hurt, and a stomachache stabbed through my body.

"Beatricci," Diogo addressed me once we were sitting down in the study. "I suggest that Juan and Bernardo depart to study at the excellent Leuven University in the Duchy of Brabant."

I said nothing, gazing out to the garden, where the wind was shaking the boughs of the trees.

"Those young men could blaze through that distance in two hours of vigorous galloping," his eyes twinkled at me in laughter.

"Prince Maximillian, the nephew of Charles the Fifth, studies there. It would be a good idea for them to make friends with him. The boys are bored in Antwerp. At the university, they will acquire an education befitting their status, and learn Latin, French and Hebrew."

"They teach Hebrew at Leuven University?" I was surprised.

"They do indeed."

***

A week later, Juan kissed my hand. "Farewell, Aunt!" he said with youthful exhilaration.

"May the angels up above accompany you on your way," I whispered. "Study well, and graduate from your studies with distinction," I added.

"Ana, don't forget us," Juan pinched her cheek.

"I'll miss you," she said shyly.

"Aunt, I'll write and tell you about our experience," Bernardo said.

"Most of all, enjoy yourselves and have fun," Brianda laughed.

"A carriage will be waiting for you once the semester break starts," Diogo called out.

Juan and Bernardo waved goodbye to us and boarded the coach taking them to the university.

"Beatricci, your cousins haven't left you. They'll come visit you over the holidays," Diogo consoled me.

***

Since my regular morning meetings with Diogo began, sometimes also attended by company agents and senior clerks, I had learned how House of Mendes conducted its commerce in Europe, delved into the promissory notes from the numerous loans made to royal houses, merchants and noblemen, tracked the scope of the debts, heard about Diogo's activity within the Vatican and his connection to monarchs and ambassadors, and most importantly, learned to respect and appreciate Diogo's genius when it came to business.

On one of those days, Diogo invited me to come see the wine cellar. He moved aside the door of the cabinet at the end of the stairs, took a crystal key out of his pocket, and inserted it in an invisible opening in the wood wall behind him. A small door opened. I found myself standing, dumbfounded, within a room housing a beautiful synagogue with a gold-covered Torah ark, *siddur* prayer books and ancient Torah books.

"In the twenty-four years since I moved to Antwerp, I've created a network of connections with noblemen and kings and founded a successful bank, but the thing I'm most proud of is the collection of holy books I've saved." He ran his hand gently over the ancient books.

The books were like children to him, the fruit of his labor. *This is where he comes to relax*, I thought as I entered the sacred chamber.

"The thing dearest to my heart," he said, "is the families and children of the forced converts that I smuggle into the Ottoman state. My brother Francisco was the first to begin the campaign to save our brothers, and I hope you will join me."

I nodded in agreement.

Diogo was a fascinating conversationalist. I enjoyed his company. I liked his mode of conducting himself and his perfect manners and admired his vast knowledge. I daydreamed about the man by whose side I would navigate the turbulent ship of my life. I had a big family to take care of, I thought, and plenty of property, which I had to protect from disappearing due to a marriage to someone who was not a family member. I trusted Diogo. With him, the fortune would stay in the family.

It was time for me to build a life for myself. Perhaps I would have another child. Mama had said that mourning a husband lasted a month. But it had been two years since Francisco passed away, and I still missed him with a passion. The black pit that had gaped in my stomach when he departed had yet to heal.

***

The flags of the kingdom and the family crest were flying high at the entrance to the palace of banker Jonathan Fuger. Gold and crystal chandeliers illuminated the giant salon, surrounded by mirrors in golden frames and murals of the family's ancestors, as well as tables set with gold dinnerware, loaded with a tasty bounty. On the stage sat an orchestra of lute, violin and harp players. A band of troubadours sang dancing songs and madrigals. The trumpeter blew his horn while the herald ceremoniously called out our names: "Señor Diogo Mendes, Señora Beatrice Mendes, Señorita Brianda de Luna."

Jonathan and Maria Fuger greeted us with much respect. I presented our hosts with a gift, a gold Venetian box patterned with roses and embedded with diamonds, in which black peppercorns were prancing. "Thank you, my dear," Maria Fuger expressed her gratitude and asked after three-year-old Ana, who had stayed behind with her governess, as well as after my cousins.

I told her that Ana was slowly adapting to her new life, chattering a bit in Flemish, and that my cousins wrote that they were studying for many hours each day.

Diogo, who proved to be an immediate draw for the ball's attendees and the many beauties fluttering around him, introduced us to his noble friends and their wives, as well as to the members of the esteemed merchant guild. From the corner of my eye, I saw three matrons exchanging whispers.

"Did you see that his rich sister-in-law brought black peppercorns as a gift?" a woman in a red taffeta dress clucked her tongue.

"Black pepper costs more than gold." Her friend, whose square décolletage was very deep indeed, rolled her eyes.

"Look at that lavish dress! And the jewelry she's wearing..." Their friend who was slim as a stalk bit her lips.

"I've heard that she's Don Diogo's partner at the House of Mendes Company!" the red-clad woman's eyes shone.

"From what I've heard, she exports black pepper and spices from Portugal's colonies." The woman with the deep neckline raised the hem of her dress.

"A woman doing business?" the slim woman's voice rang out discordantly.

"The *señora* is a widow. She must be seeking a groom..." the matron in red chuckled.

"'It's better to be a widow than a married woman.'" Their laughter rang out.

I turned back to see who had repeated the statement I had first heard from my mother, but the women had been swallowed up by the other guests.

Solemn-looking servants made their way among the many guests, serving wine in crystal goblets and beer in heavy steins.

"Welcome, Doctor Joao Rodrigues de Castelo Branco," I suddenly heard Diogo's voice as he warmly embraced my friend Doctor Amatus Lusitanus.

"Doctor, what are you doing here? How did you get here?" Diogo asked.

"Diogo! It's good to see you." He then added in a whisper, "I've changed my name to Amatus Lusitanus, a name that resembles my Hebrew name, Haviv." Diogo nodded to indicate he had understood.

"Señora Beatricci, I arrived only this morning via a tortuous route from Lisbon. Señor Jonathan Fuger heard about my arrival from the ship's captain, and invited me to tend to an ill relative and to stay in their home."

"My friend Amatus, please watch over my sister-in-law," Diogo said, handing me a goblet of wine. Before I could thank him, Diogo gallantly placed his hand on Brianda's arm and the two of them embarked on the fashionable La Volta dance.

I was not oblivious to the joyful looks my sister and brother-in-law exchanged as they twirled and leapt in courtly, agile gestures. Their movements were coordinated and graceful, and the guests were won over by their charm and effervescent joie de vivre. The orchestra increased the pace of its tunes and the audience applauded them.

"Señor Jonathan Fuger and I are happy that the *señora* has come to Antwerp and has graced us with her presence. We hope the *señora* is having fun," Madonna Maria Fuger addressed me, asking the servant to refill my wineglass.

"I'm honored to attend the ball," I replied.

Doctor Amatus Lusitanus approached me. "Señora Beatricci, I would be happy if the *señora* would oblige me with a dance."

Maria Fuger and the noblewomen waited curiously to see what my reaction would be. I smiled and gave him my arm.

"Beatricci, how are you, my dear?" he asked.

"Life goes on. I'm busy all day managing the family and the company business."

From the corner of my eye, I saw Brianda flitting like a butterfly among the guests with Diogo by her side. A moment later, they disappeared from view, and I sought them out feverishly.

"Beatricci, your sister and Diogo went out to the parlor balcony," Amatus Lusitanus told me. "Brianda looks happy."

His words tore at my heart. Thoughts swirled around in my head. Since coming to Antwerp, I had constructed several scenarios for a conversation with Diogo. I had imagined how I would reply when he brought up the future of our relationship.

Now, a troubling thought crept in among the thousands of considerations flitting through my mind. Perhaps he would want to marry a young girl. Perhaps the time had not yet come for me to marry anyone. Apparently, Diogo seemed to see me solely as a business partner.

Love Affair, 1539

Estella, who had been hired as seamstress and personal dresser to the women in the family, lowered her dark lashes. "Señora, excuse me."

I placed my quill in the inkwell. "Yes, Estella, do you need thread, buckles and more decorations?" I asked.

"No, no… The *señora* asked that I report to her about Mademoiselle Brianda's purchases…"

My sister's shopping sprees demanded nearly the same attention from me as the business of Mendes Bank. I blotted the ink from the missive stating my positive reply to His Majesty, Emperor Charles the Fifth, regarding his request for a monetary loan to finance his fight against the Protestant movement, rapidly spreading through the cities of the Holy Roman Empire.

"I'm listening, my dear."

"This week, Mademoiselle Brianda has purchased more silk taffeta fabrics, pocketbooks, shoes, brooches and scarves," Estella said quietly.

"Thank you, dear one, for your efforts." I handed her a silver coin. Estella thanked me, took the coin and quickly left the room.

The luxury and opulence of Antwerp had gone to Brianda's head. She wore the latest fashions, competing with princesses and the city's wealthiest women. Her clothing expenses had exceeded her budget. I decided to call her in for a talk.

Brianda returned from the ball and, her eyes sparkling, showed me a cane circled with purple leaves.

"I got it at the ball, from Joao the Third's royal business manager, Roy Fernandez. He said it's called sugar cane. Come on, I'll cut a piece off for you. The cane is so sweet and tasty!" she laughed, biting into it with great pleasure.

I tasted the juicy cane, but it was too sweet for me.

Brianda told me she had met the famous composer Cipriano de Rore. Three of the madrigals he had composed had been played at the ball.

"I thought they were the prettiest madrigals out of all the melodies I've ever heard in my life! Diogo introduced us, and with your permission, I commissioned two madrigals from him," she told me.

"How much did you promise to pay him for writing these melodies?" I asked.

"Beatrice, not everything is measured in money! I think we should support him financially, but I didn't tell him about my idea. I'll simply commission madrigals from him and recommend that my friends do the same," Brianda replied.

"That's nice. They'll end up calling you a patron of the arts."

"Oh, I wish! You know I've always loved music and painting, and that's why our parents gave me private lessons with the best painting and music teachers."

"Brianda, I know you're talented. Just take care not to spend too much of our money."

"Sister, stop worrying about money and start enjoying life… I forgot to tell you, I met the painter Pieter Bruegel at the party. He showed me his miniature etchings and drawings. His paintings are full of joy, and I commissioned a painting from him."

"Brianda, your expenses this week for clothing and accessories surpass your monthly allowance. How are you planning to fund these new purchases?"

"Stop it, why do you have to spoil my mood? It's not like we're lacking in money!" Brianda turned her back to me.

***

As in Lisbon, we lived as "hidden Jews" in Flanders as well, taking care to conceal our faith. I missed the Fridays back at our house, when the tambourine man would go out on the street and play the drum in order to hint that the Sabbath was arriving. Then family members and guests would sneak into the house under Grandma's watchful eye, gathering for a short, festive prayer in the secret synagogue in the cellar.

On the eve of the Sabbath, Raphael del Vino gave the servants the evening off, and twenty or so of our friends and their wives congregated in the house for an evening of card playing, around tables covered with green felt tablecloths.

"Nicely done!" Diogo applauded, complimenting Brianda, who had a knack for the game and won most rounds.

Brianda blushed. "Thank you, Diogo," she addressed him by his first name, her hand resting briefly on his own.

"I know what I'll buy Miss Brianda for her eighteenth birthday…" Diogo smiled.

"What? What will you buy her?" the women inquired.

"A pack of cards…" Diogo burst out in laughter and our guests applauded.

Suddenly, I realized what was going on. A love affair had been taking place under my very nose! I almost struck myself on the head; how had I been so blind so as not to see those two lovers? What had I been thinking—that if I sat with Diogo all day, accompanied him to meetings with merchants and bankers, carried out the company's world-spanning business by his side and acted as a full partner along with him in the rescue operation Francisco had organized, he would appreciate me? What had I expected, that if I provided for all of the needs of the *annusim*, emergency accommodations by the side of the road, mattresses, clothes, food and medicine… that if I equip my brethren, the Portuguese *conversos* with money and guides, then Diogo would value my wisdom, my industrious nature and the initiatives I had taken in my relationships with the royal houses, the merchants, the city leaders and the agents, and link his life with mine?!

I had been such a fool! Since when have men courted a woman because of her wisdom or her knowledge? Men are so stupid! They seek a beauty to walk along with them, arm in arm, to balls and other events, so they could flaunt her to their friends… They were seeking a handsome ornament rather than an independent woman with a good head on her shoulders.

Why? Why did Brianda, the flesh of my flesh, who had so many suitors, and even I myself had introduced her to many noblemen and property owners 'belonging to the letter Yod,' fancy Diogo, of all people?

At that moment, the cloud of smoke that been obscuring my eyes dissipated. Suddenly, I understood what had been going on during the long months when I had been concerned with taking care of my daughter, my sister, my cousins and the family fortune I had inherited, making sure it was not lost. While I had been worrying about gathering enough coins of currency to pay the ship owners so they would smuggle the escapees out, the inns, the guards, the spies, paying for clothes and food, the relationship between Brianda and Diogo had been taking place unhindered. Everything passed in front of my eyes in the brief moment when I saw her hand fluttering over his.

A chill ran down my spine and my eyes narrowed. All the warm feelings I had felt toward Diogo evaporated and departed my body. I felt as if I was leaving my body and watching what was going on, that I did not belong. I and that woman sitting erect and rigid on the chair like a chilly slab of ice had two different identities.

I felt a sense of suffocation and went out to the balcony. I leaned down toward a planter to smell a rose bush, bringing it closer with my hand. A thorn stabbed my finger. Drops of dark blood emerged, falling to the floor. I wrapped my finger in a white handkerchief that was soon stained. I wondered who would bind up my broken heart.

I will never forget what I felt at that moment. Instantly, I came to the decision that I would never bind my life to a man. From now on, my life would be devoted to charity, to paying the ship owners and the spies who would track the Inquisition's enforcers. Yes, my life would be dedicated to the mission of transporting my brothers to safe harbors throughout the Ottoman sultan's lands. If I did not do it, not one Jew of the *annusim* would be left on earth,

At the end of the game, Diogo went out to the balcony to summon me to pray in the secret synagogue near the wine cellar.

***

On Saturday morning, I was standing by the window. Teresa brought me a wool shawl to wrap myself in and added wood to the hearth at the corner of the room, but I was still cold. The whistling of the wind came in through the window, and gray clouds clustered in the sky.

People referred to me as a "widow and businesswoman," as if I had forgotten what it meant to be a woman. I still remembered the wondrous feeling of being desired, the fluttering in my stomach, the exchange of glances and my embarrassed face when Francisco stared at me for the first time. That sensation, which had flooded my face with a burgundy flush extending to the very roots of my hair, which trembled at the thought of my beloved, still nested in my heart.

I went into the library, closing the door after me. I knew, simply feeling it in my bones, that he would follow me. Sometimes, I knew what was about to happen even before it did.

A Marriage Proposal

I heard a light knock. The library door, with a bas-relief of the ten tribes of Israel, opened wide. Diogo, in all his glory, was standing at the threshold.

"Beatrice, please, I want to discuss an important topic with you. I hope I'm not bothering you." His voice sounded serious and formal.

"No, no, come in, please." I gestured at the red armchair by my side.

Diogo sat down on the edge of the chair, his arms lying on the armrests. "What happened, did you hurt yourself?" he asked.

I assumed a forced smile. "It's nothing… a small prick from a rose bush."

"Ahhh…" he said, clearing his throat, trying to find the right words.

I felt quite amused. It was obvious to me what he was about to say, but I had no wish to help him out.

"Beatrice, since you have arrived in our home, you've brought light, joy, and the sounds of the young nephews' laughter with you…"

You mean Brianda, don't you? I wanted to say, but held back.

Diogo cleared his throat again. "Señora, I'm asking your permission to wed your younger sister, Brianda," he said at last.

My body remained as cold as ice. I felt nothing and continued to sit erect and tall in the chair. I experienced a feeling of sadness and loneliness, like on that day when I had stood beside Francisco's bed and realized he was leaving me forever.

"Beatrice, I'm sure you know I feel deep affection toward your sister, as she does toward me," he continued, seeking some sign of sympathy in my eyes.

I wanted to stop him and say, *Mostly affection for your money, and for the respect and pleasures it brings with it,* but I maintained control of myself.

The pretty words he had written to me after Francisco's death, "Waiting for you in Antwerp," "I'll take care of you," had evaporated like the ink fading on the yellowing paper of the missives.

My plump cheeks, which my aunts liked to pinch affectionately, were sucked into the bones of my face. In a moment, my face would be swallowed within itself, and I would disappear along with it.

"You know that Brianda has many suitors…" I twirled a rebellious strand of hair that had emerged from the black shawl covering my head. "But if this is what you both wish, you have permission to do so."

Diogo's face grew illuminated. "You've made me a happy man."

"My sister does not have her own fortune, and she is dependent upon me," I said quietly.

"Beatrice, according to city regulations, the couple must register to be married, prepare a marriage contract and a prenuptial financial agreement, and file the contract at the Office of the Registrar," Diogo said. "Uhmmm…" He cleared his throat again. "I've drafted the contract, and I want you to go over it."

He doesn't waste a moment. There was a contract, and everything was ready. All I had to do was approve it.

"My sister is accustomed to a very luxurious lifestyle. If you please, I want to know the sum that you intend to write in the *ketubah*."

"I promise to provide for all her needs. Your sister will live like the daughter of royalty," Diogo replied.

"Since we left Lisbon, Brianda has been like a daughter to me. I'll take care of the wedding expenses and the dowry," I said.

"Thank you, Gracia," he addressed me by my internal, Jewish name. "I appreciate you very much. Please don't be concerned, the wedding expenses are on me." He kissed my hand.

"Meyer," I used his Hebrew name as well. "Brianda will show up at her wedding in a manner befitting her station, with a full dowry of linens, jewelry, clothing, and anything else required. I'll finance it."

I rolled the gold bracelet I had received from Francisco along my wrist. "Diogo, there's one more little thing we must settle between us."

Diogo stroked his graying beard, his brows rising in query.

"Before my marriage to Francisco, we signed a prenuptial agreement.

According to the agreement, our offspring and I inherited his property. However, in his will, Francisco left you half of his property."

"Gracia, I know this. Rest assured that I'll take care of you," Diogo nodded.

"What do you mean?"

"Gracia, I promise you'll be mentioned in my will," he stated, saying no more.

"I agree," I replied. "Let's call my sister. I want to congratulate her."

Her face flushed, prancing lightly, Brianda entered the room. Apparently, she had been standing outside the door, waiting for the right moment to make her entrance.

I wrapped my arms around her. "Congratulations, my sister, I'm glad to see you so happy. It's too bad that Mama and Papa, may he rest in peace, were deprived of seeing you in your joy." I planted a light kiss on her cheek.

"That's true, I wish Mama was here! Maybe Papa's looking down at me from heaven and is happy for me." Brianda looked up at the cloudy sky.

"My dears, I'm doing my best to smuggle your mother out of Lisbon."

Brianda clasped her hands together. "Oh, I wish, I do wish that you succeed, and Mama can attend the wedding!"

"I want to hold the wedding as soon as possible." Diogo gazed at my sister in adoration.

He has been a bachelor for fifty-four years, and suddenly he can't wait to get married. Men... I suppressed a sigh.

"Diogush, Estella showed me several models of mannequins wearing charming bridal dresses sent to her from Paris. I need several outfits: a dress for the cathedral, a dress for the ball at home and the wedding party my friends will throw me, and another outfit for the reception," Brianda appealed to Diogo enthusiastically.

"We have to take care of the invitations, the flower arrangements... Wow, so many things to do!" she called out.

"Bri, my sweet, buy the very best," Diogo encouraged her.

Diogush. Bri. Already, they had pet names for each other... I imagined our money going up in smoke as the finest treasures in Antwerp, Paris, Milan and the East were purchased.

Diogo rang the little crystal bell on his desk. The serving girls entered with a tray bearing crystal glasses and selected bottles of spirits that Diogo had apparently brought up from the cellar previously. "I left some bottles of spirits for the palace staff as well, so they can celebrate the joyous news."

"My sister, I knew you would grant your consent, and I allowed myself to make sure Ana would not go to bed, so she could celebrate with us," Brianda said.

I hadn't heard the knock on the door. Raphael del Vino let in Juan and Bernardo, who were standing at the threshold, smiling and joyous.

"Aunt, Diogo sent Thomas with the carriage to fetch us from the university."

"All our best wishes, Diogo." Juan clapped him on the shoulder, bowing to Brianda.

Diogo filled the crystal goblets with a cherry liqueur, its hue a deep red and its aroma intoxicating, which had been stored in the cellar for many years, waiting for the right moment.

I held the glittering chalice with both hands, trying to soothe my trembling body.

"To a happy married life!" Diogo hugged Brianda's waist, while she blushed.

"To love!" my sister raised the goblet.

"To you, Brianda! To you, Diogo!" We clinked our glasses together. I took a polite sip.

"Ana, Aunt Brianda and Uncle Diogo are getting married!" Diogo broke the news to Ana.

Ana ran over to her and buried her head in her lap. "I'll be a bridesmaid, right?"

Brianda twirled around the room with her. "You'll be the prettiest bridesmaid."

Juan had matured, and was familiar with the manners of Antwerp's gentry, in addition to being endowed with plenty of charm. He gave me a look indicating that he understood what was going on in my heart, but did not say a word, merely kissing my cheek.

"And what about me? You don't have a hug and a kiss for me?" asked

Brianda in her self-indulgent voice.

"I certainly do, Aunt. You know how much I love you and how happy I am for you and for Uncle Diogo. Aunt Brianda, you'll be a beautiful bride," Juan flattered her.

Shy Bernardo stood still, embarrassed. "Congratulations," he turned to me. "Now that your sister's getting married, it must be a weight off your shoulders." He was not the most intuitive of men.

Every moment felt like an eternity to me. I stayed in the room until I felt heat and shivers climbing up my body.

I excused myself by saying Ana had to go to bed and took her to her room. I covered her with a blanket and sat on the bed beside her. She snuggled into me, her small hand wrapped in mine. I caressed her sweet, lovely face, and together, we whispered the bedtime prayer:

"Shema Yisrael, Hashem e-lhoeynu, Hashem ehad.
Hear, O Israel, the Lord is our God, the Lord is One.
Our blessed angels
Michael and Gabriel
Please stay by my side as I sleep."

The way from my daughter's bedroom until finding myself in bed was erased from my memory. I could not remember Teresa washing my face, brushing my hair, helping me take off my clothes and put on the white lace nightgown, or giving me a hot beverage to drink.

I fell into bed, burying my head in the pillow. The tears arrived on their own. I felt a combination of disappointment, sadness and shame. What would become of me? A young widow of twenty-nine with a five-year-old child. Was I destined to stay surrounded by people yet lonely, traversing the world without a supportive partner by my side? With whom would I share my experiences? Who would hold me? Who would console me? On whose shoulder would I rest my head come evening time? I stifled my weeping in the pillow, which was wet from the thousands of tears that streamed down despite my best efforts.

Once, when I was thirteen, my cousin had hurt me when she called me conceited. I wept intently. My father took out an ancient book, the sacred *Zohar*, composed by Rabbi Shimon bar Yochai and purchased by my great-grandfather from Moses de León. Papa swore me not to reveal the secret conveyed in the *Zohar*, that all of us are born into this world in order to withstand trials, to make *tikkun*—rectification, and to find our destiny in life.

I did not understand what the *"tikkun"* was, or what these "trials" were, and Papa did not explain it to me. I only remember my feeling at the time. I experienced relief, and felt like a big girl, with whom adult secrets were shared.

Apparently, Brianda's engagement to Diogo was a trial I was enduring, I thought.

Up until that day, I had not known what my *"tikkun"* was. Now I understood that my destiny and my rectification in the world was to make sure that the candle of the People of Israel was never extinguished, and that the chain of generations remained unbroken. I promised myself I would never forget it.

In the few hours when I managed to fall asleep, I had a nightmare. In the corner of the room was a silver stand holding a long candle whose white light illuminated the room with a bright glow. Harsh winds shook the glass, invading the room through the closed window. The winds whistled, blew, whipped at the candle and shook it, attempting to extinguish its flame. With my slim arms, I attempted again and again to close the window, to seal the cracks under the door and to banish the raging wind.

In the morning, when I got up, I knew that this was it; I could not continue living at the estate with Diogo and Brianda. I had to leave the estate and move into a house of my own.

***

Six months after arriving in Antwerp, I was invited by Ercole de Este, the Duke of Ferrara, a duchy located to the southwest of Venice, a mild two-day ride in a coach drawn by two fresh horses, to move to Ferrara, along with Gerolamo Marta, my educated friend who dealt in gold. The duke promised that if I agreed to his request, he would grant me and my family a certificate of transit and a writ of protection for safe passage through the duchy.

In the past, I had been wary of moving to Ferrara, traveling through the Principality of Milan, as Charles the Fifth's police force had been a massive presence there, attempting to hunt down New Christians, Christian heretics and those secretly practicing Judaism. But this time, I decided to accept the invitations and wait for the certificate of transit.

In my business meetings with Diogo, I did not speak much. Diogo did not understand my silence and wanted to lift my spirits. He wrote to Daniel Bomberg, the most prominent printer in Venice, and ordered me a gift: the first edition of *Mikraot Gedolot,* or Great Scriptures, the five books of the Torah along with interpretations.

Another pain seared my heart. Time was going by, and I still had not managed to transport Francisco's bones to the Holy Land.

The Wedding, 1539

The invitations to Brianda and Diogo's wedding were written in elegant handwriting on silk paper. Brianda walked around giddy with happiness, and her joyous laughter proved infectious, spreading to all members of the household, the servants, the cooks and the gardeners.

The palace was in a flurry. The maids dusted every corner of the house, shining and polishing the numerous copperware items decorating the palace as well as the door handles with sand gathered from the garden and sliced lemon halves. Seamen at the port unloaded crates full of silk fabrics, furniture and jewelry imported from China and India. The cooks toiled over exotic delicacies, seasoned with intoxicating spices originating in distant lands. The bakers banished anyone coming into the kitchen merely to taste a cookie from the numerous pastries baked in the ovens and cooling on metal wire mesh. They filled large jars with rose cookies dipped in honey, baking semolina cookies with nuts and cinnamon. The cooks made quince and apple preserves. They sorted sacks of aromatic rice, fried cumin seeds, rolled up tiny fish balls and fried them in olive oil. Mounds of zucchinis filled with rice were packed into the wide pots.

The kitchen door was closed before those wishing to enjoy the fresh sight of miniature lemons pickled in paprika and olive oil, cucumbers in dill and garlic, and purple eggplants preserved in cardamom, mint and anise.

The wonderful scents and the quiet singing emerging from the kitchen windows filled the chambers of my heart with yearning for my parents' house.

***

Mendes Bank's profits and our wealth invoked jealousy and envy among noblemen, merchants and debtors. The Inquisition was sniffing around us, and we were afraid of informants and surveillance. Despite the danger, Diogo insisted on conducting a secret Jewish marriage ceremony.

On the night before the wedding in the cathedral, the major-domo gave the servants the night off and we entered the hidden synagogue.

A white silk canopy, embroidered with blue flowers and stars, was spread out over the heads of Brianda, who was radiantly beautiful as she had never been before, and the aristocratic Diogo. They had received this *chuppah* as a gift from the merchant Señor Leon Moshe.

Pale and emotional, I stood beside my sister. I remembered my own wedding ceremony in the cellar of our house in Lisbon, on the terrible night on which my father passed away, and my heart roiled within me.

Juan and Bernardo, in their elegant clothes, held the poles of the *chuppah*. The two other poles were held by Doctor Amatus Lusitanus, who offered me a warm smile, and the merchant Manuel Serrano.

Next to Diogo's friend Rabbi Samuel Osheki, who was conducting the ceremony, stood the witnesses, Emanuel de Orte, the accountant, and Jacob Morro.

Due to the cloud of suspicion around us, Diogo asked the rabbi to hurry up and conduct a quick Jewish ceremony. The rabbi poured red wine into a silver chalice and quietly intoned the blessing:

"In the name of the God of Abraham, Isaac and Jacob, I join you,
Meyer-Diego Mendes Benveniste and Reyna-Brianda de Luna Nasi.
May you maintain the traditions of Israel
And be endowed with boys and girls
who will maintain the Torah of Israel. Amen."

Diogo and Brianda sipped from the wine. I saw that Diogo's hand was trembling when he slipped a gold ring on the flushed Brianda's finger. The rabbi read out the *ketubah*, Diogo broke the glass in accordance with the Jewish tradition and swore:

"If I forget thee, O Jerusalem, let my right hand forget her cunning.

Let my tongue cleave to the roof of my mouth if I do not remember thee."

***

The next day, on the official date of the wedding, the sound of the bells from the Cathedral of Our Lady rang out all over the city.

Hundreds of esteemed guests gathered and came to the brightly illuminated cathedral to participate in the much-discussed wedding of the "King of Pepper" to the beautiful Brianda. Princes and princesses, noblemen, merchants serving as the company's agents throughout Europe, ambassadors and their wives, relatives and friends, including Doctor Amatus Lusitanus's brother, Philippe de Monteleto, physician to the queen of France, who had arrived from Paris—all of them were awaiting the arrival of Queen Mary, the sister of Ferdinand, king of Hungary, and Charles the Fifth, king of Spain and the Holy Roman Empire.

A murmur of excitement passed through the gentry when a herald in orange livery blew his shiny trumpet at length and declared, with a self-important expression: "Queen Mary, Queen Regent of the Low Countries!"

Queen Mary sauntered regally as the princesses who were her attendants held on to the hem of her purple velvet dress, inlaid with diamonds and embroidered in gold. Upon her head was a gold tiara spangled with pink diamonds, while her deep décolletage was adorned with a necklace with a red heart medallion.

The organist began to play while a children's choir sang hymns from the book of Psalms. Diogo held on to Brianda's arm and the couple strode slowly down the long aisle of the cathedral.

Brianda was wearing a silk dress in a deep burgundy hue, embroidered in gold. On her feet were high-heeled shoes inlaid with rubies, ordered from Venice. Her golden hair was held back in an ornamental mesh cover that matched her dress and shoes. At her neck were three long pearl necklaces, with matching pearl earrings, while her hands were adorned with bejeweled rings and bracelets, gifts from Diogo.

Ana, in a white dress with a crimson ribbon at her waist, trailed in their wake with several princesses, sprinkling the crimson petals of fragrant roses along with them.

When she passed by me, Brianda jutted her chin forward and grinned at me victoriously.

The organist ceased playing. Brianda and Diogo paused in the aisle next to the queen and bowed deeply before her.

My thoughts drifted far away. I thought about Queen Mary's declaration that she would not remarry, thus maintaining her independence.

For a moment, it occurred to me to take a lover. There were a few candidates who would be happy to oblige. However, I dismissed the thought. You could know how a love affair begins, but not how it would end. And ultimately, the lover, too, would covet my money.

During the wedding party, I saw the nobleman Don Francisco de Aragón, that squat, red-headed old man, over sixty years old, sending impudent, lusting looks at my Ana and whispering with Queen Mary. *What are they plotting?* I wondered.

Lonely Souls

When I returned to my room at the end of the wedding celebration, I felt as if I was deflating. My body was heavy and tired, and a leaden oppression spread through me. I had the dim premonition that a turning point in my life was approaching, but I could not define it. The joie de vivre and vitality to which I was accustomed had been replaced by pain and sorrow. In their place was a lonely widow sitting on the sofa with no man by her side to softly stroke her cheek, embrace her and whisper words of love in her ear. I was surrounded by family members and businessmen. Kings and earls were seeking me out, asking to conduct business with me and borrow my money. But where was the man for whom I would be the center of the universe, and who would be the dearest in the world to me?

My Francisco, where have you gone? Why did you leave me here alone? I buried my head in the pillow and my tears told him of my pain. *You left me here alone,* I sighed.

My darling, I'm missing you. Everything is different here. I thought we would grow old together, and that you would teach the son we would have to run the family business.

Look what's happening to me. I'm here, occupied with family affairs, with a spoiled sister, with our sweet daughter Ana, who was orphaned of her father. Diogo pampers her, but he has so many other occupations, especially now.

My heart was heavy, and I could not even explain to myself why. Perhaps Francisco would come to me at night in a dream and talk to me? Sometimes he came to me in dreams. I kept those dreams to myself, withholding them from everyone around me.

I consoled myself with the fact that next month, Ana and I would be moving to the palace I had rented, hoping it would help me find relief.

***

The rays of sunlight coming in through the half-shuttered blinds and the curtain struck my eyes as I dragged myself out of bed. I felt dizzy, swaying as I walked the short path to the dresser, where the bowl and water pitcher were placed. It took a major effort to raise the pitcher and pour a little water into the china bowl. Any movement sent projections of pain to my left temple. I took a towel, dipped its hem in the cool water, and laid it on my burning forehead. Suddenly, I was overcome by a spasm. I dropped the towel and vomited out coils of unfurled dreams.

I heard a light knock on the door but could not even answer. The door opened, and Teresa, whose face was now deeply lined and whose hands trembled a bit, but whose kind eyes remained the same, came in.

"Señora, what happened? Is the *señora* feeling ill?"

Teresa dipped the towel in the water pitcher again, added a bit of apple vinegar and toweled my face. She then took the bowl, went out to the balcony, poured its contents into one of the potted plants and placed it next to me.

I leaned down toward the bowl and vomited again. Teresa stroked my head. "It's a good thing you threw up. Let all the poison out. Señora, why are you barefoot? You'll get sick. Come on, I'll help you back into bed."

Teresa laid me down in the bed, covered me with a blanket up to my shoulders and told me she would ask Thomas to summon the doctor.

"Get some rest. The *señora* must be tired after the beautiful wedding."

Suddenly, I remembered the wedding, which had taken place only yesterday morning, but already seemed an eternity away.

Apparently, I fell asleep for a while, as when I woke up, Amatus Lusitanus, Teresa and Valera were all standing around my bed, their expressions concerned. I gathered my strength and sat up in bed. Dear Teresa handed me a glass of water with quince preserves. "Drink, please, so you don't get dehydrated."

"Hello, Beatricci," Doctor Amatus nodded at me in greeting.

"Valera and Teresa, please, you can go about your own business," the doctor dismissed them from standing by my side. Teresa looked at me in query.

"It's fine, I'm in good hands," I whispered.

"I'm waiting just outside the room," Teresa said.

My friend the doctor sat down in the chair beside my bed and took my hand in both of his. "I was worried about you. You were breathing heavily." He stroked my hand. "Your pulse is normal. Apparently the tension of the last few days, the wedding preparations and mainly the excitement of the wedding have gotten to you."

The doctor didn't need to tell me this. Everyone knew I had a weak heart.

"My brother, Doctor Philippe de Monteleto, brought a rare rose oil with him from Paris. It has special qualities for healing the sick."

Amatus opened a small vial, and the smell of roses enveloped the room.

"I'm preparing some medicine that will strengthen your heart and help you recover."

He poured a few drops into a glass, poured in some water from the pitcher, patiently mixed the concoction, whose color had turned a pale pink, and handed me the medicine. I sipped it slowly.

Amatus drizzled the contents of the vial into his hand and warmed the oil with his palms. "With your permission, señora, I'll massage your temples. Soon, you'll experience relief…"

His long, gentle fingers softly massaged my temples and forehead. I closed my eyes, overcome by a sensation of pleasure. The touch of his hands on my face was tender and consoling. It had been a long time since a man's hand had touched me. My stomach contracted and my breath began to speed up.

Amatus leaned in toward me. I could feel his warm breath over my face. I did not dare open my eyes, wanting to dwell within the fleeting magic for another moment.

"My dear, you know I'm here for you. You can ask me for anything you want," he whispered in my ear.

"Doctor Amatus, I know, and you are dear to my heart. Believe me, I value your friendship greatly. I want us to continue being friends," I replied quietly.

"You don't have to call me 'doctor.' I was offering you more than friendship—a shoulder to lean on. We have both been left alone. I know some people say you shouldn't marry a doctor..." For a moment, he stopped massaging my temples. I peeked out through my lashes and saw him extracting a handkerchief from the pocket of his jacket to wipe the tears that had emerged at the corners of his eyes.

His fingers continued gently massaging my face. I felt peaceful and trusting.

"Gracia, we're both lonely souls. After all, there is no such thing as chance in the world. It was not a coincidence that fate brought us together. It is a sign of two lonely souls who should come together. As the Bible says, 'It is not good that man should be alone.'"

I sighed heavily. "Amatus, my friend, you are a good person and a true friend. What would I do without you?" I mumbled, entangled in the web of sleep. The fragrant oil and his caressing touch had had an effect upon me.

I could sense his eyes surveying me, but did not see fit to open my own. It was convenient for me to let him think I was asleep, though my heart was awake.

Secretly, I hoped his hand would flutter over my cheek, that he would kiss me; my entire body was yearning for touch. However, Amatus was a gentleman, and maintained my honor. I heard him pushing back the chair and rising to his feet.

The Seeds of Disaster

On a cold, gray day, a month after leaving Diogo and Brianda's estate and moving with Ana to the palace I had rented next to St. Paul's Church, I left Ana with Allegra and went to visit my sister and brother-in-law. We sat next to the burning hearth and I asked Diogo to tell me about his arrest by the Inquisition. Diogo maintained his silence for a long time, then wrapped a fur cloak around his shoulders and recounted the tale.

"One evening, when the agent Antonio de la Ronja arrived from London for a business meeting, I heard a faint knocking at the front door. Raphael del Vino opened it, and a mother and her two young sons entered the house.

"'Our patron, the lord protecting us!' the woman wept.

"'Madam, sit down, please,' I tried to soothe her. I asked Raphael del Vino to serve her and her children food and drink, as well as provide her with warm clothes. After she calmed down somewhat, the woman told me that her name was Ermilanda Ferreira…"

"Ermilanda Ferreira was my friend," I interrupted Diogo.

But Diogo ignored me. Glancing at me distractedly, he adjusted the cloak around his shoulders and continued to describe the events of that night.

"'My eldest son, Marco, is seventeen,' the woman gestured at her short, broad-shouldered son, who was wearing a brown beret and a torn cloak, and who kissed my hand at length.

"'Emilio is fifteen.' She placed her hand on the shoulder of a brawny boy whose observant eyes were looking all around him, taking in every detail. 'And this is Jose,' she kissed the forehead of a tot who was about a year old.

"'I was living with my family in Porto. My husband, Ricardo, whose grandfather has been among the sages of Grenada, had a senior position in the city council, and wanted to be promoted and receive a more important position in order to become a part of high society. He insisted we live as Catholics at home as well, and fiercely objected to my desire that we act like Christians ostensibly, but live as Jews secretly. He forbade me to bathe in honor of the Sabbath and light the blessed candles, and demanded that I cook impure sausage for the Sabbath, after which we would eat cheese cake, violating the Jewish dietary rules.

"'One Friday evening, Ricardo caught me sweeping the house and preparing linseed wicks. He threw a fit, tossed the wicks into the fireplace and screamed at me that I was risking our lives and the future of our children.

"'The fear that Ricardo would inform on me to the Inquisition accompanied me like a dark shadow. On a night with no moonlight, I fled from the house with my three sons. With the help of friends who bribed a sea captain, I boarded a small ship in one of Porto's little fishing harbors.

"'When we got to Antwerp, the Church's hunters boarded the ship and interrogated me, asking about the purpose of our trip to the city, and whether we had come to settle in Antwerp permanently.

"'Luckily for me, just then a fire broke out on the ship's stern, and in the resulting chaos, we managed to escape. One of the people who had been on the ship, who had also fled Porto, gave me the address for Señor Mendes and told me the *señor* could help me,' the woman told me.

"I told her she could shake off her worries now and that she was in good hands. I promised her that my agents would smuggle them into Ragusa. I wrote a short missive to my accountant Jacob Morro and asked him to take care of all the needs of the woman and her sons, and smuggle them to Ragusa, a city of refuge and a part of the Ottoman state."

Diogo sighed. "As you both know, the story didn't end well. My brothers betrayed me," his voice shook.

"What happened?" Brianda stroked his shoulder.

"Emilio, Ermilanda's son, missed his father Ricardo very much. Despite the perils of the journey, he returned to Rome and appealed to the Church to help him return to Portugal. Emilio informed on me, telling them I had helped his mother and brothers escape from Antwerp to Ragusa, and that company agents, including Jacob Morro, booked their passage on the ship, provided them with addresses for accommodations along the way and with food, drink and clothes. He passed on all my secrets to the emperor's personal priest."

"Oh, no, my darling! You risked your life for him and he betrayed you!" Brianda said.

"Beatricci, they stabbed me in the heart. The son of your friend whom I saved from the Inquisition turned me in."

"That's terrible!" I said.

"The worst part was that Emperor Charles the Fifth issued an arrest warrant against me and confiscated all my merchandise for the kingdom's treasury. In addition, I underwent a grueling interrogation at the offices of the Inquisition. I thought it was best to stick as close to the truth as possible. In my interrogation I claimed that I was of Jewish origin, but lived like a good Christian, and that the aid I extended to the *annusim* was part of my routine commercial activity."

"Did the interrogators believe you?" I asked.

"They didn't have any further proof. The heads of the merchant guild intervened on my behalf. Francisco immediately appealed to King Joao of Portugal and asked him to step in. The king and the queen feared that the seizing of the merchandise would bring about the collapse of commerce in Portugal, and force the country into bankruptcy. They appealed to Charles the Fifth and to Mary, and I was released from my confinement."

"I know," I said. "Francisco let me read their letters."

Black Clouds Gathering on the Horizon

However, no one is infallible. The arrest damaged Diogo's heart. The seeds of disaster had sprouted.

The wailing of the wind infiltrated the windows of the study where I was sitting with Diogo when terrible rumors started drifting in from Lisbon regarding the auto-da-fé in Palacio Rossio Square. And tragically, some of the families 'belonging to the letter Yod' who were burned at the stake were familiar to us.

Three knocks were heard at the door. After a short pause, the knocking was repeated, three strong ones and two light ones. I exchanged glances with Diogo; we were not expecting any guests that day. We had just finished going over the accounts and discussed allocating funds to the immense wave of escapees fleeing the Inquisition in Portugal.

Aged Thomas, his face deeply lined, opened the door.

"Señor Gonzales Gomez, agent to the House of Mendes in Milan, requests to be admitted for an urgent meeting," he told us.

A short, elderly man entered the house in a state of panic. His hair was graying and he sported a small beard upon his pointy chin. His fair face was pale and his jaw was trembling. Thomas helped him take off the dusty, wrinkled green wool coat draped haphazardly upon his body.

"My dear friend Gonzales Gomez, I thought we would only be seeing you next month," Diogo said in surprise, kissing the visitor's sweaty visage. "Please meet my sister-in-law, Beatrice Mendes."

"I apologize, señora, for coming with no advance notice. I rode for days and nights in order to bring you the information in person,"

Gonzales stammered, concern reflecting in his narrow gray eyes when he began his story.

"The City Council of Milan, under the control of Emperor Charles the Fifth, king of Spain, has decided to establish a special committee to thoroughly investigate the immense wave of immigration consisting of New Christians who have come to Milan, as well as the ship owners who transported them there."

"Diogo, dark clouds are gathering on the horizon," I said.

"The clouds are already here." Gonzales Gomez wiped the drops of perspiration appearing on his forehead. "The villains wasted no time. On the day the city council reached the decision to establish the investigative committee, mass arrests of New Christians began to take place in all the territories under Charles the Fifth's rule. The desperate cries of pain of family members forcefully separated from their loved ones and thrown into jail are still ringing in my ears."

Diogo listened, his face unreadable and his arms crossed over his chest. A spasm passed across his face as he heard the terrible words 'thrown into jail.' We had known of the intention to establish an investigative committee, but the actual decision and the immediate execution were appalling news.

"I heard from one of the members of the city council that some of them are accused of receiving support from the house of Diogo Mendes,"

"We have to save them," I said.

"Those poor people. I know how terrible it is to be under arrest! I'm calling an urgent meeting for consultation," Diogo said.

"Diogo, I'm sorry to tell you that the committee is accusing you of supporting the refugees."

"No!" I cried out.

"Gracia, calm down, everything is fine," Diogo said quietly.

Diogo extracted a leather pouch full of gold coins from a drawer and handed it to Gonzales. "Gonzales, I don't want your disappearance from the city to raise any suspicion. Tonight, you'll rest in my home. Early in the morning, you'll go back to Milan. I ask that you report any new development to me, and do all you can to prevent arrests. You know what to do with the money."

"Yes," Gonzales Gomez replied.

"I suggest that we include Mickas in the meeting. It's true, he's only fifteen, but it's time to let him into the thick of things." Diogo would refer to Juan by his last name. "Bernardo is more interested in Hebrew poetry and sacred literature than in importing and exporting merchandise, so we'll leave him out of it."

"I agree. Bernardo is currently busy presenting his doctoral thesis in Hebrew and Latin," I said.

Diogo rang the crystal bell and Thomas came in.

"Thomas, please provide Señor Gonzales Gomez with accommodations, a bath and a warm meal. Call Juan and prepare the coach."

***

"Juan, I'm sending you to London in complete secrecy. You must personally inform Antonio de la Ronja, the company representative, that he's invited to an urgent assembly at my palace," Diogo informed Juan immediately when he entered the room.

Juan's face grew solemn. "What happened? Trouble with the Church police?"

"He has to know and understand everything… You'll know when the time is right. I trust you—no one can know where and why you're travelling. This is for expenses along the way." Diogo handed Juan a leather pouch full of gold coins.

"You can count on me. I'll return as soon as I can," Juan replied, turned around and left the room.

***

Three weeks later, at the beer festival, the streets of Antwerp were teeming with celebrants, fire eaters, sword jugglers, magicians, Gypsy palm-readers and fortunetellers, troubadours, drummers, and stalls offering dozens of flavors of beer and warm waffles.

Raphael de Vino gave the servants time off to participate in the celebration. Once darkness fell, under the cover of silence, a meeting took place in the secret synagogue.

Diogo lit the candles that were scattered in candlesticks throughout the room and on the round table at its center. Seeing him took my breath away. His brown hair had gone white overnight.

Juan let the company agents into the synagogue. Deep lines were furrowed into the brow of old Lupe de Provincia, the most senior of Antwerp's merchants, with whom many did business due to his decency and honesty. The silent, kind-hearted Manuel Cyrano sat down heavily in an armchair. Manuel Lopez's dark curls were peeking out under his hat. Antonio de la Ronja adjusted the black eyepatch over his eye, took off his coat and sat down as well. They were joined by the shaggy-haired, energetic Christopher Fernandez.

"Meet my relative Gaspar Lopez, who was formerly the company's representative in London," Diogo introduced us to a young dandy with a meticulously trimmed black beard, wearing a short yellow jacket, brown pants with sharp folds and boots.

"Gentlemen, the situation is dire," Diogo began. "The cruel Inquisition in Lisbon, whose establishment we were unfortunately unable to prevent, has caused thousands to flee in panic. Milan's city council has established a committee whose role is to investigate the waves of immigration, and which initiated mass arrests of 'New Christians' in all territories under the rule of Charles the Fifth. Hundreds have been arrested in Milan on their way to Ancona, Ragusa, Thessaloniki and Constantinople, the cities of the Turkish sultan. Their lives are in danger."

An oppressive silence formed around the table.

"Has Emperor Charles the Fifth gone mad? After all, you're lending money to him and to his sister Mary!" Antonio de la Ronja raised his voice.

"He hasn't gone mad. The emperor is the grandson of the evil Ferdinand and Isabella. He inherited his villainy and cruelty from them," Juan said.

"The committee is accusing Diogo Mendes of supporting the refugees." My voice was shaking.

"It's a disaster," Gaspar Lopez whispered.

"Diogo, you have to flee," said Manuel Lopez.

"I suggest you take off for Ragusa or Constantinople tonight." Antonio de le Ronja's voice expressed his urgency.

"Don't worry about me," Diogo said, a spasm passing across his face. "I gathered you here so we can decide which means to employ in order to prevent the interrogation and arrest of the New Christians. We have two main goals. First, we must smuggle our brothers to the sultan's countries. Second, we must aid them financially. They are fleeing empty-handed. If their neighbors find out, they might inform on them to the Inquisition."

"We have to prepare inns and places of refuge where they can wait until the Inquisition's police force and the spies depart," said Antonio de le Ronja, adjusting his eyepatch once more.

"My husband Francisco, may he rest in peace, would convey money to the heads of the monasteries located along the routes of trade from the sea ports to the villages and cities of Portugal, so they would serve as a temporary sanctuary for the refugees," I said.

"Throughout Europe, there's a network of inns and monasteries we work with, but that won't be enough," Diogo said.

"I'll take it upon myself to expand the network of monasteries and roadside inns," Manuel Lopez volunteered.

"What about the escapees' property?" asked Antonio de la Ronja.

"Jacob Morro, the company's accountant, will be responsible for purchasing the entire property of every family fleeing. In return, they'll receive a promissory note from us listing the value of the asset."

"All the property? From everyone?" Juan's jaw dropped in amazement.

"No comments, please. Once the escapees reach sanctuary, they can redeem the promissory note with our agents, and receive cash in return.

"Daniel Bomberg, the owner of the printing press in Venice, is willing to serve as the 'gray-market bank' in conveying the funds. Payments will be conveyed to him, seemingly as payments for printing books, which, of course, will never be printed. Daniel Bomberg will pass them on to our agents, who will convey them to the *annusim* in return for the notes and bills of exchange they are holding."

"The money will allow them to start their lives again in a new location, rent an apartment, buy food, establish a small business, and mostly, be productive, rather than becoming a burden on the community; they can even contribute to it," I added.

"Señor Mendes, what will you do with the houses, the furniture and the possessions you purchase?" asked Gaspar Lopez.

"Gaspar, why are you worrying about the property? We'll sell the assets, and with the way prices are going up these days, we'll even make a profit on the transaction. Even if I suffer a loss, it's not a disaster. I have no children of my own, other than my brother's family. My old governess, Bianca, is still in Lisbon, and I'm trying to smuggle her out of there. This is exactly what the fortune I've accumulated is intended for," Diogo said.

Lupe de Provincia filled his wooden pipe with a handful of brown tobacco leaves that he extracted from a small silver snuffbox. He lighted it with a candle burning in the sconces on the table, inhaling the smoke. "Gaspar Lopez, we are very privileged to be helping our persecuted people," he said.

"We all are," Manuel Cyrano added.

"I'm sorry," Gaspar Lopez apologized. "Of course I want to help. I simply wanted to understand how it would be carried out. I was afraid we would fall under suspicion if we suddenly began to sell off lots of property."

"We have to be patient. We'll sell off the property gradually." Diogo unfurled the map of the world that Francisco had received as a gift from Rabbi Abraham Zacuto across the table.

He marked out paths upon the map. "An escape route by land, along the roads where processions of merchants pass, and to cities interested in enhancing commerce using the knowledge and money provided by the New Christians, will include Amsterdam; Lyon and Bordeaux, France; Venice and Ferrara in Italy; Hamburg in Germany; and Lithuania in Poland. Additional routes will go to England, through the ports of Plymouth and Southampton."

"We should smuggle some of the escapees from Portugal to Morocco, Tunisia, Algeria and the islands of Madeira," Lupe de Provincia suggested.

"Your idea is accepted," Diogo said.

"The refugees interested in escaping from Europe can be smuggled through the ports of Thessaloniki, Ragusa and the Levantine cities to the Ottoman state," Antonio de la Ronja proposed.

"The Church police won't relinquish anyone. They're sending espionage vessels to pursue those who flee, even those who escape to North Africa…" I began to say. When I saw Lupe de Provincia and Antonio de la Ronja nodding in agreement, I continued, "It's important that our agents board every ship carrying refugees and help them."

"You're correct, that's very important," Lupe de Provincia said.

"That's not all," I added. "We should station agents at the mountain passes, to help smuggle the refugees to the border and warn them of undercover policemen employed by the emperor and the Church."

"That's an excellent suggestion!" I heard Manuel Cyrano whisper to Diogo.

Diogo looked at me appreciatively. "I agree with Señora Gracia. Each of you will appoint agents acting on your behalf at the ports and the border crossings. Their role will be to warn the escapees of the Inquisition's spies and administrators, to advise them on where to flee, to suggest accommodations and places to eat, and to help them cross the Alps." He was speaking quickly, and appeared to see me in a new light. For the first time, I felt that Diogo was appreciative of my suggestions, and viewed me as a full partner, rather than merely as his sister-in-law.

"I appoint Christopher Fernandez as my deputy, and he will be in charge of the rescue operations in England. He will board every ship carrying perfume that will arrive at the ports of Plymouth and Southampton. In case he finds out of danger lurking further down the road on the way to the Low Countries, he will warn the escapees," said Antonio de la Ronja.

"Excellent," said Diogo, carrying on. "If you will, gentlemen, the rescue operation requires an immense sum of money. I suggest we start a fund of 200,000 ducats to cover the anticipated expenses. If you have no objection, I'd like to appoint Antonio de la Ronja as my deputy and assistant."

Everyone nodded in agreement.

"I'll contribute twenty five thousand ducats," said Antonio de la Ronja.

Manuel Cyrano extracted a bank note from an internal pocket, filled it out with a sum of twenty thousand gold ducats, and placed it on the table.

"Here is a contribution of ten thousand gold ducats to the fund." Manuel Lopez wrote out a promissory note.

Lupe de Provincia filled out the sum on a bank note and passed it on to Diogo. "Twenty thousand gold ducats," he said.

"I can add five thousand ducats to the fund." Gaspar Lopez produced a heavy bundle of money and placed it on the table.

Diogo opened a wooden chest and placed the gold coins and the notes inside. "Señora Beatrice and I are adding 120,000 ducats on behalf of the Mendes Company, thus bringing the sum to 200,000 ducats." Diogo looked at me and said, "Gentlemen, my sister-in-law Beatrice Mendes will be my right hand."

I hoped they could not see that I was blushing.

"And Antonio de la Ronja will be appointed the treasurer of the fund for the rescue of our brethren.

"If you agree, we'll appoint Gaspar Lopez as the fund's special emissary in Italy." Diogo's voice brought me back to reality. The attendees murmured in agreement. Diogo wrote out a note in the sum of two thousand gold ducats endorsed to House of Mendes's agents in Milan, and deposited it with Gaspar Lopez. He placed the remainder of the sum in the safe, which he secured with two locks.

"Gaspar Lopez, in addition to the money, I'll also give you written instructions to pass on to the company's representative in Milan, Gonzales Gomez. Note that the money is intended for two purposes: first, to help the prisoners, to hire advocates for them and supply them with clothing and food, and second, to pay bribes to those appointed by the emperor, so the arrests and the committee's activity both come to a stop."

Diogo pulled his chair back and placed his hand on Gaspar's shoulder. "Remember, I'm putting my trust in you. People's lives are in your hands."

Diogo consulted with me quietly before addressing Juan. "These days, it's dangerous to leave our business center in Antwerp. Slowly and stealthily, we'll relocate it to Lyon. The king of France is encouraging the New Christians to settle in his country and doesn't persecute them like Charles the Fifth."

"We want you to leave for Lyon and run the company's branch there. We have faith in you," I said.

We swore to keep the meeting a secret and went our separate ways.

***

Brianda, wearing a ball gown, rose heavily from her armchair, laying down the book she was holding. "How was the meeting?" she asked.

This seemed quite odd to me. Since when had my sister been interested in business meetings? And since our arrival in Antwerp, I had not seen her reading a book.

"I thought you wanted to go to the beer festival," I said.

"I was waiting for my husband. I have a gift for him," she replied.

I was surprised. She was guarding him from me... What was she thinking, that I would steal him away?

Diogo entered at that same moment. "Hello, my wife, how are you? And how is that little baby growing in your belly?"

"Congratulations, my sister. You didn't tell me about the...?" I said, frozen.

"Diogo and I thought it would be better to wait a while before telling everyone the wonderful news," she said, immediately turning to Diogo. "Diogush, I have a gift for you."

"Thank you, my pretty, you're getting me excited," Diogo blushed.

"At our first ball, you introduced me to the painter Pieter Bruegel the Younger, and he's invited me to visit his atelier."

"Ahh, I already understand..." Diogo laughed.

"Pieter is a good, quiet man, but his paintings are original and full of joyousness. Impulsively, I commissioned a painting from him. It's a present for you."

Brianda handed him the painting propped up beside her.

"Darling, you have exquisite taste. Tomorrow, you'll help me decide in what room the painting should be hung. Bri, I have a surprise for you, too. I commissioned a madrigal for you from composer Cipriano de Rore. He will play the madrigal in your honor at tonight's ball," Diogo said.

"Thank you, darling." She kissed his cheek. "That's wonderful! We can dance together," Brianda clapped in joy.

"Gracia, it would be our pleasure if you could join us for the celebration at the palace of our partner, Jean Charles Affaitati, whose wife is throwing a party in honor of the festival," Diogo said.

My head was full of thoughts and plans concerning the rescue operation. I debated whether to courteously refuse or accept the invitation, but before I could even answer, Brianda entwined her arm with Diogo's and began to walk toward the door. "Sister, are you coming?" she turned her head toward me.

"Excuse me," I apologized, asking Thomas to prepare the coach to take me home.

On the way back home, thoughts of the secret meeting swirled in my mind, and I was filled with satisfaction. Ever since my childhood, I had wanted to leave my mark upon the world, to do something that would be remembered for generations to come. I wanted to exhibit the quality of mercy of our forefather Abraham, as I had been raised to do. This was my opportunity. When I got to heaven, and the Creator asked me, *Hannah Nasi, what have you done with the years of life granted to you?* I could reply that I hoped I had been like a tree spreading out its branches, providing fruit and shelter for my needy refugee brethren fleeing from the horror of the Inquisition.

Enough dreaming, I scolded myself. Now was no time for personal thoughts; there were so many things I had to handle in order to organize the escape and rescue routes.

***

During the next few months, Diogo and I interviewed many young and older people. We were seeking people with mental and physical fortitude, who would be willing to take risks, wait at the docks and make sure the Inquisition guards were not waiting for the escapees; if they were, the volunteers had to board the ships and inform the passengers not to leave the vessels. They even had to wait for them in mountain passes. We paid significant funds in bribes, bought safe houses, prepared blankets, warm clothes, food and medicine. We operated our ships in accordance with the needs of the escapees and conducted many fund meetings. But we did not know disaster was lurking at our threshold.

Diogo dedicated his days and nights to organizing means of rescue. However, since receiving the news of the latest accusations against him and the establishment of the investigative committee, he had not felt well and his eyes were red. Brianda and I were worried about his health.

Diogo tried many types of medicine. Brianda showed me a letter Doctor Amatus Lusitanus had brought Diogo, along with medication from Ferrara.

March 1540
Ferrara

To my esteemed noble friend, Señor Diogo Mendes,

I am sending you extract of roses, which is a special, unique medicine that has helped many patients.

Yours in appreciation and much respect,
Sebastian Pinto of the City of Ferrara

Gracia La Chica, 1540

As spring was fading away, while the scents of flowers filled the garden, a month before the expected date of the birth, Brianda was overcome by powerful contractions and Diogo sent the major-domo to fetch me.

I stroked Brianda's face, moistening her lips with a wet handkerchief. The midwife massaged her belly with hot oil, but the baby would not come out. The midwife pulled me aside. "The birth is difficult, and has been dragging on for more than ten hours," she said, wiping the perspiration off Brianda's brow.

I went out to the parlor. "Please summon Doctor Amatus Lusitanus," I asked Diogo, who was pacing back and forth in the sitting room.

"Is Brianda all right? Is the birth progressing?" Diogo asked.

"Yes. It would be better if the doctor was present as well. The contractions are very strong," I replied, returning to the room.

When Doctor Amatus Lusitanus arrived, Brianda was soaked in sweat, and had begun quietly murmuring a prayer.

The doctor extracted a special oil with a pungent odor from his bag and handed it to the midwife. She applied the oil on Brianda's belly, forehead and temples. Several minutes later, Brianda calmed down and the birth continued.

"Brianda, you have a daughter!" the midwife lifted up the baby girl who had made her way into the world.

"Congratulations, my sister! Welcome to the world, child."

Tears of joy were rolling down Brianda's cheeks.

The midwife cut the umbilical cord, toweled down the baby with warm water, swaddled her in the white wool blanket that Brianda had knit during the months of her pregnancy, placed her briefly in Brianda's lap, then transferred her to my arms. I embraced the sweet baby with the clear face and the strands of flaxen hair, like her mother's.

Then I placed her in her pretty crib.

Brianda bit her lips and groaned, continuing to moan in pain. The midwife oiled her belly once more, her eyes gaping wide. "Doctor, I think that… that there's another baby!" she called out.

Amatus examined Brianda again. "You're right, the birth isn't over. There is another baby."

"Twins? Maybe a boy?" Brianda murmured with difficulty.

The birth was stalled. The midwife continued to encourage Brianda, who was weak and exhausted. The midwife placed her elbows on Brianda's belly and applied pressure on the womb in an attempt to push the baby out into the world.

"One more little effort!" she cried out.

After twenty long minutes or so, the baby emerged into the world. His face was blue.

"A boy," the midwife murmured, flipping him over and lightly tapping his behind. A yellow fluid was ejected from the baby's mouth. "He's not breathing." The midwife grew pale.

Amatus placed his mouth on the baby's and tried to imbue him with several life-giving breaths.

Brianda bit her lip. "Do something, save my son!" she begged.

After a minute that seemed to last an eternity, the doctor informed my sister, with much sadness, that her baby had passed away.

"No! I want my son…" Brianda mouthed soundlessly.

The midwife propped the baby up against her shoulder, with only a black strand of hair on his head peeking out from under the blanket that would never warm his tiny body, and turned to leave the room.

Tears appeared in Brianda's eyes, and her lips whispered the prayer she had heard from Mama.

"My poor, tiny baby,

May the blessed angel escort and protect you."

I walked over to embrace my sister, but she signaled to me that she wished to be alone. I wandered off. Diogo entered, his legs barely carrying him, to sit beside his wife.

"Darling, don't cry, I'm with you always," he wiped away the tears rolling down her cheeks.

During the first few days, Diogo walked through the palace quietly, celebrating the birth of his daughter and mourning the death of his son. Brianda stayed in her bed for most of the day.

***

In the beginning of June, the nobility and the city's dignitaries swarmed to the Cathedral of Our Lady to take part in the lavish christening. Brianda was radiant with the peace of a young mother. Her earlobes displayed the diamond and sapphire earrings she had received as a gift from Diogo, which matched her turquoise taffeta dress and the white ornamental mesh embroidered with pearls that held back her hair. Brianda dressed the baby in a white damask silk christening gown with lace embroidery ordered in advance from an Italian embroiderer, while Diogo walked around like a proud peacock, rejoicing in his beautiful daughter. Jean Charles Affaitati, Diogo's partner and good friend, was honored with being the baby's godfather.

Thousands of candles were burning in the cathedral. The new baptismal basin was made of pure silver, its sides engraved with the baby's name in elaborate cursive letters: Beatrice Mendes.

In order to differentiate me from the smiley baby with the sweet round face and the flaxen hair, we called her Beatrice La Chica, or Little Beatrice, from her very first day—"La Chica" for short.

I wanted to hold her in my arms. Brianda agreed to let me cradle her for a moment. I brought her pale pink cheek to mine; she smelled fresh, like the beginning of life.

***

Raindrops had been drizzling down all morning, and the weather was gray and cloudy. I was perturbed by the fact that a House of Mendes ship that had been scheduled to arrive from Lisbon to the Port of Antwerp a week ago was still delayed, but I did not let this fact disrupt my plans, accepting Brianda's invitation to a light afternoon meal.

Allegra dressed Ana in a plaid dress and tied red ribbons in her hair. Seven-year-old Ana chose to give one of the new dolls I had bought her from a Venetian merchant as a gift to Brianda's ten-month-old daughter, La Chica.

I kissed Brianda on her cheek. "This new dress really suits you well."

"Thank you. It was sent from Venice," Brianda told me, embracing Ana.

Sweet La Chica, in a pink wool dress and white socks, was crawling on the rug toward the doll Ana had brought her. She laughed happily when Ana crawled after her and tried to catch her.

Brianda asked Allegra to take Ana and La Chica to the playroom, inviting me to see the new paintings she had purchased.

"Diogo is boasting to his friends that his beautiful wife is a patron of the arts," I said.

Brianda blushed. "It thrills me to discover young, talented artists and support them," she said. "Come on." She strolled leisurely toward her study.

Large windows had been installed in the big, lovely room, letting in the sunshine. The hearth, spreading a pleasant warmth, and the wall behind it had been covered with *azulejos* tiles with a pattern of pale blue flowers.

"Diogo gave me this room and I renovated it from the ground up," she told me. She walked among ten easels made of thick, full wood, displaying paintings that were full of light. Brianda paused next to a painting depicting a group of village children at play.

"A painting by Pieter Breughel," she said. "He's daring enough to paint children playing, rather than portraying them as angels. Look how colorful the painting is, and full of light, and how accurate the details are. Here's one boy doing a headstand, while another is rolling around, and there are girls playing hide-and-seek. I'm certain his paintings will be worth a fortune," she said.

I examined a landscape depicting the Scheldt River, bearing Brianda's signature.

"I prefer this painting of the river that you drew. There's a vitality to it," I said.

"Thank you," Brianda said, "but I believe these painters will be famous one day."

"It's wonderful that you're investing your money in artists whose paintings you like and appreciate."

"I intend to host an exhibition of select paintings soon."

"That's lovely, sister. If you need help with the preparations, I'll be happy to pitch in."

Brianda placed her hand on my arm. "Gracia, thank you. I'll be happy to have you helping me," she smiled. "Come on. It's time to dine."

We sat at the round table, set with delicate china plates bearing fragrant cheese pastries and pear preserves as well as goblets of warm wine.

Raphael del Vino, the major-domo, appeared at the doorway of the small dining room.

"Doña Brianda, I apologize for the interruption."

"I asked that we would not be bothered," Brianda said.

Ana placed her pastry on her plate and looked at me. The major-domo bowed. "Doña Brianda, Don Diogo asked that Doña Beatrice come urgently to the stock exchange,"

"What is so urgent that my sister has to leave in the middle of a meal?"

"Madam, I do not know. Don Diogo's coach is waiting at the entrance."

"Beatricci," Brianda placed her hand on my own, "please, stay with me. Look what a fabulous meal I've prepared."

"Mama, please, I want to stay…" Ana requested.

"Brianda, I'm sorry, but I have to leave."

"Beatricci, does it seem reasonable to you that my husband spends more hours of the day with you than with his wife and daughter?" she suddenly blurted out in anger.

"I'm sorry," I apologized. "Something urgent must have happened. Ana, you can stay with Aunt Brianda. I'll come back soon to pick you up."

Where?

Jacob Morro, agent of the House of Mendes, was waiting for me at the entrance to the stock exchange. The courtyard was abuzz. Groups of merchants who were members of the spice guild were huddled together, whispering discreetly, their faces clouded with uncertainty and concern.

"Doña Beatrice, the captain of the ship that arrived from Lisbon is waiting for you in the office; you should hear the news from him. I'll join you in several minutes," Jacob Morro said.

I entered Diogo's office.

"Madam," the captain doffed his hat to me. His face was seared by the sun. "The ship did not sail on time from the Port of Lisbon as a royal decree required us to get to Palacio Rossio Square," he lowered his eyes, "in order to witness the first auto-de-fé."

A sense of bleakness took over the room.

Diogo placed his finger on his lips, closed the windows carefully and peeked beyond the door. After making sure no strangers were eavesdropping on the conversation, he signaled the captain to resume.

"The cruel Inquisition in Portugal has accused one of the most respected and wealthy New Christians of heresy and of secretly practicing Judaism. The auto-de-fé ceremony was scheduled for the eve of the day holy to... those belonging to the letter Yod," he added in a whisper. "After the wretch was brutally tortured by the Inquisition, he admitted to affixing placards to the cathedral doors in which he called their messiah 'a false messiah.' The cries of that wretched man as his body went up in flames are still ringing in my ears."

The Lord protect us and save us from all strife, I prayed silently.

Diogo struck the table with his fist. "The Church, the king and the nobility are trying to disrupt the unity and good relationships among the forced converts, so that they don't become too wealthy or occupy positions of authority within the state. They want to break their spirit. On the one hand, they forbid us from marrying the Old Christians in order to preserve the purity of blood, *limpieza de sangre*, so that no Jewish blood is mingled in with the blood of the Old Christians, while on the other hand, they accuse us of heresy in order to seize our property and inflict us with fear."

"The Inquisition's interrogators have begun to infiltrate the villages. They're encouraging the inhabitants to inform on the heretics. Thousands are fleeing to the ports. I managed to smuggle out about a hundred people with me. Jacob Morro is looking after them," the captain resumed.

Diogo produced a heavy bundle of coins. "I want you to sail for Lisbon again immediately, and load as many escapees as possible on deck."

"Excuse me, señora, I have to return to my ship," the captain said, hurrying to depart.

Jacob Morro came in, sitting down heavily in one of the chairs.

"The merchants are in a state of turmoil. We've just received news that Emperor Charles the Fifth has led his army into Ghent, the city of his birth, which is not far from here. The emperor has punished the residents of the city who rebelled against him, captured the leaders of the rebellion and forced them to march barefoot in front of him, with a choke collar around their neck. The merchants are afraid the emperor will also invade Antwerp and treat them in the way he likes to boast about, 'an iron fist in a velvet glove,'" Jacob reported.

"But his mother, 'Joanna the Mad,' gave birth to him in Ghent. How dare he conquer the city of his birth?" I wondered.

"His mother is Spanish, his father is German, and he was born in Flanders," Diogo said. "Apparently, he feels more Spanish than Flemish. In one of my meetings with the emperor, I heard him laugh and say, 'I speak Spanish to God in heaven, Italian to women, French to men and German to my horse.'"

"Where shall we go? I'm afraid to stay in Antwerp. It would be better if we moved to the Duchy of Ferrara. Duke Ercole de Este is encouraging the New Christians to settle in Ferrara and allowing 'those belonging to the letter Yod' to live there openly."

"Don't get too excited. Their situation remains tenuous everywhere. The German priest Luther is disseminating terrible hateful sermons directed against them all over Europe."

"Why don't we relocate to one of the Ottoman states? Perhaps Thessaloniki or Ragusa?" I lowered my voice.

"It's too soon. First, we must collect on all the debts owed to the House of Mendes. It would be better to relocate to the city of Lyon in France."

"I suggest that Jacob Morro set out for Lyon and help Juan. Jacob, your wife told me that both her sisters live in Lyon."

"They do. They love the city," Jacob replied.

Diogo sat down at the desk and composed an appointment letter for Jacob. "Leave for Lyon with your family next week. Watch out for the emperor's soldiers on the way. If they stop you, tell them you are going to visit your sister-in-law."

Diogo produced a pouch of money. "Please, rent two roomy residential houses near the center of the city, in a discreet manner, preferably within walking distance from each other."

"Best of luck, Jacob. Augustino Henricks will join you and your family," I said, then rose from my seat. "Brianda is waiting for me. I have to leave."

"I'm going out to speak to the merchants. No one in Antwerp has any intention of rebelling against the emperor, and I should try to calm them down," Diogo said, extracting a letter from the drawer. "Read this." I recognized my mother's rounded handwriting.

Beatricci and Brianda, my dear daughters,

Our beloved Grandma Reyna has passed away. I am ill, and I do not think we will ever meet again.

Missing you and loving you,
Mama

"I said goodbye to my mother, your Grandmother Reyna, twenty-three years ago," Diogo said sadly.

"Grandma Reyna is gone. We have to make use of our connections and smuggle Mama out of Lisbon." I struggled to keep the tears at bay.

I picked up a sheet of paper and quickly composed a short missive. "I'm writing to the agents of House of Mendes to instruct them to make every effort to get Mama out of Lisbon."

I folded the letter and handed it to Diogo. "Ask the young courier to convey this to the captain."

I went out to the carriage. The rain began to come down, dripping down the steamed-up windows. *Even the sky is crying over Grandma Reyna's departure*, I thought.

When I entered the parlor, I found Brianda sitting and embroidering there, untypically quiet. Ana and La Chica had fallen asleep on the sofa. Diogo walked over to Brianda and kissed her cheek.

"Hello, Brianda."

Brianda gazed at me coldly.

"How nice of you to bother to return. Your meeting took three hours. The meal has gone cold," she said bitterly, placing the embroidery on the table beside her.

"Brianda, I'm sorry. I did want to spend the day with you."

She moved over to the window, watching the hard rain come down relentlessly. "You wanted to… but you chose to leave," she said, ringing the bell.

Allegra and Rapahel del Vino entered the room.

"Señora," Raphael addressed Brianda.

"Please prepare the carriage. Allegra, please take Ana. Make sure she doesn't get wet; it's raining outside."

"Mama sent us a letter," I said, trying to appease her somewhat.

"If Mama sent us a letter, why did you receive it, and not me?"

"Mama writes that…"

"There's no need for you to tell me," Brianda interjected. "Leave the letter on the table. I can read it myself."

"Grandma Reyna… Mama…" I could hear Brianda crying as I left the parlor.

The Agreement, 1542

It had been six months since we sent Jacob Morro to supervise Juan in Lyon. House of Mendes's business in France had expanded. Juan forged connections with the French royal court. He requested that we approve a loan of 150,000 gold ducats to King Francois the First, in return for securities and high interest. We happily approved the loan, as we could see the importance of creating a relationship with and a stake in the French monarchy, which did not persecute the New Christians like the emperor.

I proposed to Diogo that we send Bernardo to Lyon as well. He had now graduated from the university and been appointed to manage the trade of fabric and wool.

***

The vessel we had ordered from the shipyard was still not ready. The certificate of transit to the Duchy of Ferrara had still not arrived, although it had been sent to me. The clerks at House of Mendes were busy working on the annual accounting, and I asked the accountant, Emanuel de Orte, to hand it over to me for perusal.

"I believe the *señora* will be very pleased with the profits," Emanuel de Orte said as he handed me the annual balance sheet. I went over the books; the profits were indeed immense. However, gradually, I realized that the fortune Ana and I had inherited had gone into the House of Mendes account and been subsumed within it, so that I did not know what my part of the profits was. The massive fortune I had invested in the House of Mendes had funded Diogo's and my business ventures, for loans, purchases and expanding the import and export business to new markets. Our business had developed and grown, and the company was earning vast profits.

I was concerned about Ana's future. When she turned sixteen, she could wed and receive her part in her father's inheritance, but I was besieged by doubts. Diogo was not healthy. What would happen to my private fortune, which I had brought from Lisbon and London, now that Diogo and I were running the company together? It was nearly impossible to separate the capital I had invested in the company from the immense fortune accumulating in the company's coffers.

And if Diogo passed away, heaven forbid? How would the assets and the liquid capital be divvied up?

Brianda and Gracia La Chica would inherit the company's assets. Who could guarantee that my daughter and I would receive our relative portion of the House of Mendes fortune?

I decided not to wait. The next day, when Diogo arrived at the office in my home, bringing along documents to be signed, I addressed him.

"Diogo, I have a request. I want to know my current portion in the company's assets."

"Gracia, you know that's nearly impossible." Diogo coughed, his face flushing.

"Diogo, we've been working together for three years now. You have a family of your own and I'm a widow. I want to secure Ana's future."

Diogo wrapped his wool scarf tighter around his neck. "I'll ask Emanuel de Orte the accountant to try and calculate the profits from the capital you brought with you."

At first, I thought his cough was a symptom of embarrassment, but later, I understood that he had a cold. I rang the bell and asked the maid to prepare some plum wine spiced with cinnamon and honey for him.

Diogo apologized for being unable to stay as he was hurrying to have dinner with Brianda and La Chica.

***

A week later, Diogo returned to my office. Once again, he was coughing heavily and deeply.

"Why don't you ask Doctor Amatus to come and examine you?"

"Don't worry, it's only a little cold," he soothed me.

I asked the serving girl to serve us warm water with a cinnamon stick and rose extract.

"I'm sorry," Diogo said, "but Emanuel de Orte claims that due to the cyclical nature and process of financial transactions and the cashing of the promissory notes we gave the escapees, it would be very hard to calculate your relative portion of House of Mendes's capital. He says that if he went on vacation for six months and dedicated night and day to the books, he might manage to perform the calculations."

I looked him straight in the eye. "Diogo, you understand that I must receive securities in return for the funds I've invested in the company, whose value is now significantly higher."

Diogo added a teaspoon of the rose extract to his cup of water and sipped slowly.

"Do you have a proposal?" he asked.

I, too, sipped the fragrant water.

"I think you should sign a document stating that Doña Beatrice Mendes and her daughter Ana Mendes are entitled to half of the company's assets."

"I don't think Brianda will like that idea. I want to consult my solicitor." Diogo finished drinking, placing the cup on the platter. "Brianda wants to invite you and Ana for a meal on Saturday afternoon. La Chica enjoyed playing with Ana yesterday, and we would be happy to have you over. This time it will only be our immediate family," my brother-in-law changed the topic.

I did not reply, preferring to keep silent. I knew that Brianda must not find out about the agreement.

✳✳✳

On Saturday, in the middle of the meal, Diogo began coughing intensely, and I thought I saw drops of blood on his handkerchief.

"Diogo, your cough is not going away. Why don't you ask Doctor Amatus to come over?" I said.

"Gracia," Brianda's face grew flushed, "please, don't interfere! You're not his wife. You don't have to tell him what to do." Her voice grew high.

"I'm sorry, but his cough…"

"Stop it! I don't want to hear you," she blurted out. "It's quite enough that Diogo is with you for hours every day, spending more time with you than with his wife…" She burst out in tears.

"Brianda, please," Diogo stroked her hand. "We only work together…"

"Mama, why is Aunt Brianda crying?" Ana asked.

"Sometimes, adults are sad too," I replied.

"I wish Mama was here. She wouldn't allow you to interfere in my life this way," Brianda cried.

"Brianda, calm down, the girls can hear you," I said. "And you should know we're doing our best to smuggle Mama out of Lisbon to Antwerp," I said.

"'We?' Are you and my husband one entity now?"

I hugged Ana. "Come on, let's go home."

"No, I want to play with La Chica. You promised me!" Ana stamped her feet.

"Ana, come on!"

∗∗∗

Throughout that month, Diogo worked from his offices at the estate. Doctor Amatus Lusitanus tended to him, ordering him to stay in bed. Once he had recovered, he came over to visit me.

"Gracia, what's wrong?" Diogo asked when he saw my melancholy expression.

"Sadly, an hour ago I received the news that my beloved mother, your sister, who was supposed to board a ship that would bring her here to us in Antwerp two weeks ago, has passed away."

Diogo sat down in a chair heavily.

"We have to let Brianda know. Could you come see her with me?"

I did not have the strength to talk, merely nodding.

"I thought I would make you happy…" Diogo said. "Instead of rejoicing, we're receiving such painful news…

"I wanted to tell you that while I was ill, I had time to think. The idea you proposed seems entirely fair to me, and I asked my solicitor, Johan von Frederick, who has returned from America, to draft an agreement."

From his briefcase, Diogo produced a document signed in his own hand as well as by Johan von Frederick, with the seal of House of Mendes stamped upon it.

"In the event of my death, Doña Beatrice Mendes and her daughter Ana Mendes are entitled to half of the property of House of Mendes," Diogo read out a paragraph of the agreement.

"May you live a good, long life," I wished him, and we departed on our way to tell Brianda the bitter news.

Libel, 1542

The summer of 1542 did not bring good news with it. The City Council of Brabant, the seat of Emperor Charles the Fifth, published a horrific list including the names of a hundred and fifty New Christians burned at the stake at an auto-de-fé in Lisbon, including some of our friends and family members.

The news affected all of our moods, primarily Diogo, who was still coughing and suffering chest pain. The seeds of disaster had sprouted, growing thorny, venomous leaves.

Brianda told me that Diogo was experiencing nights of restless sleep.

"Memories of the brutal interrogation the inquisitor inflicted on him return to him at night, and sometimes he shouts out in his sleep," she told me.

One warm morning, I was awoken by noise from the yard. I rose from my bed, wrapped myself up in a robe and shifted the curtain aside to better see through the morning mist. An old coach was standing at the entrance to the house. The coachman rubbed his calloused hands, gazing at the door to the house.

The doors opened. Thomas made his way to the black coach, received a missive from the coachman and placed several coins in his hand. The coachman quickly mounted his carriage, whipped his horse and hurried off.

Teresa and Valera entered the room, and after they had dressed me in an orange morning gown and efficiently brushed my hair, I went down to the dining room.

"Good morning, señora," Thomas greeted me, placing the missive on the table.

"Good morning, Thomas. I hope this letter bears good news," I replied.

"Let's hope so, señora. Don Diogo Mendes sent you the letter, and asked that you come to their home."

I opened the envelope. The letter was written in code. Anything but more trouble, I hoped. However, prayers are not always received and accepted in the House of Prayers.

I brought the paper closer to the candle's flame and read it.

Milan
For Señor Diogo Mendes

Gaspar Lopez has been arrested in Milan for practicing Judaism. In order to save himself from arrest and torture, he has turned over the names of all the participants in the secret meeting and revealed the secrets of the fund to save the annusim, as well as plans for action and the names of the agents. He falsely accused the participants by saying the purpose of the meeting was a plan to murder Emperor Charles the Fifth.

Gaspar revealed the secret prayers on the Sabbath and the Jewish holidays taking place at the secret synagogue at your home. He informed the Inquisition that Brianda orders kosher meat for the estate's kitchen from a Jew, as well as of the existence of a community of annusim in England. All meeting participants must flee Antwerp.

Run!

Your friend, Gonzalez Gomez

May the Creator of the World preserve us and save us from all strife, my lips whispered as I was on my way to Diogo's estate.

La Chica roamed the house sadly. She could not understand why her mother was crying all day while her father stayed in his room, and why she was not allowed to visit him, or why the servants were tiptoeing around.

Diogo was pale and was coughing constantly. Brianda was sitting next to him, trying to convince him to sip the plum wine spiced with cinnamon and honey, a cure for coughing.

"He can't sip the wine!" she said.

With a massive effort, Diogo managed to sit up in bed. "That traitor, that liar! Gaspar Lopez dares accuse me of plotting a murder!" he called out after straining to speak.

His fever spiked. Doctor Amatus Lusitanus was summoned, but Diogo continued to burn up, coughing and spitting blood.

Amatus performed a bloodletting, treated him with leeches, infused an extract of healing herbs into a glass of water and massaged his chest with olive oil, yet Diogo's cough persisted until he seemed unable to breathe anymore.

"Gracia, I've been betrayed," his lips whispered. "Wh…en I'm be…tter we'll leave Flan…ders…"

"Rest, Diogo, don't worry. Please, get better," I pled.

"You should wait outside," Brianda said. "I want him to sleep."

"She's not bothering me," Diogo whispered, but Brianda insisted I leave.

"Lord, please heal him," was the only sentence I uttered.

***

"Diogo, wake up!!!

"My darling, Diogo, wake up!!!"

Brianda's loud cry echoed frighteningly through the walls, shocking me. I dropped my wineglass, causing a dark stain to spread across the table. I pushed back my chair and ran to his room.

Diogo was lying in his canopy bed, covered by a blanket with only his head exposed. He was staring at the ceiling. Brianda was leaning over him, her face white.

"He's not waking up…" she stammered.

I helped her rise and hugged her. I asked the serving girl to seat her in a chair and pour her some apple juice spiced with rosewater, but Brianda would not leave, entwining her hand with Diogo's bony, lean fingers.

"Diogo," I whispered, but he did not answer. His breathing was labored, his mouth slightly open.

"The priest is at the door," Rapahel del Vino announced. *Just like when Francisco died, the priests are the first to catch the scent of death*, I thought.

"Send him away," Brianda said, her voice shaky yet assertive. "Tell him it's not time yet."

But the priest insisted on coming in. After much effort, promising him we would call him immediately if the situation worsened, we managed to get him out of the room.

Diogo's breathing gradually became heavier and slower.

"My son, dearest to my heart, say your confession," Diogo's old governess, Bianca, whispered in his ear.

"Forgive me, Lord, for all my sins," his lips moved soundlessly.

Brianda leaned in toward him. He seemed to be whispering, "*Shema Yisrael, Hashem e-lhoeynu, Hashem ehad*. Hear O Israel, the Lord is our God, the Lord is one."

Suddenly, his hand dropped from the bed to the ground.

I embraced Brianda, who seemed confused and lost.

"Farewell, darling," she whispered. "I loved you. I will not see your face again." She kissed his cold forehead.

I gently led her away and closed his eyes.

Bianca emptied all the water from the vases and poured it outside to banish the evil spirit. She then tore a small rip into the lace slip Brianda was wearing under her green silk gown, in the traditional gesture of mourning.

The bustle outside the room increased. Servants had gathered from all over the house. I drizzled rosewater over an embroidered handkerchief, letting Brianda inhale the sweet scent, and asked the serving girl to pour her a glass of water with cinnamon and honey.

"Diogo would want us to go on with our lives," I said. I don't know where I found the strength to say such things. "We can't allow ourselves to be beaten down. We still have a lot to do in this world."

I had already "chosen life" once before, when my Francisco ascended to heaven.

"That's true," Brianda sighed through the tears misting her pretty eyes. "But I can't help it, I already miss my Diogo."

Brianda sat La Chica in her lap, hugged her and held her close to her heart. They both cried.

I embraced my sister and her daughter and cried along with them.

Now there were so many things to tend to. Thomas took it upon himself to dress Diogo in the linen shroud that Diogo had ordered from a workshop in Amsterdam on the day he married my sister, a charm for longevity. As it turned out, it did not do him much good.

The sorrow and pain over his people's betrayal and the way they had informed on him had gotten the better of him.

Cookies Tasting of Salty Tears

My funeral garb consisted of the black taffeta dress and lace gloves I had worn to Francisco's funeral.

"The *señora's* hair looks reddish brown in the light," said Teresa, weaving my hair into a long braid and rolling it around my head. She affixed the black lace shawl to my hair with black hairpins.

The *señora* is noble," she added, but the words landed upon my cold heart. I felt all alone in the world. My loved ones were gradually disappearing and leaving me, I thought, and now the heavy burden lay solely on my shoulders. From now on, I could not share the load of the family, the business and organizing the rescue mission with anyone.

I asked Teresa to instruct the cook to prepare hard-boiled eggs and lentils, fry sardines and bake cookies tasting of salty tears.

Brianda looked pretty in the black silk dress emphasizing her clear face. Before we left the estate for the funeral, the immediate family member stood next to Diogo's casket in the living room. Brianda whispered a prayer of goodbye that our family members in Lisbon would recite in the house of the deceased before the funeral procession left for church.

"The angels of heaven will accompany you
On your way to your eternal resting place
Baruch dayan ha'emet. Blessed be the True Judge."

The bells of the cathedral rang out. We left Diogo's estate, along with Juan and Bernardo, who had returned from Lyon. Diogo's sudden death suppressed the accusations against him, evoking feelings of regard and admiration, and many had gathered in order to pay him their final respects. Queen Mary, the bishop, various princes, the city's dignitaries, noblemen, merchants, an emissary from Emperor Charles the Fifth, the Pope's legate and ambassadors from many countries walked in the wake of the carriage pulled by black horses in which Diogo's lavish casket had been placed, covered by wreaths, following it to his grave near the cathedral.

The bishop sprinkled water on the coffin, lit incense and began the mass.

A heavy weight lay on my heart when I closed my eyes and silently repeated the words I remembered: "Lord, forgive our loved one's soul."

***

During the meal of condolence, the first meal eaten following the interment of the deceased, everyone was quiet, immersed in the sorrow and pain of death and loss. The table was set in an understated manner. I encouraged Ana to eat. "During a period of mourning, at my parents' home, they would eat lentils and hard-boiled eggs, which are round and symbolize the cycle of life. They wouldn't add salt to the food, in order to feel the bitterness of loss."

La Chica, who sensed the oppressive atmosphere, burst out in bitter tears, and Brianda's weeping increased. Bianca picked up La Chica, placed her in her lap and sang to her until she calmed down.

I stroked Brianda's arm. Her eyes were brimming with tears, and she was having a hard time biting into the egg.

"My sister, you have to eat. You haven't eaten a thing since yesterday. You need to be strong," I implored her.

"Papa, Papa," La Chica called out and began to cry again.

Brianda hugged her daughter, tears rolling down her cheeks. "Papa's in heaven now," she said.

"Aunt," Ana turned to Brianda. "Please, do as I do," she requested, placing one hand on her heart while pointing at the gray sky with the other.

"Place your hand on your heart, look toward the sky, and think about the good things you shared with Uncle Diogo," she said quietly.

Brianda put her hand on her heart. For a moment, she closed her eyes and focused. La Chica imitated her. She placed her little palm on her heart and closed her eyes. *Charming orphan girl*, I thought.

"Thank you, my sweet," Brianda kissed Ana excitedly. "I really do need to think about the good things I had with him."

"Ana, you're amazing, so young and so smart," Juan said.

I noticed that he was looking at her differently, no longer like a cousin. *Well*, I thought, *we should start bringing them together, and make sure he stops flirting with the daughters of the Christian gentry.*

The servants cleared the table, replacing the dinnerware with pitchers of warm water with cinnamon sticks, cups, and white plates with cookies tasting of salty tears.

I dipped the edge of the salty cookie in warm water, thinking sadly that we were two sisters raising orphan girls who would never know their fathers.

I felt an overwhelming desire to get out of Antwerp. If I could, I would pack a few possessions and flee. However, new trouble landed at our threshold. A letter from the city council arrived at my office, accusing Diogo of "practicing Judaism" and ordering the initiation of an investigation, including a summons to a trial.

It was obvious to me that the long arm of the emperor and his sister Mary was to blame. They were hoping to seize Diogo's property and to avoid paying back their debts.

My head was spinning with ideas and thoughts on how to bring about the cancellation of Diogo's trial.

I called Juan in for a meeting at the offices of the company, which I had renamed "Mendes Brothers Heirs," and explained the emperor and his sister's intentions to him.

"It's obvious to me that Charles and his sister, Queen Mary, have got their eye on Diogo's inheritance. They're planning to seize his property, and are accusing Diogo, even after his death, of heresy and of secretly practicing Judaism."

Juan opened the liquor cabinet and poured us a dry red wine. "Aunt, I've never heard of accusations being brought against a deceased person," he said, sipping the wine. "I've heard from my friend, Prince Maximillian, that the emperor wants to declare war on France and is bragging, 'Francois the First and I are in perfect agreement. He wants Milan, and so do I,'" Juan told me.

"There's one thing I know: money blinds people. The emperor's wars will prove to be our salvation. Charles needs gold coins to fund his wars against the Protestants, the heretics and France. This will also play in our favor. With gold coins, you can solve problems."

"What are you thinking?" Juan asked.

"I'll approach Emperor Charles and offer him a generous monetary loan in return for repealing the accusations against Diogo. You'll talk to your friend Prince Maximillian, the emperor's nephew, who will encourage the emperor to accept my proposal."

Juan poured himself another glass of wine, drinking it down quickly.

"Aunt, how large of a loan were you thinking of?"

"I'll start with a suggestion of fifty thousand gold ducats."

"Fifty thousand? That's a fortune!"

"Juan, do you want us to lose all of the property? The emperor and his sister are determined to seize control of the inheritance." I picked up the goblet and drank a little of the wine. "The emperor won't agree to a loan of fifty thousand ducts. He'll want two hundred thousand gold ducats, and at the end of the negotiations, we'll compromise on a hundred thousand ducats with no interest."

"A hundred thousand?"

"A hundred thousand, or we'll lose it all," I said, placing the goblet of wine on the table.

The Will, December 1542

The morning on which Diogo's will was read was gray and cold. Chills were running through me. I asked that some wood be added to the fireplace, but could not stop shivering. I wore a dark blue wool dress and wrapped a black wool shawl around me, descending the stairs to the coach waiting for me, Juan and Bernardo.

An oppressive cloud of grief and a heavy aroma of tobacco hit me in the face when we entered the elegant offices. Many books were aligned in perfect order on the gleaming wood shelves.

Johan von Frederick was wrapped in a green silk cloak. His face, sporting a gray goatee, and his small eyes, framed by dozens of tiny wrinkles, were solemn.

"Doña Beatrice Mendes, Don Bernardo and Don Juan Mickas, hello. Please sit down."

"Hello," we replied. A servant pulled back the chairs for us and we sat around the mahogany table.

Brianda sat at the middle of the table, on the edge of her seat. She was wearing a black dress, her face flushed with crying. Next to her sat Augustino Hendricks, who had come to the funeral from Lyon. He nodded sadly, rising from his seat for me.

A servant placed a tray on the table, bearing a pitcher of water, glasses and a plate of cookies. Juan was the only one who tasted them. Johan von Frederick poured me a glass of water.

"Doña Brianda and Doña Beatrice, I'm sorry about the tragic loss that your family has suffered. I had great appreciation and respect for Diogo Mendes. His departure is a great loss to all of us," Johan von Frederick began the meeting. He filled his wood pipe with tobacco and blew gray smoke rings into the room. I held myself back from coughing.

"Ladies and gentlemen, if I may, I've decided to call you to my office and reveal the will discreetly before it is read in public tomorrow at Grote Market."

"We thank your honor," I replied. I was glad not to have to hear the contents of the will for the first time in public.

Juan edged the glass of water that I had not touched closer to me.

"Aunt, please drink." A warm smile graced his lips. I felt relief. *I can always count on him*, I thought. Bernardo, meanwhile, was sitting quietly and solemnly, as was his habit,

The solicitor nodded his head and broke the red wax seal stamped on the will, which was wrapped in a red ribbon.

"Uhmm... Uhmmm..." he cleared his throat.

"Before I begin reading, I wish to note that the will was drafted two years after the birth of Beatrice La Chica, the daughter of Don Diogo and Madame Brianda." The solicitor looked at Brianda, whose hands were clenched in fists.

"Don Diogo Mendes wanted to secure the future of his daughter, the family business and his dear wife."

Frederick tapped his pipe against the table. "I'll read the will," he said.

I, Diogo Mendes Benvenishte, hereby instruct that after my death, one thousand, six hundred Flemish liras are distributed to the poor. Every year, a hundred liras will be distributed to the poor of Portugal or Flanders. A third for the needs of prisoners, a third to clothe the needy, and a third for charity for impoverished brides.

Brianda coughed lightly, perhaps meaning to speed up the reading of the will.

The property of the family and of the House of Mendes company will be distributed as following:

Half of the fortune will be given to my sister-in-law, Señora Beatrice Mendes, in accordance with the conditions of the will of my brother

Francisco Mendes and the agreement between us.

I appoint my sister-in-law Doña Beatrice Mendes as trustee for the remainder of the property and in regard to the inheritance of my daughter, Beatrice La Chica Mendes Benveniste.

I recommend she rely on the help of Juan Migois and my assistant Augustino Henricks, both of whom I trust.

To my beloved wife Brianda Mendes I return the amount of her dowry.

The solicitor placed the will on the table, while the room was engulfed in silence.

Brianda's face looked jaundiced. Augustino's fingers were stroking his beard. I was astonished. Diogo had not left his wife even one ducat! It was unbelievable where my life was leading me. A thirty-three-year-old widow, I owned the Mendes Bank, the second largest bank in the world, a fleet of merchant ships and multiple assets. Power and control were now in my hands.

A heartbroken cry shocked me.

"You witch! You did everything you could to get me disinherited! Diogo was my husband—why on earth would you be the trustee for my daughter? Who's ever heard of such a thing? You villain, what did you do to convince Diogo to transfer my inheritance to you?"

"Madame Brianda, I'm sorry for the terrible calamity you've experienced. Please, this is your husband Diogo's will," the solicitor tried to calm her down.

"To everyone except his wife? I don't believe it! Didn't Diogo trust me?" Brianda picked up the will. "Who was I married to? What does our marriage mean if he forgets his own wife in his will?" she wept.

"Brianda, Diogo inherited his fortune from his brother Francisco," I said.

"Who do you think you are? Do you think my daughter's inheritance is yours? Only yours? Don't you worry about my daughter, do you hear me? I'm her mother, not you. You should realize that, and the sooner, the better!"

Brianda paced around the room as if delirious. "Both of you betrayed me. Your secret meetings were merely a cover for the affair you were conducting."

"Brianda, heaven forbid!"

"Don't deny it! How could a husband be so cruel, unless you, you witch, cast your spell on him?!"

"Diogo has only appointed Doña Beatrice as trustee in regard to your daughter's inheritance, and she is entrusted with it only until La Chica turns fifteen," Augustino Henricks tried to talk to her logically.

"Knowing her as I do, she'll never transfer the inheritance to La Chica. She'll find a thousand excuses and won't convey the inheritance. Blood is thicker than water! Do you hear me?" she struck the table with her hand angrily. "The inheritance belongs to our daughter, Beatrice La Chica. When has a mother's guardianship over her daughter ever been torn away from her and given to another woman? When has anything like that ever been heard of in the world? You poisoned his soul," she wept. "Witch!"

Her words trickled like drops of venom into my ears.

"You'll be hearing from me," she spat out at me, standing up across from me with both her hands propped up on the table.

"Madame Brianda," Augustino Henricks hurried to follow her, "out of all the women in the world, Diogo chose you as a wife. He waited for the love of his life until he was fifty four."

"Why, then? Why is she the trustee? If Papa was still alive, this would not have happened. Papa would have taken care of me."

"Madame, I have known your sister since she was a girl, and I taught her history in Lisbon."

"What does that have to do with anything?"

"Your sister is a good woman. She has always taken care of you. I remember your parents arguing whether to send you away from Lisbon with your sister, or leave you with the family. Your mother thought that Beatrice, a widow taking care of a baby, would have a hard time fleeing Portugal with you and both your cousins, but your sister insisted on taking you with her."

"Why is she inheriting my share? Isn't she rich enough?"

"Madame, please, don't compare yourself to your sister. Señora Beatrice is managing the company."

"It's my inheritance! Mine! She convinced my husband to only return the dowry to me. She left me penniless."

"Madame, time will heal the pain. You're strong. You must gather up the pieces and take care of your child."

"My Diogo, I can't believe you left me. Left behind an orphan child. Why? Why did you leave me?" Brianda burst out in tears.

The Christmas Ball, 1544

A drab autumn wind struck my face when I opened the window. The garden was covered with a reddish pallet of leaves that the wind had blown around in its fury. I breathed in the chilly air. The church bells rang in a new morning.

"Oh, no, the *señora* might get sick!" Teresa called out in fright, hurrying to shut the window. "It's cold in here," she said, adding logs to the fire in the hearth.

A light shiver went through me. Teresa wrapped my shoulders in a wool shawl and handed me a warm cup of cocoa. The cocoa beans had been transported by our ships, which had begun to deal with the natives in America.

"*Por favor, señora*, drink. The beverage will warm you up."

The night before, Christmas day, 1544, we had attended a ball. Burning torches illuminated the garden, while hundreds of candles burned brightly in the crystal chandeliers. Red and white wreaths of flowers filled the Affaitati family's lavish ballroom, and clowns in broad, red-and-yellow striped trousers juggled balls.

Brianda greeted me with a chilly nod. She was wearing a silver brocade dress woven with gold. Her fair hair was pulled back with a black scarf embedded with pearls. She was the most beautiful woman at the ball, and fluttered like a butterfly with a broken wing among the opulently dressed and bejeweled guests. Brianda had magnetized a group of young noblemen to her.

A musical band burst out in a cheery madrigal. The English ambassador, a bachelor of forty or so, bowed to Brianda and invited her to join several couples who had milled into the dance floor, coming together in a line dance.

I was surrounded by a circle of guests interested in the gems and spices I was importing. I conversed with English and French merchants about ways of improving commerce between our countries. The ambassador from Venice and his wife joined the group, drawing attention with their stylish attire and mostly with the latest innovation: the ambassador's wife's high-heeled shoes, which matched her red dress. The ambassador himself wore a short red topcoat and blue velvet pantaloons ending at his knees, tied with red drawstrings, and brown shoes.

"Señora Beatrice Mendes," he addressed me, "we would be happy to host the lady in our fair city of Venice."

"Thank you. I've heard your city was one of the most beautiful cities in the world," I replied, beginning to contemplate the idea of leaving for Venice.

"It's a wondrous city. They are waiting for you in Venice," the ambassador's wife smiled at me.

Father Sebastian, wearing a white and golden pointed cap and a white silk shirt under a red cloak, his cheeks sunken, his nose long, his jaw sharp and his brows unruly, turned to me. "Señora Beatrice Mendes, lovely as always. It's good to see her." He kissed my hand.

Since Diogo had passed away, I visited the cathedral infrequently, and had been avoiding his sermons.

"Good evening, Father Sebastian," I replied. Privately, I wondered what that fox was scheming to achieve with his flattery.

"Greetings, my friends. Please excuse me. With your permission, I shall steal the *señora* away for a few minutes," he buttered them up with his tongue.

My friend Doctor Amatus Lusitanus, who was dancing enthusiastically with a plump, giggly girl, tracked us with his eyes.

Father Sebastian offered me his arm. We drifted away from the bustle of the dancers, standing near one of the windows. A gale was storming outside. Lightning illuminated the sky, and raindrops glittered in the trees of the garden, lit by torchlight. Father Sebastian's slim fingers played with the 'waft and weave' at his neck and he coughed slightly. "I'm sorry that the *señora* is not coming to mass at church on Sundays," he said.

I fluttered my red fan in a failed attempt to cool my blazing face. "Father, you know that due to my health, I cannot always attend the prayers."

"It's good to see that the Mendes sisters are getting over their grief upon the loss of Diogo. It's a shame your brother-in-law was deprived of celebrating with us."

"We all miss my brother-in-law."

"I understand that the *señora* is successfully running the Mendes Brothers Company that she inherited from her brother-in-law, and is visiting the ports and the merchant guilds," the fox continued.

"Father, excuse me," I interrupted. "I have been meaning to tell your eminence for quite a while that in honor of the New Year, I have decided to donate five thousand gold ducats to renovating the worship hall in the church."

"Thank you. The *señora* is a good disciple."

"I'll always be happy to assist the church."

"Yes," the fox cleared his throat. "There's one more little thing. I have an excellent proposal for the *señora*."

Juan picked up a glass and approached us. "Hello, Father Sebastian," he said.

"My son, it's good to see you. I see you have grown into an impressive man and a successful businessman."

"Thank you, Father Sebastian.

"Please serve Father Sebastian a glass of cherry liqueur," Juan asked the headwaiter, who was hovering near us. "Our company privately imports it from Bordeaux."

"Thank you, but I don't drink."

"That's too bad, its excellent liqueur."

"Juan, there you are! I've been looking for you…" said Señora Affaitati. "The wife of the French ambassador wants to introduce their daughter to you."

"I beg your pardon," Juan apologized, hurrying after Señora Affaitati.

"Señora, allow me to help your family," said Father Sebastian.

"Help me?" *What is that old fox up to?* I wondered.

"The Church and the monarchy know that your daughter Ana is now of age. I want to propose a member of the nobility to the *señora*, a close friend of Queen Mary."

"Father, thank you for taking an interest, but you can rest assured that I'm taking care of my daughter. She's only ten," I replied in a chilly voice.

"Señora, Don Francisco de Aragón, an offspring of the royal house of Aragón, has personally escorted Princess Isabella, the sister of King Joao the Third, during her first meeting with her future husband, Carlos-Charles the Fifth, King of Spain. This nobleman impressed Princess Isabella with his impeccable manners and demeanor."

I pretended to be interested, but my soul was in a state of turmoil.

"Señora, I have the honor of proposing Don Francisco de Aragón as a match for your daughter. I am certain the *señora* can see the great honor in marriage to a Spanish nobleman."

My lips curved in a half-smile. "As far as I know, Don Francisco de Aragón is illegitimate."

Father Sebastian's small eyes stared at me. "Señora, don't believe the malicious rumors. The nobleman is slightly over forty, and is an excellent match. I'm certain that the noble de Aragón will secure her future and take good care of her."

I leaned against a post. "I'm sure you mean he will secure his own future."

"Señora, you may rest assured that Emperor Charles and Queen Mary will support the match as well."

A servant holding a tray with glasses of wine approached me. "Señora, please," he smiled at me.

I took a glass and twirled it in my hand, observing the red hue of the wine.

"Señora, I'm certain that if your husband were alive, he would be happy to marry into the royal family." The priest cleared his throat, adding, "Especially in light of the fact that your brother-in-law was accused of the severe offense of 'practicing Judaism.' The *señora* knows that a person can still be investigated and accused after his death…"

I felt the familiar pain rise and grab hold of my stomach and my chest. Father Sebastian tapped his fingernails against the glass, and a drop of wine splashed on his cassock. "The *señora* knows that after Diogo's death, new evidence against him was uncovered, and he was accused of heresy."

I sipped the wine, which warmed my chilled body. "Father Sebastian knows that those accusations were ludicrous, and that they were repealed."

"Señora, rumors claim that a large ransom was paid to make them disappear."

The guests' enthusiastic applause at the end of the dance camouflaged my silence.

"Señora, this marriage would be your salvation. It would eliminate the accusations of heresy and covertly practicing Judaism that have been plaguing your honor and her family."

After a brief pause, the orchestra launched into a sweeping melody. I felt dizzy and held tightly onto my wineglass.

"If I may, madam," the fox took my glass from me, placing it on a side table. "I'm certain the *señora* does not wish to risk…" he coughed briefly before adding, "…any false accusations."

The drumming of the dancers' feet on the gleaming wood floor beat at my head. Amatus Lusitanus walked over and extended his arm to me.

"Father Sebastian, excuse me, I see that you're engrossed in an important conversation, but today is a day of joy. Allow me to steal the *señora* away briefly and invite her to partake in her favorite dance." Without waiting for an answer, Amatus gathered me to him and swept me off to the dance floor.

"His body language seemed intimidating to me," he told me.

"Thank you, you came just in time," I whispered in his ear.

The difficult conversation and Father Sebastian's implied threat filled me with anxiety. I felt safe and protected in Amatus's strong arms, and drank down his words of endearment thirstily.

Challenging Queen Mary, 1544

In June, Juan returned from Lyon as I'd asked him to, burst excitedly into my study, took off his elegant hat and kissed my hand. The maid served him apple preserves and a cup of warm wine.

"Juan, the ground is burning under us. Queen Mary and her brother Charles the Fifth have decided to do anything in their power to take over Ana's inheritance and marry her off against my will. Mary holds immense power, and her brother Emperor Charles supports her. I'm afraid they'll send their soldiers to arrest Ana and force her to wed against her will. In their fury, they might hurt the family."

"I heard the rumor and so I rode almost nonstop. I've heard the queen has summoned you for a meeting."

"The queen has invited me to her palace, but that doesn't mean I have to go there. Read my reply."

Juan's eyes opened wide in astonishment as he read.

March 1544
Antwerp

To Her Majesty Queen Mary, Regent and Queen of the Lowlands

Your Majesty,

I'm honored to receive your esteemed invitation to come to the palace for an important discussion. I would be very pleased to meet Her Majesty Queen Mary, my dear friend, but unfortunately, I am not well. Therefore, I cannot arrive for a meeting with Her Grace The Queen.

Respectfully,
Doña Beatrice Mendes

"I think your letter is a personal insult to the queen," Juan rubbed his beard.

"I'm not her vassal! The queen will not decide on my behalf whom my daughter is to marry!"

Juan ran his hand through his black, gleaming hair. "It is not the custom in Flanders to forcefully marry off daughters. The emperor wouldn't dare."

"It is the custom in Flanders to draft marriage contracts between babies. Ana is ten. I'm worried. The situation is very perilous."

"I'm sure you haven't simply let the situation be, without coming up with a plan to save us from trouble," Juan said, sipping his wine. "You still haven't received the certificate of transit from the Duchy of Ferrara, and what about the hundred thousand gold ducats you loaned the emperor? If we leave, the emperor will not repay the debt."

"I've been waiting for Charles to repay the debt for two years now! I didn't send you to study in the royal court with Prince Maximillian and the rest of the nobility so you can tell me what the problem is. If you have an idea, now is the time to suggest it."

"My friend Countess Catherine told me she heard that Queen Mary is very angry at you because you are avoiding a meeting with the queen, and no one has ever dared disobey her."

"Who is Catherine? Her name is not one of those 'belonging to the letter Yod.'"

Juan produced a tiny oval silver box and opened it. "Catherine is one of Queen Mary's ladies-in-waiting. She belongs to one of the most ancient Christian families in the city, and her brother is head of the civil police. She sent me her portrait. Look how beautiful she is."

"Juan, be careful. If she's sending you a picture, she'll be lusting after you and your money."

"I take care of myself. This is not the only portrait I have," Juan laughed, showing me three portraits of beautiful noblewomen he kept in his valise. "Catherine snuck me a copy of the missives exchanged between the emperor and Queen Mary."

"Why didn't you say that immediately?"

Juan opened his valise and extracted two rolled-up missives.

April 23, 1544
My good sister,

I am writing to you in the matter of the niece of Diogo Mendes. Don Francisco de Aragón, who served me faithfully in Spain, wishes to marry her and requests our assistance. If the marriage takes place, he will bestow upon me, in return for our help, a loan of two hundred thousand gold ducats. I want to help Don Francisco in return for his service, and particularly due to the loan, which I need for the expenses of the war.

I ask that you do all you can to bring about the marriage, and will grant you fifty thousand gold ducats from the two hundred thousand.

I pray that all your wishes come true.
Your brother, Emperor Charles the Fifth

"That sycophantic snake, Don Francisco de Aragón! Promising the emperor a loan of two hundred thousand ducats from my daughter's inheritance. The nerve of him! Selling my daughter to that dirty old man in return for money for his war efforts! I won't have it!"

I opened the second missive.

May 12, 1544
Brussels

Emperor,

Sir, I am willing and ready to obey His Majesty and provide any assistance I am able to offer in promoting the service extended to him, in the form of a loan of the two hundred thousand ducats that are currently so essential to us.

Don Francisco de Aragón asked me to speak to the mother. However, Beatrice Mendes is a very delicate woman, and is always apologizing that she is ill and cannot come to the meetings. Nobleman de Aragón wants to compel the mother to acquiesce to the marriage, and is pressuring us to threaten her that if she persists in declining, the emperor will take action against her property.

If we enforce this marriage upon Beatrice Mendes, the merchants of Flanders will fear that you may marry their daughters off against their will, and will flee Flanders and the countries of Your Majesty's kingdom. I am afraid we will evoke outrage and that the girl will run off, taking all her property with her.

I hereby inform His Majesty that if necessary, I will travel to Antwerp to meet the mother, Beatrice Mendes, but I have to know how I should conduct myself there in regard to this matter.

Your sister, Mary

"She's wise," I said. "She writes that I'm very delicate and that I apologize for being sick and not accepting her invitations. She understands that I'm not interested in meeting her.

"Unbelievable! Queen Mary is willing to travel all the way to Antwerp to meet me!" I laughed. "Juan, your friend Prince Maximillian is exhibiting religious tolerance. He needs your support in his alliance with the Lutherans, which his father Ferdinand and his uncle Emperor Charles oppose."

"Maximillian told me that the emperor believes he will not join the Lutherans and betray the Catholics. The emperor has offered him his daughter Maria as a wife, and appointed Maximillian as ambassador to Spain after he won a medal of honor in the campaign against France."

"That's excellent. Ask Maximillian to talk to his uncle Charles and try to influence him."

Juan removed a sword hanging on the wall and began to battle an imaginary enemy. "Next week, Maximillian and I will fence against each other. It's not easy to beat him," he said, stabbing at the air. "He's called 'the lord of fencing.'"

Thomas knocked at the door, his expression solemn.

"An emissary on behalf of Her Majesty Queen Mary has arrived from Brussels," he said.

The queen's emissary, dressed in his immaculate uniform and accompanied by two soldiers from the Queen's Guard, addressed me.

Juan and I exchanged looks.

"Señora Mendes, if you please, a royal invitation." The emissary broke the seal and ceremoniously read out his message.

June 1544
Brussels

For Señora Beatrice Mendes,

The señora is invited to the royal palace for an important discussion taking place on Monday, June 25, 1544.

Best Regards,
Queen Mary
Regent of the Lowlands

The die had been cast. I could not continue avoiding meeting the queen. Her letter made it clear that if I did not show up for the meeting at her palace, she would send armed soldiers to take me to her.

A Royal Meeting, June 1544

The morning brought a whiff of childhood memories with it. Teresa entered the room smiling, singing "Open the Door" in Ladino. This was the song my Grandma Reyna liked to sing when she baked bread early in the morning.

"The breakfast that the *señora* likes is ready, little buns with honey and cinnamon," she informed me with a smile.

I knew that Teresa had given her heart to Raphael del Vino, Brianda's major-domo. I believed she was very dear to Raphael as well, and the two of them frequently sought excuses to leave Brianda's estate or my house and visit each other.

"Thank you, I'm not hungry."

"The *señora* has to eat before the meeting at the palace. If she doesn't eat, she'll get dizzy, and in addition, everyone is waiting for her in the dining hall."

"Teresa, did you take care of the guests in the house's cellar?" I asked.

"*Si, señora*, the refugees have received warm clothes. We laid out mattresses and blankets for them, and I personally am making sure they receive food and drink."

"You're doing a good job. And how are the baby and his mother?"

"He cries a lot. His mother doesn't have enough milk, and his father is among those who have been arrested. It's a good thing Ana is playing with him; she's the only one who can soothe him."

"Look for a wet nurse for him."

Ana had begged to join me for the meeting with the queen, but I preferred to leave her at home. Her beauty might turn the heads of the princes and noblemen in the royal court.

***

When I arrived in Brussels, I was overwhelmed by the sight of the opulent palace that Charles, the queen's brother, had bestowed upon her as a gift. I now understood why the emperor needed such large loans. In additions to the funds dedicated to preparations for war against the Ottoman sultan, the castle must have cost a fortune.

The royal hall in which Queen Mary was sitting was immense in size and impressive in its gleaming green marble floor and soaring ceiling. I looked at the wall of arches, adorned with massive paintings depicting battles, separated by immaculate marble statutes of the kings of the empire.

In the center of a stage surrounded by short columns, under a red velvet canopy sporting the flags and crest of the country, Queen Mary sat upon her towering royal throne, carved with gold etchings. To her left were her dozen advisors, while to her right stood princesses, ladies-in-waiting and other members of her entourage, impressively dressed in the latest Flanders fashions.

The soldiers of the Queen's Guard, clad in their armored uniforms and bearing long bayonets in their hands, were stationed on both sides of the hall.

"Doña Beatrice Mendes!" the herald called out my arrival. Two ladies-in-waiting, about seventeen years old, approached me and escorted me to the stage. I stopped about ten meters before the queen and curtsied to her deeply.

Her face was narrow and long, her eyes black and piercing and her lower lip somewhat fleshy. The queen was wearing a crimson silk dress with a high collar, embroidered with gold thread in a flowered pattern. Cloth ribbons embroidered in gold adorned her sleeves. Her reddish hair was elaborately braided and covered with a black cap inlaid with diamonds and pearls. At her neck was a red heart medallion.

I had heard that after her much-admired husband, Louis the Second, king of Hungary and Bohemia, had been killed in 1526 in the battle of Mohács against Sultan Suleiman, who had headed the Ottoman army invading Hungary, Mary vowed to always wear the medallion that her beloved wore into battle.

I assumed she was quite lonely without a man by her side. I had heard she rejected her brother Charles's proposal that she marry King James the Fifth of Scotland, as well as King Frederick of Bavaria. Mary preferred to stay ensconced in her memories and faithful to her dead beloved.

I curtsied deeply once more.

"Welcome, my friend. Queen Mary is pleased that you are feeling well. It has been a while since we met. I've missed our conversations." The queen sounded quite pleasant. Apparently, she was trying to capture me with honey, I thought.

"Greetings, Queen Mary. I'm honored to be visiting Her Highness in her new, beautiful palace. My queen, I've brought you a little gift, perfume sent to me by my friend Madame Esther Kira from the sultan's harem in Constantinople, especially for you," I said, presenting her with a silver box containing ten perfume bottles in exotic scents.

"Bless you," the queen replied. Her lady-in-waiting opened one of the vials, and a sweet aroma of mysterious, faraway lands spread through the hall.

"Señora Beatrice, thank you. The queen appreciates your gift. The perfume has an exotic scent," she said.

"Doña Beatrice Mendes, I've invited you to discuss the future of your daughter, Señorita Ana. My advisors report that she is beautiful, kind and well educated. It would be an honor for Señora Mendes to be joined by matrimony to the royal family," the queen began.

"Your majesty, I dedicate most of my time to taking care of my family. My daughter is still young. I might consider it in the future," I replied.

"Queen Mary would be very pleased to marry Señorita Ana Mendes to a nobleman of the royal court, Don Francisco de Aragón," the queen continued, while her ladies-in-waiting gently applauded.

I tensed, all my senses and my very being sharpening. I had to fight and save Ana! I knew I was putting myself at grave risk; the queen might instruct the soldiers of the guard to arrest me and throw me in jail. However, I gathered my courage and addressed her directly: "Is Her Majesty Queen Mary referring to the proposal brought up by Father Sebastian, to marry my daughter off to that notorious old man, Don

Francisco de Aragón? I don't know who authorized him to interfere in my family's life."

The advisors, the princesses and the ladies-in-waiting all exchanged astonished gazes when they heard my brazen answer. In a moment, they would whisper to the queen that she should have me arrested.

"The Queen is quite certain that Doña Mendes wants the best for her daughter. Therefore, the Queen is suggesting an excellent match for your daughter. The Queen is well familiar with the nobleman de Aragón; he is one of the best and most respected gentlemen in the royal court."

I felt a light tingle. Red hives appeared on my face and hands.

"Your majesty, my Ana is young and beautiful; she's only ten years old. The man your highness is proposing as a match for my daughter is an old, ugly ne'er do well."

A murmur of astonishment spread among the royal entourage.

"Doña Mendes, we want the best for your daughter. His Majesty, my brother Charles, King of Spain and Emperor of the Holy Roman Empire, 'the empire on which the sun never sets,' gives his blessing to the marriage as well."

The thoughts whirled through my mind. *What exactly is she thinking, that if she lists all of her brother's titles, she can intimidate me?*

"Thank you, your majesty," I replied.

"Doña Mendes, think about it. From the moment this marriage takes place, your grandchildren, your great-grandchildren, all your descendants will be royals, and their futures guaranteed." The queen clapped gently, and all the attendees joined her.

"It's also possible that we can marry your little niece to a member of the gentry. I've heard she's named after you, Beatrice Mendes La Chica."

I was appalled. They were already scheming to take over La Chica's fortune? All those assembled stared at me, awaiting my answer.

The court jester, in his puffy colorful trousers and his blue chemise, sat down in the corner, his face, painted in white, assuming the expression of a scolded puppy.

I thanked the Creator of the World that her threats did not affect me. I felt strong and sure of myself. The king and the queen needed me; they needed monetary loans for their wars against the Ottomans, France and the Protestants. *By the grace of our foremothers, give me the strength to guard my daughter from falling into their clutches*, I whispered a prayer in my heart. Afterwards, I gazed directly at the queen.

"Forgive me, your majesty the queen." I paused briefly before adding, "I would rather have my daughter drown in the sea than marry that old man!"

The advisors, secretaries and ladies-in-waiting present in the royal hall all let out cries of astonishment.

"The impudence!"

"She's quite brazen!"

"Shhhh… quiet!"

I believe no one had ever dared speak to the queen in that tone and in such harsh words. The queen's hands were forcefully gripping the armrests of her throne and her face looked jaundiced. I saw rage coursing through her, yet she kept her silence. Apparently, she realized there was no chance I would accept her proposal.

The queen gazed at me with a hawk-like expression. "Queen Mary reminds Señora Mendes that she and her sister were very lucky that the accusations of heresy and practicing Judaism brought against her brother-in-law, Diogo Mendes, were repealed after many efforts on my part. Otherwise, all of her property would have been seized on behalf of the state treasury."

Her predatory eyes reminded me of what everyone said about the queen: "Mary never forgets and never forgives." My throat grew tight. The choke collar was tightening. The queen was threatening me. *Good Lord, help me! The ground is burning under our feet.* They would do anything to marry my daughter off to that dirty old man and get their hands on my fortune.

"Her Majesty Queen Mary knows that my brother-in-law Diogo Mendes was a devout Catholic who contributed generous funds to the Church. The accusations of heresy and practicing Judaism brought up against him were revealed to be false," I said in a clear voice.

A chilly silence spread through the room.

The queen's face assumed a scowl and her lower lip trembled. With a gesture of her black-gloved hands, she signaled her advisors to approach, and exchanged whispers with them for a long interval. Finally, she addressed me.

"The Queen asks that the Mendes Bank provide the throne with a loan of two hundred thousand ducats, as well as sacks of wheat, sugar, salt, black pepper, saffron, cinnamon, cloves and an additional list of spices that the major-domo will convey to the bank's representative."

"My queen, the House of Mendes must prepare for granting such a considerable loan. I'll ask Don Juan Mickas to handle the preparation of the contract. Does a two-year loan appeal to her majesty, or would you rather repay the loan in three years? In either case, the loan will be granted with no interest."

"Queen Mary asks that a contract for three years be prepared."

"As her majesty wishes. As for the supply of spices, the Mendes Brothers Heirs emporium is awaiting the arrival of the merchant ship *Hispania*, which is scheduled to sail in from Madagascar. I'll contact my secretary, who will handle the queen's request as swiftly as possible.

"Thank you, Madam Queen," I curtsied deeply.

This was the most appropriate moment to make my request. I chose my words carefully.

"Her Majesty Queen Mary, I do have one small request," I said casually, attempting to sound natural and hide the fact that my breathing had become rapid and wheezy.

"The queen knows that I am not well, and suffer from many ailments. The doctors have recommended rest. I wish to request that her majesty allow me to leave for a short trip with my family and my staff of servants, to convalesce in the healing waters of the hot springs in Aix-la-Chapelle."

I waited for the queen's response with apprehension. This was not the first time we had gone on a healing vacation to the hot springs nestled among the verdant forests of the town of Aix-la-Chapelle. This was a highly common custom among people of our station. But perhaps she might suspect that this was merely an escape plan?

The queen huddled briefly with one of her advisors and decreed: "The Queen knows that the air in Aix-la-Chapelle is restorative, and will help Señora Mendes. The Queen allows her to depart in a week and return four weeks from today. The Queen suggests that during her leave of convalescence, she dedicate some thought to the crown's generous proposal."

I curtsied to the queen.

"Thank you, my queen. I will consider her majesty's offer," I replied.

The queen turned to her personal secretary. "Under orders of the queen, prepare a certificate of transit to Aix-la-Chapelle for Doña Beatrice Mendes, her family and her servants. This permit will be in effect for three weeks, starting next week."

The secretary left the room and returned several minutes later with a certificate of transit stamped with the royal crest. The secretary leaned over the escritoire, picked up a quill, dipped it in the inkwell and wrote down our names and the dates.

Bowing, the secretary handed the certificate to the queen, still extending his quill in the air.

The queen read the certificate attentively, narrowed her eyes into slits and gazed at me at length. My heart skipped a beat. I prayed the queen would not change her mind. Mary took the quill, signed the certificate and stamped the royal seal upon it.

I heaved a sigh of relief. We engaged in more polite conversation. The queen inquired about Beatrice La Chica's education before moving on to discuss Juan. She told me that at one of the balls thrown by Prince Maximillian, she had been introduced to Don Juan Mickas, who had impressed her with his nobility and his manners.

I was troubled by Mary's interest in my cousin Juan. Who knows, perhaps she saw him as a solution to her widowhood and her financial concerns? I knew that princesses and noblewomen were interested in him and wanted him as a match for their daughters. Perhaps the queen would want to marry Juan off to one of the members of her entourage, thus gaining control of the family's fortune?

I knew that connections with the queen resembled life with a queen bee, who bestowed honey but was also capable of stinging.

The queen signaled with a motion of her hand that the conversation was now over.

I strode three paces back, among the happiest steps of my life.

***

I, Doña Gracia Hannah Nasi, a thirty-four-year-old widow, a secret Jew, had challenged Queen Mary and the all-powerful Emperor Charles the Fifth, had overcome royals and stood up to them!

Certificate of Transit

Now I felt a sense of relief. I had managed to save my Ana and had a transit certificate to Aix-la-Chapelle. I felt that I had to notify Brianda of the good news and let her know about at least some of my future plans. Since the death of my brother-in-law Diogo and the will he had left behind, the meetings between my sister and I had been reduced to the necessary minimum, much to the chagrin of Ana and La Chica.

Outside the music room, I could hear Brianda playing the lute and singing to herself with her melodious voice.

A dove flies across the sky
With no comfort, I tremble and sigh
He's left me and won't come by
In his heart there's no mercy for me.
Darling, let your tears flow
Your sorrows are many, I know,
And your family is cruel and low
They will not let us be.

I entered the room. La Chica was the first to see me. She leapt from the armchair, opened her arms wide and ran toward me.

"Aunt Beatricci!" she called out. I hugged her and breathed in her good scent. "Did Ana come with you?" Her eyes sought out her cousin.

"Sweetheart, soon you'll spend plenty of time together," I whispered in her ear.

Brianda stopped playing and laid the lute down.

"Brianda, hello."

"Hello," she replied in a chilly voice, then picked up knitting needles and yellow yarn from the basket beside her and began knitting vigorously, the needles clinking against each other.

"What brings you to my home?" she addressed me coldly.

I signaled to my sister that the exchange was not meant for La Chica's ears. Reluctantly, she rang the bell. Allegra came in, took La Chica's hand and asked her to come with her.

"Brianda, I came to let you know that we've received Queen Mary's permission to travel to convalesce in Aix-la-Chapelle."

"What do you mean by 'we'?"

I produced the certificate of transit and pointed at the line stating "Doña Brianda Mendes and her daughter Beatrice Mendes."

"I can't believe how impudent you are! How dare you decide without asking me? Did you ask me if I want to go on vacation?"

"Brianda, don't raise your voice at me," I said.

"You're not a queen that everyone needs to bow down to." She stabbed the ball of yarn with her knitting needles.

"The queen has permitted us to go on vacation. It would be dangerous for you to stay in the city and be seen in society despite receiving a certificate of transit."

"You could have at least consulted me." Her face grew flushed. "I wonder what's behind your idea to go on vacation…"

"The queen is insisting on marrying Ana off to that bastard, Don Francisco de Aragón."

"What's so terrible about marrying a Christian nobleman from the royal family?"

"Stop this mockery. Have you forgotten we only marry those who are 'one of ours,' 'those belonging to the letter Yod'?" I lost my temper. "La Chica is in danger, too. Queen Mary explicitly said, 'It's also possible that we can marry your little niece to a member of the gentry. I've heard she's named after you, Beatrice Mendes La Chica.'"

Brianda dropped the knitting needles. The ball of yellow yarn rolled across the wooden floor, while the knitted rows in the vest began to unravel one by one.

"Today they want to force Ana to get married, while tomorrow, your daughter may be taken from you. They'll make her get engaged to a fat old duke, and the funds of her inheritance will pass on to the crown. The decision whether to join us or stay on in Antwerp is yours."

Brianda grew pale. "They wouldn't dare. I'm not coming. I'm happy at my estate. We're staying."

I considered not answering her, but decided it would be better to share my plan of escape with her.

"My final destination is Venice."

At last, I saw some light in her eyes. Stunned, Brianda maintained her silence.

"Brianda, you have to decide about the jewelry and the few works of art you'll take with you. Let Raphael del Vino and the staff know that you've decided to renovate the estate, that you're having a hard time with your memories of Diogo, which stare back at you from the paintings and the various possessions."

I suggested to Brianda that she ask the major-domo to assign at least three people to pack each crate, and that she accurately list and number each object.

"Why do you think I don't know how to manage the palace and the packing? You're not my mother. Stop ordering me around!"

Brianda had no idea that I was planning on selling Diogo's estate in the future. Since she did not ask, I did not volunteer the information.

***

When I returned home, I convened the household staff and instructed them to start packing clothes and linens in preparation for the journey. I decided to pack the jewelry myself, with the help of my cousin Bernardo.

I invited House of Mendes agent, Augustino Henricks, to come over along with Juan, and asked them to start discreetly selling furniture, rugs, musical instrument and works of art, converting them into gems, diamonds and gold coins. I told them that if any questions came up and people were curious, they should tell them that we were renovating the house, as during the harsh winter, water had leaked into the palace, damaging the roof. I decided that in order to avoid raising suspicions regarding our intention not to return to Antwerp, we must maintain the appearance of business as usual, and instructed the gardeners to freshen up the garden, planting new flowers and greenery. In the kitchen, the cooks were preserving fish in salt, baking bread and dry cookies, making cheese, preserves and jams for the trip.

I sent missives to all agents of the Mendes Brothers Heirs company, asking them to immediately present me with an updated, confidential report listing all our assets, merchandise, list of debtors and our own debts to suppliers and merchants. In order to avoid suspicion regarding the reason for my request, in case the letters were intercepted by Charles's soldiers who were following the House of Mendes agents, I wrote to them that a religious war between Catholics and Protestants was about to break out in Europe, and therefore I needed an accounting of the assets and the fortune. I added that I had heard news that the Ottoman sultan, Suleiman the Magnificent, intended to continue his campaign of conquest in Hungary, and I wanted a current assessment of our financial situation.

***

Thomas opened the door. "Señora, Doctor Amatus Lusitanus and House of Mendes agent Augustino Henricks wish to see you. They're waiting in the foyer."

"Please let them in."

Amatus Lusitanus managed to bring a smile to my face.

"Darling, I heard you fought the queen like a lioness and bested her. Nicely done!" The handsome doctor kissed my hand, making me blush slightly.

"Pardon me, what caused you to arrive so urgently?" Juan asked.

Amatus produced a handkerchief and wiped the perspiration from his forehead. "We just came from the port. I was summoned to tend to a woman in the throes of labor who was having a difficult time and was unable to disembark from a ship arriving from Portugal."

"While Doctor Amatus was tending to the woman, I walked around the port," Augustino Henricks told us. "I saw the soldiers of the Queen's Guard stopping dozens of frightened passengers with drawn bayonets and binding their arms with steel chains. There was yelling, screaming, crying. Sailors, priests and peddlers milled about, encouraging the soldiers of the guard with calls of:

"'Burn them!'

"'Throw these *Cristianos Nuevos*, these New Christians, into the bonfire!'

"You wouldn't believe who I saw there," Augustino Henricks continued. "Don Francisco de Aragón was standing on the pier with his two assistants, supervising what was going on. When he saw me, his narrow eyes twinkled, and he asked to send you his best regards."

"The bastard isn't wasting any time, and has decided to take his revenge against us," Juan said.

"Don Francisco de Aragón is very dangerous. I saw about forty of them, women and men, being taken away to the jailhouse near the city square," Henricks said. "We managed to smuggle away the woman who was giving birth and the baby, as well as ten more children, two women and two men, without the guards noticing. At the moment, they're all packed in together on the floor of the carriage," Amatus said.

"Juan," I handed him a heavy bundle of money, "leave for city hall immediately and bail out the detainees. Don't spare any expense. After a difficult, dangerous sea journey, those wretches won't be able to survive even a single day in that terrible jailhouse.

"Augustino Henricks, I have a writ of appointment for you." I gave him a missive sealed with the red wax stamp of the House of Mendes.

Reddish blotches of excitement spread across his plump cheeks and thick neck.

"My brother-in-law Diogo, may he rest in peace, recommended in his will that I should allow you to help me. I'm appointing you as the company's representative in Venice. I'm sure you'll prove a faithful delegate for the House of Mendes."

His brown eyes were scurrying about rapidly. I could see that he was debating whether the offer would serve him well or whether I merely wanted to distance him from me.

Juan placed a hand on his shoulder. "We have faith in you."

"Your wife liked the city of Lyon. She'll fall in love with Venice, and your children will receive an excellent education. In addition, I'll raise your annual salary and increase the commission on every deal you make."

"Señora Beatrice, in honor of my friend Diogo and in your honor, I accept the position. With your permission, I request twenty percent of every deal I bring in."

I did not like to be bargained with over wages, and found a demand of twenty percent to be excessive, but I did not have another agent I could send to Venice. I did have to increase his commission, but had no intention of multiplying it fourfold.

"Twenty percent is a very high sum. I'm willing to pay you ten percent. I'm certain you'll be successful, and produce lots of deals. You're also responsible for collecting debts, which will increase your commissions, of course."

"I agree. The day after tomorrow, we'll be on our way to Venice." Augustino Henricks took an almond cookie, and he and Juan left the house swiftly.

I called Thomas in. "Thomas, ask the coachman to park the carriage by the servants' entrance, and provide the people inside it with food and drink. During the night, we'll smuggle those poor souls into hiding places. We'll conceal them until we arrange travel permits and lodging for them."

"Beatricci, you're putting yourself at risk. The Queen's Guard is searching for them," Amatus Lusitanus warned me.

"I know, but I have to help them."

***

Our travel cases were piled up one on top of the other, filling up the room and ready to be loaded on the coaches.

The way to Venice was open to us. I debated what to do, how to veer off the road to Aix-la-Chapelle and travel to Venice without causing the queen to send her soldiers after us. Suddenly, an idea occurred to me—to stage a chase after the pair of "lovers," Ana and Juan.

"We'll spread the rumor among all friends and acquaintances that you and Ana have embarked on a love affair, and you've decided to run away from home and elope, much to my chagrin."

"Mama, I can't believe you came up with such a strange idea..." Ana snickered.

Meanwhile, Juan burst out laughing, kneeled at Ana's feet and kissed her hand.

"Ana, I'm assuming you don't want to marry that old bastard."

"Yes, Mama," Ana replied, trying to stop giggling.

"Juan, get up. Hear me now, and listen well. Under cover of darkness, you'll sail in the direction of Venice, introducing yourself as a couple that wishes to elope. Instead of leaving for Aix-la-Chapelle, I'll follow you, chasing you down in order to prevent the marriage."

"I'm sorry, Aunt, I don't think the queen will believe this fantastical story."

"Do as I say! Go and prepare a small travel case. At the appointed time, Thomas will drive you to the port, where a fleet ship will be waiting for you."

Ana and Juan looked at each other, their eyes lighting up with mischief.

"But you won't be sailing for Venice. That's merely the cover story I made up... I want you to be seen sailing off together. In fact, I'll meet you on the way. Now, excuse me, I have to write the queen a letter."

To Her Majesty Queen Mary

Regent Queen of Hungary and the Lowlands

Your majesty, my only child, Ana, has fled in the dead of night with her beloved, Juan Mickas, heading toward Venice.

I was amazed and am shocked that they managed to conceal the connection between them, taking place under my own nose.

My queen, I have thought of your honorable proposal and saw fit to suggest it to my daughter. Unfortunately, daughters these days do not obey their mothers, and she came to a different decision.

Madam Queen, we are both mothers. I am sure the queen will under-stand a mother's pain. I have no choice but to pursue the couple and try to overtake them.

I request her majesty's pardon.

Respectfully,
Beatrice Mendes

On the night before my departure, I changed my plans. As I had not received a permit to settle in Venice, I decided to take a risk and stop in Lyon, using my stay there to collect debts from merchants and debtors who owed money to the House of Mendes, while hoping I would soon receive permission to settle in Venice.

PART THREE

From Antwerp to Venice, 1545

On Paths Unknown, January 1545

It had been six months since we left Antwerp, never to return. The oppressive heat had been replaced by winter chill.

Two widows and their orphaned daughters had escaped the long-reaching and greedy clutches of Charles the Fifth and his sister Mary, who had not been impressed by my letter and sent their armed soldiers after us.

Twenty-one-year-old Juan and twenty-three-year-old Bernardo quickly galloped upon their horses to Lyon, fleeing the emperor's soldiers.

My little family—Ana, who would soon turn eleven, twenty-four-year-old Brianda, her five-year-old daughter La Chica, and I, thirty-five-year-old Beatrice Mendes Gracia Nasi—had managed to escape with cases full of gold and silver coins, gems, pearls, jewelry and expensive clothes. We left behind many friends, memories and plenty of property.

We traveled in a caravan of coaches including thirty escorts, of whom six were armed guards we had hired to protect us against highwaymen. We kept away from the main paved roads and chose to travel on more desolate routes. We experienced rough mountain passages, traveling along unknown paths and secret routes known only to the residents of the mountains and the villagers, trying to shake off our pursuers.

The carriages got stuck in the mud and the rocks, and we almost flipped over several times. The guards accompanying us cleared our path and removed the stones, rocks and trees that had collapsed and blocked our way. The coach was our home and shelter on warm summer days, and now, with the arrival of the intense cold, our eyes burned and grew red from the travails of the road, and a chill invaded our noses and mouths.

The girls were coughing constantly, even though we covered their mouths with a handkerchief. On rainy days, the raindrops battered down upon the roof and windows, as if trying to find any opening to enter and soak us. The snow that began falling as we approached the outskirts of Lyon, our city of refuge, made it harder for the carriage to forge a path.

Throughout the peril-filled road, I maintained a confident façade, believing that we would get through the journey successfully. However, fear stabbed at me, impaling me with its sharp needles. I could hear its voice.

Señora, even with a detail of soldiers escorting you and your family, all of you are not safe here on the road, in the mountains, from the soldiers of the emperor and the queen pursuing you.

Tell me, the voice continued, *aren't you afraid that the soldiers will try to assault you? After all, the rumor of a lady highly rich in property traveling along the roads is sure to reach their ears very soon.*

No, I answered the fear, *since I distributed the property among many carriages. Some of them have already preceded us, and I left some of my possessions in various towns, with loyal people.*

The voice taunted me again. *What were you thinking when you claimed responsibility for the entire family? You're dragging them along on perilous, rough roads, sleeping at the houses of relatives, in inns and roadhouses with various odd characters...*

I tried to silence the pain and convince myself I had done the best I could for my family, but the fear stabbed at me more deeply and more painfully. *What were you thinking, that you were capable of making the best decisions on behalf of everyone? Look at Brianda: you left her penniless. All her property was left behind in Antwerp: the palace, the furniture, the expensive rugs and the precious works of art, and of course, the memories of her husband Diogo.*

That's enough! I protested. *I take care of her.*

You call that taking care? The voice contained a note of bitter mockery.

What do you want from me? I asked, trying to ignore the pain. *The journey is taxing for her.*

What are you talking about? The journey is taxing for her? From now on, she's entirely dependent upon you!

Not really... Only until we get to Lyon, and from there to Venice, I answered the bothersome pain.

Is that what you wanted? She and her daughter, with no property or money, under your exclusive patronage?!

I'm only carrying out my brother-in-law Diogo's will. It was his decision to have me handle the funds. He knew they would evaporate if they ended up in his wife's hands.

Don't play the innocent. The pain stuck another needle straight into my heart. *Can't you see that Brianda is ensconcing herself in silence? You're sitting together in the same carriage, shivering in the chill of the roads, tired, living next to each other in paltry rooms in out-of-the-way roadhouses and the homes of friends, eating peasant bread, a wedge of cheese and vegetable soup, all in the same plate. It has been six months since you left Antwerp, and your sister is still ignoring your presence. You might as well be air as far as she's concerned. She doesn't say a thing to you other than the most essential words.*

I was wracked with shivers. I wrapped my body in the thick wool blanket, but the cold would not release its hold on me.

She'll get over it by the time we get to Venice, I tried to soothe the pain. *You'll see, she'll flourish there. Living in an international city will suit her.*

It's time for you to wake up... The voice was relentless. *She and her daughter are entirely dependent upon your tender mercies.*

What could she do to me? I defended myself. *She has to behave herself and enjoy life. I take care of all her needs. What do you want from me? I promised Mama I would take care of her, and I'm keeping my promise.*

Very faithfully indeed... the voice mocked me.

A gray shadow infiltrated the closed carriage windows and settled upon my heart. Brianda was as stubborn and chilly as Queen Mary.

"That's enough, get out of here!" I called out in panic, trying to silence the voices scurrying inside me.

"Mama, Mama, are you all right? What happened? Did you have a bad dream?" Ana asked, frightened.

"Everything's fine, my sweet, it was just a dream I had," I whispered, my lips dry.

I looked at Brianda, sitting across from me in the carriage. Her face was frozen, her eyes gazing into the distance through the carriage windows.

The fierce chill invaded our bones. Mists covered the small houses scattered among the hills and the trees.

"Brianda, we can't maintain this silence," I said.

Brianda pulled at the wool blanket, covering her shoulders. "I actually quite like it."

From the wicker basket beside me, I produced two thick slices of bread spread with cheese, with an egg between them, given to us by the innkeeper that morning before we left. I offered the bread to Brianda, but she shrugged and ignored me. Finally, she said, "Try to listen to me for once: we're not together. I didn't choose to share a carriage with you."

"Please. You're my sister. It's hard for me when you're angry with me."

"It's hard for *you*? I'm at your mercy."

"Do you really believe I wouldn't take care of you?"

"Don't patronize me. I'd rather take care of myself."

"Brianda, please, if not for me, then for our daughters. Talk to me."

"About what, exactly?"

"Please. You're my only sister. We're in great danger. It's clear to me that the queen and the emperor will be fuming when they find out we've violated their decree and didn't return to Antwerp from the hot springs, and once they hear the rumor that we've come to the Duchy of Lyon."

"I thought we were on our way to Venice! Did you change that without asking my opinion as well?"

"I'm sorry. I'm hoping the messenger from the Venetian Council of Ten will bring our permit to settle in Venice, which I purchased back when we were still in Antwerp, to Lyon. We'll run the risk of stopping in the Duchy of Lyon."

"You think of everything..." Brianda said bitterly.

"There are merchants who owe us money in Lyon, and if I don't collect it directly from them, that money will be lost."

I was not anticipating the ensuing storm. Brianda struck the wall of the carriage with her hand.

"The moneys owed to the House of Mendes belong to La Chica! And who gave you permission to change the company's name from 'House of Mendes' to 'The Company of the Heirs to the Brothers Francisco and Diogo Mendes'? Did you consult me?"

"I decided to commemorate their names…"

"'I decided, I changed…'" she threw out at me, wagging her finger in front of my face. "Everything revolves around you. Does it not occur to you to consult others? To ask? To share?"

Brianda cracked the window open. Red leaves swept along by the wind swirled above us, then were blown out again just as quickly.

She closed the window with a sharp motion, bringing her face close to mine. "Listen to me. That money belongs to me and is supposed to come to my daughter and me." She pronounced the words slowly.

"Excuse me, the money belongs to The Company of the Heirs to the Brothers Francisco and Diogo Mendes, of which I am manager," I said.

"That's what you think! I'll collect those debts! Diogo compiled a detailed list of debtors for me, along with the precise sums they owe. The monetary debts of Avelardo Salvietti, Bartolomeo Panciatichi, and Nicola and Carlo Antenori belong to me and my daughter."

Ana and La Chica trembled in their seats.

"Calm down and lower your voice. Not in front of the girls."

"Get your hands off the property that belongs to me and to my husband Diogo, may he rest in peace. You've been plotting behind my back. Explain to me how you forced Diogo to sign such an insane will?" Her eyes were spitting fire, her voice becoming thin and discordant.

A cold wind whipped at the carriage. I kept my silence.

"What's wrong? Can't you hear properly anymore? You asked to talk to me—well, now we're talking."

I stayed quiet.

Brianda turned her head and gazed out at the desolate hills.

A void gaped open in my heart. The carriage rocked from side to side on the path of sharp stones, threatening to overturn. Among the whistling of the wind, I could hear the whimpering of animals. Lightning flashed, its brightness cutting through the gray sky. An enormous bolt of thunder rolled over the hills, and raindrops began to fall.

The horses whinnied in fear. I held on to the walls of the carriage with all my might, hugging Ana to me. Brianda cradled La Chica in her arms, covering her with a blanket.

The solemn commander of the guard escorting us knocked on the wet window and opened it. Raindrops whipped at his helmet and armor.

"Señoras, are you all right?" his question was carried through the gusting wind.

I glanced at Brianda, who was pale and frightened.

"Thank you, we're fine," I said, but in my heart, I knew that we were not fine. The rift that had formed between my sister and me was deep and painful to both of us, and would not be healed anytime soon.

"Why don't we stop by the side of the road and rest?" I requested.

The commander of the guard pointed at the cloudy sky. "Madam, heavy rain is about to come down. We should get to the duchy before dark."

The Duchy of Lyon

In thundering silence, we approached the Duchy of Lyon, crossed the river and climbed the hill toward the center of the city. I felt very tired, my body aching from the bumpy journey. I could not enjoy the narrow alleys and the plazas with fountains that we passed on our way to the house that Jacob Morro had rented for us.

Jacob Morro's kind wife and her sisters had taken care to fill the pantry with loaves of freshly baked bread, milk, cheese, eggs and vegetables, and had also prepared a steaming vegetable soup for us.

During the long weeks I spent in Lyon, I supervised the relocation of the company's center of activity and guided Juan and Jacob Morro in expanding the operations of our bank in the city and carrying out the monetary transfers.

Juan grew popular among members of the local gentry, particularly the noblewomen. He forged connections with wool and silk merchants and the owners of workshops specializing in dyeing and weaving silk, many of whom belonged to the Spanish and Portuguese New Christian community.

One of his successful ventures was hiring Christopher Manuel, a plump Frenchman with a bulbous nose and red hair. To my relief, Christopher Manuel was diligent in collecting the many debts owed to us by merchants.

The stacks of sacks full of gold coins, placed in chests and kept under guard, enraged Brianda, who thought, of course, that the money belonged to her and her daughter.

Bernardo, in charge of the trade in fabrics and who spent his free time at literary salons and poetry recitals, acquiesced to Brianda's request and went with her to meet three of the company's debtors. In the meeting, Brianda demanded that the merchants convey the funds to pay off the debt directly to her. The merchants, who hosted her graciously in their offices, were surprised by her request and politely explained to her that as far as they knew, the manager of the Mendes Bank's branch in Lyon was Juan Mickas, while the manager of the company was Doña Beatrice Mendes.

I was furious at Benardo for interfering in matters that were none of his affair, but he played the innocent, apologizing by saying he had only honored his aunt's request to accompany her to a meeting, and claiming there was no reason why he shouldn't continue to escort his widowed aunt to meetings.

When Brianda entered my room at the guesthouse, her face was clenched, and her words rattled like rocks rolling downhill.

"How dare you? Who do you think you are? Inciting everyone against me! The money belongs to me, you domineering woman! If Diogo were alive, this would not have happened! I would make sure he threw you out of the company! You're jealous and mean. I know you fancied Diogo, but he chose me!"

"Stop whining. The person who founded the company is Francisco."

"You take care of and help everyone, they call you a 'saint,' a 'virtuous woman' or '*la señora*,' but I'm the only one who knows the truth. I'll tell everyone what a cruel woman you are. Money has blinded you."

Brianda picked up the silver hairbrush and turned the mirror toward me. "Look in the mirror. 'Purloining the moneys of widow and orphan,' that's who you are."

"Stop it, get out of my room!" I raised my voice.

"You want to humiliate me. That's the only way you feel like you're worth something, how mighty you are."

"Brianda, stop it."

"Don't you tell me to stop it! I know very well why you don't get married…" She laughed bitterly. "You're afraid they'll take your ducats… You're in love with money and not with people!"

Brianda opened a red velvet reticule and turned it over. Dozens of gold ducat coins scattered with an ominous noise across the green marble floor.

"Take it, gather up your lover, hold him tight and cling to him at night instead of a husband." Her voice trembled as she left the room, slamming the door behind her.

What have I done wrong to make her behave so harshly toward me, without appreciating all I've done for her? I thought.

"Come back here!" I called out after her, but she no longer heard me.

I sat in the armchair, utterly drained.

Apparently, the argument was heard throughout the house. Juan came in, gathered the coins and put them in a small box.

"Aunt, I'll return these to her. She needs them," he said.

"She'll never have enough…" I said. "Let the merchants know that if they don't pay their debt to the bank, I can't continue to provide them with credit to purchase wool and silk."

Two weeks later, after exhausting negotiations, I agreed to postpone collecting a third of the debt till next year. The debtors conveyed the remainder in gold coins to our bank's branch in Lyon.

***

The morning brought some joyous news. A Venetian emissary, dressed in colorful elegance, personally handed me my permit to settle in the Republic of Venice, granted to us by the Council of Ten, which ran the republic.

"We're leaving early tomorrow morning," I informed Brianda.

"In Venice, I want us to use our maiden name, de Luna, rather than Mendes. I don't want the news of the arrival of the 'Mendes sisters' in Venice to reach the ears of Emperor Charles the Fifth. It would be better for them to hear from their ambassadors about the arrival of Doña Beatrice de Luna and Doña Brianda de Luna," I said.

The cup of plum wine Brianda was holding trembled in her hand, and splashes of dark wine stained the settlement permit and her dress.

"You've even decided for me what my last name will be?!" Her eyes were glazed as she looked at me. "So what if that's what you want! I don't have any right to decide whether it suits me to be called Señora Mendes or Señora de Luna?" Brianda rose from the table furiously, wiping the drops of wine off her dress.

"I would pay a lot to leave for Venice without you, but you've taken over my inheritance," she gritted out.

I blotted out the stains from the settlement permit with a napkin.

What I saw when I raised my eyes took my breath away. Juan was standing in the doorway along with Queen Mary's royal emissary. The messenger extracted a sealed scroll from his bag, broke the seal, unfurled the scroll and began to read.

Señora Beatrice Mendes has violated the conditions of the certificate of transit given to her by Her Majesty Queen Mary, and did not return to Antwerp at the required time.

Therefore, Señora Beatrice Mendes and Señora Brianda Mendes are required to appear at a hearing before the Council at its seat in Brabant.

The emissary placed his hand on the hilt of his sword, handed me the royal summons and departed.

"Look how you've embroiled us in trouble. Because of you, we've been summoned for a trial," Brianda scowled.

Juan placed his hand on Brianda's arm. "Aunt, everything's fine," he said quietly.

"No, nothing is fine. If we don't appear before the council, the emperor will send soldiers to arrest us!" Brianda covered her face with her hands and burst out in tears.

"Brianda, I promise you we won't be arrested. We're leaving for Venice this week, like I promised you."

"You promised Mama to take care of me, and instead, you stole my and La Chica's inheritance. Because of your greed, I'll live like a peasant in Venice, dependent upon your mercies," she wept.

PART FOUR

Venice
1545-1548

Venice, Capital of the World, 1546

Golden and reddish rays of twilight sunshine and the flames of the torches carried by the noblemen's servants flickered upon the black water canal, illuminating the residents taking part in the celebration of spring in a soft, enchanted light. The women braded strands of gold into their hair, their outfits brightly colored and adorned with lavish embroidery. Venice, the capital of the world, the city we had heard so much about, was revealed before our eyes.

I had intentionally timed our arrival to the date of the celebrations, hoping the procession of gondolas in which we entered the city would not attract unnecessary attention and would blend in with the atmosphere of joy in the high-spirited city.

A gondolier wearing a black beret was standing at the end of a long, narrow gondola, decorated with horses and with the emblem of the winged lion, patiently navigating with his single oar among the colorful gondolas cruising the Grand Canal, while singing a love serenade in a tuneful voice to the young people sitting at the stern of the gondola.

Ana held on tightly to La Chica's hand, her gaze tracking the lovers.

Our procession of gondolas sailed slowly along the long, twisty canal. I tried to take in the city. The buildings sporting capitals, cornices, etchings, balconies sculpted with white lacy stone and nooks displaying angel statues seemed to me to be the handiwork of an embroiderer of marble lace.

"Hey, look!" Ana pointed toward the pier. A clown dressed in broad striped yellow-and-red pantaloons, his face made up in white, his nose red, a pointy cap upon his head and gold boots on his feet, jumped around and began to walk on his hands. A tall, fat African tilted back his head and slowly inserted a long sword into his mouth, as if he were eating macaroni. Next to him stood a slim gypsy with a gold earring, pouring a beverage into his mouth, after which he immediately spit out a yellow flame.

"Turks, Ottomans…" the gondolier noted, pointing at two men with curling black mustaches, wearing long cloaks, broad sashes tied around their waists, and sporting turbans on their heads, who had just exited a stately building bearing the sign *Fondaco dei Turchi*, the Turkish commerce center.

"Is that where you want to take us, the place with those Levantine Orientals?" Brianda spat out between pursed lips.

"In the countries of that 'Levantine' sultan, we could live openly according to our faith. Would you rather live your entire life behind a mask?" I asked.

Brianda shrugged and did not reply.

Among the houses perched shoulder to shoulder and painted in autumnal hues stood a beefy man holding a glass pipe and breathing life into it, cutting the warm material with a scalpel, and amazingly, ending up holding a reddish vase,

We passed by the Palazzo Ducale di Venezia, the doge's stunning palace, and by St. Mark's Basilica, its domes adorned with gold mosaics, overlooking the square bustling with celebrants, some of whom wore white masks on their faces.

The gondola stopped at the front entrance of a lavish palace. The carved wooden doors opened before us. Juan, Bernardo, and Augustino Henricks, the representative for House of Mendes, doffed their hats to us in an elaborate display.

"Welcome, señoras, to La Serenissima, the city of the sea, Venice!" Juan gestured ceremoniously.

"Aunt, let me help you." Benardo extended his hand and helped us off the gondola and into the ground floor.

"Ladies, welcome to Palazzo Gritti, the palace of Doge Gritti, now deceased." Augustino Henricks took off his black hat; apparently, he had gone somewhat bald.

He placed his hand on the staircase bannister. "Please go up to the *piano nobile*, the nobility's living quarters."

Ana extended her hand to La Chica and the two of them ran up the stairs. They roamed wide-eyed through the opulent guest lounge, its walls covered with gilded wood etchings, golden mirrors and portraits. A sparkling chandelier hung from a ceiling adorned with frescoes of angels. Green and black marble tables and red armchairs were scattered throughout the hall.

"The doge's secretary recommended Palazzo Gritti to me. He said the ladies would love it." Augustino Henricks patted the little potbelly he had grown. "Luckily for you, I was the first to see the palace owner's representative walking around in Piazza San Marco, holding a tree branch, a signal for property offered for rent or for sale. I conducted brief negotiations with him and rented a palazzo appropriate for your stature," he said in satisfaction.

"I hope you provided a separate house for me," Brianda said.

"Brianda, I want you and La Chica, who is like a daughter to me, to live comfortably and reside with us in Palazzo Gritti," I lowered my voice.

"La Chica is my daughter. Don't you dare say 'she's like a daughter to me'! Do you hear me?" Brianda raised her own voice.

La Chica burst out in tears, hugging her mother.

A dim sensation of fear and worry began to climb up my gut. What was my sister plotting? Why was she allowing herself to scold me, and daring to humiliate me in front of Augustino Henricks?

Juan opened the window. "The location of the palace is excellent. It looks out on Piazza San Marco, the Doge's Palace, the government and commercial offices, the Basilica and the Grand Canal. You can go everywhere on foot, or sail in a gondola."

"The rumors that you've fled Antwerp and are not fulfilling your duty to the Church are spreading like wildfire among the members of the city's high society. I thought that if you lived near the Basilica, the Venetians would calm down and stop talking about you," Augustino Henricks explained.

People who talk abundantly and rapidly usually made me suspicious, but I did have faith in Professor Henricks, the company agent whom Diogo had recommended in his will that I rely on, and who had been my professor in Lisbon.

"You did well," I said.

"Augustino, please make an appointment with the doge for me," Brianda requested.

"Why do you need an appointment with him?" I intervened.

Brianda turned her head away from me and looked toward the canal.

"Stop interfering in my life."

Juan examined his new hat in the mirror, alternately tilting it left and right on his head and stretching out the little peacock feather.

"I have to look my best," he said. "Tomorrow is the La Serenissima celebration, the marriage of the doge and the sea. 'The city that rules the sea,' that's what Venice is called, and the entire city will take part in the celebration."

"I'm not certain we'll come," I said.

"You killjoy," Brianda gritted out. "La Chica and I will go, and Ana will come with us," she added loudly.

Ana and La Chica clapped enthusiastically.

"The doge and the city's dignitaries will be happy to meet the 'wealthy ladies' who have arrived in Venice, and will do anything to keep you in Venice," Juan said, stretching the hem of his cape in front of the mirror.

If I had briefly considered not going, I now rejected the idea. As far as I was concerned, a celebration was an excellent opportunity to meet the city's aristocracy and dignitaries, as well as the ambassadors of foreign countries. Obviously, I had no intention of allowing Brianda to meet the doge by herself.

The tolling heard from the bell tower filled the piazza, preventing us from continuing the conversation.

"Look at the statues of the black people on the tower. They're striking the bells with their hands and welcoming us upon our arrival in Venice!" La Chica, who had gone out to the balcony, called out.

An older man of fifty or so, lame in his left foot, entered the room while doing up the two rows of silvered buttons upon his black jacket.

"Welcome, señoras and señoritas," he bowed before us. "Señora, my name is Luciano de Costa. Señor Augustino Henricks hired me to be the major-domo," he said, running his hand over his head, a signal that he was among those 'belonging to the letter Yod.'

I exchanged looks with my sister. *Thank God*, I thought. *He's one of us.*

"Of course, the employment of the major-domo is temporary, until the two of you decide whether you're interested in continuing to employ him," Augustino Henricks added immediately.

"Augustino Henricks, pardon me for asking, but have you agreed with the major-domo on a monthly wage?" Brianda asked.

"I leave that to your consideration, señoras," Augustino Henricks tried to evade the question.

Brianda turned to look at me.

"Madame, who is paying my wages?" Luciano asked.

I produced a leather pouch. "The wage is in accordance with the standard accepted in the city, with a bonus of one-tenth of the wage," I said, placing a gold coin in his hand. "An advance on your salary."

Brianda reached out to stop me, but Luciano de Costa was quicker, swiftly tucking the coin into his pocket.

"Tell us about yourself," I requested.

"My family is from Vino de Castello," he recounted. "I studied law, Latin and the sciences at Salamanca University. I worked in commerce until my partner in the fur trade informed on me, claiming that I was practicing Judaism. When I found out that the Inquisition had sent priests to interrogate us, I fled with my family to the port. On the way, highwaymen forced us to stop our carriage, and my wife was killed. It was a miracle that I managed to escape, with five orphans I must care for."

I asked Luciano de Costa to make sure the servants' entrance was opened to the staff that had faithfully escorted us and the soldiers of the guard, and to provide them with food, drink and lodging. I emphasized that for us, they should prepare fish, vegetables and fruit.

"Augusting Henricks, please inform Lord Marco de Mollino that I have arrived in Venice and would be happy to see him," I added.

Augustino Henricks knitted his brows in perplexity.

"Yes, señora. I hope he's home," he said, leaving the house.

"I didn't know you knew him, Aunt," said Juan.

"He was recommended to me. Marco de Mollino belongs to a respected noble family, among the Old Christians, and is a Venetian citizen who has been paying taxes to the city council for over twenty five years. He has connections with all the heads of government and commerce in the city. Since Venice's city council has imposed commercial limitations on the New Christians, the Portuguese *conversos*, we are not allowed to purchase merchandise and sign contracts. Marco de Mollino will sign contracts for the House of Mendes merchandise," I explained to Juan.

A young serving girl entered the hall, bearing a silver tray with a red glass dish containing nuts and dates, fragrant cookies and beverages.

"If you please," she said, curtseying.

"These are Venice's famous almond and cinnamon cookies. Please, try the lemonade as well, made from freshly squeezed lemons," said the major-domo.

The refreshing drink and the crispy cookies opened my eyes and bestowed me with renewed vigor after the exhausting journey.

"Please come in." Luciano de Costa opened the elaborate brass doors of the palazzo's inner rooms before us.

The study had a wooden floor, surrounded by a library consisting of hundreds of books. Perfumed candles illuminated the sleeping hall whose arched windows overlooked the canal, with a canopy bed at its center.

"Señoras, please, let's go out to the pretty balcony." Luciano de Costa opened the doors. I leaned against the banister and gazed out at the gondolas sailing in the waters of the Grand Canal.

Augustino Henricks had made a good choice, both with the Palazzo Gritti palace and with his major-domo. Luciano de Costa was quiet and businesslike, and I liked him.

I gave de Costa the list of crates, each of which was marked to note whether it should be unpacked or left sealed, as well as to whom it belonged. I instructed him to make sure the servants would unpack the crates, as well as to station two inspectors who would ascertain that the contents of each crate would be placed in the closets and cupboards, and that an inventory was conducted in accordance with the lists he held, so that nothing would be misplaced or vanish.

"Stop ordering everyone around!" Brianda erupted at me.

"But, Madame Brianda, the lady asked us to only open the boxes marked…" de Costa said.

"I'm the mistress of this house, and the major-domo is required to carry out my orders. Doña Beatrice will soon be moving to another house," Brianda spat out through clenched teeth.

"Please unpack all the crates," I said. As I left the room, I heard Brianda asking de Costa to instruct the cook to prepare a warm vegetable soup.

I did not rest all afternoon. I walked between the rooms to make sure everything was being done to my satisfaction. When I discovered that the box in which I kept select pearls imported from the East had disappeared, I was furious. I did not agree to sit down and eat lunch with everyone until the crate was found. I turned the house upside-down, surveying every crate with de Costa, but the precious box had disappeared.

"Mama, please, don't take it to heart. It'll make you ill. Pretend you gave it to charity," my Ana requested, but I could not calm down. I had saved up so much money to buy the most beautiful pearls, worth a fortune, so I would have security in the future! And now the pearls had disappeared, seemingly into thin air. I was sure they had been stolen, but did not know if it had happened on the way to Venice or in the palace.

The Yellow Badge

"I have nothing to wear! The women of Venice wear vibrant, colorful clothing from soft, light fabrics and wear high-heeled shoes," Brianda said as we were hosting Señora Carina, the small, opinionated wife of Augustino Henricks, my representative in Venice.

I was not considering arriving in Venice dressed inappropriately. During our stay in Lyon, I had ordered us and the girls dresses with sleeves that were puffed at the shoulder, their narrow waist adorned with a pearl belt, and precious stones embroidered into the front of the garment, from the waist to the hem of the dress.

"Madame Brianda, excuse me, I know a wonderful seamstress, called 'Esterika, the clothes magician.' She lives in the 'ghetto,' the Jewish neighborhood. If you agree, I'll ask my maid to invite her here, but she charges a very high fee," Carina offered.

"Please, I'll pay any sum she asks for," Brianda said.

"Don't be frightened when you see her. She wears a yellow badge on her coat."

"A yellow badge? What's that?" Ana asked.

"It's the mark of the Jews, a yellow piece of cloth shaped like a circle or with six corners, sewn onto the front of the garment, or else a yellow or red hat that they must wear, meant to differentiate the Jews from the Christians. They may walk around the city, but are required to wear the mark."

The girls' eyes opened wide.

"I've never seen a Jewess." La Chica clung to Ana.

"But if the Jews are free to move around the city, why do they live in a separate neighborhood?" Ana asked.

"Good question! My cousin is smart," Juan smiled.

"The rulers of the city want to isolate the Jews and prevent them from competing with the city's citizens. They're prohibited from buying houses and land. They're only allowed to deal in rags or be moneylenders," Carina explained. "Esterika has to be back at the ghetto before the bells toll. At ten at night, the gate to the ghetto is closed, and anyone left outside is at risk due to the hoodlums and the authorities who might throw them in jail."

"Poor thing…" La Chica whispered.

Listening to her made me sad. If I had thought that in Venice, I might return to Judaism, I now understood I would have to postpone my plans. I had no intention of living in the ghetto and walking around the city with an identifying mark that would leave me and my family vulnerable.

After Carina left, I felt a strong need to strengthen Ana's connection to the family's history. She was twelve, and the time had come to reveal the secret to her.

***

On Friday night, I took Ana into my study, where Brianda was waiting, closing the door carefully.

"Ana, congratulations," Brianda embraced her.

"Congratulations? Why?" she asked.

I sat down across from her, holding both her hands.

"Ana, I want to reveal the family secret to you."

"Secret?" Ana looked at Brianda and me in wonderment.

"My Ana, you're Jewish."

"I'm Jewish?"

"Yes, and your name is Reyna-Malka Nasi Benveniste. Ana is your outside name in society."

"Are Juan, Bernardo and La Chica Jewish too?" she asked.

I nodded, and gave her a brief account of our family's history.

"I wish Papa were with me," Ana said.

"Reyna, your father is looking down at you from heaven and is proud of you," Brianda consoled her, offering her candy.

I clasped a gold necklace around Reyna's neck, with a pendant embedded with a blue sapphire at its center, surrounded by six white pearls.

"Reyna, my daughter, swear to me now that when the day comes, you will pass on the Jewish faith, as well as this pendant, to your daughter, who will in turn pass them on to her daughter."

Brianda poured oil onto the wicks, we covered our heads with white kerchiefs, and lit the blessed wicks.

"Reyna, repeat after me," I requested.

"Blessed are You, the Lord our God,

Who has sanctified us with His commandments,

And commanded us to light the blessed wicks,

in honor of and for the glory of the Holy Sabbath.

Amen.

Shabbat Shalom—a peaceful Shabbath."

Reyna closed her eyes, covered them with her palms just as we did, and repeated the blessing.

I was surprised by the maturity and solemnity with which Reyna accepted the secret. I hugged her and kissed her.

"Reyna, the candle will never be extinguished. The chain of generations of the People of Israel remains unbroken."

***

Several days later, at ten in the morning, when I entered the reception lounge, still troubled by the loss of the chest of pearls, I found two noblemen, dressed in the manner of Venetian dandies, waiting for me. The older of them was gaunt, his face elongated and his nose aquiline. On his head was a green cap adorned with a blue feather, while his body was clad in a red tunic, striped trousers and leather boots.

The younger, a bouncy lad of seventeen or so with a red mane of curls and laughing eyes, was wearing a chemise with one white sleeve and one sleeve striped in pink. A silvered dagger hung from his belt.

The guests doffed their caps to us and bowed.

"*Buongiorno*, my name is Marco de Mollino. I'm honored to meet the esteemed lady, Doña Beatrice Mendes…"

"If you please, Señor de Mollino, my name in Venice is Beatrice de Luna." I had a different name in every place, yet I was still the same person. I smiled internally.

"A thousand pardons, Señora Beatrice de Luna. Welcome to the city of freedom. Finally, after a long correspondence, I'm so happy to meet the *señora*."

His melodious voice was full of vitality and energy. "This is my son Nicola," he introduced the young man.

I was glad that the connections I had forged were bearing results. I reached an agreement with Marco de Mollino that in return for his services, he would receive a monthly wage as well as a commission for every deal he carried out. I decided to test his efficiency.

"Señor de Mollino, yesterday a ship arrived at the port bearing a cargo of sugar and pepper intended for me. Could your honor accompany my representative, Augustino Henricks, and myself to the custom house in order to release the merchandise?"

"Señora, with your permission, I prefer that the *señora* and her representatives not come to the customs house or to the port. Señora, if the staff at the port and at customs discovers that the delivery arriving belongs to New Christians, the release of the merchandise will be delayed for reasons that will remain unclear. And in general, if the merchandise is intended for merchants who are Jewish…" he spat out the word contemptuously, "…the sailors and the porters humiliate them and vandalize their cargo. Please, give the documents to Nicola. My son will leave for the customs offices to release the merchandise."

"Madame, I'd be honored. I will be happy to assist you in any matter and issue," Nicola said.

I asked Luciano de Costa to fetch the file of documents lying on my desk, with a cover stating, "Delivery number 01-1546 to Venice."

In the meantime, seventeen-year-old Nicola was curiously eyeing the beautiful Ana and La Chica, who were holding hands, clad in fashionable dresses.

De Costa passed the file to Nicola, who took off at a run to the custom house, while still sneaking in another glance at Ana.

I thought to myself that I must make sure the young redhead did not develop any romantic ideas about Ana. He had to understand that she was out of bounds for him. He should be kept away from the house.

"I'd be honored to escort the ladies to our city's annual celebration and introduce you to its dignitaries," Marco de Mollino offered.

"Thank you," I smiled, nodding in agreement.

The Eternal Union Between Venice and the Sea

A variety of characters from all over the world were milling about in the bustling square in celebration. A miscellany of languages—Italian, English, French—reached our ears. Men with overgrown mustaches clad in turbans were conversing in Turkish.

"Do women walk around in the city on their own?" Brianda asked in reaction to the sight of a woman of thirty or so, wearing high-heeled shoes and holding a small velvet reticule, entering the Basilica.

"This is Venice, the city of freedom," Marco de Mollino laughed.

The numerous ships and gondolas at the port made my head spin with a variety of ideas. The Port of Venice would make an excellent docking point for the ships unloading merchandise, which would then be conveyed to warehouses I would purchase next to the port in order to store them. It was time I realized my dream of building a fleet of ships. Why should I be dependent upon others' vessels? I could have the ships repaired in Venice, which was sufficiently centrally located.

Hundreds of men, women and children dressed in their colorful festive clothing were standing in the front courtyard of the doge's palace, above which a tarp had been stretched out to provide shade.

"Mama, look!" Ana pointed at a ship adorned with gold decorations, with a gold canopy at its center, its red curtains pulled back. It was sailing seaward.

"That's the *bucentaur*, the state barge of the doge and his wife. The statuette at the bow is designed in the pattern of the doge's crown," Juan said.

Doge Francesco Donato stood in all his royal glory at the stern of the boat, wearing the *corno*, the doge's traditional crown, on his head. The bushy gray brows shading his brown, piercing eyes and his white beard bestowed him with a dignified air.

A red silk cape, embroidered with gold leaves and adorned with gold buttons, was wrapped around his neck and flowed down to his ankles, which were clad in leather boots. Next to him stood his wife, a blonde wig on her head, its curly strands cascading to her shoulders. A companion shielded her with a white parasol.

In my heart, I laughed as I imagined the wind blowing the blonde wig off her head in a moment or two, but that was not the case.

The doge raised his hand, sporting a red ruby ring upon his finger, and showed the crowd a gold coin. The sounds of laughter and cheering stopped; all grew silent.

The doge threw the coin into the blue waves, stating: "I hereby declare the eternal union between Venice and the sea. You, daughter of the deep, are now sanctified to me."

The exuberant celebrants, most of whom were wearing amazing masks, cheered at length: "Bravo! Bravo!"

Peddlers roamed among the attendees, selling sweets. We stopped by a small stall offering warm chestnuts in a cloth bag. The girls loved their nutty flavor.

"Señora Beatrice de Luna and Señora Brianda de Luna, please clear some time in your schedules. This very moment signals the opening of La Dolce Vita, the 'sweet life' festival, which will consist of two months full of parties, celebrations and balls to which the city's dignitaries and their wives will invite you." Marco de Mollino chuckled. "My wife and I will be your companions, if you wish."

"Thank you, that's wonderful! A celebration that never ends." Brianda was enthusiastic, her eyes greedily taking in the city and its people. "I have to order some sets of clothing and accessories."

Many eyes followed us as we strolled along the canal. We were the only ones walking through the city with six armed guards. Most of the gazes focused on beautiful Brianda and handsome Juan, with the little peacock feather adorning his cap. He was wearing a yellow velvet cloak, with the short sword he had received from Prince Maximillian at his waist.

De Mollino introduced us to the doge and his wife, who received us very warmly, inviting Brianda and me to visit their palace.

A group of people with a yellow patch sewn onto their cloaks passed us by, bidding us hello. "Jews," Juan lowered his voice.

"Those poor people, they have to wear a badge," Bernardo whispered, wrapping his blue cloak tighter around his shoulders.

An intoxicating aroma of coffee reached us from the entryway of one of the lavish houses.

"The smell is coming from the coffee house," de Mollino explained.

"I've never heard of a coffee house." Brianda peered in through the lounge windows.

"Please, let's go in," she urged me.

"Señoras, you're welcome to go in. My guards will wait outside for you. Don't worry, the Jews can't enter here…" Marco de Mollino winked at Bernardo and Juan.

The gazes of the patrons turned to us as we entered the beautiful salon, with reddish brass candlesticks and wood tables carved in geometric patterns. Noblemen and their wives sat around the tables, drinking a dark beverage in delicate glasses, accompanied by fragrant pastries.

The owner approached us with alacrity, wiping his hands on the white apron tied at his waist. "If you please, the *señoras* are invited to try some coffee, the beverage prepared from the best coffee beans in the world!" he declared in his melodious speech.

His eyes twinkling jovially, the owner of the establishment seated us at a table at the center of the salon. The open windows looked out upon the Basilica in all its beauty. A pleasant breeze brought the scent of the sea with it. Seagulls and pigeons soared and frolicked over the lagoon. The owner explained that only adults were permitted to drink coffee. He suggested lemonade for the *señoritas* and offered all of us melty meringue cookies, *torta di pinoli*, pine nut cake, and *amaretti*, almond cookies that had just come out of the blazing oven.

I savored the hot, bitter coffee. How little was needed to be happy! My family, good coffee and the wondrous *amaretti* cookie. I enjoyed the relaxed, pleasant atmosphere. As I sat in the salon, I realized another important thing: coffee was worth its weight in gold. It was not only a beverage, but an actual social event!

I decided I would not confine myself to importing sacks of coffee beans, but would purchase coffee plantations from the natives, supervising the coffee beans and their quality from the moment they were planted and until they arrived in Venice. That way, I could control their price.

Several dignitaries approached us and introduced themselves. We asked them to pull some more armchairs over to the table and invited them to sit with us. Their wives exhibited plenty of interest in us, asking where we had come from and whether the girls were sisters. I saw that their minds were already working on coming up with matches for the girls. Brianda was flushed and happy over the interest stirring around her.

I introduced us as sisters from the de Luna family and did not expand much. I remembered what Francisco had taught me our sages once said: "Blessings will only be found in that which is hidden from the eye."

A pretty woman of thirty or so paused outside the coffee house. From her expression and by reading her lips, I understood that she was asking her husband to go inside. The husband, a brawny man with dark eyes, took care to button up his cloak, concealing the yellow badge affixed to his white shirt. He shrugged and shook his head.

The owner of the establishment, noting the exchange between the couple, wiped his hands on the hem of his apron and stationed himself at the opening of the salon, his hands on his hips.

The man placed his hand on the crook of the woman's arm. She glanced at me furtively, strolling slowly beside her husband until she disappeared from our view.

***

In one day, we were introduced to the city's nobility, almost in its entirety, as well as to the ambassadors of foreign countries. Brianda's and my engagement calendar had been filled. For me, it was mainly business meetings during the day and balls in the evenings, while Brianda was invited to card games, morning meetings, dances and masquerade balls. We met many of the city's dignitaries, and when we returned home, I wrote down the names and positions of all the people I had met in a notebook.

***

At night, thinking of the Jews living in segregated neighborhoods, wearing the Jewish badge and prohibited from entering the coffee house and enjoying the bitter beverage, left me sleepless.

I tossed and turned, my face covered with cold sweat. Rising from the bed, I wiped my face, took the candlestick and walked to the library by its flickering light. I opened the desk drawer and took out the little Torah book I had been given by my father, which I took with me everywhere.

I paged through it, reading the first verse my finger landed on.

"And Moses took the bones of Joseph with him: for he had sworn the children of Israel, saying, God will surely visit you; and ye shall carry up my bones away hence with you."

This is it. I decided the time had come to convey the bones of my loved ones who were buried in Portugal to Venice.

I wrote to the Pope that my parents and my husband had been loyal Catholics, and were buried in the cemetery in Lisbon. Unfortunately, I could not visit their graves and honor their memories, and I was requesting His Holiness the Pope's permission to bring their caskets to Venice to be interred in the cemetery next to the church whose construction was currently being funded by my donation.

A month later, I received a missive in reply.

At the Pope's request, the Church in Lisbon will be happy to assist the Pope's protégé, Señora Beatrice Mendes de Luna.

I felt much relief. I would bury Francisco's and my parents' caskets in Venice. And who knows? Perhaps in the future, I would manage to transport their bones to the Mount of Olives in Jerusalem.

Madame Brianda

Venice suited Madame Brianda, as my sister was called, who was constantly celebrating. A procession of seamstresses, embroiderers, goldsmiths and wig and hair dye experts arrived at the house, their arms loaded with packages of fabrics, leather, jewelry and a variety of accessories. They spent many hours in her company, selecting clothes for every event to which she was invited, and the list was endless.

Her engagement calendar was full of invitations to parties, masquerade balls, plays, recitals and card games, and she was received as the guest of honor in all of them.

The major-domo, Luciano de Costa, reported to me that he had met the goldsmith from whom Madame Brianda ordered jewelry, who complained to him that it had been three weeks and she had still not paid off her debt to him. In addition, I heard rumors of her debts to furniture stores.

One afternoon, I found an open letter in Brianda's rounded handwriting on her dresser, and couldn't hold myself back from reading it.

Dear Roxanna,

Please procure for me the hair pins and reticule with inlaid sapphires and rubies, as well as the perfume you purchased for Mary Queen of the Lowlands. It has an intoxicating scent.

I hope my miserly sister won't limit my shopping. I'm sick of being dependent on her.

Respectfully,
Your friend Brianda de Luna

**

Reddish rays of light were twinkling in the waters of the Grand Canal, visible through the windows. I sat down to chat with Ana and La Chica and sip hot water seasoned with rose petals, and adorned with more colorful petals. The cook served us thin, well-baked squares of dough, topped with slices of tomato and fried peppers, with a scent of basil, along with mozzarella cheese. "Venetian bread," the cook said proudly. I tasted the dough and fell in love.

Brianda entered the room, her steps light and her pretty face glowing in the twilight. She sat down next to La Chica, her fingers gently undoing the ribbon around a small, ridged silver box in the shape of a flower, engraved with a delicate floral pattern. She raised the lid, which had a flower-shaped mirror inside it.

"I bought it from the best watchmaker in Venice," she said, winding the watch's spring with her fingertips.

"Mama, can I see it?" La Chica sent a tentative hand toward the box.

"Did you pay the watchmaker?" I asked.

Brianda did not reply.

"Girls, please go to your rooms," I said in a voice that bore no questioning.

"Brianda," I addressed her after the girls reluctantly left the table. "Please explain to me how you have money to pay for that watch."

"You killjoy. You don't have one word to say about the watchmaker's work of art?" Brianda closed the box.

"The watch is beautiful, but you've exceeded your monthly allowance, and I've received complaints that you're not paying your debts."

Brianda leaned forward in her chair, her brows rising in a scowl. "You should be ashamed of yourself," she thrust her finger before my eyes. "With three black peppercorns, you could pay all my debts and raise the paltry allowance you've granted me! Do you want me to live in Venice like a plebe, a commoner?" She gathered up the box containing the watch and exited the room.

I hurried out after her, wanting to conclude the fight today. I searched for her in the music room, which was her favorite, but there was no sound of playing coming from the room.

The door to her study was open. I went in.

Brianda's portrait, painted by Titian, hung on one of the walls. I was surprised—he had managed to capture the very texture of her soul with his paintbrush, an exuberance tinged with sadness reflected in her pretty eyes.

I wondered if the sadness was a result of the heavy debt weighing on her shoulders, and the rage over losing guardianship of her daughter La Chica's inheritance.

I walked to Brianda's room and knocked lightly on the door.

"Come in, please," she called.

I opened the door and saw Brianda sitting next to the ancient escritoire.

"My sister, I want to talk to you," I said quietly.

"I thought you were…"

"Please, let me say a few words."

"You're already here. You might as well talk."

"My sister, I love you, but it's beneath your dignity to owe money. I miss talking to you, and I miss the way we could always laugh together."

Brianda picked up the red fan lying on the escritoire's marble surface and waved it in front of her face.

"The past is the past," she replied quietly.

"Brianda, Mama and Papa would have liked us to live peacefully. I promised them I would watch over you and take care of you for the rest of my life."

A veil of tears shrouded her eyes.

"I miss Mama and Papa. If the king had allowed Mama to leave Portugal, she wouldn't have let you treat me so patronizingly."

"Papa passed away and Mama isn't here. I was widowed at a young age and became mother to my daughter, to you, my sister, to Juan and to Bernardo."

"You forget that I'm a widow too, and that Diogo disinherited me, and put you in charge of my daughter's money. That isn't normal! Under the law, a mother is her daughter's sole guardian."

"Brianda, my sister, I want you to be happy. We live here together. It would be easier for both of us, and mostly for our daughters."

"Mostly, I'm tired. I'll think about it." Brianda's gaze drifted to the Grand Canal.

"I'm tired too. It breaks my heart that we don't talk like we once did." I sat down in a chair, covering my eyes, which were glazed with a mist of tears.

"My sister, you're dear to me. I'll increase your monthly allowance so you can maintain the standards suitable to women of nobility. Come to my room; I want to give you five thousand gold ducats to cover your debts. Next week, when we're a bit calmer, we'll talk again and decide on the sum of the monthly allowance." I reached out to her.

Brianda hesitated briefly, then rose and hugged me.

Guardianship

The peace between us did not last long. Brianda was surreptitiously consulting Venetian solicitors who frequented our home, and plotting behind my back. I stayed one step ahead of her, and presented a request for an urgent hearing before the Venice Court of Foreign Affairs.

A cool morning breeze was blowing when a black gondola stopped at the entrance to the palazzo. A guard of the republic, wearing a long sword at his waist, leapt off the gondola and entered the gates of the palazzo.

"Señora, the court messenger requested that I present you with an invitation to a hearing."

***

On the next day, a small cloud was floating in the sky as the city woke into the day's bustle. "Good morning, señora," the gondolier paddling through the gray water of the canal greeted me.

"A pleasant morning to you, too," I replied, sitting down on a red velvet pillow, holding a case containing the documents summoning me to the hearing.

The gondola stopped at the entrance to a large brick building, with brass lettering stating, "Venice Court of Foreign Affairs." Jacob Morro, who had arrived from Lyon, was waiting for me, and gave me his hand to help me off the gondola.

A courteous guard in an orange uniform opened the gate for us. We climbed up to the courtroom, its front doors embossed with Venice's winged lion emblem. I handed the hearing summons to the guard.

"Madame, please come with me," the guard instructed, signaling Jacob

Morro to wait outside the courtroom. The hall housing the court and its ceiling were coated with gold leaf. A stunning chandelier dangled from the center of the ceiling, and the windows looked out on the Grand Canal.

The esteemed judges sat around a gilded, arc-shaped table, wearing dark blue cloaks with gold ribbons.

The guard gestured at a padded armchair, striped in red and gold, positioned on the reddish carpet in front of the judges.

The elderly judge leafed through the documents lying on the wood table before looking up.

"Señora Beatrice de Luna," the elderly judge began. "The court has agreed to your request to conduct an urgent hearing. What does the *señora* want?" the judge addressed me in an authoritative voice.

"Gentlemen, esteemed judges, I wish to confirm my guardianship over the inheritance of my niece Beatrice Mendes, the daughter of Diogo and Brianda de Luna Mendes," I said.

I struggled with the clasp of the case, which refused to open. I produced a copy of Diogo Mendes's will and presented it for the judges' consideration.

The elderly judge drummed his fingers on the table.

"The court is authorized to discuss the request. The *señora* is required by law to present proof of residency in the Duchy of Venice," I heard his throaty voice.

I presented the judges with the permit to settle in Venice which I had received from the Council of Ten, with wine stains at its edges.

The judges perused the documents, whispering among themselves.

The elderly judge examined me at length, "Señora, the documents you have provided state your name as Mendes, while you introduced yourself in court under the name de Luna."

I handed the judge my wedding certificate, which included my maiden name, Beatrice de Luna.

The judges' gazes alternated between me and the documents as they conversed with each other.

"The Court of Foreign Affairs approves Señora de Luna Mendes's guardianship over the inheritance of Señorita Beatrice Mendes, the daughter of Diogo and Brianda Mendes," the elderly judge declared in a hushed voice. He marked the documents with the court's stamp, adding his signature.

I thanked the judges and left the court hall. Jacob Morro kissed my hand, happy for my success, and requested my permission to go to the shipyard to check the condition of one of the ships, whose sail had been torn.

The city was quiet, its residents and visitors out to have lunch in their homes and in taverns.

Brianda was waiting for me in the living room, her hands on her hips and her eyes blazing.

I didn't know how she found out what had taken place before I even got home.

"How dare you go behind my back and renew the guardianship over my daughter's inheritance?!" she yelled.

I carefully closed the room's windows and door.

"My younger sister…"

"Don't patronize me. I have a name!!!"

"Brianda," I lowered my voice. "I'm spending a fortune in order to avoid charges and prosecution for heresy. If I don't save every ducat, how do you think I'll have thousands of gold ducats for the emperor and his sister Mary, so that they rescind the accusations against us?"

"How can you even dare to think of saving yourself and Ana with the money from my daughter's inheritance?"

"I'm saving you and La Chica from a heresy trial as well. Do you want her to be forced to marry someone who doesn't 'belong to the letter Yod'?"

Brianda stationed herself right next to me. I could smell her jasmine perfume.

"It's none of your business who my daughter marries! You're not her mother! When will you understand that?"

"Diogo trusted me to manage her funds well, and granted me guardianship over her assets."

"What are you trying to say, that my husband didn't trust me? That I'm not a good mother?"

Brianda sipped from the glass of lemonade on the table and sank back into the sofa, exhausted.

"Brianda, you're a wonderful mother, but when it comes to financial matters…"

"But… But…" Brianda picked up the file of documents lying on the table, scattering the papers everywhere.

I heard a light knock on the door.

"Yes?"

"Excuse me, attorney Don Titiano Verdi is waiting for Madame Brianda in her study," the major-domo announced.

"You'll be hearing from me," Brianda gritted out and left the room.

I opened the windows and breathed in the fresh air. Later in the day, I would find out that Don Titiano was a Venetian solicitor belonging to one of the Old Christian families, who was happy to appeal to the Court of Foreign Affairs on Brianda's behalf, requesting to repeal my guardianship over La Chica's funds and to transfer it to her natural guardian, Brianda. I also found out that he was not among the best attorneys, and had lost many of his trials.

The atmosphere in Palazzo Gritti was oppressive. When La Chica saw me, her eyes drifted away, trying to evade my gaze and my questions. She no longer told me about her strolls and her various experiences in the city, as had been her custom.

"Ana, what's going on with La Chica?" I inquired with my daughter.

"Mama, she was crying and secretly told me that Aunt Brianda is forbidding her to talk to you. She begged me not to tell you."

Brianda's solicitor failed in his efforts to convince the Court of Foreign Affairs to overturn my status as trustee of La Chica's inheritance, and Brianda roamed the palace in a state of turmoil, leaving for and returning from meetings, sending missives, and mostly ignoring my presence. Finally, she informed me she had rented a small residential palace, and that she and La Chica would be moving there in a few months.

***

I tried to occupy myself with company affairs for most of the day and not to let the battle with my sister affect business.

In the meantime, Juan began to manage the business of maritime commerce. He tracked the fleet, took care of shipyard repairs, and paid storage and custom fees in the ports, as well as marital insurance for the ships and merchandise.

I put company agent Duarte Gomez, who has studied medicine in Salamanca University and had a brilliant mathematical mind, in charge of the *lettres de change*, the company's bills of exchange and credit. He called them "the engine of the economy," claiming they were vital to commerce just as air is vital to the human body.

I asked him to teach Ana mathematics and science twice a week, in addition to her literature, poetry and philosophy lessons with writer and poet, Alonso Núñez de Reinoso.

***

The sun was illuminating the lovely city in a soft light. Many families were strolling along the Grand Canal. I decided to go for a walk with Ana.

"Mama, please, La Chica wants to come with us." Ana begged when she came in wearing a pink dress that suited her well.

"I don't think Brianda will allow La Chica to come on a walk with us." I took my velvet reticule and we prepared to leave.

"Madam, forgive me for the interruption." The major-domo handed me a missive sealed with the emperor's insignia and departed.

I broke the royal seal, read the missive, and felt the world collapse around me.

Brabant
May 1546

For Señora Beatrice Mendes and Señora Brianda Mendes

As the señoras *have violated the royal summons to appear before the Council of Brabant at the date decided upon, the* señoras *are accused of heresy against the holy Catholic faith.*

Their possessions, including forty chests and boxes full of treasures in Antwerp and three crates in Germany, have been sealed with the stamp of the king and seized on behalf of the Holy Roman Empire.

Emperor Charles the Fifth
Emperor of the Holy Roman Empire

The room was spinning around me. I held on to the sides of the table.

"Mama, what happened?" Ana asked.

"Let's postpone our walk. Call Juan," I asked her.

"He told me he was sailing to Murano Island."

I drafted an authorization appointing my cousin, Juan Mickas, as my delegate. Around noon, Juan returned, storming into the room. "What happened?" he asked.

"The emperor has accused us of heresy against the holy Catholic faith and seized the forty crates full of gems, diamonds and gold that I deposited with merchants in Antwerp." I showed him the missive.

"Juan, I'm appointing you as my official delegate before Emperor Charles the Fifth and his sister Queen Mary. You must act to repeal the accusations of heresy against Catholicism, undo the seizure of my property, and bring the forty crates to Venice. Offer Charles and Mary loans and monetary gifts, but make sure not to scatter my money needlessly to the winds."

"At your service, Aunt."

I rested my hand on his shoulder. "Tomorrow, first thing in the morning, you'll leave for Antwerp. I'm placing a great deal of responsibility on your shoulders. I have faith in you."

Don Juan Mickas

The days passed by. I waited eagerly for news from Juan. The ship docking at the port finally brought me a bundle of letters.

Antwerp
June 1546

Dear Aunt, as we agreed, I returned to Antwerp as your delegate to save the property left behind and seized by the crown.

Enclosed is a letter I received from my friend Allegria Toledano, the daughter of the royal goldsmith.

Juan

The enclosed letter read:

Brussels
June 1546

Juan my dear,

I miss you. I enjoyed dancing in your arms at the ball. Juan, you are the best and most noble dancer I know, and I hope to dance in your arms again.

You asked if I could write you stories about what takes place in the palace. Luckily for you, I have an excellent memory. I remembered that the day after Queen Mary met with your aunt Señora Beatrice Mendes, I came to the palace to personally deliver to the queen a ruby broach that my father had designed for her. The royal court was bustling with activity. Servants were loading chests and furniture onto coaches.

One of the women courtiers told me that Don Francisco de Aragón was angry since his marriage to Señorita Ana Mendes had not taken place. He had decided to leave the royal court with the gold coins he had promised to convey to the queen if the marriage had occurred.

I was waiting for the queen outside the reception hall. Luckily for me, the door remained partially open.

"Marranos—pigs, conversos," the queen called out as she gazed out through her window and watched Francisco de Aragón's carriage depart from the palace courtyard.

"It's too bad my brother Charles is busy with his wars against the king of France, and had no time or wish to handle the matter properly," the queen said, and ordered the clerk to write:

To His Honor, the Holy See
From Mary Queen of the Lowlands

The New Christians are poisoning our children's souls. The Inquisition should tighten its rein and interrogate those sailing the seas between the Italian principalities and the Balkan shores. I request that the Pope address this matter as expediently and thoroughly as possible.

Thus it ended.

Yours, missing you and hoping this information from the palace is of use to you.

Your friend, Allegria Toledano

***

Antwerp
July 1546

Dear Aunt,

I managed to meet Queen Mary, who greeted me in a very chilly manner.
I want to tell you about the meeting in detail:

"Don Juan Mickas," the herald declared when I entered the reception
hall, accompanied by brawny guards.

Queen Mary was sitting on the elevated platform at the top of five
broad marble steps. On the right side of the hall sat advisors and
dignitaries, while at its left was a large musical orchestra.

I bowed deeply.

"Welcome, Don Mickas. Have you come to my palace to tell the
queen that the Mendes sisters, who fled Antwerp, taking with them
merchandise that does not belong to them but to the merchants of
the city, are returning to stand trial before the Council of Brabant?"
the queen asked loudly.

Taking care to conceal my apprehension, I bowed again and said:
"Your Majesty Queen Mary, Señora Beatrice and Señora Brianda
are not the emperor's subjects. The señoras arrived in Antwerp from
Portugal of their own free will and by their own efforts, intending
to conduct business in the city."

I have no idea how I had the audacity to claim you were Portuguese
subjects who were not under the emperor's rule.

The guards drew their swords and surrounded me. I was afraid they would arrest me, or worse, stab me.

The jaws of everyone present dropped in amazement, and they looked tensely at the queen.

The queen narrowed her eyes into sharp slits. Very fortunately for me, she signaled the guards to return to their spots with a slight wave of her hand.

The queen demanded that you and Brianda come to Antwerp and return the merchandise you took from the city without permission, paying your debts to the merchants.

"Your highness, before Señora Mendes left, with your majesty's permission, on her way to Aix-la-Chapelle..." I began, attempting to continue despite the calls of:

"Traitor!"

"Ran away from the city..."

"Violated the decree," and so on.

"...Señora Mendes paid all her debts to the city council and merchants, and left funds with her agents so that they can handle her commercial affairs."

"Don Juan Mickas, you claim the señoras acted properly. Why, then, do they not return and face the council to refute the accusations of heresy brought against them, as they were requested to do?" the queen raised her voice. Her eyes were blazing in anger. "Señora Beatrice Mendes has been charged with the severe accusation of consorting with the Ottoman enemy." After a short pause, the queen continued: "The accusations against Diogo Mendes were even more severe. The deceased was accused both of heresy and of secretly

practicing Judaism."

"Your majesty the queen, the Mendes sisters are faithful, dedicated Christians who donate many funds to the Catholic Church. Señora Beatrice Mendes has contributed significant funds to His Highness the Emperor to support his battle against the dissemination of the Protestant movement and Lutheran ideas.

"Your loyal servant standing here before your majesty, Don Juan Mickas, is willing to stand trial in place of my aunts, the ladies of the house of Mendes."

But the queen was not impressed by my willingness. Mary suppressed a tiny smile and said, "Young man, your readiness and desire to take the accusations upon yourself are very noble indeed. However, the señoras are requested to return immediately and answer the accusations of heresy."

I thought a bit of flattery might help. I bowed my head and said, "Your majesty, Queen Mary, it is a well-known fact that your highness rules with much wisdom, and has led the kingdom to many accomplishments. Commerce is thriving, the economy is flourishing, and many noblemen, merchants and tycoons wish to settle and live under your majesty's patronage.

"The forty crates containing precious diamonds and gold coins seized by the monarchy in Antwerp, as well as the three chests confiscated in Germany, belong to the House of Mendes. A large part of their contents is intended for paying debts to merchants.

"I wish your highness to know that no businessman will consent to having his assets seized, and following the seizure of this property, I am afraid that merchants might leave the city."

At this point the queen lost her patience. She furrowed her brow and wagged her finger in front of my face. "Young man, take care. You have the audacity to tell the queen things that no one before you has ever dared say."

I apologized and continued. "I beg your majesty's pardon. The widowed sisters are not rich at all. In their wills, their husbands bequeathed only fifteen thousand gold coins to each of them, while the rest of the property belongs to their daughters. The girls are still young, and cannot stand trial."

The queen gestured her advisors to approach her and huddled with them. Finally she said: "The crown is willing to rescind the accusations of fleeing. But due to the harm caused to the city's merchants and the debts left behind by House of Mendes, the Queen demands that the sisters face the City Council of Brabant and answer the questions they are asked. In addition, they must pay a one-time fee of one hundred thousand gold ducats, to be conveyed to me immediately."

"Excuse me, honorable queen, the señora does not possess such a fortune," I apologized. "But as a gesture of goodwill, as a delegate of Señora Beatrice Mendes, I'm willing to offer a sum of thirty thousand gold ducats, a sum that is already beyond our means," I said. The queen insisted on a hundred thousand ducats and threatened to have the two of you arrested.

I was unwilling to concede. I apologized and said we did not have the ability to pay such a large sum.

I bowed even deeper. "Majesty, forgive us, but..."

The queen's eyebrows rose. "The crown sees the sum of a hundred thousand ducats as a low one for a family that has violated the queen's instructions and which consorts with the Ottoman enemy."

I explained that the House of Mendes's connections with the Ottomans were merely mercantile ones, and suggested that I would appeal directly to Emperor Charles the Fifth, with the hope that we would reach a satisfactory agreement. I thanked the queen for the valuable time she had dedicated to me, stepped back while still facing the queen, and departed. Behind me, I heard the attendees' cries of astonishment. Later, one of her ladies-in-waiting told me that genteel Mary was upset, and sipped a full goblet of wine.

Your cousin Juan

***

August 1546
Regensburg, Germany

Dear Aunt,

Per your recommendation, I sent a missive to the emperor and requested an urgent meeting. My good friend Prince Maximillian urged the emperor to accommodate my request.

The emperor saw me in a new, three-story citadel surrounded by towers with embrasures, the construction of which has just been completed. He must have spent a fortune on building it.

Every time I meet the emperor, I feel excited. His black piercing eyes, his narrow nose, the mustache and the short, black beard beginning to go gray, his furrowed brow, all grant him a demeanor of power and dignity, and I believe his courtiers' admiration for him is genuine, and does not stem from flattery.

I myself cannot believe I enjoyed such royal honors. I received a title of nobility! I kneeled down before the emperor and bowed my head.

My knees, resting on a red pillow, were trembling. The emperor laid his sword, embedded with jade and rubies, upon my head.

Carlos King of Spain—Charles the Fifth, Emperor of the Holy Roman Empire, bestows the esteemed title of knight upon Don Juan Mickas!

His personal secretary presented me with a scroll bearing this declaration along with the king's elaborate signature.

Prince Maximillian raised a goblet of red wine and congratulated me, "Welcome, my good friend and companion, Don Juan Mickas, to the ranks of nobility." The princes, noblemen and advisors present at the ceremony drank wine in silver goblets and cheered for me.

To my surprise, the emperor was open with me, and told me about the difficulties he is experiencing. On the one hand, the need to recruit funds for the war against the Turks he detests, headed by Sultan Suleiman, and on the other hand, his cooperation with Henry the Eighth, king of England, against the king of France.

The emperor described to me his numerous efforts to reach a truce between the Catholic and Protestant princes, in order to prevent a Protestant majority in the German royal council. "My friend, you are young, but it would behoove you to learn how to deal with your opponents." The emperor clenched his fist. "Always remember: an iron fist in a velvet glove," he said, gulping down a stein of dark beer in one sip.

I told the emperor about my conversation with Queen Mary, noting that the sum the queen was requesting was beyond our financial abilities. I asked the emperor to repeal the accusations against you, telling him I was willing to pay thirty thousand ducats, as I had promised the queen.

Aunt, I carried out your instructions, and as usual, you were right. It was a lucky thing you insisted that we do not concede. Happily, the agreement with the emperor was signed today.

The main points of the agreement:

All accusations against Brianda and yourself will be repealed, and you do not have to face the Council of Brabant.

The emperor and Queen Mary will together receive a grant of sixty thousand gold ducats before the end of August. The Mendes Bank will loan the emperor two hundred thousand gold ducats with no interest, for one year, to assist with the expenses of the war against the Ottomans and the Protestants. The kingdom's income will be a guarantee for the return of the loan.

The forty crates with the diamonds and gold coins seized from the palace in Antwerp, and the three crates seized in Germany, will be returned to us!

And most importantly, Queen Mary is not permitted to cancel or alter the agreement.

At the end of the conversation, King Charles briefly laid his sword against my shoulder and told me honestly that as the expenses of the war against the Ottomans were emptying the state treasury, he needed gold coins to fund his war against the heretics. And since, luckily for me, he liked me, although his sister Queen Mary would not approve of the agreement, the emperor would sign it.

"Remember, the Goddess of Luck is like a woman: the more you chase after her, the further away from you she gets."

The emperor burst out in laughter and the entire audience joined him.

He added his looping signature to the agreement and stamped the royal seal with his ring.

Aunt, the house is empty and lifeless without all of you. I miss Ana's carefree laughter and the conversations with you. Prince Maximillian asked after you both, and asked when I would see Ana again.

The merchants and the noblemen wonder when you'll return. There are rumors flying around town that you have fled, and that you're sailing to the land of the Ottoman enemy.

Your cousin,
Juan Mickas

***

I expressed my joy over the repeal of the accusations of heresy and the decisions to return the precious chests into my possession, along with my reaction to temporarily part from two hundred thousand ducats and a gift of sixty thousand ducats to Charles and Mary, by drowning all my emotions in a glass of wine.

Then I drank another glass in honor of the title of nobility bestowed upon Juan.

Living Without Fear

Brianda was putting us in danger. She refused to attend the Sunday mass at St. Mark's Basilica, and invited a father confessor to come to the palazzo.

"With our status and thanks to our legendary wealth, we can afford to establish, in addition to the church we've built, a private chapel in one of the rooms of Palazzo Gritti. That way, I won't have to make excuses why we don't come to mass," Brianda said. I accepted her reasoning, and to be honest, wondered why I myself had not thought of this.

I called in an architect specializing in building churches to design a lavish chapel in the palazzo. The architect ordered stained-glass windows, while Brianda purchased a small organ for the chapel, which La Chica liked to hear played.

Dozens of golden incense candles in gold candelabras illuminated depictions of the six days of creation in the stained-glass windows. The St. Mark Basilica Choir, and the basilica's organ player, Fra Manuelo, greeted the city's dignitaries—bishops, priests, merchants, ambassadors, writers and poets—who had been invited to the chapel's grand opening.

In the dining hall, formal tables had been set with gold dinnerware and silver platters overflowing with roasted chicken, meat, fish, fruit, cakes seasoned with ginger and cinnamon and fine wines. The noblewomen and the wealthy merchants gossiped about love, infidelity, and losses and victories in card games and duels.

As our guests imbibed the wine, their tongues grew looser. Around the table, complaints were aired about the Portuguese *conversos* who were immigrating to Venice en masse, taking over the city's commerce, pushing out the merchants who were long-time Venetian citizens, the pure Christians, growing wealthy at their expense, causing the prices of houses and stores to go up, while some of them were "practicing Jews," carrying out the Jewish customs

***

"I heard the pope was applying pressure on the Venetian senate to forbid the republic's subjects from maintaining connections with the Portuguese *conversos*," Juan told us after the guests dispersed. He had arrived with Bernardo especially for the grand opening of the chapel.

"But… we're Portuguese *conversos*, too. Do you think the Venetian merchants will be prohibited from dealing with the House of Mendes?" Bernardo asked.

"The Venetians are proud of being first and foremost Venetians, and only then Christians. They won't listen to the pope," Brianda said.

"Things change. We can't cling to the illusion that they won't hurt us. We have to be prepared for every calamity," I said.

"What do you mean?" Brianda asked.

"I want to live my life without fear. I dream of returning to our parents' faith and living openly as a Jew," I said quietly.

The room grew silent.

"Even back when we lived in Lisbon, Francisco and I were planning on moving to the land of the sultan. When we were living in Antwerp, Diogo also began preparations to move to Turkey. It's time to travel east," I said.

"East?! I'm happy in Venice. I have no intention of migrating again," Brianda said.

"We're not moving yet, but we must be ready for every eventuality," I said.

"Listen," Juan said. "I met with King Henri the Second of France and with Queen Catherine de'Medici in the Palace of Fontainebleau. The king is an impressive man with a grayish mustache and a goatee around his chin. His voice broke when he talked about his father, King Francois the First, who lost a battle to Charles the Fifth and was taken as a prisoner to Madrid along with his sons, seven-year-old Henri and his brother, for four years. He said the time has come to take revenge on the emperor, and reclaim France's conquered lands, and asked for a loan to fund his war upon Charles the Fifth."

"France still hasn't repaid the loan that Francois the First borrowed from Diogo," I said.

"In Paris, I met Diane de Poitiers, the king's beautiful mistress. She's older than him, and some say she's the one who rules the kingdom. Diane asked me to make sure that Mendes Bank approves the loan, and promised that in return, we'll receive trade benefits.

"I also met the Duke of Florence, Cosimo de'Medici and his wife, Eleonora de Toledo, and made friends with them. The duke agreed to my request and granted the Portuguese *conversos* freedom of action and commerce. We agreed that House of Mendes would expand its dealing in Florence."

"Juan, I'm proud of you. You've managed to forge connections with the French monarchy, which will help us to make loans with good interest rates, and increase our profits."

Juan smiled and thanked me.

I asked him to use his connections with Duke Cosimo de'Medici and leave for Florence to open a branch of Mendes Bank. I informed him that I was sending two of our senior agents to Constantinople to purchase a residential palace for me, as well as office buildings and warehouses, and forge relationships of commerce with the heads of the regime and the merchants.

Brianda listened to the conversation quietly, without making a sound. From that evening on, we were no longer troubled by questions on why we were not attending mass at church.

The Ghetto, 1546

Simone Scopio, a member of the guild of maritime insurers, looked at me curiously, leaned back in his seat, and opened a round snuffbox. The sweet scent of tobacco filled the lavish office.

"Señor Simone Scopio, I request a price quote for maritime insurance of ten chests of silk fabric transported from Venice to Ragusa, as well as fifty sacks of black pepper, cloves, ginger and cinnamon transported from India to Venice." I placed a list on his desk specifying the merchandise, the names of the ships, ports, and departure and docking dates.

Simone Scopio slid his glasses up his nose and surveyed the list.

"Señora Beatrice de Luna, if I may, I'll present a proper price estimate to the *señora* tomorrow."

"Señor, the estimate should reflect the significant scope of the trade carried out by my company, House of Mendes."

"I will certainly take that into consideration in my offer." Simone Scopio filled his pipe with tobacco, packing it in with his fingers.

"The members of the insurers' guild would consider it an honor if the *señora* would consent to take part in a team of arbitrators in a trial between two Jewish Portuguese merchants."

"Señor Scopio, before I arrived in Venice, I had never conducted business with Jews, and I'm not familiar with their customs."

"Señora de Luna, you requested a price quote from a Jew." Scopio drew the tobacco into his mouth, a smile igniting in his gray eyes.

"I've never taken part in arbitration."

"The *señora* is renowned for her wisdom and fairness."

"I'm not looking to make enemies."

"The *señora* is a businesswoman whose reputation has spread world-wide. Her verdict will be received with appreciation." Smoke rings were rising from the pipe.

Through the windows of his office, I saw my Venetian business manager, Marco de Mollino, signing confirmations of receipt for House of Mendes merchandise, which had just been unloaded from a ship arriving from India, for the custom clerks.

"Who are the members of the arbitration team?"

"Rabbi Joseph Raphael, the Levantine merchant Marcello Domini, and myself."

I felt a slight tickle in my throat. Spinning the necklace of the gold pendant I wore, I considered his offer. It made me curious to get to know Jews more closely, and experience arbitration. I decided to agree to his request.

Simone Scopio placed the pipe in a silver box. "Thank you, señora. The arbitration will take place tomorrow at my home."

"At your home?"

His gray eyes examined me. "The *señora* should have no fear. Many Christians visit the ghetto. My wife Fortuna would be happy to host the *señora* and her sister Señora Brianda as part of her literary salon, which will be held at the end of the discussion."

"Thank your wife for the invitation on my behalf."

"I'll wait for the *señoras* by the gates to the ghetto once they open."

Although my relationship with Brianda was chilly, I didn't want to be impolite and decline the invitation, and so I asked her to join me. After some hesitation, she finally agreed.

＊＊＊

The next morning, we wrapped our shoulders in wide silk shawls, I kissed the sapphire in my gold pendant, and we departed Palazzo Gritti. Our legs were shaking as we crossed the small bridge over the green water canal. Brianda slowed her steps, knitting her brows. "Maybe we should go back?"

The bells of St. Mark's Basilica rang loudly. The guards opened the heavy locks upon the closed gates, shifted the latch, and the iron gates groaned and opened wide.

Rays of sun peered through the wispy clouds, illuminating the sign beside the wall:

Ghetto Ebraico di Venezia—Jewish Ghetto of Venice.

The guard's eyes, red with fatigue, passed over us. I was afraid he would detain and interrogate us, but he and the other guards were busy conversing with a woman whose face was heavily painted.

People in yellow caps and others with a yellow badge on their clothes were hurrying out of the ghetto on their way to the printing presses and stores on the Rialto Bridge, in which they dealt in used clothing. Men wearing the traditional black, flat Venetian hats were entering the gates of the ghetto.

"*Buongiorno, señoras,*" Simone Scopio hurried toward us.

We strode on the black stone tiles in the narrow streets between the cramped houses, with *mezuzahs* affixed to their entrances. My eyes were drawn to one of the doors on which a bas-relief of a menorah, the traditional Jewish candelabrum, was carved.

Curious women and children gazed down at us from the narrow balconies and windows. Strands of pasta were hung to dry in the wind on a rope stretched upon the roofs of the houses.

In the middle of a small plaza between the houses, stood peddlers dealing used clothing. One of the stands offered candlesticks, goblets, lanterns and ancient gold and silver jewelry.

"*Señora, por favor,*" the elderly hands of the peddler, wearing a simple cloth dress, stroked a beautiful silver candlestick. "Please, señora, look at the ancient candelabra," her black eyes shone.

Her husband handed me the candlestick. "It possesses a rare beauty," he said.

"Señora, the candlestick is a bargain," the old woman said. "It belonged to a rich family in the old homeland of Hispania," she sighed, her eyes fixed upon me. She elbowed her husband's waist.

"Shlomo, look how much the lady resembles Hannah." She gestured in my direction.

"Which Hannah?" Her husband narrowed his eyes, turning to look at me.

The old woman left her spot behind the stall, approaching us.

"My friend, Doña Hannah Nasi," she said, her wrinkled hand coming to rest on my own hand.

Her words took my breath away. Could it be that the elderly peddler was a friend of my Grandmother Hannah, after whom I was named and whom I resembled?

"Was the lady acquainted with...?" A strange woman's elbow struck my waist, interrupting the conversation.

"Señora, a thousand pardons," the woman apologized, taking a pair of silver earrings from the stand. "Excuse me, how much are they?" she asked the peddler.

I placed the candlestick back on the stand and nodded with a frozen expression. "Thank you."

"Brianda, come on," I said.

"Why? I want to buy the bracelet." She showed me a gold bracelet.

I left the stand. I felt the old woman's eyes piercing the back of my neck, but did not turn around.

"Ladies and gentlemen, Lord of Forgiveness...[9] It is the month of Elul, and Rosh Hashanah, the Jewish New Year, is almost upon us!" A young book peddler was holding a crumbling volume.

Men wrapped in a tallit were exiting through the door of a small building upon which a sign stating "Synagogue" was affixed. Brianda stopped across from some women and servants bearing straw baskets, who were bustling in and out of a small store with a sign beside it declaring, "Kosher Butcher Shop."

Next to the *sottoportego*, the covered passageway, stood a building with a small red flag upon its roof. Christians and people of many nationalities were entering and exiting its doors, holding red bills.

"The bank is required to loan money to poor Christians at a low interest rate of five percent only, and hang the Jewish mark outside. The

---

9   *Adon Haselichot*, or Lord of Forgiveness, is a hymn traditionally sung on the days of the month of Elul and during the ten days of repentance in the month of Tishrei, beginning with the Jewish holiday of Rosh Hashanah and ending with the conclusion of Yom Kippur.

Red Bank is the largest. The Green and Yellow Banks are smaller, and are named after the color of their bills," Señor Simone Scopio explained.

At the center of a large public square, a group of old men were sitting on the lip of a well with a bas-relief of a lion, examining us curiously.

The Scopio family's home was a nine-story mansion whose windows looked out on the canal. The *portier*, a liveried doorman, bowed before us and opened a retractable iron door adorned with the symbol of the scorpion. We climbed up the winding stairs that led us straight into the sitting room.

"Please, meet Señora Fortuna, my wife," he introduced us to a round-faced, golden-haired woman, wearing a taffeta dress in earth tones with green beaded embroidery.

"Welcome, señoras!" Fortuna opened her arms wide and kissed our cheeks. "I've heard so much about you!"

"Señora Fortuna is beautiful," Brianda complimented her, and receiving a compliment relating to beauty from her was a rare honor indeed.

"My wife is both pretty and smart. She composes rhymed poems," Señor Scorpio boasted.

"There are more educated women in Venice: Jewish painters, poets and writers," Fortuna blushed.

"My wife's Christian friends try to persuade her to convert and move to the center of the city, but she refuses, of course."

"Madame Brianda, I've heard that the lady supports artists. I want to show you the paintings of Señora Rosa, the daughter of Sage Baruchin."

"Her friend converted to Christianity!" I heard a voice behind me. I turned around, but did not locate the speaker.

"Rabbi Joseph Raphael," Señor Scopio introduced me to the rabbi, who was holding a thick book in his hands.

"Señora de Luna, I've heard many fine things about the *señora*'s activity." His warm gaze won me over.

"Thank you, Rabbi Joseph Raphael."

"Merchant Marcello Domini is a member of the arbitration team," Simone Scopio introduced me to a man with intense features and a double chin.

"Come on, let's go into the library, Señor Avraham and Señor Moshe are waiting for us."

"Señor Avraham, please present the case to us," said Simone Scopio.

Avraham stated that he dealt in gems. He had insured a small chest containing thirty-eight pearls he had imported to Venice from Alexandria with Moshe the insurer. However, a shipwreck occurred opposite the coast of Cyprus, and a boat sent to collect the merchandise in the sunken vessel found the chest inside a sealed sack of black pepper. The chest was opened in the presence of witnesses and contained only twenty-five pearls. Avraham was demanding compensation for the thirteen lost pearls.

The next to testify was Moshe the insurer. He said he was opposed to paying compensation for the missing pearls, and claimed it was not even certain that there had been thirty-eight pearls in the chest.

I listened to their claims, and then consulted the rabbi and the other mediators and let them know of my decision.

"The insurer, Señor Moshe, will deposit seventy gold ducats, compensation for the lost pearls, in favor of the insured, Señor Avraham," I suggested, and my verdict was accepted by the other arbitrators.

After the discussion, I was invited to enter the lavish salon. A murmur passed among the people present and all eyes turned to me, including those of some of my Christian acquaintances.

"Dear guests, I'm happy to be hosting our friends as well as our distinguished visitors, Señora Beatrice and Señora Brianda de Luna, in our home."

Brianda flitted among the guests, charming everyone with her beauty and her manners.

"Meet the head of the Venetian printers, Señor Daniel Bromberg." Simone Scopio introduced me to a man with reddish hair.

"The *señora* is invited to my modern, sophisticated print shop, to see the new typeset letters." Daniel Bromberg opened a small notepad he extracted from his pocket.

"Señor, what kind of books does your honor print?" I asked, sensing eyes staring at me from behind. I turned around, but did not see anyone in particular listening in on the conversation.

"The Jewish community has asked me and my friend, printer Geronimo de Vargas from Ferrara, to print *siddurim* and *mahzorim*, prayer books for Rosh Hashanah and Yom Kippur. Eliyahu Bachur, a hardworking young man I employ, is proofreading the *siddur* these days. I'm hoping to publish it soon."

I produced my own notepad. "I'm free on Monday at eleven. If it's convenient for the *señor*, we can meet."

"I'd be happy to meet. I'll send my gondola to fetch the *señora*."

Simone Scopio introduced me to Rabbi Yitzhak Lucato, the community's rabbi, a Jew with a bent back and a kind face.

"Señora," he addressed me quietly. "We're collecting donations to establish another synagogue in the ghetto."

"The Ashkenazi and Sephardic congregations don't get along, and can't pray in the same synagogue," I heard someone comment behind me.

"Madam, the Sephardic and Levantine Portuguese Jews are merchants, while the Ashkenazis are moneylenders," Rabbi Lucato smiled.

"Rabbi Lucato, I donate to the Church," I replied sharply.

Maids in white aprons and lace kerchiefs on their heads roamed between the guests, holding silver platters with tiny cookies and glasses of wine and liqueur.

"Dear guests, please sit down, and with your permission, my wife will begin the evening with a poem she wrote."

Señora Fortuna stood in front of us, holding a notebook. "This is a short poem about the soul," she said, and began to read:

"A man trezads upon the earth,
A heavenly soul lights his path.
When his days are through and his light goes dark,
The Creator reclaims his soul's divine spark."

The guests applauded politely and then began to discuss the essence of the soul and its fate at the end of life.

"The soul should be free, and live without masks," said someone who was sitting several rows behind us.

"The soul wishes to fly like a butterfly, while the body stops it, like the ghetto we live in," said Señora Fortuna.

"Shush… mind what you say."

"Ladies and gentlemen, the soul is the thoughts within us, the desire that motivates us to create and take action. A man's soul is always free. No one but yourselves controls your soul," said Rabbi Lucato.

The guests responded with exclamations of agreement and wonderment.

"And what is the body?" the merchant Marcello Domini asked.

"The body is the vessel, the home in which the soul dwells…" Rabbi Lucato replied.

"The body is a vessel?" Brianda marveled.

"Yes. At the moment of our birth, the Creator of the world gave us the soul, which entered our body, as a gift, as a deposit."

"I don't understand what the rabbi means," Brianda whispered in my ear.

"Then who am I? Who is man?" Avraham asked.

Rabbi Lucato opened the bible he was holding. "Man is the soul. The Book of Genesis states, '*And the Lord God formed man of the dust of the ground, and breathed into his nostrils the breath of life.*' Just as a craftsman breathes air into matter and forges vessels of glass, so the Creator imbued a spark of His soul into humanity."

"What happens when a person dies?" asked printer Daniel Bomberg.

"When a person sheds the follies of the world, the body, which was the vessel in which the soul resided, returns to the soil from which it was formed. As the bible states, '*For dust thou art, and unto dust shall thou return,*' while the soul ascends to the heavens."

Señor Moshe the insurer clasped his hands together and shook his head in disbelief. "Rabbi, I can't accept that the soul lives on after death."

"Ecclesiastes says, '*Then shall the dust return to the earth as it was: and the spirit shall return unto God who gave it,*'" the rabbi quoted.

Brianda suppressed a tiny yawn with the palm of her hand. "I want to go," she said.

What is the soul? Where does it come from and where does it go? I wondered on my way home. *Does the soul really live on, rather than disappearing? If the soul is eternal, what is the meaning of my life in this world? And what are the implications of my deeds on my life in the next world?*

A sensation of fatigue and heaviness engulfed me. Would I be remembered after I was gone? I held on to the banister of the little bridge, gazing at the water, bifurcated by golden rays of light. Tiny droplets of water splashed from a stone thrown by a tot into the water. Perhaps I should do more for my persecuted brethren?

Winds of Hate Rising From the Abyss, 1547

It had been a year and a half since we arrived in Venice. The cold was gradually melting away, the rains decreased, a light breeze bore the scent of flowers, and a pleasant sensation of spring engulfed the city.

I looked up from the beautiful wood escritoire I had received as a present from the doge, "as a token of appreciation for Señora Beatrice de Luna's business endeavors on behalf of the Republic of Venice."

"Marco de Mollino, what's wrong?"

A pallid smile surfaced on my business manager's face. "Señora, the Great Council has decided to establish 'the Holy Office' in Venice."

Inquisition?! I suppressed the cry that was about to emerge from my throat. A black drop of ink leaked from my quill to the accounting ledger documenting the import and export of black pepper. I meticulously soaked up the drops of ink staining the page.

"Señora, the members of the Council believe they must take firm action against the Portuguese *conversos* who are heretics against the Catholic faith and live secretly as Jews."

The air in the room seemed to stand still; I heard my heart beating loudly. I kept running away from the Inquisition, but it was still breathing down my neck.

"The *señora* should have no fear. The rumor is that the doge's brother, who is a good man, will be appointed as head of the Holy Office," Marco de Mollino said quietly.

My fingers fluttered over my pendant. I knew that every word I uttered would have the weight of gold.

"Marco de Mollino, I want to expand the company's business to export paper and leather. I want you to prepare a bid proposal to be distributed to the guild members."

"Señora, tomorrow I'll look into the pricing of merchandise at the paper and leather manufacturers' guild. *Arrivederci*, señora, have a good day." He doffed his hat and went on his way.

I swallowed. "*Arrivederci*."

Venice was sinking! La Serenissima had succumbed to the pope's pressure. It was dangerous to stay here! I knew I had to advance my plans to travel east to Constantinople. I picked up a sheet of paper, and with a trembling hand, wrote down the most urgent tasks:

Summon Juan for an urgent meeting.

Collect from the king of France the hundred and fifty thousand ducats that King Francois the First had borrowed from Diogo for one year, and despite the many years that had passed since, had yet to repay.

Collect the debts of private merchants.

Write to the Duke of Ferrara again and ask for a certificate of passage and a permit to settle in the duchy.

The list was growing long. I placed my quill in the inkwell and walked over to my sister's room.

"Brianda," I sat down in the armchair by her side. "The Great Council of Venice has approved the establishment of an Inquisition in Venice."

"No one would dare harm us. We're rich," Brianda said, her face pale.

"The money won't protect us. We have to leave."

"You're willing to leave all this beauty?" Brianda pointed at the gondolas sailing in the quiet waters of the canal."

"Under La Serenissima's mask of beauty, in the midst of the course of our lives, winds of hate are rising from the abyss."

"Where will we go?" Her voice trembled.

"To Ferrara, a two-day sail up the Po River."

Brianda shrugged. "Don't pull the wool over my eyes. You want to immigrate to the Sultan's barbaric land."

"Brianda, believe me, the House of Mendes has been dealing in sugar and bolts of wool with the Duke of Ferrara from back in the days when we still lived in Antwerp."

"Why can't we stay in Venice? La Chica and I are happy here, and I have a wonderful circle of friends, male and female."

"Especially a certain Venetian male companion…" I hinted to Brianda that I had heard of her relationship with a Venetian nobleman.

"Stop that, he's just a friend. I want to live and die in Venice. I'm tired of roaming."

"Brianda, do you understand the meaning of the Inquisition? They'll be tracking our every move."

"And you want to live with the Muslims?" was her reply.

"When our parents were young, the Muslims controlled Spain, and they had a good life. Those who 'belong to the letter Yod' in Ferrara have a synagogue, community institutions and freedom to work in any form of employment they desire."

"I'm not a little girl. You won't decide on my behalf where I'm going to live."

"I want you and La Chica to come with me."

"No! I won't let you take my daughter!" she said, leaving the room angrily.

***

In the balmy heat of summer, the stone tiles were blazing, and steam was wafting up from the waters of the Grand Canal. The rumors of the establishment of the Inquisition shocked the Portuguese *conversos*, spurring them to seek ways to escape Venice. Undercover police officers and Venetian Guard soldiers filled the ports. They tracked the ships, hunted down those fleeing, and threw them in jail.

I set up a meeting with Juan to discuss the dire situation. During the meeting, the major-domo handed me a letter.

Città di Ancona

To Señora Beatrice de Luna,

I am happy to inform you that Pope Julius the Third has permitted the Portuguese conversos to live unmolested in the city of Ancona in the pope's domain.

Best regards,
Merchant Marcello Domini

I read the letter repeatedly, again and again. The unbelievable was taking place in front of our eyes! The pope was responding to the generous monetary grants he was receiving from the House of Mendes and from the merchants, granting the *conversos* the rights to settle and conduct commerce in his realm. We decided to lease three ships that would transport the refugees to Ancona, as well as to Ragusa and Thessaloniki, which were controlled by the sultan, and from there to Constantinople, the capital of the Ottoman Empire.

I instructed Juan to gradually and discreetly shut down House of Mendes's businesses in Lyon, Florence and Paris. I kept my businesses in Venice running as usual, in order not to raise suspicion among the city authorities that we were planning to leave.

Much to my disappointment, the certificate of passage that the Duke of Ferrara sent me appeared to have been lost, and Brianda firmly refused to consider moving to Ferrara. She appealed to the Court of Foreign Affairs and requested to challenge Diogo's will and receive the natural guardianship over her daughter's inheritance.

I met the members of the Council of Ten and the senators, trying to repeal the hearing summons, but was unsuccessful.

The two incidents, the disappearance of the certificate of passage to Ferrara and the fact that I had to stay put in order to attend the court hearing, broke my heart. I felt lost and lonely, and had no choice but to stay in Venice.

The Arrest, 1548

Some dates imprint themselves upon your memory and never let you go. Saturday, August 30, 1548, was such a date.

A loud knocking shook the walls of the palazzo. I exchanged frightened glances with Brianda, looking out through the curtains. A gondola bearing five monks wearing brown habits, with brown hoods covering their heads, as well as six soldiers from the Republic Guard, armed with swords, had stopped at the entrance of the palazzo.

My heart was beating wildly. *The Inquisition's interrogators*, I realized.

Brianda held on tightly to the windowsill. "What are they doing here?"

The soldiers shoved the gatekeeper, burst into the palace and galloped up the staircase. They pushed aside major-domo Luciano de Costa and Thomas, who entered the study in fright. The Guard's soldiers raised their swords, surrounding me.

My body trembled in terror. I felt the Inquisition's heavy clutches gripping my throat.

"Ahh… Ahh… Excuse me, I request an explanation," I finally managed to say.

"Señora Beatrice de Luna Mendes is requested to accompany us," an elderly monk addressed me in a sepulchral voice. His white hair was visible under the hood on his head.

"Have you come to arrest us?"

The old man's shriveled face scowled. "My name is Pedro Niño, and I am a *familiar*, a civil collaborator of the Holy Office. I request that the *señora* speak only when she is granted permission to do so," he commanded in a chilling voice.

The *familiar* produced a parchment scroll, broke La Serenissima's orange seal with the emblem of the winged lion, unfurled the scroll and began to read its contents out loud:

August 30, 1548
Republic of Venice
The Court of Foreign Affairs
Summons to an Interrogation

In accordance with the order of the Court of Inquisition Investigations, and following information provided to us, Señora Beatrice de Luna Mendes is summoned to an interrogation at the court.

The Government of the Republic of Venice declares that until the accusations become clear, the property of the accused Beatrice de Luna Mendes shall be placed under the guardianship of the republic.

The Republic of Venice

I had been betrayed.

Had one of my acquaintances slipped a note into the maw of the winged lion, informing on me? The weeping began to climb up my stomach and into my throat. I thought my body was about to fall to pieces, but I did not have time to break down. I talked to myself: Gracia, stay strong, don't let them see you fall apart. You are strong, and will find your way out. Everyone else is leaning on you.

Greedy villains. I would not let them destroy my business and take over my fortune and my property. I had to save my family! Without anyone noticing, I slipped the key to the locked room into the hand of my major-domo.

"Make the chest disappear and let Juan and my business manager and partner de Mollino know that I've been arrested," I mouthed soundlessly.

Luciano de Costa nodded and snuck away from the soldiers of the Guard. I trusted him to conceal the precious chest containing the gold coins I saved for an emergency, and to convey the message.

After a long interval, I heard the whistle of the gondolier.

"What are you doing? Leave the *señora* alone!" I saw Juan's silhouette in the doorway, but the guards unsheathed their bayonets and pushed him back.

The whimpering cries of the serving girls interrupted the silence. They looked at the Republic Guard soldiers, stunned, as the soldiers began to place valuables in crates.

Estella came in with a coat and draped it over my shoulders.

"I'll take care of the girls!" Brianda called out.

"Mama, Mama…" I heard the terror in Ana's voice as she looked at me, pale and frightened, holding on to La Chica's hand while the younger girl burst out in tears.

"Go back to your rooms immediately!" I called out, but it was too late. One of the soldiers grabbed hold of their arms and dragged them out of the room.

My body was trembling. I tried to get a hold of myself so they would not see the shivers wracking through me, but I doubt if I managed to conceal them. Worry was gnawing at me. What would happen to my only child, my Ana?

Who had informed on me? Who had turned me in?

Follow the money, Francisco's voice echoed in my head.

"Señora, you are under arrest. You may not talk to anyone. Please, come with us."

Familiar Pedro Niño cleared his throat. "The *señora* is accused and subject to interrogation, but based on my acquaintance with the methods of interrogations and the torture that accompanies it, I suggest that the accused confess her sin, and thus the *señora* can avoid the difficult interrogation."

Under Arrest in Palazzo Ducale

I tried to shake off the heavy hands of the soldiers of the Guard, roughly grasping my arm, to no avail. With frozen expressions, they shoved me into a black gondola bearing the sign of the 'weave and weft.' The windows were covered with black curtains. The only sound was the oar striking the water.

Tears rolled down my cheeks as I silently mouthed the prayer I had learned from my grandmother. "My Lord, who heard Daniel in the lion's den, hear my prayer and please save me from incarceration."

The gondola stopped at the entrance to Palazzo Ducale, the Inquisition building, which had assumed this role in the city only six months before. I disembarked from the gondola slowly. A large crowd of people gathered around me. Their gazes of amazement surrounded me.

"*La Señora* Beatrice de Luna!"

"The rich *señora* has been arrested!"

"That's Doña Beatrice Mendes!"

"Unbelievable!"

The whispers echoed around me.

I held on to the hem of my dress to keep it from getting dirty as I was led through a side entrance of the palazzo. The guards were holding torches burning with red and yellow flames, which illuminated the darkness of the moist, drab, twisting corridors. A gray, furry rat passed just a breath away from me, and I reared back. A heavy wooden door opened.

"Go in!" the guard commanded me.

"The *señora* should be thankful she was not tossed into one of the cells under the Grand Canal. It's dark there day and night, and the rats and mice and the murmur of the waves are the prisoners' only friends," the *familiar* Pedro Niño whispered in my ear, closing the door behind me.

***

The First Day

I walked into a small room whose windows had been sealed. A small opening covered with iron mesh let in a thin ray of light, which illuminated a table, a narrow bed, a stone bench and a wall bearing drops of dried blood and signs of carving. A musty smell filled the air, and the spirits of the wretches who had been locked inside hovered in the room. I approached the wall and tried to read the letters that had been erased. I recognized the word "Esther." That poor soul must have meant to appeal to our Queen Esther in his or her prayers.

I sat down on the cold bench, trying to suppress my trembling and choke down the weeping climbing up my throat. I wiped away the tears. I did not want to give them the pleasure of watching me break down during my darkest hour.

Through the window, I saw a star shining in the distant sky. I believed it was the angel the Lord had sent to illuminate my path and watch over me.

I heard the heavy footfalls of the inquisitors, the shuffling of prisoners' feet and the shrieks of pain of the poor men and wretched women tortured by the Inquisition's interrogators in the musty cellars under the Grand Canal.

Through the terrible screams, I managed to hear the words "secret Jew," "Sabbath," "prayer," "Moses," and "Martin Luther." Apparently, the Inquisition was also persecuting those who believed in Luther, who had opposed the indulgences, or writs of pardon, offered by the Catholic Church and demanded to burn the holy Talmud books.

The smell of the slices of pork roasted in fat made my stomach turn. I refused to eat the meat or the tasteless vegetable soup. I drank water and ate a little dried fruit, constantly praying to God to save my soul.

At night, before falling asleep on the cot with its thin straw pallet that retained the scents of the hundreds of prisoners who had slept on it before me, covered by a thin blanket, I was overwhelmed by a barrage of thoughts. I imagined a storm taking place in the skies of Venice, with kings, ministers, ambassadors and delegates from other lands, the pope, friends and debtors all exchanging urgent letters and discussing my arrest.

Who turned me in? The thought gnawed at me again.

Follow the money, the voice repeated.

I woke up when the first rays of light filtered in through the mesh window. A brown chameleon crawled in under the door, rearing up, its round eyes fixing upon me.

Good morning, Señora Gracia, you should get used to your lovely new abode as soon as possible… it seemed to be telling me. I held onto my head with both hands, hoping I had not gone mad. *Lord of the Universe, please help me, how low have I sunk that a chameleon is talking to me?* The chameleon crawled toward me and jumped on the bench. It assumed the color of stone.

Stay, I silently asked it, but it leaped and disappeared under the bed.

I was apprehensive about my monthly cycle. I always had maids and attendants, but here, I was alone by myself. What would happen? How would I manage? As it turned out, my body was smart. It was considerate of me and slowed down its activity. Oddly, on one hand I was happy, but also upset, afraid my femininity was escaping me.

The door opened. A *familiar*, his face covered with a brown hood, stood with his back obstructing the peephole in the door. I clung to the opposite wall, my legs shaking and fear clogging my throat. What was he planning to do to me?

The *familiar* looked at me, then quickly extracted a bundle wrapped in a pillowcase from under his cloak and waited. I undid the clasp of the gold bracelet on my wrist and dropped it on the bed. The *familiar*'s black pupils widened. He placed the bundle on the bed, swiftly collected the bracelet and exited.

I unwrapped the bundle and was engulfed with the aroma of home. I took out a soft wool blanket and placed it against my cheek, trying to breathe in its scent and preserve it. A blue jar with macaroni and pecorino cheese also awaited me in the bundle. Finally, comfort food from home.

It was important to me to display that I was in full control and was managing the House of Mendes from my prison cell, as well. French merchants who had dealings with the company owed me significant sums of money. I was afraid that the merchants would take advantage of my circumstances and would not repay their debts.

I leaned against the door, obstructing the window. Raising the edge of my outer dress, I undid part of the hem of the slip. Each of my slips had a double hem containing emergency gold coins, which I never used. I extracted a gold coin wrapped in paper. Tearing a small rip in the mattress, I searched through the straw and found a slightly thicker stalk. I dipped it in the milk that remained in the cup I had received that morning, and wrote down three letters on the paper that had surrounded the gold coin. I hoped they would place the paper above a candle flame and read my letters.

Ana, my daughter,

Don't worry. I'm fine. I'll be out soon.

Love you,
Mama

✳✳✳

Marco de Mollino,

The ship Albatross will reach the Port of Venice tomorrow from India, with a cargo of black pepper, ginger and precious spices. It's important that you direct it to the Port of Ancona.

Beatrice de Luna

✳✳✳

Juan,

Please urgently convey my instructions to Christopher Manuel, my representative in Lyon:

"Señora Beatrice de Luna hereby authorizes Christopher Manuel to collect her debts from the French wool merchants as soon as possible."

Beatrice de Luna Mendes

***

When the *familiar* entered to empty the chamber pot under the bed, I snuck the gold coin wrapped in paper into his hand.

"Please pass this on to my major-domo, Luciano de Costa."

***

The Second Day

On the morning of the second day, the chameleon climbed the wall and stood next to the window, its eyes briefly alighting upon me.

"Hey, chameleon, I envy you," I found myself talking out loud to the creature whose body had assumed a black-brown color, like the hue of the iron mesh. The chameleon's eyes opened wide.

"You're a free little creature, while I, what am I? All the gold coins, the silver, the diamonds, the jewels and the property I've accumulated can't bring about my release. Others' greed to attain my fortune is the reason for my own misfortune."

The chameleon seemed to be twisting its mouth in a bitter smile. A second later, it disappeared behind the iron mesh, escaping to the street.

My stomach hurt. I did not even taste the slice of meat served for lunch. I sipped a little of the tepid minestrone soup and tore apart a slice of bread to dip in it. To my surprise, a note peeked out from the loaf of bread.

Dear Aunt,

I'm doing all I can to bring about your release. I approached Moshe Hamon, Sultan Suleiman's physician, asking that the sultan take you under his patronage. Bacadelli, the pope's legate, has informed the Council of Ten that "the pope is appalled by the possibility that the fortune accumulated in the Kingdoms of Christendom shall pass on to the Turkish infidels." Our agents are using their connections to ensure your release.

Juan

✻✻✻

The Third Day

The taps of a cane against the stone floor, accompanied by tentative steps as well as the clumsy footfalls of the *familiar*, woke me from my sleep and raised a dim fear within me. They were coming to take me to the torture chambers. I had heard so many horror stories about the torture: people were hung naked from a wheel and spun and then.... The key turned in the lock. My heart was beating wildly. I leaped from the bed, adjusting my dress.

The door opened. A mustachioed, portly *familiar* stood at the entrance to my cell. "The accused has a visitor, Doctor Philippe de Monteleto, the physician to the Queen of France, Catherine de'Medici. He has received permission to conduct a doctor's visit," he announced officiously.

The *familiar* then produced a round pocket watch from his trousers and sprang the lid open. "Doctor, you have half an hour." The wooden door closed.

To my surprise, leaning on his cane, the hem of his striped cloak riding high on his back, my friend Amatus Lusitanus entered the room.

"Doctor Lusitanus… I thought your brother Philippe…" I was so happy to see a dear, familiar visage.

The doctor's face turned pale. "Ssshhh…" He removed his hat and pointed fearfully at the walls, implying they might have ears. "I had to come in using my brother's identity. In Ferrara, I returned to our ancient faith. I am a Jew…" he whispered.

I approached him, lowering my voice. "I wish I could make my dream come true as well. To be as brave as you…"

"The news has reached the Venetian authorities," he whispered.

"You put yourself in danger for me… You…"

Amatus stroked my face. "Darling, I've been worried about you and have missed you." He held me close to his heart.

I rested my head in his lap. "Amatus, I've missed you…" I said, tears forming in my eyes. His large, warm palm caressed my cheek softly. If there was love between us, why had my beloved wandered far from me, and I had not plucked this love?

Amatus held my hand.

"I've changed, Amatus. My hair is scattered with gray," I said.

"Beatricci, the white strands in your hair endow you with dignity."

Amatus had never seen me cry, but now, I could not hold back the tears.

"I'm so sorry." He produced a white handkerchief from his pocket, tenderly wiping the teardrops away and kissing my cheek.

"My friend, it's not your fault." I snuggled into him. "Please, sit down." I pointed at the stone bench.

He rested his cane beside the stone bench and sat down beside me. Taking both my hands, he brought them to his warm lips and kissed them.

"Have you seen my Ana? I'm very worried about her."

"Darling, I was afraid to go to Palazzo Gritti. The Inquisition is sniffing around it. I met Juan briefly at the port. He let me know that Ana was fine, and that she and La Chica are praying for your swift release."

"Did Juan say anything about Brianda? How is she doing? It's fortunate that she wasn't arrested along with me. My sister is a delicate, sensitive woman."

"Juan is taking care of the girls and of your sister, and moving heaven and earth to bring about your release. He won't leave Venice until he sees his aunt set free.

"Venice is abuzz. No one believed the authorities would dare arrest 'the richest woman in the world.' The city's dignitaries, its nobility and merchants are all intervening on your behalf. There are rumors going around that a Turkish warship is about to depart from Constantinople to Venice. The Republic Guard is patrolling the port, and fear is evident on the streets," Amatus told me.

"The thought that I've been arrested is gnawing at me. As the days go by, the fear grabs hold of me and paralyzes me. My body is becoming lifeless." In my loneliness, I allowed myself to share my deepest fears with Amatus.

"My dear, have your stomachaches stopped?" he asked tenderly.

"Unfortunately they haven't. And my eyes hurt, too."

"Let me see your eyes," Amatus requested, concern evident in his voice. "Darling, the pain is a result of the immense mental tension you're experiencing. You mustn't strain your eyes and read by candlelight." Amatus pointed at a volume of the New Testament that the interrogator had left next to my bed. I opened it every night, so that they would see that I was reading it.

Amatus took a small vial out of his bag. "I brought you a new pain medicine," he said, drizzling a few drops into the water cup on the shelf. The sweet scent of roses spread through the room. "Infuse seven drops into a glass of water and drink it three times a day. It will help."

"Thank you," I said, and drank the water like a parched man in the desert. "Have you met Duke Ercole de Este? Have you talked to him?"

"The Duke of Ferrara is making diplomatic efforts to assist you. He promised me he would issue a certificate of transit to the duchy for you."

"When?"

Cries and weeping heard above us interrupted him. The tormented prisoners of the Inquisition passing through the Ponte dei Sospiri, the Bridge of Sighs linking the doge's palace and the prison, pierced through the stone walls.

"Beatricci, your acquaintances and many you have helped and saved are praying for your release. You'll be out of here soon," he consoled me.

"Would you like to pray with me?" I asked hesitantly. With our backs to the door, we knelt next to the bed. "Lord, answer our prayer as You answered the prayer of Queen Esther," we whispered. A key turned in the lock, and the door opened. "Señor Philippe de Monteleto, the meeting is over!"

Amatus rose, sneaking a gold coin into the guard's hand.

"Five minutes," the guard said, departing.

"My Beatricci, I'm waiting for you," he whispered in my ear.

I wrapped my arms around his neck and inhaled his scent. "You're dear to me," I whispered.

"Please, don't cry, and take care of yourself." A tear appeared in his eye.

A jangle of keys. The iron door opened.

"Doctor Philippe de Monteleto, this visit is over, please get out," the guard commanded.

Amatus quickly limped out of the cell. The rapping of his cane echoed down the corridor.

Love is light as a feather, here one moment and gone the next. I wet the pillow with my tears.

The Trial

The Fourth Day

I was carving a notch in the wall to mark my fourth day under arrest when the heavy door opened. A *familiar* accompanied by two armed soldiers from the Republic Guard stood at the entrance to my cell, his hands on his hips.

"The accused, Señora Beatrice de Luna Mendes, is being summoned to her trial," the familiar declared with frightening officiousness.

He led me wordlessly down the long, dark corridors to the courtroom. Guards armed with bayonets opened the large wooden doors. I entered a massive hall with an arced ceiling and climbed five steps to a raised platform. On this stage was a table covered with a red tablecloth, with an open notebook and an inkwell lying upon it. Next to it, on a tall chair, sat the head inquisitor. His face was flat and elongated, his bulbous nose and cold eyes resembling those of the doge's greyhound. The inquisitor was wearing a red cloak and a red hat. He was flanked on both sides by three bishops in black cloaks and hoods, sitting as erect as wooden poles. A giant painting of souls condemned to hellfire hung on the wall behind the interrogators.

A monk dressed in a brown cloak and hood stood tautly with his fingers entwined beside a pole from which a rope hung down. At the end of the rope was a heavy weight. On the wall beside him hung a large wheel with a wooden handle at its centers, pliers and iron tongs.

My legs were shaking, barely carrying me. *They're about to torture me…* I closed my eyes.

Stay strong, I repeatedly told myself. Through the fog enveloping my heart, I heard the inquisitor's barks.

I stood by the accused's stand, placed my hand on the Gospels and swore to tell the truth.

A bald priest, wearing a short black cape, leaned over the table and swiftly moved his quill over the thick journal to note down everything that was said in the trial.

"On the fifteenth of the month of September, the year 1548, in Venice, during the first seat of the Office of the Holy Inquisition in the Court of Foreign Affairs, in the presence of Inquisitor Giovanni Nunez de Cruz, the accused Señora Beatrice de Luna Mendes, widow of Francisco Mendes, was brought before us, and swore upon the Holy Gospels, on which she placed her hand, and was required to tell the truth, which she has promised to do."

The inquisitor fixed his scowling eyes upon me, his nostrils quivering as he barked out, "The accused is asked whether she wishes to confess her sins."

I felt thin, sharp needles piercing my heart, which had grown petrified within me. "I have no sins to confess. Forgive me, I am a Portuguese subject, and the court has no authority to investigate me," I heard myself replying in a clear, legible voice. I had thought that perhaps that way, I might soothe that short-tempered man.

"The *señora* has received a permit to settle in Venice. Does the accused recite Jewish prayers?"

"I was born in Portugal to a Catholic family, and I am a faithful Catholic, and familiar only with Christian prayers."

"Has the accused lit candles on the eve of the Sabbath?"

"No, your honor."

"Does the accused wear a clean white blouse in honor of the Sabbath?"

"I wear my regular clothes, in accordance with my station," I replied.

The vein in the inquisitor's neck swelled and trembled. "The accused was not asked about her station. The accused will respond only to the questions asked of her.

"Has the accused mortified herself with fasting on Yom Kippur, celebrated Passover and participated in the fast of Esther?"

"No, sir." I shook my head.

"Has the accused refrained from eating pork, blood and fish without scales, as is the custom of the Jews?"

"No, your honor."

"Does the accused pray before she goes to sleep?"

"Yes, your honor." I entwined my fingers forcefully under the witness stand.

"Does the accused believe in the Holy Trinity and in Christ our savior?"

"Yes, your honor." I entwined my fingers even harder.

"The court advises the accused, with much compassion, to consent to confess her sins and state the entire truth in regard to them, reminding her that she has sworn to tell the truth, and informing the accused that the court has heard testimony that she has abandoned the holy Catholic faith and is practicing the rules of Moses, and the rituals and faith of the Jews. Therefore, the court warns the accused to open the eyes of her soul to our Lord, and attempt to find balm by offering a true, complete confession of her crimes, revealing all her sins against our holy Catholic faith, as well as the names of the people with whom she has forged connections, and to avoid perjury in regard to herself and to others. She must do all this to clear her conscience, to save her soul and to enjoy the mercy this court habitually bestows upon true, worthy confessors," the inquisitor said.

"The court calls upon *familiar* Gabriel Battista, the jailer in charge of the accused, to testify."

So that was his name. *He must have thought it was beneath him to introduce himself to me by name, or perhaps that was their method to allow us to wander around in darkness,* I thought.

After he had been sworn in, the *familiar* began to testify that I had been served slices of pork roasted in fat, and that I had refused to eat them, claiming that my stomach hurt and asking to eat fish.

The *familiar* recounted that when he brought me fish with no scales, I once again refused to eat, claiming that I had a stomachache.

He continued his tale, stating that he had tried to talk to me and convince me to confess to being secretly Jewish, and that I had refused, and told him that I was a faithful Christian.

The interrogator thanked the *familiar*, who left the courthouse, and fixed his threatening hound eyes upon me.

"Has the accused asked her cousin Don Juan Mendes to close the branch of the Mendes Bank in Lyon, and make preparations for relocating to the Turkish state, Venice's enemy?" he asked furiously.

I looked directly at the interrogator. "Your honor, I wish to know who has testified against me."

"Doña Beatrice de Luna Mendes is the accused in the Court of Foreign Affairs, and you do not have permission to ask questions. Please answer the question."

A pain pierced my stomach. I pictured the faces of the people who might have known the secret, wondering which of them had betrayed me and informed on me.

"I'm sorry, your honor, could you please repeat the question?"

The inquisitor's eyes narrowed into two furious slits. "The accused is asked to focus," he said. "Did the accused make preparations to leave Venice and move to the enemy country of Turkey?"

"No, your honor, my business is in Venice."

"Has the accused moved funds out of Venice and violated the laws of La Serenissima?"

"No, your honor."

"Are House of Mendes ships trading with the Balkan states passing information to the sultan, undermining the security of La Serenissima?" the inquisitor barked out.

"Your honor… never."

"Did the accused order thirty copies of *siddur* prayer books in Hebrew, translated into Portuguese, from the printer Daniel Bomberg?"

Dryness crept up my throat. "No, your honor."

"Did the accused donate funds to the building of a Sephardic and Portuguese synagogue, as she promised Rabbi Lucato she would do?"

I had been right; someone had been tracking me during my visit to the Scopio family.

"The accused is asked to answer the question."

"No, your honor. My donations to St. Mark's Basilica and other churches are common knowledge," I replied.

"Does the accused wish to convert to the religion of Moses and live as a Jew?"

I entwined my fingers as hard as I could. "No, your honor." I gritted the words out like gravel.

The inquisitor rose from his seat, tossed his cape with a dandified gesture and barked out submissively. "The court wishes to call Madame Brianda de Luna Mendes, widow of the esteemed merchant Señor Diogo Mendes, to testify."

A murmur passed through the courtroom. *What is Brianda doing here?* The words struck me and I grew dizzy. *She must be coming to testify on my behalf...* I thought.

Brianda sauntered into the courtroom in high-heeled shoes and a green dress with a red velvet sash knotted under her chest. A pair of emerald earrings swayed at her earlobes. She looked fragile, younger than her twenty-seven years. It did not appear as if she had previously been under arrest.

Why isn't she looking at me? I wondered as she passed by me and came to a stop by the witness stand. *Perhaps she's nervous?*

The inquisitor's smile exposed his yellow teeth. "Due to the circumstances of this case and its importance, the Court of the Inquisition is diverting from its habit of maintaining confidentiality in regard to the names of the witnesses, and asks witness Madame Brianda Mendes to swear upon the Gospels to tell the truth and nothing but the truth."

The courtroom seemed to spin around me. I grabbed my head. *No, this is impossible. My sister wouldn't testify against me; she would never do that!*

Brianda removed her black gloves and placed them on the stand.

"I, Brianda Mendes, widow of Diogo Mendes, swear to say nothing but the truth," she whispered.

"The witness is asked to repeat the testimony she presented to the court."

Brianda ignored me, fixing her eyes upon the priest who meticulously wrote down every word. *My sister, what are you doing?!* I wanted to cry out.

"I, Brianda Mendes, as a devout Catholic, body and soul, see it as my duty to inform the court that my sister...' Brianda paused briefly, coughing. The investigator handed her a glass of water. She took a few sips, then continued: "My sister Beatrice de Luna has been living as a Jew in secret."

I felt the air evaporating from my body, which was gradually shrinking.

"To the best of my knowledge," Brianda went on, "Beatrice is planning to move to Turkey, an enemy of the Republic, and return to Judaism openly. She has begun packing her valuables and sent emissaries to purchase a house and warehouses for her in Turkey. Your honor, my daughter and I wish to stay in Venice, where we can continue living as good Christians."

The rustle of the quill pen with which the priest was inscribing Brianda's testimony for the protocol was the only sound heard in the courtroom.

The interrogator examined Brianda affectionately. "Madame Brianda, your daughter will soon turn fifteen, and will be entitled to receive her inheritance."

"My daughter, Beatrice Mendes, has many suitors. I want to marry her to a Venetian nobleman. We wish to stay in Venice as good Christians, but my sister, whose permission I have to ask for every expense, wants to flee Venice with all her property and with my little daughter's inheritance, and, in her immense cruelty, would leave us destitute."

"What are you requesting, señora?"

"I want the Court of Foreign Affairs to declare me as the legal guardian and financial manager of my daughter's inheritance. I also request to receive all the funds I am owed as part of my daughter's inheritance, which are half of the property and fortune of the House of Mendes. All this in order to ensure that my daughter and I can live as devout Catholics."

My cold body became meaningless. My sister Brianda, my own flesh and blood, had informed on me. I wanted to sit down, but could not afford to reveal my weakness. I held up my weightless body with the force of my will, struggling not to fall onto the stone floor.

I continued to stand, frozen, at the accused stand, tracking the bony fingers of the inquisitor, which were drumming on the table. The pain in my head sharpened. A misty veil covered my eyes. *Traitor!* I choked the scream that wanted to burst out of me.

"The court advises the accused, with much compassion, to admit to her sins and find balm in confessing her offenses and saving her soul." The hound eyes looked at me indulgently. "Does the accused have anything to add?" the interrogator addressed me.

Who would heal my broken heart? My beloved sister, for whom I had been like a mother since she was sixteen years old, had betrayed me, revealing the secret of our faith that we had sworn to conceal in our hearts forever. Did she not understand that those who betray their families betray themselves?

"I am faithful to the Church. My sister Brianda has concocted a despicable plot against me in order to take over her daughter's inheritance. My brother-in-law Diogo was familiar with his wife's spendthrift nature and luxurious, extravagant lifestyle, and out of concern for his daughter's future and the integrity of his assets, assigned me with guardianship over her inheritance until she married. Jealousy gnaws at her to an extent that has made her slander me with lies."

"The court declares a day-long break in the proceedings. The accused shall be returned to her cell," the inquisitor declared.

I tried to stop the uncontrollable tremor in my legs. Two heavyset *familiars* flanked me on both sides and, with ponderous steps, led me back to that terrible room.

I lay down on the bed, raised the blanket in order to cover myself, and saw a tiny, rolled-up note. Which one of the guards had snuck it in? I turned toward the wall, so that the eyes of the *familiar*, who peered in every hour through the small window in the iron door, would not see me.

The letter was written in French and encoded as well. The first letter had been switched with the last, the second with the next-to-last, and so on.

Aunt,

Sultan Suleiman the Magnificent had sent a missive to the doge and demanded that his Portuguese subject, Señora Beatrice de Luna Mendes, be handed over to him.

Juan

I felt encouraged. Juan was employing our entire network of international connections. I put the note in my mouth, chewed it and fell asleep.

***

The Fifth Day

Whimpers and choked cries coming from the corridor shocked me from my sleep.

"I'm Catholic! I'm not Jewish!" The voice sounded familiar to me. "Leave me alone! I'm a loyal Christian. Return me to my daughter! Bring me back home!"

The thuds of the guards' rough boots, approaching my cell, frightened me. I heard the jangle of keys. The door opened, and the torch's flame illuminated Brianda's jaundiced face.

My eyes gaped open in amazement, and the shock made me unable to speak. The guards brought another bed covered with a thin blanket into the cell, and placed a plate containing slices of bacon and vegetables on the table.

"From now on, you have a roommate," they said, slamming the door behind them.

You Cannot Sew a Broken Heart

I stood motionless under the window. We did not exchange a word. The silence was oppressive. A slender ray of sunshine tinged the cell yellow, stretching an invisible rope between us.

"My sister, someone turned me in for being a secret Jew," Brianda murmured as she sat on the end of her bed, crying.

"I'm not your sister." I turned my head away from her.

Brianda extracted an embroidered handkerchief and wiped away the tears. "Beatricci, I'm sorry."

"People are responsible for the words that come out of their mouths, and are masters of their own fate," I said.

"Please, for Mama and Papa's sake, can you ever forgive me?"

There is a moment in which life changes. A sister becomes a stranger, love becomes animosity.

"You cannot sew a broken heart," I replied.

∗∗∗

The Sixth Day

An autumn wind was moaning, droplets of water entering through the window. The jangle of keys disrupted the deathly silence that had reigned in the room for two whole days since she first entered it.

The *familiar* pushed open the door and placed the burning torch in a stand on the wall. The yellow flames flickered, illuminating his rigid face.

Perhaps I'm being released today? I thought hopefully.

The *familiar* looked directly at us, the nostrils of his fleshy nose quivering as his fingers unfurled a short missive.

The court has decreed that Señoritas Ana and Beatrice La Chica should be removed from the destructive influence of their mothers, Beatrice and Brianda de Luna Mendes, both accused of heresy.

Based on the demand of the head inquisitor and with the consent of the pope, out of a desire to educate Señoritas Ana and Beatrice La Chica in a Christian environment, the girls will be taken to continue their education in a convent.

"No! Please, I want my La Chica!" Brianda cried.

I was appalled. "My Ana!" An exclamation of pain burst out from the bottom of my heart.

The *familiar* dropped the missive on the bed, picked up the torch and left the cell, locking the door with a thud.

The rain increased, along with the wailing of the wind. Lightning flashed, illuminating Brianda, who had collapsed on the bed, covering her eyes with both hands. I grabbed hold of her hands and pulled them off her eyes.

"Look what you've done!" I said with suppressed rage. "Where have you brought us?"

"I… I didn't know that… I'm sorry…" Her crying increased.

I grabbed hold of her shoulders and shook them. "Because of you, we'll lose Ana and La Chica! Now they'll hand them over to the nuns, do you understand?! How did you dare turn me in?!"

"I want my daughter, get me out of here!" Brianda beat her clenched fists against the wall. "La Chica, my baby, how will you get along in a convent?" Brianda cried.

"Cry! Maybe the tears will cleanse your sins and the disaster you've inflicted on us. You only think of yourself. The constant pursuit of money has blinded your eyes."

"You left me no choice… You deprived me of my natural right to be my daughter's gua… guardian." Her face reflected pain and bitter resentment.

"How impudent! How dare you accuse me?!"

"I didn't think they'd be abducted to a convent… I was wrong. What are we going to do?"

Lord, please help me, on behalf of my forefathers and on behalf of the secret Jews I helped. Please, save my daughter and my niece, I requested in my heart.

"Forgive me," Brianda's lips murmured.

The room was spinning around me. My body was overcome with weakness. I leaned against the wall and slowly slid down, sitting down, utterly depleted, on the cold stone floor.

***

The Seventh Day

The turning of the key in the door woke me up. The *familiar* pushed the door open. Weak morning light fell upon my face.

"Come in, please," he said.

Teresa's small, slim form appeared at the entrance of the cell. She was holding a little package wrapped in a blanket.

"You have ten minutes," the *familiar* declared loudly.

Teresa shuffled in. Her small body was shaking from head to toe when she hugged us and burst out in tears.

"Señoras, I can't believe you're living under such conditions." Her hands undid the bundle. "Our cook sent you risotto. Eat it before it gets cold."

"Teresa, what about... La Chica... and Ana?" Brianda wept.

"Teresa, sit down, tell us everything you know," I requested.

"A few days ago, I don't remember what day it was anymore, I'm getting all the days confused, six Republic Guard soldiers and two old nuns, with white hair peeking out under their habits, burst into Palazzo Gritti. Without asking permission, they went into the music room, where Ana and La Chica were playing their instruments." Her lips trembled as she began her tale.

"'Señoritas Ana and Beatrice La Chica, we are here to escort you to a convent where you'll be educated from here onward,' one of the nuns informed them, showing major-domo de Costa the decree from the

Court of the Inquisition. La Chica was frightened and burst out in tears," Teresa recounted.

"'Mama, no! Please, not to a convent!' Ana tried to remove the nun's hands from her arm. 'You're hurting me, leave me alone!' But the nun grasped her tightly."

"My baby…" Brianda sobbed.

Teresa stroked her cheek. "I extended my arms to her, but the Guard soldiers waved their axes in front of my face and ushered her away from me. The nun told me to prepare clothing and some personal possessions for the girls, and that there was no need for fancy dresses. 'Bring the package to the gondola waiting outside,' she ordered me.

"'Where are you taking us?' Ana cried, trying to extract La Chica from the nun's rough hands, but she only grabbed her tighter.

"'To the convent, where you'll receive a proper education. Your mothers are ruining you,' the nun scolded her, and her sharp voice tore at my heart.

"I went into the girls' room and quickly packed some clothes in a small chest, and dear Thomas helped me take it down to the gondola.

"I wanted to hug the girls, but those villains pushed me away. The girls' eyes were begging me to save them. The horrid feeling of being unable to help my beloved girls won't let go of me." Teresa beat at her heart with her fist.

"Teresa, listen to me carefully." I looked in her eyes. "Ask Luciano to send Juan an urgent message to do whatever it takes, and quickly, to free Ana and La Chica. He should contact the Portuguese ambassador in Venice and remind him that we're Portuguese nationals. I want him to find me another place of residence immediately. Start packing my possessions. I'm not going back to Palazzo Gritti."

"Will the *señora* be released?" Teresa's dark eyes gaped open.

"Do as I say." I hugged her.

The door opened wide. "The meeting is over," the *familiar* grunted, hastily ushering Teresa out.

"The risotto," she mouthed silently.

I undid the rope securing the blanket and opened the small container. The strong aroma of rice in saffron reached my nose. I stirred the yellow rice with the wooden spoon, and felt something firm. At the bottom of the container was a piece of leather. I picked it up, but saw nothing. *It can't be, there must be something there!* Using my fingernails, I gently peeled off the external layer, suddenly exposing a letter on which the tracks of tears had left their mark.

I strained my eyes to read it.

My Mama,

How are you? Mama, I'm writing to you from the scary convent in Murano, to which the nuns and the Guard soldiers took La Chica and me by gondola.

I'm watching over La Chica, who can't stop crying and wants to return home. She misses Aunt Brianda very much.

Being here is terrible. The convent is surrounded by a wall, there's nothing but water behind it, and there's nowhere to escape to.

The place is sad and bleak, the corridors are long, there are dozens of rooms, and you barely see anyone, only statues and paintings everywhere. The food is dreary, and the twelve girls who live here are punished for every infraction of the rules. The nuns treat us well, but I can't be here.

Mama, I beg you, please save us.

With love,
Ana

My Ana and La Chica were being held by nuns. The tears dropped down upon the page. The green ink smeared, blurring the letters. Would they be forced to eat pork and pray to their messiah?

I handed the letter to Brianda. "Why? Why?"

"You have to understand, it's my right to receive my natural guardian-ship over my daughter. The Venice authorities claimed that my chances of winning custody were slim, unless it turned out that the rumors that my sister was practicing Judaism and was a heretic were indeed true."

"Now you're blaming the interrogators?"

"You don't have to believe me, but you left me no choice."

"And you had to confirm their suspicions and inform on me." My words assailed her.

Brianda rose from her bed and sat down next to me. Her hand touched my cold palm. I drew my hand away.

"God punished me," Brianda sighed. "I hired an agent in Lyon, the son of a Roman family who boasted about his connections with the mistress of King Henri the Second. He promised to collect the debts that the merchants in Lyon owed me. But the agent coveted my fortune, and informed the Church that I was secretly Jewish."

I listened without saying a word.

"The French authorities have frozen all our assets in France," she said.

What we had feared had indeed come to pass. Diogo had worried that if the money fell into Brianda's hands, she would swiftly lose it, but not quite this swiftly! And now all the profits and the family fortune I had accumulated were frozen in France.

The *familiar* entered the prison cell and slowly unfurled the notice he was holding.

"The *señora* is released!" he declared with a self-important expression.

I rose from the bed swiftly, adjusting the hem of my dress.

"No, no, excuse me," the *familiar*'s hand slid to the sword hanging from his belt. "Only Madame Brianda de Luna is released from confinement today," the *familiar* smirked.

The room spun around me. Brianda opened her arms to embrace me. I stepped back, turning my face away. I heard the patter of her heels on the stone tiles.

I dozed off. The large form of *familiar* Pedro Niño stood at the opening of the room. "The *señora* is summoned to the courtroom," he declared.

***

Despite being about fifty years old, the inquisitor strode nimbly into the courtroom, holding a parchment scroll in his hand. He climbed the stairs, and before he could settle into his chair, one of the dignitaries of the city's Council of Ten burst into the hall, a missive signed with the seal of La Serenissima in his hand.

"A missive from the doge," he told the interrogators at his side. The inquisitor broke the seal. "A Turkish warship is on its way to La Serenissima. The sultan claims that Portuguese national Doña Beatrice Mendes is his subject, and threatens to conquer Venice if the *señora* is not released," he whispered to the judges, drumming nervously on the table.

The inquisitor summoned the priest who served as the court's secretary and exchanged whispered words with him. The secretary dipped his quill in the inkwell and wrote down his statements. He blew on the page to dry the ink and handed the parchment to the inquisitor, who read it in aggravation:

In the presence of Inquisitor Giovanni Nunez de Cruz and the judges, the court hereby declares the release of Señora Beatrice Mendes.

"There's some justice in the world!" I thanked the sour-faced interrogators and rushed out of the courtroom, unescorted this time.

✳✳✳

I blinked as the sun's rays alighted upon me, breathing the clear air of freedom in deeply.

"Aunt, thank God!" Juan, who was waiting for me, hugged me.

We began to walk toward the gondola awaiting us, but my legs collapsed after the prolonged stay in the prison cell. Juan linked his arm with mine and helped me walk.

"I'm finally free." I dipped my hands in the cold water of the canal. "Juan, when your freedom is stolen from you, you realize that even in the bondage of prison, your thought and will are free. No one can control them."

"Aunt, you've become a philosopher..." Juan laughed.

"Have the girls returned home? I have to see them," I said.

"The doge signed a writ for their release. Augustino Henricks and the soldiers of the Guard have set out to fetch them. They'll arrive in two hours or so."

"I've worried and missed them so much that I couldn't sleep at night. This is the first time in their lives they've been alone, on a desolate island, in a cold convent with nuns who are strangers to them."

"Aunt, they feel fine. I sent two of our agents to the convent, accompanied by their wives, masquerading as peddlers and nuns, and I gave them your regards."

"I knew I could count on you."

"The sultan came to your aid. I'm sure Amatus Lusitanus told you that he sent a warship to escort you to his land."

Amatus's name brought a blush to my cheeks, but Juan did not notice.

"Aunt, the Venetians are very angry. They want to continue their 'dolce vita,' their sweet life, and don't want the Ottomans to declare war against Venice because of a feud between two sisters."

"The conclusion is clear: this is the time for action, rather than words, and it must be swift. If the situation deteriorates, the Venetians won't merely blame the Mendes sisters for the war, but all of the Portuguese *conversos*."

I gathered up the hem of my dress and disembarked from the gondola. The servants, headed by the major-domo, Thomas, Teresa and Estella, were standing in a line and received me with curious gazes. Teresa ran toward me and hugged me, her face ecstatic.

"Blessed be. We were worried about you."

I never thought I would see a tear in the eye of one who ran the house so imperially.

My heart fluttered within me as I passed the threshold. Chests and crates were piled up on the ground floor, waiting to be moved to my new home.

In the family's quarters, the ancient rugs, the heavy curtains, the wood tables and the decorations that had yet to be packed greeted me like good friends happy to see me again. But without Ana, the Palazzo Gritti was not a home to me.

"Where is she?" I asked.

"Excuse me, whom is the *señora* referring to?" Luciano de Costa asked.

"You know very well whom I mean." I couldn't even utter her name.

The thought that I would have to stay in the same house with her even for one day made me shudder with revulsion.

"Madame Brianda accompanied Señor Marco de Mollino. She didn't want the girls to be alone with the Republic Guard soldiers," de Costa said, removing an invisible speck of dust from his blue uniform.

"She'll meet my daughter before I do," I said angrily.

"Señora, from the day Madame Brianda returned from Palazzo Ducale, her eyes are dim, and I don't hear her singing and laughing," Teresa said.

Good, I thought to myself.

"Luciano, as of today, she'll be eating her meals separately, in the small dining room," I informed him.

"Señora, you've lost weight. Your face is so thin. Did they not feed you over there?" Estella asked.

The smells of cooking drifting from the kitchen embraced me, bringing tears to my eyes "I've missed your food. The macaroni with the pecorino cheese you sent me was delicious!" I told the cook, who flushed with happiness.

"Thank you, señora. In honor of my lady, I've prepared sardines in marinade with pine nuts and raisins, fried eggplant and artichoke in lemon sauce and mint. And I'll also make the saffron risotto that the *señora* likes."

I looked out through the windows. "I can't eat until I see the girls."

"It will be a while before they arrive. Please, señora, I drew you a bath. Don't let them see the wrinkles and dust on your dress," Teresa said.

I gave in to her pleas and went to my room, which was full of chests and crates that had been packed with my possessions. Teresa helped me take off my dress. I dipped in the perfumed water while she vigorously scrubbed my body with a small towel until my skin reddened. I knew that she was doing all she could to remove the memories of the days of imprisonment from me.

After the bath, Teresa dried me off with a towel that had been warmed by the hearth, dressing me in a blue taffeta dress that improved my mood.

"I ask that from this moment on, you report every one of my sister's actions to me: where she goes, when she gets back, and whom she meets. I don't want to run into her during the day."

"Madam, a sister's envy of her sister is as fierce as hellfire," Teresa sighed.

I paced back and forth in the guestroom, eagerly awaiting my daughter and niece.

"Mama! You're free!" My Ana ran into my open arms. For long moments, I breathed her in, enveloping her with kisses and hugs.

"How are you, my sweet? I missed you so much."

"Aunt," La Chica opened her arms to me and hugged me. I held her close to my heart.

"La Chica, come to your room," said Brianda, who had stationed herself at the entrance to the room.

"Mama, I want to be with Ana and Aunt Beatricci," La Chica begged, but Brianda turned her back to us and left the room, and La Chica followed.

Marco de Mollino gallantly doffed his hat and warmly kissed my hand. "Doña Beatrice, welcome back. It's good to see you."

"De Mollino, thank you for going out to fetch the girls."

"Señora, a Venetian nobleman fulfills his duties."

"Do you know why Brianda was freed before me, and the charges against her were dismissed?"

"Señora, the court accepted the claims of Madame Brianda's solicitor, that she was a good Christian and that she wanted to stay in Venice. Her agent turned her in to the Church because he wanted to win a portion of her funds that had been seized."

Clouds of War

Juan looked out through the windows. "Sultan Suleiman's royal fleet is approaching!" he declared.

I went out to the balcony. A fleet of black warships, their masts flying red flags and Sultan Suleiman the Magnificent's banners with their curly gold script, were revealed to me through the gray clouds hovering over the city.

Battalions of Republic Guard soldiers, armed with spears and guns, marched in formation to the port.

Men, women and children went out to the balconies of the palazzos, while others swarmed to the port, looking in amazement at the Turkish fleet sailing toward shore.

The entire household staff, clerks and servants, stopped their work to gaze out the windows. Cries of disbelief were heard from every direction.

"I'm scared…"

"An entourage from the sultan!"

"Run! The sultan is coming to conquer the city!"

"The sultan wants to sign a maritime alliance with Venice."

"He's dangerous! His soldiers conquered the city of Boda in Hungary and laid siege on Vienna!"

Juan, who was the first to notice the approaching fleet, hastened out of the palazzo. He returned a long while later, his expression concerned.

"The *shawish*, the sultan's delegate, accompanied by two janissaries— infantry soldiers—wearing swords, just entered Palazzo Ducale to give the doge a personal missive from the sultan."

"Do you know what happened at the meeting?"

"The doge's secretary told me that the doge is pacing in his offices like a caged lion. He's furious about the 'the sultan's impudent demand' to allow you to leave Venice. He's concerned about the economic damage the republic will sustain if you leave with your property, and fears that if he doesn't acquiesce to the demand, the Ottomans will conquer Venice. He's convening the Council of Ten for a discussion.

"There's another problem as well. Augustino Henricks visited the doge's palace and managed to convince the scribe to swiftly copy the missive:

With the grace of Allah

I am Sultan Suleiman Han, son of Sultan Saleem Han and grandson of Sultan Bayezid Han, sultan and ruler of the Mediterranean Sea and the Black sea, of Rumelia and Anatolia, Kurdistan, Azerbaijan and Persia, Damascus, Aleppo, Egypt, Mecca and Medina, Jerusalem and all of Arabia, Yemen and many other countries conquered by my glorious forefathers and myself.

To the Doge of Venice Francesco Donato,

I have been informed that my subject, Señora Beatrice Mendes, is about to marry her daughter, Miss Ana Mendes, to the son of my personal physician, Moshe Hamon.

I command you to arrange the departure of Señora Beatrice, her sister Señora Brianda, their daughters, her servants and her possessions from Venice.

The shawish, the sultan's delegate, is on his way from Constantinople to escort them to the wedding that will take place, Allah willing, in Constantinople.

As I'm certain you know, we live upon our sword, and have never hesitated to embark upon a campaign of war.

Our horses are always harnessed, and our swords are always at the ready.

May the almighty Allah grant justice!
Sultan Suleiman Han Hazretleri
The Sublime Porte of Constantinople

Juan straightened slightly and smiled. "Thanks to the good connection I've forged with the sultan's Jewish doctor, he's been whispering in the sultan's ear and convincing him to intervene on your behalf. And now Venice is trembling in fear of the caliph. Aunt, our situation is good!"

The wineglass trembled in my hand, and drops of wine splattered on my hand and on the table. "Our situation is good? Our situation is very dire!"

Juan hurried to wipe the drops off my hand.

"Who asked Moshe Hamon to inform the sultan that Ana is about to marry his son? The investigation against me hasn't been concluded yet, and the news that Ana is marrying a Jew puts us in danger. No one, not even the sultan, will control me and decide when I should leave. I'm the only one who decides!" I said.

Drops of perspiration appeared on Juan's forehead. "I'm sorry, I thought you were planning to move east as soon as possible."

"I still haven't shut down the House of Mendes businesses the way I want to. There are debts to collect, property to sell, merchandise about to arrive." I wrapped my shawl tighter around my head. "We can't fall into the sultan's honey trap. I don't want to declare the extent of my assets and fortune to the sultan, the way Ottoman law requires."

"And what happens if the sultan reneges?"

"He won't. He's very interested in me arriving with my fortune in Constantinople." I twirled the bracelet I had received from Francisco. "We mustn't make Venice into our enemy. We need to deny the news about Ana's engagement to the son of physician Moshe Hamon."

Juan scratched his forehead. "What do you propose?"

"Write to Efendi Moshe Hamon, the sultan's doctor, and tell him that we thank him for his proposal of marriage, but that Ana is too young to get married."

Juan raised an eyebrow and laughed. "To the Turks, a fourteen-year-old girl who hasn't married is an old maid..."

Juan contacted our agents, missives flew back and forth, and the next communications no longer mentioned a marriage between the two families.

***

A cold, late-November wind was blowing. I bundled myself in a fur coat over my red brocade dress and wrapped the fur tighter around my neck. The wind rocked the gondola leading me to the lavish home of Monsieur de Marvelier, the French ambassador, and his wife. Also present were Monsieur Bacadelli, the pope's legate, and Charles the Fifth's ambassador. The main topics of conversation were the sultan's threats and the clouds of war over Venice.

Madame de Marvelier turned her eyes to Juan, who was talking enthusiastically to a beautiful noblewoman. "Manuela, the daughter of the ambassador from Florence, is interested in your handsome cousin. Such a fine young man, and a favorite among the women," she smiled at me pleasantly.

Monsieur de Marvelier poured fine, amber-hued cognac into round crystal glasses, and after dinner, the doors to the ballroom were opened.

I lingered by the hearth, which was emitting a pleasant heat. My friend Don Angelino approached me with a glass of cognac in his hand. "Please," he handed me the glass, his eyes looking around.

"Doña Beatrice, I have received information that you should know about. But it cannot be revealed that you received it from me," he whispered.

I put down the glass and nodded.

"My dear," Don Angelino lowered his voice, "in two weeks, the court will rule in favor of your sister Brianda and charge a considerable monetary payment from you."

I grew pale, clinging to the cornice of the fireplace. "Thank you, my good friend."

I took a deep breath, picked up my cognac glass, and we returned to the hall, which was bustling with guests.

PART FIVE

Ferrara
1548-1552

Strands of Love, 1548

Rays of sunlight peeked out through the folds of clouds. I leaned against the rail of the ship swaying down the Po River, spread out my arms and breathed in the air of freedom. *Gracia, you've made it! You've reached safe harbor!* I said soundlessly to my image reflecting in the blue-green water. *You're free, and have escaped Venice. The Inquisition does not view your actions as heresy! You hold a certificate of transit to Ferrara.*

Ana came up to the deck, snuggled in a fur coat, and curled into my shoulder. "I want La Chica." The wind carried her words away and tousled her hair.

The paths of the two girls who had not parted for even one day in recent years had diverged. A broad river now separated them. I wiped Ana's cheek of the water droplets that mingled with her tears.

Ana shifted my hand away. "You should have conceded to Aunt Brianda."

"Each one of us makes choices in life. Brianda chose a life of artificial glamor in Venice, while I chose to live in a place where I would not be persecuted or thrown into jail."

The wind whipped at the sides of the ship, the mast creaked, and Ana furrowed her brow.

"Juan and Bernardo have left me too," she said.

I smoothed the furrow with my finger. "Juan stayed behind to release the House of Mendes funds that were seized, and will be in Ferrara soon. And Bernardo's in Lyon, managing the export of wool and wine."

The ship approached the soft, verdant hills.

"Ana, you're with me. The Venetian chapter of our life is over and done with. We've reached Ferrara, the city of freedom."

The captain cast the anchor, and the sailors tossed the ropes and tied the stern of the ship to the bollard on the bustling pier.

"Welcome! Madam, always at your service." The face of my friend the printer Geronimo de Vargas lit up. Geronimo and Gerolamo Marta, who dealt in gold, had been negotiating with the duke on my behalf, and had managed to obtain the much-yearned-for certificate of passage to Ferrara for me and my family.

Christopher Manuel, the company agent who had moved to Ferrara at my request, reached out and helped us board a carriage upholstered in white velvet, his reddish hair disheveled by the wind.

The coach passed through sleepy villages. Crimson roses and climbing grapevines adorned the yards of the wooden houses, dogs barked, cows and sheep lowed in their pastures, and shepherds and elderly village women waved to us.

On both sides of the main street, three-story houses rubbed against each other. Residents of many nationalities, wearing their native costumes, strolled around and chatted in Italian, French, Spanish, Portuguese and Ladino on the busy street. Lavish carriages transporting esteemed ladies and gentlemen hurried on their way, while wagons overflowing with merchandise tried to bypass them.

I noticed that no one here was wearing a yellow cap or a Jewish badge on their clothing, like in Venice, but I didn't say a word in Christopher Manuel's presence.

Ana gazed in indifference at the people who watched our procession of opulent carriages curiously, her eyes as empty as trees that had shed their leaves.

"The palace of the Duke of Ferrara," Christopher Manuel pointed at an intimidating fortress with four towers, surrounded by a high wall and a moat.

The bells of the cathedral rang out, echoing into the distance.

"St. George's Cathedral," he said as we passed by the large statues of the lions lying in front of the cathedral's impressive façade.

"I'm sure we'll meet the *señora* at the beautiful cathedral on Sunday," he said, the freckles on his face flushing. I smiled to myself and did not reply.

The carriage approached a two-story palace covered in earth-toned terracotta tiles. The arced façade was flanked by two white marble columns. The second floor featured rounded windows, with triangular cornices made of white marble above them.

"Palazzo Manianinni," he declared in a voice suffused with self-importance. "Duke Ercole de Este demanded that the owner cancel the rental to his friend Sebastian Pinto, and rent it out to Señora Mendes for two hundred ducats a year. I negotiated successfully to rent the palazzo for two-and-a-half years, until after Easter 1551. When the duke heard that I'd rented the palace, he summoned an architect to renovate and design the palace especially for you," Christopher Manuel boasted of the good deal he had obtained for me.

"Christopher Manuel, do you know about the war that broke out between the dukes? All of them wanted my mother to live in their principality." Ana briefly allowed the shadow of a smile to surface on her face and disembarked from the carriage.

"Thank you," I said. "Please convey two hundred ducats to the duke's secretary today, payment in advance for a year's rental, and I want you to start negotiating for the purchase of the palazzo. If the duke recommended the palace and had it renovated for me, it would be proper for me to own it."

The gates opened. I savored the sounds of the carriage wheels clattering as it entered the roofed passageway into the large courtyard, with several large urns containing red poppies at its center.

Guillaume Fernandez, with his curving eyebrows and thick mustache, hurried to open the carriage doors. He had managed to escape from Lisbon with his family, but the ship had gone down with all its passengers. Guillaume had clung to a log for three days in the stormy sea. A House of Mendes ship on its way to Venice saved him, bringing him on deck. I was impressed by his courage and determination, and had smuggled him into Ferrara.

"Christopher Manuel, ask to have my personal chests unpacked immediately. They're numbered one to ten. Please make sure the servants lay them down gently in my room," I said.

"Yes, señora." Christopher conveyed his orders in Portuguese, and the crates began to be passed from hand to hand.

Halls covered in gold and stunning murals greeted us. Wealth and luxury were evident in every corner. Chandeliers dangled from the murals on the ceiling, and velvet sofas, silk armchairs and bright marble and wood tables were arrayed on the marble floor and the soft rugs.

I paused by one of the gold-coated Venetian mirrors, gazing at my reflection. A white hair was poking out under my pink hat.

Ana excused herself, saying she was not feeling well, and followed Teresa up the opulent marble staircase to the living quarters.

I entered the large kitchen. A pan with fried fish was sizzling on the range. Boxes of fresh fruit and vegetables were stacked up on the long table. Pots in an assortment of sizes and copper pans stood on long shelves, with the sparkling lids hung on hooks.

A line of liveried servants and aproned serving girls with immaculate head scarves dipped their heads and bowed and curtsied politely.

"Welcome, *La Señora* Mendes," they greeted me in Portuguese. I was still excited to be addressed as "*la señora.*"

I smiled at them. "Hello to all of you. The *señora* expects dedicated, efficient and responsible work from all of you," I said.

"Thank you, *la señora,*" they replied in tandem.

"The major-domo, Guillaume Fernandez, will be in charge of your personal issues. Please talk to him concerning any problem and request.

"I want to let you know that I intend to establish a monetary fund dedicated to the needs of the staff of Palazzo Manianinni," I began, surveying them with my eyes. "Maids will be endowed with a dowry of twenty gold scudo, so they can marry respectfully. Single male servants will receive a marriage bequest of twenty-two gold scudo."

The staff burst out in happy cheers, displaying broad smiles.

"Señor Christopher Manuel, the House of Mendes's agent in Ferrara, will pay each of you an advance on your wages today," I said.

The staff members, touched by this gesture, bowed and curtsied deeply. "*La señora! La señora!*" they called out in chorus, moving me to the point of tears.

Christopher Manuel undid a heavy bundle of money and took out coins. The servants burst out in cries of amazement. He passed between them, placing a silver coin in every extended palm.

I said goodbye to the staff and they returned to their work. As I climbed the stairs to my room, I met hardworking servants who were polishing the copper handles of the doors, and maids brushing the curtains and dusting the furniture.

I went out to the balcony overlooking the well-tended garden, surrounded by cypress trees. I closed my eyes, breathing in the fresh scents and listening to the water burbling in the fountain.

"My darling," I heard a familiar voice. The strong arms of Amatus Lusitanus wrapped around me.

I blushed. "I was hoping you would come."

"I promised to wait for you. A gentleman keeps his promises. Let's stroll together in the pretty garden." Amatus offered me his arm.

"I'd love to." Ambling leisurely, with Amatus leaning on his cane, we descended to the reception hall.

Guillaume Fernandez opened the wide doors leading to the garden. The wind toyed with the vines and fruit-bearing trees, which were shedding their leaves. Arm in arm, we strolled through the magical garden, among the beds of flowers and the statues.

I glanced at his face. "Tell me how you're doing."

"My lovely, I've been appointed professor of medicine at the University of Ferrara, and have invited researchers to witness an experiment I conducted."

"An experiment?"

"I used a straw to inflate a vein with air, and showed the amazed researchers that the air flowed from the veins to the heart!"

"Excuse me?"

Amatus looked at me directly. "I've discovered that blood does not disappear! Instead, it flows upward to the heart at a uniform rate, and the veins contain valves that prevent it from going down!"

I grasped both his hands forcefully. "Your discovery is dangerous. The Church will accuse you of heresy."

Amatus sighed, leaning heavily on his cane. "I know. That's why I only published the experiment, and not the conclusions."

"Let's sit down," I suggested, and we settled on a bench in the garden.

"I apologize for being weak. I underwent circumcision a few days ago," Amatus apologized.

"You underwent circumcision? Are you in pain? Do you feel all right?" I asked immediately.

"I'm fine."

"You're brave." I stroked his arm.

"It's not a matter of bravery. I wanted to be a Jew like my forefathers." His face grew solemn. "And how about you, my dear?"

"I'm apprehensive. I still haven't received a writ of patronage from the duke."

Amatus stroked my face with his hand. "Beatricci, I'd like to continue sitting beside you my whole life."

The loneliness was peeled away from me. There was no need to say a word. A moment of contentment occurred in the pretty garden between me and the dear man at my side.

Amatus wrapped his hands around my own. "Darling, I want strands of love to link my life with yours."

There is nothing I'd want more than to live with him, I thought to myself.

"I promise you I'll think about it," I heard myself say.

Amatus rose and extended his hand to me, a glimmer of sadness in his eyes.

"Beatricci, I'm returning home. I hope you'll miss me."

Beatrice La Chica

The treetops, the balconies and the roofs were covered with white. I opened a bottle of sherry and breathed in the sweet aroma of cherries. Pouring the beverage into a goblet, I sipped a bit. My body filled with warmth.

"Mama, look." Ana took my hand and led me to the window.

A messenger galloping in on a gray horse, his black cloak swept up by the wind, was making his way down the snowy path. He stopped at the gates of the palazzo, leaping off his horse.

The bells of the cathedral rang twelve times. Heavy footfalls echoed on the stairs.

"Señora, excuse me, a messenger from the Venetian court." Guillaume Fernandez gestured at the stranger.

Ana curled up in an armchair, her eyes staring at him. The messenger stepped inside, his hand holding the hilt of the sword at his waist, taking off his helmet, which was covered with snowflakes.

"Doña Beatrice de Luna Mendes?" The stranger was breathing heavily. I nodded. "*Sí.*"

"The Venetian Republic's Court of Foreign Affairs has asked me to hand your honor the verdict."

From the leather valise attached to his silver armor, the messenger extracted a missive sealed with the stamp of the winged lion and placed it on the desk.

316

The Republic of Venice
December 15, 1548

The Court of Foreign Affairs

Doña Beatrice Mendes has left the Republic of Venice without a certificate of transit and has not shown up for the continuation hearing regarding her case. The Venetian Court of Foreign Affairs has decreed that Doña Brianda Mendes shall receive the natural guardianship over the inheritance of her daughter, Beatrice Mendes.

Doña Beatrice de Luna Mendes is required to deposit one hundred and fifty thousand gold ducats to the credit of young Beatrice Mendes, which shall be kept in the Venetian Treasury until she turns fifteen.

The seizure of the property and fortune of House of Mendes, deposited in the Venetian Treasury, shall be repealed only after Doña Beatrice Mendes appears before the court to continue the hearing and carries out the court's decision.

The Court Secretary

I drained my glass of sherry.

"Mama! Do they want to arrest you?" Ana asked anxiously.

"No, no, they don't even mention the accusations of practicing Judaism and heresy."

"Then why does he write that you have to appear before the court in Venice to continue the hearing?"

"They want to make sure I deposit the hundred and fifty thousand ducats in the Venetian Treasury."

Ana's black eyes opened wide. "That's a fortune!" she said.

I gazed out through the window. The messenger was speeding away, disappearing from view.

"Luckily for us, La Chica wasn't awarded half of the House of Mendes fortune, but much less," I lowered my voice.

"So we're going back to Venice to deposit the money?"

"No, I won't let Brianda take your inheritance. The profits are a result of my business ventures. I could have spent my time attending balls, playing cards and squandering the money, and then we would have been left penniless."

"Mama, why don't you deposit the money, and the two of you can stop fighting?"

"Are you not listening to what I'm saying? I'm guarding your inheritance. One day, you'll run the company. Don't be naïve."

"But I'm only fourteen," Ana shrugged.

"You have to understand, the House of Mendes is under financial pressure due to my arrest. Henri the Second, king of France, has not repaid the immense debt of a hundred and fifty thousand gold ducats that his father borrowed from us. A merchant who bought sacks of cocoa and black pepper disappeared without paying. A ship that was supposed to unload perfume at the Port of Ancona abandoned its planned route and sailed off to the new continent. Don't forget that we also have to pay the providers at the colonies for the spices, the silk fabrics and the ornaments the company has purchased."

"I don't want you to be arrested."

"Don't worry." I kissed her forehead and grew alarmed. She was burning up with fever, her body trembling. I laid her down on the sofa and asked the servants to summon Doctor Amatus.

Amatus entered, placing his cane and his doctor's bag next to the sofa. He leaned over Ana, examining her tongue and her pupils.

"Ana, how are you?"

"All... ri... ght...." she murmured, a glaze of tears in her eyes.

Amatus stroked his beard. "Please, apply vinegar poultices to her forehead. It seems like a slight cold."

He placed two vials on the desk. "Mint extract for the cold, and extract of chamomile flowers to soothe her. Please make sure she drinks plenty of hot water with cinnamon and honey.

"Beatricci, I'll come again in the morning to see how she's doing. I'm sorry for being in a hurry. The duke asked me to tend to his wife, Duchess Renée. She's not feeling well," Amatus apologized.

Teresa returned bearing a silver platter with a plate of cookies and a cup of hot water with cinnamon and honey. Ana sipped the water slowly. I placed a rag dipped in apple vinegar on her forehead. The sour smell woke me up.

I replaced the hot poultice with a cool one, remaining to sit in the armchair by Ana's side and contemplate my position. Brianda was a wounded eagle; her feathers had been plucked in the battle over the property and guardianship. A wounded eagle could inflict fierce revenge. Once she won the trial, she would try to take control of the merchandise that my ships would unload in Venice, and collect the House of Mendes's debts. Worst of all, Venice's noblemen would descend upon her and La Chica with proposals of marriage.

I had to act swiftly. I picked up a sheet of paper with a heading displaying the emblem of the House of Mendes and, in gold lettering, the words "The Company of the Heirs to the Brothers Francisco and Diogo Mendes." I opened my silver inkwell, dipped the quill in the ink, and wrote down my request. I folded the sheet of paper and put it in an envelope.

When I rang the bell, Guillaume Fernandez showed up immediately, gazing at Ana, whose breathing was rapid.

"Relay this letter to printer Geronimo de Vargas. Ask him to convey it to the duke's personal secretary," I instructed him, and remained sitting by Ana's side all night long.

The clatter of the carriage wheels woke me up from the sleep that had taken over me. The maids shifted the curtains and the gray light of a winter morning dawned. The garden was covered with wisps of dew and the tops of the cypress trees were swaying in the wind. I heard familiar footsteps. Teresa opened the door.

"Aunt, what happened?" Juan kissed my hand and looked with concern at Ana, whose breathing was still labored.

"Ana's ill."

Juan stroked her black hair, cascading around her pale face. "Ana, Ana..."

Ana opened her eyes slowly. "Juan?"

Juan sat down beside her. "Yes, it's me. How are you, sweetheart?"

Ana made an effort to smile. "I'm glad you're here. Will you be living with us?"

"I rented a nice residence, not far from your palazzo."

"How's La Chica?"

"She misses you very much."

Juan turned to me. "I managed to obtain a copy of a report that France's envoy in Venice sent to King Henri. It cost me a pretty penny, but you should read it."

Six months ago, Beatrice Mendes sent her trusted agent to France to withdraw the majority of her fortune from Lyon and other locations in your kingdom. The details of the matter remain unclear and I cannot establish the truth; however, it is obvious that these developments are shrouded in mystery.

The tapping of a cane was heard in the staircase. Teresa opened the door.

"Doña Beatrice, Don Juan, Señorita Ana, good morning."

"Hello, doctor," Juan shook Amatus's hand.

"The *señorita* is feeling better. I believe her new medication was helpful," Amatus laughed, clapping Juan on the shoulder.

Ana nodded, her pale face blushing.

Amatus examined the pupils of her eyes and the color of her tongue.

"The girl will recover," he nodded. "Please make sure she drinks warm water with cinnamon and honey, as well as the extracts that will make her stronger."

"I'm off to a meeting. You'll be all better by the time I come back." Juan stroked her cheek and left the room.

Amatus and I went out to the balcony. A flock of birds began to frolic above our heads.

"How are you, darling?"

"I was very worried about Ana," I said.

"Ana's experiencing an immense amount of tension. Try to soothe her."

"I'm having a hard time," I sighed.

"What is it, dear?"

"The court in Venice has appointed Brianda as trustee of La Chica's inheritance, and is forcing me to deposit a real fortune, a hundred and fifty thousand gold ducats, in her name."

Amatus linked his arm with mine. "I'm sorry to hear that."

"La Chica is only eight, and I know Brianda will end up throwing the fortune that I earned, and which belongs to Ana, to the wind."

"What do you intend to do?"

"I'm in trouble. If I want to reclaim the House of Mendes's immense fortune that was seized by the Venetian authorities, I need to appear for the continuation of the hearing and deposit the money."

"What does Ana think about it?"

"Ana wants me to deposit the money and end the feud with my sister."

"Darling, do as you see fit, but if you ask my opinion," his eyes dove into mine, "for your own health, put an end to this battle that is doing harm to your body and your soul."

A bluebird left the flock, descended to sip water from the fountain, then returned to its companions.

Amatus handed me an invitation bearing the seal of the University of Ferrara. "I'd be happy if you could accompany me to the reception the university is holding in honor of my book, *The First Century*, in which I described the first hundred medical cases I've handled."

My heart was beating in excitement like a young girl before her first romantic outing. *This will be the first time I appear in public as his date,* I thought.

"I await your answer…" he whispered in my ear.

Lost Debts

I leaned back in the armchair and reread, again and again, the missive Augustino Henricks had sent me a day after the court reached a verdict. My fears had come to pass: Brianda was trying to take over the assets of the House of Mendes.

Republic of Venice

The soldiers of the Republic Guard surrounded the House of Mendes ship Doña Bella, which arrived from India. Madame Brianda hired armed soldiers who took over the ship and seized the bags of black pepper and cinnamon.

I have found out that Brianda has appealed to Henri the Second, king of France, requesting that he seize the assets of House of Mendes and transfer them to her.

Augustino Henricks
House of Mendes representative in Venice

Teresa entered the room. "Excuse me, señora, there's a carriage parked across from the palazzo, accompanied by an armed guard!"

I laid down the account ledger concerning grain export.

Christopher Manuel, whom I'd sent to Lyon on my behalf, had returned.

"Señora, I'm afraid that Madame Brianda's agent will collect the debts from the French merchants before I can." The freckles on his face flushed.

"Tell me succinctly," I said.

He handed me a notebook. "I managed to collect some of the lost debts. At this moment, Guillaume Fernandez and Thomas are supervising the transfer of the crates from the carriage to the safe room."

I straightened in my chair and opened the notebook. On the first page was an orderly table specifying the names of the debtors and the sums actually collected.

I skimmed the list quickly.

Avelardo Salvietti—53,749 gold scudo.
Bartolomeo Panciatichi—64,152 gold scudo.
Nicola and Carlo Antenori—22,525 gold scudo.
Total—140,426 gold scudo.

I leaned back in my seat. "Teresa, ask the major-domo to fetch a bottle of wine from the cellar."

The major-domo entered bearing a gold tray with two goblets and a bottle of wine engraved with the words "Castello Estense 1540." The servant poured the wine and handed the goblets to me and to the excited Christopher Manuel.

"Let's raise a toast to your success," I said, inviting him to enter the safe room with me.

The guards protecting the safe room, armed with short swords and bearing shields in their hands, shifted aside. Guillaume Fernandez and Thomas, who had been awaiting my arrival, left the room. I locked the door after us.

Three metal crates, secured with heavy locks, stood on the marble table.

"Every crate contains close to fifty thousand gold coins. It wasn't easy to collect the debts." Christopher Manuel stood tall.

"It's not easy for anyone. Each of us does his duty."

He opened the crates. Hundreds of gold coins winked at me.

I took a deep breath. Eleven years ago, I had smuggled part of my inheritance out of Lisbon.

It was a shame that Francisco hadn't lived to see how I managed to expand the fortune I had inherited.

We counted the coins together.

"As a reward for your efforts and your success, I'm doubling your wages."

"Thank you, *la señora.*" Christopher Manuel's face grew flushed.

I wrote the date December 21, 1548, on the receipt and sealed it with the stamp of The Company of the Heirs to the Brothers Francisco and Diogo Mendes. I did not sign my name, so that if things veered off track with Brianda, the authorities would not seize the crates on her behalf.

Duke Ercole de Este the Second

Guards wearing tight, colorful trousers and silvered helmets sporting a white feather were standing tautly at the entrance to the watchtower. They clutched a spear in one hand and a shield in the other. My friend, printer Geronimo de Vargas, handed the certificate of transit to the officer of the guard. The iron chains creaked. The wooden bridge was lowered, and the carriage entered the courtyard of Castello Estense.

We ascended the broad, twisting staircase, passing by halls whose arched ceilings and tall walls displayed breathtaking paintings and decorations. Noblewomen in rustling gowns, knights and court clerks who came across us slowed down, sending curious glances in my direction.

In the gilded reception hall, under the duchy's blue crest of nobility, featuring a large white eagle, its wings spread wide, its beak and claws made of gold and sporting a gold crown on its head, sat Duke Ercole de Este the Second, stuffed into a knight's full armor. His face was angular, his nose sharp, his ears large, his hair curly and his black beard well-groomed. Next to him sat Duchess Renée, the daughter of Louis the Twelfth, king of France, in a purple velvet dress. Rumors claimed that beautiful noblewomen fluttered around him, but Duchess Renée guarded him closely against the variety of women circling him.

I curtsied lightly. "Greetings. I wish to thank the duke and duchess for opening the gate of the lovely Duchy of Ferrara before me."

"Doña Beatrice Mendes, the Duke and Duchess de Este are happy to host the lady in the Duchy of Ferrara," the duke said, his voice hoarse.

The duke was surprised when I presented him with the first book of madrigals by composer Philippe Verdelot.

"Doña Beatrice, Philippe Verdelot is my favorite composer."

I handed the duchess a jewelry box made from mother of pearl, containing an ivory butterfly broach inlaid with diamonds and rubies. The duchess's hand flitted gently over the broach.

"Thank you, I love the flight of butterflies." A smile sparked in her eyes.

The duke looked sharply at Queen Renée, who was rumored to be well-educated and open to the Protestants' liberal ideas, in contrast to his own opinions. Under her influence, Ercole had allowed the Jews to live openly, without being required to wear the Jewish badge.

"Doña Beatrice Mendes requested an urgent meeting. The duke awaits to hear of the matter at hand," the duke nodded in encouragement.

"Your majesty the duke, although I am a woman, my brother-in-law Diogo Mendes placed his full trust in me. I was his right hand, and we managed the House of Mendes together. In his will, he appointed me as trustee of his daughter Beatrice La Chica Mendes's inheritance, as well as granting me authority to manage the House of Mendes, and courts in Antwerp and Venice have confirmed the will."

"What is your request?" he asked.

"My duke, after I left Venice for Ferrara, the court in Venice repealed Diogo Mendes's will and my status as trustee of his daughter's assets." I presented the duke's secretary with a file of documents, including Diogo's will and the verdicts of the courts in Antwerp and Venice.

"My request is that the duke, in his benevolence, renew my guardianship over the inheritance of my niece La Chica, confirm my authority to manage the House of Mendes, and grant me and my family a certificate of patronage. I want to note that Diogo feared that his wife would squander the company's funds and his daughter's inheritance. He knew I would successfully run House of Mendes affairs, as I have indeed been doing."

"I will pass your request on to the duchy's solicitors, and they will grant it serious consideration."

"How is your daughter?" Duchess Renée asked.

"Thank you. Doctor Amatus Lusitanus has tended to her, and Ana is recuperating."

The duchess's face lit up with a smile. "Professor Amatus Lusitanus is a talented physician. I'm sure you witnessed this at the reception the university held in honor of his new book, *The First Century.*"

My face assumed a scarlet hue. "Indeed." I handed the duchess a gilded invitation in an attempt to camouflage my embarrassment.

"I would be grateful to the duke and duchess if they would accept my invitation to be the guests of honor at a literary salon in my palace, where writers and poets are invited to read the best of their work to the audience."

A spark of curiosity ignited in the duchess's pretty eyes. She placed her hand on that of the duke. "Thank you, we happily accept the invitation."

***

At the end of the month, Geronimo de Vargas brought a letter from the duke.

January 28, 1549
Duchy of Ferrara
Castello Estense

To Señora Beatrice Mendes,

The Court of the Duchy of Ferrara approves the will of Diogo Mendes read in Antwerp in the year 1542.

Doña Beatrice Mendes is an exceptional and multi-talented woman. Although the authority of guardianship is not granted to a woman who is not the child's mother or grandmother, the court has decided to grant her the guardianship bestowed upon her in the will over the assets of her niece Beatrice, as well as the authority to manage the funds of her inheritance.

The court grants Doña Beatrice de Luna Mendes the authority to manage and employ agents throughout Europe on behalf of the House of Mendes company.

The duchy's accountants shall look into the House of Mendes's account ledgers and verify that the funds of the inheritance are being properly managed.

Respectfully,

Duke Ercole de Este the Second

The Portuguese Conversos, 1549

The month of January bore disturbing news to Palazzo Manianinni upon its cold wings regarding waves of hatred toward the Portuguese *conversos*. That morning, Guillaume Fernandez placed an urgent missive on my desk.

Venice

For Doña Beatrice Mendes,

I regret to inform you that the Great Council has discussed the large waves of immigration from Portugal to Venice and intends to deport the Portuguese conversos from Venice.

Augustino Henricks
House of Mendes representative

I paced back and forth in my office, distraught. The sun was setting on La Serenissima. Brianda and La Chica, who were also *conversos*, were in danger. What would become of them? Would they flee?

Venice

Aunt,

I've proposed to the Venetian senate that they assign one of the desolate islands in Venice's lagoon as a residence for the Portuguese conversos.

*That way, they can continue to engage in commerce profiting the
Republic of Venice. Our brothers have no respite. Even after converting
to Christianity, we're being deported.*

Juan

The New Christians' circumstances grew even more dire. Urgent missives landed on my desk, informing me of the fickle treatment of the Portuguese *conversos* in Europe.

Aunt,

*My friend Cosimo de'Medici the First, Duke of Tuscany and Florence,
has agreed to my request and signed a decree permitting the
merchants among the Portuguese conversos to conduct business
within the realm of the duchy.*

Juan

***

Paris

Aunt,

I have met with the king of France, Henri the Second.

*I've done it! I convinced the king to publish a bill of rights for the
Portuguese conversos, allowing the conversos to settle in his country, to
engage in commerce and to purchase assets.*

Juan

***

Venice

Aunt,

I'm very sorry. The senate of the Republic of Venice has decided by majority vote to banish the Portuguese conversos from Venice. A convert caught within the borders of Venice after the decree of deportation takes effect shall be bound up in chains and sold into slavery, and his property will be seized.

Juan

***

Snowflakes began to fall. The servants increased the blaze in the fireplace. In the kitchen, chestnuts were roasted, their scent spreading through the house, but it did not ease the oppression weighing on my heart.

Amatus Lusitanus rested his carved cane against the windowsill. "Beatricci, pardon me for arriving with no advance notice," he apologized.

"I'm always happy to see you."

"For you, my darling." Amatus presented me with an oblong box of flowers. I undid the golden ribbon, removed the lid, and was left breathless. On the silk paper lay a spectacular flower, in hues of red and striped in white, cradled by two long green leaves.

"Thank you!"

"A lovely flower for a lovely woman," Amatus smiled. "The sea captain from whom I bought the tulip told me that in the gardens of the sultan's palace, tulips bloom. They originate in Persia, and are called *tulban* due to their resemblance to a turban."

"Are you hinting that the time has come for me to learn Turkish…" I laughed, inviting him to sit next to the hearth.

Amatus Lusitanus took off his coat and scarf, both covered in snowflakes, and handed them to the servant. He removed his gloves and brought his hands close to the fireplace.

I filled a crystal vase with water and gently placed the tall stalk inside.

The serving girl lowered a silver tray onto the table, bearing crystal goblets with cherry liqueur and tiramisu cake sprinkled with cocoa powder.

"Beatricci, I've received three offers for a position as a physician."

I curled my hands around the crystal goblet. "I'm listening."

"The new king of Poland, Sigsimund Augustus the Second, has invited me to be his personal physician," he said with a nod of his head.

"The question is whether you want to move from vibrant Italy to Poland."

Amatus hesitated, his face growing solemn. "The council of the Republic of Ragusa, under the reign of the Turkish sultan, has offered me the position of 'city doctor,' the option of continuing my medical research, and a full tax waiver."

"An interesting offer," I said, sinking into the depths of the armchair.

"I prefer Ragusa, where I can live as a Jew openly. Unfortunately, I still haven't received a certificate of passage," he sighed.

"And what's the third offer?"

"Pope Julius the Third has requested that I come urgently to Ancona and become his family doctor, tending to his sister. He has offered me handsome wages and a tax waiver."

I waved an ivory fan with a pattern of poppies. "Is it not dangerous for a Jew to live in the pope's country?"

"The pope has promised me immunity from accusations of heresy."

I affixed a hairpin to a strand of hair that had draped over my forehead. "Oh," I choked a cry of pain. "Amatus, are you leaving me...?"

"Ancona is on the coast, close to Ragusa and Constantinople." Amatus's warm hands wrapped around my own. "Beatricci, come with me."

"I wish I could."

Amatus looked at me sadly. "Well, then, our paths must diverge now. I hope that eventually, we'll meet again. Farewell, darling, take care of yourself." Amatus kissed my hand and rushed off.

"I hope we meet again soon..." I leaned against the windowsill and sadly tracked Amatus's carriage, which was already disappearing in the distance. I wondered if I had made a mistake by giving him up and choosing to remain a widow and the manager of a business.

***

A month later, I received his letter.

Ancona

Beatricci,

Through the windows of my clinic, I saw a flag with two gold stripes and a lion between them waving from the mast of a ship that docked at the Port of Ancona today—the emblem of the illustrious House of Mendes.

I thought perhaps you had arrived in Ancona and hurried to the port. I waited by the ship's gangway, hoping to see your pretty face, but my hopes were dashed.

Yours,
Your friend, Amatus Lusitanus

The days filled with the pain of my loneliness. My soul yearned for Amatus's embrace, but he was far away from me. I had been left on my own. In addition, Thomas, my beloved and faithful servant, grew ill and passed away.

I was worried about La Chica, Brianda and my *conversos* brethren— the refugees who had escaped en masse in the cold, rain and snow. I buried myself in my work. Palazzo Manianinni became the headquarters of a covert smuggling network.

Sacks of wheat, jam, cheese, blankets, jugs of water, clothes, coats, bandages and medicine were all loaded on House of Mendes ships, intended for the *conversos* escaping the lowlands and Venice. Agents were sent to central ports to warn them of undercover policemen, inns were rented, and bribes were passed from hand to hand. The knowledge that I was doing good deeds and saving the persecuted imbued my days and nights with sweetness.

"*La señora*, excuse me, if I may, early in the morning, two children knocked on the kitchen door, after having snuck into the palace in a coach delivering fresh milk. The girl's eyes were red, and she begged for a bit of bread and cheese, and asked that we allow them to sleep in the stables," the cook said, wiping her hands on the hem of her apron.

"Let them into the kitchen," I said, making my way there.

The cook went out to the storehouse and returned with two frightened children, wearing torn, ragged clothes, hiding behind her voluminous dress. I handed them two slices of bread from the fresh pastry basket. The girl took her brother's slice of bread and hid it in her coat pocket, tore the other slice in two and gave half of it to her brother.

I sat them down at the servants' long dining table, and asked the cook to pour them some warm milk and serve them slices of bread with butter.

The children gobbled up the food, staring at me with beseeching eyes.

"What are your names? Where are you from?" I asked.

The children lowered their eyes to the ground.

"Don't be scared," said Ana, who had joined us and sat down next to them.

The boy hugged his sister. "*La señora*, my sister, Clara Gonzales, is ten, and I am Hector Diaz, eight years old."

"Where were you born?"

"We were born in Lisbon. Our father disappeared one day. It was said that drunks murdered him," Hector mumbled, his eyes red.

"Poor little things," Ana said, asking the cook to give them a slice of cake. The children devoured it ravenously, storing the crumbs in their pockets.

"How did you travel to Ferrara?" I asked.

"We fled with Mother in a ship transporting pepper to Venice, and were waiting for a ship that would take us to Ferrara, but the Inquisition's policemen caught Mother and yelled at her that she was a Portuguese *converso* and a secret Jew," Clara recounted quietly.

"'Run away to the home of the generous Señora Beatrice Mendes in Ferrara,' Mother whispered to me before the police dragged her away. I hope it's all right that we arrived at the *señora*'s house," she said, embarrassed.

I stroked Clara's black hair, to which dust and dirt were clinging. I liked Clara and her brother. My palace was large enough to house two orphans, I thought.

"Clara and Hector, from this day onward, I'll take care of all your needs. You'll live in my home, serve my family and receive proper wages. When you're ready to wed, you'll receive a dowry from me, twenty gold scudo for Clara and twenty-two gold scudo for Hector. Now go and see the head of the staff. He'll take care of you," I said.

"*La señora*, thank you, thank you." The two knelt down on the marble floor and kissed the hem of my dress.

The Ferrara Bible

In addition to dealing in black pepper, perfume and wool, and simultaneously to granting loans, I immersed myself in the business of publishing books and manufacturing paper, which were very profitable for the company.

I collaborated with my friend, printery owner Geronimo de Vargas, who had returned to the Jewish faith and was called Yom Tov Atias. The price of books, which had been high, so that only the wealthy could afford to purchase them, had decreased radically due to the invention of the printing press. Many people began to purchase holy books, literary books and art books. My circle of buyers increased, along with our profits.

Yom Tov Atias, who did business in Ferrara in cooperation with printers Avraham Osheki and his son Samuel, invited me to visit their new offices on Via San Romano. I brought Ana along with me, hoping she would find interest in book publishing, thus easing her intense yearning for La Chica.

A guard in a short cloak escorted us to their well-lighted offices, infused with the smell of ink. At the center of the room was a bronze printing press. "It's the first printing press ever made. I purchased it from the heirs of Johannes Gutenberg." Yom Tov Atias stroked the wood frame of the device.

My gaze fell upon a bundle of pages with a heading written in beautiful Portuguese handwriting: "Solace of the Trials of Israel." Avraham Osheki placed his hand on his son's shoulder. "Samuel is writing a poem about the travails of our people."

I picked up several pages and skimmed the rhymed lines, describing the history of our people.

"Samuel, I'm truly moved. Thanks to your book, readers will find out about the glorious history of our people. I hope you continue to write about the heroes, male and female, who took their fate into their own hands and defeated our enemies."

"I hope so, Señora Mendes, may it happen in our own day and age," Samuel Osheki said, looking at Ana, who blushed.

I extracted a bundle of money from my reticule and handed it to Samuel. "A grant for the publication of your important book."

Samuel smiled, flustered. "A blessing upon the *señora*'s good hands."

"Gentlemen, I thought about asking you to print the bible in a Ladinotranslation. I want our brothers, the secret Jews who have forgotten their language and cannot read Latin, to be able to read the bible."

"That's dangerous!" Avraham Osheki shook his head.

"Under no circumstances!" Yom Tov Atias blinked.

"Henry the Eighth, king of England, accused William Tyndale, who translated the bible from Latin to English, of heresy, and had him executed!" Avraham's voice grew choked.

"We're in Ferrara, not in the England of thirteen years ago. When I visited London on my way from Lisbon to Antwerp, I saw a bible translated into English in a church," I tried to soothe them.

"We're frightened. I don't think the authorities want the Portuguese *conversos* to study the bible," said Avraham Osheki.

"It would never occur to me to put you in danger. I've received the patronage of Duke Ercole de Este the Second, the grandson of the pope, as well as an expression of support from the Church for translating the bible into Ladino."

Yom Tov Atias and Avraham Osheki exchanged tentative glances.

I produced the writ of patronage from Duke Ercole the Second and showed it to them.

Yom Tov Atias fingered his short beard for a long while. Finally, he nodded at Avraham Osheki, who expressed his agreement.

I smiled. "It's important to me that the translation be accurate and clear, and that the quality of the paper and ink is of the highest level. All expenses will be paid by me." I took a bundle of money from my leather bag. "There are thirty thousand gold ducats here. An advance payment for your expenses."

Yom Tov Atias poured cherry liqueur for all of us, and we drank to the success of the translation and distribution of the Ferrara Bible.

"The first copy of the Ferrara Bible will be given to me. We'll give another copy, which we'll print in Latin, to the Duke of Ferrara, in thanks for the rights to settle that he bestowed on my family and our brethren, and in honor of his grandfather, Duke Ercole the First, who invited the Jews exiled from Spain to live in the duchy, and protected them from blood libels."

A shiver ran through me. Was every boy or girl among those 'belonging to the letter Yod' familiar with the Hebrew prayers? Were the Jewish prayers doomed to evaporate and disappear from the world? I had to translate the prayers into Ladino as well.

"We'll also translate the *siddur*, the prayer book," I said. "So that the prayers can be understood by everyone."

Avraham Osheki nodded, and we decided we would translate the prayer cycle, as well as a prayer book for the holidays.

At the end of the meeting, I invited Yom Tov Atias and Avraham Osheki to Palazzo Manianinni on Monday at ten o'clock to update me on their progress.

***

On Monday, at a quarter to nine in the morning, Guillaume Fernandez entered my study. "Señora, I apologize, but publishers Yom Tov Atias and Avraham Osheki are asking to speak to you urgently."

"*La señora*, I'm sorry we're early," Yom Tov Atias apologized, raising the hem of his cloak, which had clearly been put on in haste.

"I require your urgent assistance." Señor Osheki wiped the perspiration from his forehead. "An hour ago, I found out that my brother, his wife and their two daughters, who had been summoned for interrogation by the Inquisition, which has come to Castello Branco, have managed to evade the investigation, fleeing Portugal by ship. Tragically, a French pirate ship has taken over the vessel, robbed its treasures, and since my brother and his family are *conversos*, the pirates have taken them prisoner. They are now bound in iron chains in the hull of the ship, which is docked not far from the Port of Ancona."

"Oh, no, may the Lord protect them and save them from all strife," I said.

"The pirates are demanding a ransom of one hundred gold ducats for the parents, and a hundred gold ducats for every daughter. They are threatening that if they do not receive the ransom within a week, the men will be sold to slave traders from the new continent, and the girls will be sold into prostitution. Only three days remain." Avraham Osheki wiped away a tear.

"*El ombre yeva mas ke la piedra*. A man's soul bears more than a stone," Yom Tov Atias sighed.

"The sum of the ransom is very high. Could the *señora* consult Don Samuel Abravanel and Doña Benvenida? They are the virtuous people who ransom prisoners," Christopher Manuel suggested.

"I'll do that, but not now. Now we have to save your family," I said decisively. "Christopher Manuel, please give Señor Osheki three hundred gold ducats."

Señor Osheki kissed my hands. "Blessed are you among women, *la señora*."

Christopher returned, handing over a heavy bundle to Yom Tov Atias.

"Take care of it. I've written a receipt for you, for some books that House of Mendes purchased from you, so that you won't be accused of theft," I said.

"My cousin Don Juan departed yesterday at my bidding to visit the House of Mendes's branches in Lyon, Antwerp and Venice. If any problem occurs, you can contact him," I added.

That entire night, I tossed and turned. We were hated as Jews, we were hated as impure Christians. The time had come to fulfill my dream and live openly as a Jew. But who would be able to advise me on this matter?

Don Samuel and
Doña Benvenida Abarvanel

The sky was cloudy. Grayness covered the street and sprinkles of rain were carried along by the cold wind, streaming over the garden and dripping down the windows. I don't think I had been as excited to meet Queen Mary as I was to meet the son of Don Isaac Abarvanel, whom my late father had admired, along with his wife, Doña Benvenida.

Don Samuel greeted me with a vigorous stride. He stood erect, although he was more than seventy years old. His wide forehead, which was furrowed with wrinkles, his silvery beard and the spark in his black eyes all made him resemble a prophet.

"Señora Beatrice Mendes, welcome to our abode."

"Greetings to those present," I replied, using a form of address I remembered from my parents' home.

Doña Benevida, whose slim form was almost swallowed by the red velvet armchair, stuck the needle and the purple embroidery thread in the blue silk fabric she held in her hand, signaling me to sit in the armchair next to her. "My dear, I'm happy to see you," she said in a soft voice.

"Doña Benvenida and Don Samuel, I've heard you ransom prisoners and help orphans and the poor with your charity fund."

"We do our duty. When we were forced to wear the Jewish badge in Venice, we left the city, and luckily, were granted permission to take our property with us. But many fled empty-handed, and it is a privilege to help them," Don Samuel said.

"We've heard of the *señora*'s good deeds and acts of kindness, and how immediately upon her arrival, she carried out the religious duty of *pidyon shvuyim*—the redemption of captives," said Doña Benvenida.

"Has the rumor spread already?"

"Businesspeople know everything." A slight smile flickered upon Don Samuel's lips.

"My father, Alvaro de Luna, admired Don Isaac Abarvanel and his interpretation of the Torah."

Don Samuel gently extracted a thick volume in a brown leather cover, its pages yellowing, from among the many books filling the shelves of his wood bookcase.

"An interpretation of the book of Genesis in the handwriting of my father, Don Isaac Abarvanel." Don Samuel carefully handed me the book.

I brought the book close to my face, breathing in the scent of the pages. In my mind's eye, I envisioned his father, Don Isaac Abarvanel, the Jewish minister of the treasury, standing tall before Ferdinand and Isabella, passionately attempting to convince the monarchs of Spain not to exile the country's Jews. At night, he returned to his home, and while bent over his desk, wrote interpretations of the Torah by candlelight.

"Doña Benvenida, I have a request. I heard that you were the admired teacher of Leonora, daughter of Don Pedro, viceroy of the Spanish rulers of Naples."

"It's true. Leonora was recently named Duchess of Tuscany, but she still calls me 'Mother' and has granted us trading rights in Tuscany," Doña Benvenida smiled.

"I'd be happy if you could teach me and my daughter Ana the Torah and the prayers."

Doña Benvenida rose gracefully from her armchair and kissed both my cheeks. "Señora Mendes, I will help you whole-heartedly."

"Your parents would have been proud of you," said Don Samuel Abarvanel.

"We'll meet every Friday at ten in the morning in my home. Your daughter Ana is invited every Tuesday, about which it was said 'it was good' twice in the bible, at nine in the morning," Benvenida said, warmly embracing me. The dimple in her cheek made her look mischievous.

***

I took care not to miss any of the Friday meetings, in which two of Doña Benvenida's friends also took part: the fragile Pomona Modina, a humble, quiet woman, who studied a page of the Talmud every day with her son, the poet Avraham, and her sister-in-law Bat-Sheva Modina, who had black, piercing eyes and a radiant face, and who delved into the mystical Book of Zohar and the writings of Maimonedes.

The meetings ran on for many hours, and I attended every single one. We were served cherries, lemon liqueur and delicate almond cookies. Doña Benvenida taught us the weekly Torah portion, Bat-Sheva told us about the Prophet Deborah, Queen Shelomtzion Alexandra, and the heroes of the bible, while Pomona taught me prayers and religious duties.

We laughed, exchanged stories about children and husbands, and my friends boasted of their grandchildren while I praised my daughter Ana. We had a funny agreement, permitting us to talk about one child and one illness every time. This was not a problem for me, as I only had one daughter, while they had been blessed with sons, daughters and grandchildren.

During one of our meetings, Doña Benvenida coughed constantly, telling us that Doctor Duarte Gomez had concocted a special medicine to help her combat the cough.

"It's too bad that the pope invited Amatus to Ancona to tend to his sister. If he hadn't gone, we could have consulted him."

"If you're referring to the doctor by his first name, you must be close friends." Pomona flashed a subtle smile.

"We've known each other for many years," I replied.

"The doctor did not invite you to come with him?" Bat-Sheva asked.

My face grew flushed. "Amatus did ask to link his life with mine," I murmured.

"The doctor is in love with you," Pomona smiled.

"How do you feel?" Doña Benvenida placed her hand on my shoulder.

I wrung my hands. "I… I… love… like him very much," I said, fanning myself to cool my blazing face.

"*Kuando la fortuna te espande un dedo, espandele la mano.* When fortune extends a finger to you, extend your entire hand to it," Doña Benvenida winked at me.

"Why don't you marry him?" Pomona asked.

"I can't marry him, and it is beneath me to live with him without marriage."

I watched the birds, which began to frolic dizzyingly through the garden. "As a widow, my rights are equal to those of a man. I may compose and sign letters, engage in commerce and manage the company. If I married him, I would lose my independence and would not be able to manage the House of Mendes."

"Life is a choice between options, between love and business," said Doña Benvenida.

"Go with your heart," said Bat-Sheva.

"The Torah says: 'It is not good that man should be alone.'" Pomona placed her hand on her heart.

Doña Benvenida poured lemon liqueur into my goblet. "Drink, my dear."

I grew fiercely attached to the three women. Before I met them, I did not know how much I was missing the company of educated women, full of wisdom and joie de vivre. I was lucky to have found such friends at my age.

"I'm making preparations to immigrate to the Land of Israel," Bat-Sheva informed us one Friday.

"You're lucky. I'm too old. I wish I could relocate to the Land of Israel as well," Pomona sighed.

"Isn't it dangerous to live there?" I asked.

"For Jews and *conversos*, it's dangerous everywhere," Bat-Sheva replied.

"Where will you live?" Doña Benevida asked.

"In the holy community of the city of Safed."

"Do you have relatives in Safed?" I asked.

"My sister and her husband live in Safed, near the home of Maran Rabbi Joseph Karo, whose family originated from Toledo, like my family. They've rented a house for us near the synagogue. My husband will open a workshop for weaving wool and will teach at Rabbi Moshe Cordovero's Tomer Devorah Yeshiva."

"Why Safed and not Jerusalem?" I asked.

"I've heard that the air in Safed is healthy and clear, its waters are healing, and its mountains overlook the Sea of Galilee and Tiberias. In Jerusalem, the Turkish pasha taxes the Jews heavily, and the Arabs abuse the Jews," Bat-Sheva said.

"Safed will be the source of salvation, and the messiah will appear there. As the Talmud says, 'The Sanhedrin moved... from Jerusalem to Yavne... to Tiberias, and from there shall salvation come,'" Pomona quoted.

"Don't you want to live in Constantinople?" I asked.

"I'll tell you a short story. When I was a child, I met a traveler, a gaunt, dark-faced man named David Reubeni. He dreamed of establishing a Jewish state in the Land of Israel and founding a Hebrew army. Ever since I heard of his intentions, I've dreamed of relocating to Israel," Bat-Sheva replied.

Doña Benvenida's eyes grew misty. "I, too, believed in him. I sewed him a blue silk flag and embroidered the Ten Commandments on it in gold thread. On his way to a meeting with the pope, he rode a white mule through the streets of Rome, waving the flag, which he held in his hand. Next to him strode dozens of admirers, including Shlomo Molcho, a New Christian formerly known as Diogo Pires, who returned to Judaism and was believed by some to have viewed himself as a messiah," she told us.

"I was fifteen at the time. I remembered what an uproar his meetings with the king created. There were arguments at home. My father claimed that David Reubeni and Shlomo Molcho were false messiahs," I said.

A storm of thunder and lightning was tearing through the gray sky, causing the windows to shake.

"David Reubeni suggested forging a military alliance between the Jews and the Christians to conquer the Land of Israel from the Turkish sultan. But the Church and the emperor were leery of the hopes of salvation that David Reubeni and Shlomo Molcho evoked in the *conversos*, and arrested them. David Reubeni was exiled to Spain and died there. Shlomo Molcho was arrested and burned at the stake in Mantua." Benvenida wiped away a tear.

"Such daring—I wish he had succeeded! Imagine if there was a Jewish state," I said.

"Beatrice, why don't you move to Safed too?" Bat-Sheva suggested.

"First I'll move to the sultan's land, and then to Tiberias."

"Tiberias?"

"Yes. I want to wake up every morning and see the Sea of Galilee from the windows of my home, and then bathe in the Tiberius Hot Springs, which would do my bones good."

"Well, I'll wait for you with a hot phyllo-dough *borek* with cheese, straight from the oven, in my house in Safed," Bat-Sheva laughed.

The Emperor's Decree,
Summer – Winter, 1549

The river of life raged and stormed, threatening to drown my secret Jewish brethren, exiled from Venice and the domain of Charles the Fifth's and Queen Mary's empire. The emperor's decree of expulsion instructed the Portuguese *conversos* who had arrived in the empire during the last six years to leave the kingdom within a month. The frightened, panicked *annusim* hastily packed their belongings and began to wander, seeking a place to lay their heads.

I was not worried about the rich, including my sister Brianda. I knew they could purchase passage aboard a ship or hire a coach and move to Ragusa, Thessaloniki or Constantinople. But I was highly concerned about the fate of the poor, the orphans and the elderly, who did not have the means and did not know to whom they could turn.

I remembered my parents' stories about the expulsion from Spain, the travails of the road during the hot days, and the old stomachache tore through me. However, I knew I had no time to wallow in the pain and that I had to take action. I sent letters to all House of Mendes agents, asking them to make every effort and spare no expense in helping the refugees to leave for the few countries and cities opening their gates to them, primarily in the Ottoman Empire, Poland, North Africa, and a few cities and duchies in Europe.

Juan had to leave Venice for Brussels. I received a letter that made me fear intensely for his life.

June 30, 1549
Brussels

Aunt,

I've arrived in Brussels. The writ of expulsion against the conversos
is now in effect throughout the domain of Charles's empire;
Portuguese and Ladino are no longer heard around the city, and
fear reigns in the streets.

I'm staying with friends at their residence, awaiting an interview
with Queen Mary. I hope I can convince the queen with my reasoning
and the hefty monetary endowment she will receive to cancel the
writ of expulsion and return the exiled.

Juan

I was very worried about Juan, to whom the writ of expulsion concerning
the Portuguese *conversos* also applied. I wrote to him that it was dangerous
for him to stay in Brussels or anywhere within the emperor's domain, and
asked him to depart for Ferrara immediately. But Juan was a stubborn
young man; he wouldn't turn back, and promised he would write to us
after meeting the queen.

In mid-July, I was invited to Castello Estense, for an urgent meeting
with Duke Ercole de Este.

The duke cleared his throat and informed me that my sister Brianda,
who was also subject to the writ of expulsion published by the Venetian
senate, along with La Chica, had appealed to him in a request for a
certificate of passage to Ferrara.

I was surprised. I hadn't thought Brianda would want to live in Ferrara
with me, and politely answered the duke that I was concerned about my
sister's and niece's welfare, and that I would do anything to help them.

The duke's secretary leafed through a pile of documents and handed
the duke a letter in Brianda's handwriting.

The secretary adjusted his white wig. "Your sister has offered the duke an endowment of forty thousand gold ducats if he intervenes on her behalf in the battle between the two of you over guardianship. She even sent an advance payment of twenty thousand ducats with a messenger."

I fanned myself vigorously, trying to dispel the heat that had risen within me. Bribing the duke and turning him against me? How dare she?

The duke looked at me and gently said, "Your sister is complaining that when you left Antwerp, you didn't allow her to bring the jewelry boxes she had received as gifts from her husband, containing an emerald necklace and gold coins. She claims you didn't even provide her with money for cheap ink and a proper bedspread, and she's forced to live on loans. What I don't understand is how your sister writes that she does not have the money to buy cheap ink, while also offering to pay me tens of thousands of ducats."

I froze in my place. The personal details and lies she had recounted to the duke stunned me.

Quickly, I came to my senses, saying, "I'm sorry we had to involve your highness in our personal problems. Since we left Portugal twelve years ago and until she got married, my sister was raised in my home as a daughter of nobility. Her frustration stems from the fact that I was appointed trustee over her daughter's assets."

Brianda's financial offer was appealing to Duke Ercole, and to my surprise, he decided that despite the dispute between her and myself, he would agree to her request and grant her and her servants a certificate of passage to Ferrara. As for her request to be appointed trustee over her daughter's inheritance, he would consult his solicitors. The duke concluded the conversation in this manner.

**

"Aunt Brianda and La Chica are coming!" Ana began to jump with joy when she heard of their arrival. "Mama, I want them to live with us in Palazzo Manianinni!" She stamped her feet.

I stayed silent.

In the handsome guest rooms, the maids laid out Egyptian cotton linens and filled the crystal vases with white and red tulips. The scents of baking drifted out from the kitchen. I hoped the excitement of the reunion would displace the unresolved friction between us, but I knew this was merely wishful thinking. Brianda would not relent until she could resume her status as trustee over the property; but that was not to be.

A loud exchange interrupted my work. I finished summing up the Income column and exited my office.

Brianda looked older. Small wrinkles were etched at the corners of her eyes.

"Hello, my sister Beatricci," she kissed my cheek faintly.

"Welcome. I'm very sorry about the cruel writ of expulsion. I'm glad the two of you came to me." I kissed her twice, once on each cheek.

Beautiful nine-year-old La Chica and fifteen-year-old Ana were excited by their reunion. Holding hands, they sat down on the sofa and caught up with each other's exploits.

"I won't stand for it! The esteemed *señora* deserves a more respectable sleeping hall," The sharp voice of Luciano de Costa, who had managed Brianda's household in Venice after we left, intruded upon us.

"Madame Brianda and her daughter have received the most lavish guest rooms," insisted my major-domo, Guillaume Fernandez.

"Madame Brianda deserves the best," de Costa argued.

"Luciano de Costa looks after me," Brianda blushed, looking away from me.

I eyed her harshly. "Brianda, Guillaume Fernandez is in charge of the household. De Costa needs to know his place."

The next few weeks proved that I had not been wrong. Much to my annoyance, de Costa trailed Brianda like a shadow, indulging her every wish and whim and addressing her fawningly. He interfered in Guillaume Fernandez and Christopher Manuel's work, berated the servants, and tried to change household arrangements on her behalf. Much to my amazement, he even escorted her to a card game once. I warned him not to dare do so again.

***

About two weeks later, Brianda pranced lightly into the dining room, waving a gilded invitation imprinted with a gold crown.

"I received an invitation for two from Duchess Renée de Este to a ball in Palazzo Schifanoia," she called out in exaltation. "Finally, we'll see the palazzo's murals and breathtaking ceilings, word of which has made its way even to Venice."

"The ball is in September. You have two months to get ready," I spat out.

Seamstresses, goldsmiths, cobblers, expert hairdressers and a variety of artists ascended to Brianda's bureau in the weeks preceding the ball. Finally, a silvery silk fabric and a fur cloak were decided upon.

The Plague

The commotion heard at the servants' entrance disrupted breakfast. I laid down the wedge of pecorino cheese on my plate. Guillaume Fernandez entered, his eyes frightened. "Excuse me. The cobbler's assistant is at the servants' entrance, and has informed me that the cobbler is ill, and cannot deliver the silvered silk shoes that Madame Brianda has ordered for the ball in time."

"I won't have shoes that match my dress?"

"Mama, why don't you wear the white silk shoes that you wore to the masquerade ball in Venice?" La Chica suggested.

I still had not finished the cheese when Guillaume Fernandez entered again, his steps hesitant, holding a small package.

"I beg your pardon. The goldsmith's wife arrived at the servants' entrance and left a package for Madame Brianda." Guillaume handed the package to Brianda. "Her face was red and full of sores, and she was crying and saying that her husband had made Madame Brianda earrings and a bracelet before he died, but he did not have time to finish the emerald necklace, and she doesn't have money for burial expenses and food for the orphans…"

The package dropped from Brianda's hand as her face grew pale. A servant quickly picked it up and placed it on the table.

I asked him to pay the poor woman her husband's wages for the jewelry and give her some food.

Guillaume left and immediately returned, reporting that that seamstress's daughter was now waiting at the servants' entrance as well. "She's coughing constantly and begging for a bit of food. She told me that her mother, her husband and her two little brothers passed away in agony overnight."

The cup of milk slipped from Brianda's hand, cracking the china plate.

"Provide her with some supplies. Check the reserves of food in the storehouse and allocate a daily amount of provisions for the cooks, then leave immediately to summon Doctor Duarte Gomez and Christopher Manuel, my agent in Ferrara," I instructed him.

Doctor Duarte Gomez entered with a mask smelling intensely of vinegar covering his face, and dropped into an armchair in exhaustion.

I asked him to update me on what was going on in the city.

"Señora, there is someone ill in almost every household, mostly children, women and the elderly. The number of funerals per day is rising at an alarming rate. The University of Ferrara has shut down, the city's wealthy residents have hired ships and escaped its borders. The streets are empty, and the residents are barricading themselves in their homes. I'm sure a plague has broken out."

"Heaven help us, what will we do?" Brianda called out.

"I hope you have vinegar…" Duarte Gomez mumbled.

"Yes, we have a six-month supply of vinegar in the storehouse in our yard," I said.

"Have all the jugs of vinegar brought to the kitchen. Cover your faces with vinegar masks, eat cloves of garlic, and under no circumstances should you leave the palazzo for the street. Nuns are tending to the sick throughout the city, but to no avail. The bodies of the dead are being tossed from the houses and are piling up on the streets. The stench of the dead, with no one to bury them, is enveloping the city."

The girls exchanged frightened looks.

"If any of your family members or servants are coughing, spitting blood, experiencing nausea, stomachaches, chills, or exhibit reddish-brown blotches on their body, they need to be quarantined immediately, preferably in one of the structures in the yard," he said.

"What happens if we catch it? Will we die?" La Chica hugged Ana.

"No, heaven forbid," Brianda said, her voice trembling.

"Take care of yourselves." Doctor Duarte picked up his bag and left.

The city's bells rang out, calling for a prayer for the recovery of the sick.

The church bells rang out as well, calling believers to pray.

Christopher Manuel rushed in, saying that rumors were spreading in town about a couple of Portuguese *conversos* who had come to the duchy from Germany, suffering from a high fever and chills, coughing harshly and spitting blood, with red spots appearing on their hands. They were the ones who had brought the plague. The priests and the enraged residents were now protesting in front of Castello Estense, demanding that the duke expel the Portuguese *conversos* from the city.

We were appalled when he told us that Samuel Osheki, the son of my friend the printer Avraham Osheki, as well as five merchants from among the Portuguese *conversos*, had been accused of spreading the plague, and had been arrested and thrown in jail, and all of their property had been looted.

The situation worried me. It was clear to me that the duke would not be able to withstand the pressure from the protesters and would expel the New Christians who had arrived from Portugal, just as the rulers of Venice, Carl the Fifth and Queen Mary, had done. I understood that we had to leave and escape the city.

I instructed Christopher Manuel to hire, immediately and at any price, a ship and its entire crew, rent a summer house on one of the islands, and hire guards to watch over Palazzo Manianinni. I handed him a heavy bundle of money and told him that if necessary, I would add more.

The next day, a messenger showed up at my palace and handed me a personal missive from the duke, which appeared to have been hastily written.

9.14.1549
Castello Estense
Duchy of Ferrara

Esteemed Señora Beatrice Mendes,

The riots and demonstrations against the Portuguese who brought the plague to Ferrara are expanding.

"The Portuguese conversos" who have arrived in Ferrara in the last four

months will be expelled from the city once the writ is published. They will be loaded onto three ships docking at the harbor.

Doña Beatrice and Doña Brianda Mendes, along with their daughters and servants, will be required to leave the city along with all the Portuguese by tomorrow at midnight.

Respectfully,
Duke Ercole the Second

Christopher Manuel arrived immediately after the messenger, wearing a vinegar mask and shaking all over. He said the duchy's soldiers were sweeping through the homes of the Portuguese *conversos*, forcing out men, women, children and the elderly and herding them on board three ships docked at the end of the harbor. The duke, his wife and their courtiers had abandoned the city and sailed to their summer house in the coastal city of Comacchio along with the city's gentry and the senior priests.

Luckily for us, after many efforts and in return for a true fortune, he had rented a rickety ship that would take us to a nearby resort town. He had also found six discharged soldiers, holding steins of beer in their hands, one of them lame, one of them one-eyed and another who was sixty years old, who had agreed to guard Palazzo Manianinni in exchange for an entirely exorbitant fee. He promised to double it if the palace was not looted in our absence.

We left the palazzo urgently, taking along a chest of jewels and a few chests of clothes, and departing for the ship, which was waiting for us at the port.

The eyes of Ana, La Chica, and mostly Clara and Hector, who were experiencing the terrors of expulsion and the escape from Portugal once more, told me how frightened and panicked they were. Luckily, I had made preparations in advance and found us a way out.

When we arrived at the port, lit torches were illuminating the pier, and the sights revealed to us were brutal. The guards patrolling back and forth yelled at the masses forced into the port: "Hurry up! Board the ships quickly. You must leave the borders of Ferrara by midnight."

The girls, Clara and Hector looked in terror at the guards and soldiers stabbing with their bayonets at men carrying crates on their hunched shoulders and elderly people attempting to hang on to their bundles and shuffling toward the harbor. Old women collapsed in exhaustion on the banks of the river. Mothers held weeping babies to their hearts, children hung on to the hems of their tired mother's dress. A burly guard stopped a dignified woman, tearing a gold necklace from her neck. The cries of the wretches trying to defend their bodies and meager possessions from the soldiers who were stabbing the men and women crowding onto the ship, grabbing bundles and crates from their hands and robbing their money, were piercing the very heavens.

I felt sorrow for being unable to do even a little to ease the fate of the exiles, whose tormented faces, cries and beseeching were breaking our hearts.

I grasped Ana's hand, and along with the managers of our household and the servants, we hurried to board the ship. Immediately after we boarded, the captain asked Guillaume Fernandez to increase his fee due to the risk he was taking upon himself by sailing with Portuguese *conversos*. I instructed Guillaume to pay him, but promised myself he would never work for any of my acquaintances again.

For an entire day, we sailed to the resort town in which Christopher Manuel had managed to rent an old, small villa. I encouraged Brianda and the girls, who were devastated by the expulsion and the paltry villa, saying we had to believe that things would turn out for the best. I promised them that those who had hope would attain everything in life: *kon la esperansa, todo se alkansa.*

For five long months, we lived modestly in the villa. Guillaume Fernandez and Luciano de Costa purchased flour, fish, eggs, milk, cheese and vegetables for us from the villagers and from the old woman who was the house's caretaker and lived in one of the rooms. The girls went for a short walk in the wooded hills every day, accompanied by Brianda, Clara and Hector. Sometimes, despite my disapproval, Luciano de Costa came with them as well, continuing to fawn over Brianda.

I spent most of my time going over the company's account books, which I had taken with me. It felt strange being disconnected from the management of my business, reminding me of the days I had spent in the Inquisition's prison. I thought about the fact that although the duke had invited me to settle in the Duchy of Ferrara, he still had not granted me and my family a writ of patronage and protection that would allow me to settle in the city and leave it whenever I desired. I came to the conclusion that I did not want us to be persecuted our entire lives, and that I must put an end to my business in Italy and in the Italian branches of the House of Mendes. I began to plan the relocation of my family to the sultan's cities, Ragusa and from there to Thessaloniki. When the right moment arrived, once I had a writ of patronage from the duke and could travel safely, I would carry out my plan.

✷✷✷

It had been months since I had heard from Juan.

One day, a sweating, weary messenger arrived on horseback from Antwerp bearing a missive from him.

Aunt,

I was arrested by Queen Mary's guard. Don't worry about me: I managed to secure my own release and am waiting for an interview with Emperor Charles the Fifth.

Juan

After five long months, the plague subsided and the number of infected decreased. I received permission to return to Ferrara with my family and some of our servants. Luciano de Costa and a few other servants who had still not received permits allowing them to return stayed on in the villa.

Brianda rented a residential palace not far from Palazzo Manianinni, and my life returned to its previous state of turmoil.

The duke permitted the release of my brothers the Portuguese *conversos* from the ships. Sailors carried off the corpses of the wretches, mostly elderly men and women, who had died due to the overcrowding and hunger prevailing on the ships.

The first thing I did upon our return was appeal to the duke for the release of Samuel Osheki and the five Portuguese merchants accused of spreading the plague, and for severely disciplining the guards who had robbed and looted their property when they were under arrest.

As Luciano de Costa was behaving improperly and I could not convince Brianda to keep her distance from him, I asked the duke to forbid him from returning to Ferrara, and the duke confirmed my request. However, Brianda requested an interview with the duke. She cried to him that she was a widow and could not manage without her major-domo, and requested a temporary permit that would allow him to return to the city. Much to my chagrin, the duke could not withstand her tears and pleading, and de Costa received a temporary permit that ultimately became permanent.

I was more successful in the case of Samuel Osheki and the merchants. The duke agreed to my request and released them. The merchants chose to return to their business and continue living in Ferrara. In contrast, writer Samuel Osheki distributed the prophecy of Jeremiah among our brethren the New Christians who had returned to Ferrara:

"And I will persecute them with the sword, with the famine, and with the pestilence, and will deliver them to be removed to all the kingdoms of the earth." He influenced many to set out on the road again, fleeing the environment of religious intolerance and hatred directed at them, and escape to the sultan's lands.

I worried about Juan after we did not receive any additional letters from him, and continued to assist the refugees and supply them with equipment and food. In the dead of night, we smuggled them on board House of Mendes ships owned by us and transporting grains, wool, leather and spices to the ports of Ragusa and Thessaloniki.

Arrest in Antwerp, 1550

On a cold morning, February 12, 1550, I was invited to have breakfast in the palace of the Duke of Ferrara, Ercole de Este the Second.

The servants led me to the sun porch, overlooking a garden whose flowers and trees were speckled with dewdrops. The duke's wife, the beautiful Duchess Renée, was waiting for me by a table set with blue china.

"That's a lovely pendant. I've never seen anything like it," the duchess admired the gold pendant I was wearing.

"Thank you. It's nearly my only memento from my mother, who passed away in Portugal."

The duchess offered me hot cocoa and muffins with cream, jam and honey.

"Duchess Renée, Doña Beatrice, good morning," Duke Ercole de Este greeted us, entering with vigorous strides. "I see the two of you are managing perfectly well without me."

"Darling, women's talk," the duchess replied.

"Doña Beatrice, we're honored to grant you a writ of patronage," he said, handing me a parchment scroll tied with a red ribbon.

A feeling of elation spread through me. I'd done it! In a world of zealots and religious persecution, the liberal, justice-seeking and unusually kind duke had chosen to swim against the current, stay true to his values and grant me a writ of patronage!

I unfurled the scroll, the words flickering in front of my eyes:

The Duke of Ferrara, Ercole de Este the Second, welcomes Doña Beatrice Mendes to the Duchy of Ferrara and grants her, her family and her servants a writ of patronage.

Doña Beatrice is entitled to practice Judaism and may not be arrested and accused of heresy.

Doña Beatrice is entitled to leave Ferrara and take all members of her household, her servants and her entire property with her, without paying custom fees.

Signed,
Duke Ercole of the House of Este
Duke of Ferrara

"Thank you, duke and duchess. My family and I will never forget the kindness of your grace."

"Doña Beatrice, one more small matter," the duke said before I left.

"Yes?"

"Tomorrow at nine I wish to summon you, your sister Brianda, and printer Geronimo de Vargas for a discussion on an agreement of conciliation between you and your sister."

I thought to myself that Yom Tov Atias, otherwise known as Geronimo de Vargas, had done well not to publicize the fact that he had returned to Judaism, and that I would have to postpone the move to Ragusa until I managed to reach an agreement with Brianda, and regained possession of the chests containing gems and coins that I had deposited in the Venetian Treasury.

***

"Mama! Juan is back!" Ana stormed into my office in excitement.

Wearing a white lace shirt and a blue wool cloak, with a short sword at his waist, Juan rushed in.

"Dear aunt," he kissed my hand.

"We've been worried about you! Tell me everything." Ana gazed at him in admiration.

"I've been worried about you, too. I heard you were exiled from the city," he said.

"Your arrest shocked me. You should have listened to me and left Brussels for Ferrara immediately," I said.

Juan sat down and leaned back in his seat, his voice growing hushed.

"I was hoping I could convince Queen Mary or the emperor to cancel the decree. I rode to Antwerp two days in rain and wind, but as I was waiting to be received for an interview with the queen, on October 2, 1549, on a cold, dark night, when I was leaving the home of friends, I was assaulted by a guard of soldiers armed with bayonets and spears. They asked to see identification and a permit to stay in Antwerp. '*Converso!* The writ of expulsion against Portuguese *conversos* is now in effect, and you are not allowed to be present within the borders of the Holy Roman Empire!' the officer of the guard roared at me, and whistled out a command."

"No!" Ana's face grew pale.

"His soldiers forcefully bound me with handcuffs. I fought them, and the armored officer raised his bayonet and injured my arm." Juan pulled his sleeve up and showed us a deep wound on his arm. "I was arrested and placed in an isolated citadel."

"You were injured! Why didn't you write to us?" Ana called out.

"I didn't want to worry you. The merchant guild and the members of the city council came to my aid and demanded I be transferred to confinement at an inn. Their pressure helped, and I was moved to an inn at the outskirts of the city. As a protest against my arrest, my many friends joined me for lunch at the inn. They brought baskets full of food and drink, spreading out the loaves of bread, meat and pastries on the inn's tables. And as the place was small and crowded, some spread out their lunch on the inn's staircase and ate with me. The rumor of this demonstrative protest took wing and spread throughout the city.

"Following the protest and the many appeals to the emperor, Charles the Fifth decided, 'in a gesture of goodwill,' to free 'the knight Juan,' as he calls me, and to see me for an interview."

"The knight Juan…" Ana was blushing slightly.

Juan filled the goblets with semi-dry wine that Bernardo had sent us from Lyon and served it to us.

"Lovely Ana." He twirled the glass of wine between his fingers.

Embarrassed, Ana cast her eyes to the floor, blushing even more.

"Not only did the emperor receive me for an interview at his palace, he also consented to my request and repealed the writ of expulsion!"

"You convinced the emperor to cancel the writ of expulsion? What are you, a magician or a hero?" She smiled at him in exuberance.

"I'm neither, but I do have charm." He glided his hand over the ivory hilt of his sword. "Your mother is a brave woman. She taught me not to be afraid." Juan raised his goblet. "To courage!"

"To your release and the repeal of the writ of expulsion!" I called out.

"Juan, the House of Mendes is in trouble. The scope of the loans Charles the Fifth and his sister are requesting from us has decreased significantly, and our profits have followed suit," I said.

Juan looked through his case and extracted a rolled-up map. "A map of the New World. I received it from a noblewoman, the sister of Emperor Charles the Fifth's advisor," he said, unfurling the map on the escritoire.

At the top of the map was the emblem of Carlos, King of Spain, otherwise known as Emperor Charles the Fifth: a black eagle with two heads, its beak and claws red, with red swords and a gold royal crown above the heads, and the emblems of the kingdoms under his reign at the center. The Pillars of Hercules, with a red ribbon winding around them, flanked the eagle on both sides.

Ana bent over the map, pointing at the motto engraved in gold letters on the ribbons, *Plus ultra*.

"What's the meaning of 'Plus ultra'?"

Juan leaned over the map, his head touching hers. He placed his hand on Ana's, then twirled the ruby ring on his finger and said, "'Plus ultra' means 'further beyond.' It's Charles the Fifth's motto. He wants to encourage the sailors to dare sail to the New World, and has promised them there are more countries beyond the Strait of Gibraltar, and that they should not be afraid to set sail. Charles canceled the previous script, '*Non plus ultra*'—'nothing further beyond,' which warned seamen of the dangers of crossing the Strait of Gibraltar."

Ana smiled at him joyfully. "You know so much."

I smiled to myself; the two of them were growing closer to each other.

Juan drew an imaginary line between Spain and the new continent, America.

"Pinto Moses, one of Charles the Fifth's clerks, who was detained at the inn with me, told me that ships loaded with gold are sailing from the new continent to Spain and Portugal, and that they're filling up the king's treasuries with gold bars and decorative items, until they're at full capacity."

"That explains why the scope of his loans from us has decreased, and our profits along with it," I said. "Have you made any progress in collecting the immense debt of one hundred and fifty thousand ducats that Francois the First, king of France and Henri the Second's father, borrowed from the Mendes Bank?"

"Not yet, but when I met Henri the Second in Paris, he boasted that France and England had reached an agreement to put an end to the wars between them, and promised to repay the debt soon. By the way," Juan chuckled, "he looked ecstatic. Queen Catherine de'Medici just gave birth to their fourth son, and is pregnant with the fifth. In addition, he has a daughter with his mistress, Diane de Poitiers, who is twenty years older than him."

"The king has an older mistress?" Ana was surprised.

"He has two... He's got no time for wars, he's too busy with his mistresses... And when there are no wars, there are no loans. The agreement between France and England hurts our income," Juan said.

"We can't rely on business with Europe. We have to expand our business to include the countries of the East, and relocate our headquarters to Istanbul, called Kushta or Constantinople." I pointed at the capital of the Ottoman Empire.

Juan raised an eyebrow. "Do you intend to leave your chests of ducats in the treasury in Venice?"

I shook my head. "What are you thinking? I'll fight for every single ducat. I'm preparing to relocate, and intend to shut down our entire business in the West. But only after I've regained possession of the chests I deposited in the Venetian Treasury, as well as all the merchandise that Brianda confiscated from me in Venice, Lyon and Paris, and after the king of France repays his debt. Only then will we move east."

The Conciliation Agreement

An unseen hand shifted away the darkness of night, sending caressing rays of light to illuminate the day.

This was it. The time had come. I donned a silvery dress and prayed that the efforts and many hours put in by the duke's barristers, the important solicitors I had hired and Brianda's own solicitors would bring the conflict between us to an end.

The bells of the cathedral rang nine times. Duke Ercole de Este entered the golden conference hall wearing a red cloak and a gold chain at his neck. He sat down in his carved chair at the head of the round conference table. His personal secretary sat at his right, taking down notes. To his left sat the duchy's barristers in their white wigs, while Brianda and I sat across from them.

Throughout the discussion, Brianda sat with her lips pursed, arguing every statement and suggestion the solicitors made. After hours of negotiations, we reached an agreement on all details.

The bells of the cathedral rang twelve times. The duke raised his hand, and the conference table grew silent.

"Ladies and gentlemen, this is a moment of reconciliation and peace between the Mendes sisters." He gestured at the secretary. "Please read the summary of the conciliation agreement reached in the discussion, and attached to the ten-page detailed agreement."

The duke's secretary stroked the curls of his white wig, raising the certificate that bore the duchy's eagle emblem stamped in gold.

"Uhhhmm," the secretary cleared his throat ceremoniously and began to read the document out loud:

Ferrara, June 4, 1550.

Conciliation agreement between the Mendes sisters.

Doña Brianda Mendes agrees to remove the liens she has placed on House of Mendes merchandise in Venice, Lyon and Paris.

Doña Beatrice Mendes shall deposit in the Venetian Treasury, within three months, one hundred thousand gold ducats in the name of the young Señorita Beatrice Mendes La Chica, constituting the funds of the inheritance bequeathed to her by her father, Diogo Mendes. When she reaches the age of fifteen or upon her marriage, she will be entitled to receive her money. Guardianship over the management of young Señorita Beatrice Mendes's inheritance fund shall remain in the hands of her aunt Beatrice Mendes, in accordance with the will of Diogo Mendes and with the consent of the Court of Foreign Affairs in Venice.

The secretary handed the duke a golden quill, and the duke inscribed the agreement with his elaborate signature. I took the quill and added my name.

Brianda hesitated, her gaze roaming around the room helplessly.

"Madam, please sign," the duke addressed her gently.

Her hand trembling, Brianda signed her name.

The secretary passed the document to four bankers from Florence and five from Venice who were waiting outside the hall. They read it attentively and signed their names as guarantors to the execution of the agreement.

***

I was engulfed with peace. The conciliation agreement had been signed to my satisfaction. Brianda and La Chica departed on a long excursion to the healing hot springs in Aix-la-Chapelle. I appointed my loyal agent, Doctor Duarte Gomez, who possessed a certificate of passage, as House of Mendes's agent in Venice. I sent him to confirm the conciliation agreement I had signed with Brianda in a Venetian court, but was bitterly disappointed. He reported to me that the Court of Foreign Affairs in Venice refused to approve the agreement, claiming it had been signed in Ferrara, outside the jurisdiction of Venice. The court once again declared Brianda to be the sole trustee of her daughter's inheritance, and demanded I show up at the court for further discussions.

Even worse, Brianda violated the agreement and appealed to the French court, demanding that House of Mendes assets that had been seized in Lyon and other cities be turned over to her.

Duarte Gomez reported to me that the ambassadors of foreign countries in Venice, primarily the French ambassador, Monsieur de Marvelier, were highly interested in the 'sisters' feud' and intended to take advantage of it to seize the property of the House of Mendes within their countries.

I paced back and forth in the living room. Things were veering out of control.

The thoughts were racing around in my head. I understood that I had no choice but to return to the den of the winged lion, Venice. If I did not make sure that the agreement we had signed was approved, my seized possessions in the Venetian Treasury would evaporate like smoke in the wind, which would have repercussions upon my plans to relocate my business to the Ottoman countries.

I was afraid that if I returned to the Duchy of Venice, the senate would want to keep my fortune in the city, and would prevent me from leaving, even though I held a letter of patronage from Duke Ercole de Este. It was clear to me that if I wanted to move east in confidence, it was important that I obtain a writ of patronage from the pope.

I sat down to write a letter to Pope Julius the Third. I asked for his protection, promising him that I would personally make sure that the ships of House of Mendes and other Portuguese *conversos* merchants would dock at the Port of Ancona, guaranteeing his city high revenue from taxes and custom fees.

I signed the letter and sent Christopher Manuel to Rome, along with a chest of gold ducats to be donated to the Church.

I decided to teach the Venetian authorities a lesson and cause them financial harm. I instructed all House of Mendes ships not to stop at the

Port of Venice, causing the city to sustain heavy losses, as the high taxes we paid for every ship docking in the port and the custom payments for the merchandise ceased abruptly.

I sent Juan to Paris, proposing that he contact Diane de Poitiers, Henri the Second's mistress, who was the one pulling strings and actually running the kingdom. I suggested he ask her to exert her influence on the king so that he would repeal the seizure of House of Mendes's assets and merchandise, in return for a very handsome sum.

Augustino Henricks also departed on a mission to Lyon and Paris on my behalf, to collect debts from the cities' merchants before Brianda or Henri the Second could get their hands on them.

***

Six months had passed since we had signed the agreement. White and violet blossoms covered the garden. Thousands of birds that had migrated to warmer climates were now swirling over Ferrara once more. I received another summons to attend a hearing before the court in Venice.

On a sunny day, an emissary from Rome brought me a letter from Pope Julius the Third.

"Ana, it's unbelievable. I've received a papal privilege—a bill of rights!" I showed her the letter.

Pope Julius the Third has confirmed the authority of Doña Beatrice Mendes to relocate her business to Rome or any other territory ruled by the Church, and to settle there temporarily or permanently, under the patronage and protection of the Church.

I asked the servant to pour Ana and me some cherry liqueur.

"To us! The duke's writ of patronage along with this amazing writ of protection from the pope will allow us to return to Venice and save your inheritance funds!"

"I'm afraid to go back to Venice." Ana shrugged. "Do you think a document can protect us? Do you trust Venice's secular authorities to respect a writ of protection from the pope? The decree of expulsion against the *conversos* is still in effect in Venice, after all," she curbed my enthusiasm.

"I never believe anyone. Learn to trust no one but yourself. We have one more important card in our hand: the writ of protection we'll receive from the Ottoman emperor, Suleiman the Magnificent."

My friend Amatus Lusitanus sent me the powerful Physician's Oath he'd composed. In his letter, he told me that he would soon complete his role as personal physician to the pope's family, and would relocate to Ragusa, where he intended to live openly as a Jew and continue his medical research. I envied my friend the doctor for not being bound to his business and his fortune, which allowed him to live according to his faith.

I asked Guillaume Fernandez to pack the trappings of my life into chests and crates. I appealed to the duke and requested his permission to sublet Palazzo Manianinni, so I would not lose the rent I had already paid.

Taking Off the Mask

My friend Doctor Amatus Lusitanus, who had been invited by the duke to give a guest lecture at the University of Ferrara, attended the farewell ball held in my honor by publishers Yom Tov Atias and Avraham Osheki. A sharp stab tore through my heart when he introduced me to his friend Michaela, a slim beauty whose green eyes gazed at him with constant admiration, and who responded to his every statement with a giggle.

My friends Doña Benvenida and Pomona Modina, who had been invited to the ball and felt my pain, buzzed around me like bees. They chattered on about nothing, amused me with their stories and did not allow me to feel lonely even for a moment. I bid farewell to all my friends, knowing in my heart that I would probably never see most of them again.

During the month when the crates and chests piled one on top of another, nearly threatening to break under the accumulated weight, I thought that before we returned to Venice, I should take off the mask and return to Judaism openly. I shared my decision with Ana, and explained to her that no one there must know of it, as if the Venetian authorities discovered our secret, we would be forced to live in the ghetto, would be accused of heresy, and our property would be seized forever.

Ana, who had matured into a beautiful, serious girl, kissed my cheek and promised to shroud and seal our secret in her heart.

***

On the Sabbath before Yom Kippur, the Holy Day, the moment arrived, and much to my joy, Amatus Lusitanus came to accompany us to the synagogue.

I caressed the sapphire in the center of my gold pendant and the gems that shone at me. "The chain remains unbroken," I whispered, brushing away a tear. I covered my head with a white lace kerchief and kissed the large silver mezuzah at the entrance to the synagogue.

My friends Doña Benvenida and Pomona Modina, whose heads were also covered with white lace kerchiefs, were surprised to see Amatus, but did not say a word. They imprinted kisses upon our cheeks and held us close to their hearts.

My legs were trembling as I stepped on the red marble diamonds of the synagogue floor. It was the first time in my life I had entered fearlessly into a synagogue where Jews were praying openly. The candles burning in the crystal chandelier brilliantly illuminated the gold-covered Torah ark, decorated with the Seven Species, the grains and fruits listed in the bible as products of the Land of Israel.

"*Shabbat shalom*, a peaceful Sabbath," Don Samuel Abarvanel and other worshipers, each wrapped in a tallit, greeted us.

Amatus Lusitanus kissed my hand. "Good luck, my dears," he said, entering the prayer hall.

I held on tightly to the gleaming wood banister leading to the women's section.

A tall woman with a wide, tan face and a dimple in her cheek examined me curiously.

"Welcome. I'm Sarah, the wife of Rabbi Benveniste," she said softly, pointing at the rabbi who was standing next to the podium. "You and I are distant relatives, and I've heard a lot about you," she said, seating me, along with the excited Ana and my friends, on a wooden pew, in the first row of the women's section.

Rabbi Benveniste wrapped his head with a tallit and began to pray. I opened the ancient *siddur* my father had given me as a gift and we prayed.

A Prayer of Moses the man of God,
Lord, thou hast been our dwelling place in all generations.
Before the mountains were brought forth,
or ever thou hadst formed the earth and the world,
even from everlasting to everlasting, thou art God.

Thou turnest man to destruction;

And sayest, Return, ye children of men.

For a thousand years in thy sight are but as yesterday

When it is past, and as a watch in the night.

Three distinguished rabbis climbed up to the podium. They sat down in front of the worshipers, each of them covering his head with a tallit.

"When a person leaves the gaol, untying the bonds of untruth and returning to the Torah of Moses, he recites a confession.

"Gentlemen who are praying and dear ladies, I shall ask you to keep the ceremony taking place before you as a secret, as human lives might be at stake."

A dignified silence filled the synagogue. "You're brave," Benvenida whispered.

"Ladies, please repeat the following sentence after me," the rabbi with the silvered beard and the soft eyes said.

"*La señora* Beatrice de Luna Mendes shall henceforth be called in Israel: Doña Gracia Nasi, Hannah Nasi.

"Ana, daughter of Doña Gracia Hannah Nasi, formerly Beatrice de Luna Mendes, shall henceforth be called in Israel: Reyna-Malka Nasi, of the house of Benveniste."

"Amen," we whispered, deeply moved.

"Today, we shall recite the prayer for the annulment of vows in honor of your return to the fold of the People of Israel," Rabbi Benveniste said. "Please repeat after me.

"*Hear me, oh masters, expert judges. I hereby present my statement before you*

And annul, from here onward, any vow or oath I have sworn

And I regret all that is mentioned here," the elderly rabbi called out, his voice shaking.

Ana firmly pressed her palm against mine, and we repeated the Hebrew words, our pronunciation somewhat imprecise.

The rabbis declared three times:

"*All are annulled for you, all absolved for you, all permitted to you.*

There are forgiveness, absolution and redemption here.

All are null and void, like a broken vessel, and a thing of no substance.
As we grant annulment in this court on earth
So shall they be annulled in the Court on high."

"Amen," the women replied, in awe and excitement.

Ana looked at me, and briefly, I saw Francisco's gaze reflecting in her eyes. "Congratulations, Mama," she whispered to me.

"At long last, we're Jewish." I hugged and kissed Reyna, warm tears rolling down my cheeks.

"Gracia, Reyna, congratulations, you are our sisters," my friends said.

After the prayer, we were invited to Kiddush, the blessing said over the wine, in the synagogue hall. The aroma of *hamim*, the Jewish *cholent* stew, spread through the hall, filling me with yearning.

Doña Benvenida and Pomona hugged my daughter Reyna. We all brushed away tears, knowing it was a moment of parting, and that we might never meet again.

PART SIX

Venice

1552

A Stranger in Venice

Venice had changed its façade and lost some of its vitality. In Piazza San Marco and the Rialto, there were fewer passersby. The sound of the Portuguese language was not heard. Many of the stores of the Portuguese *conversos* were locked and bolted, and hooligans had thrown stones and eggs at them. Other stores had been broken into and looted.

Autumn rains washed over the city and fog covered the Palazzo Gritti. The bustle of visitors, merchants, bankers, messengers arriving to deliver invitations to balls, literary salons or musical recitals, and beggars seeking alms had decreased. Venice had turned its back on me; I was a stranger in a familiar town.

An elusive reddish light glinted from the stained glass windows, the golden mosaics, the decorations and the precious stones in St. Mark's Basilica.

"Señora de Luna Mendes, you've returned to us? We didn't have time to say goodbye!" Adriana, the notorious gossip, declared with a quiver of her fleshy chin.

"Hello, Señora Adriana," I said in a chilly voice,

"The *señora* never left us, she simply departed for a few years and has returned for good," muttered Marco de Mollino, my business manager in Venice.

"Everyone is hoping that the sisters' feud will come to an end," Valera winked to her friends.

"I see that the *señora* is well versed in others' lives," Marco de Mollino raised his voice.

Priests, city dignitaries and noblewomen gathered around. It was impossible to miss their whispering.

"The *señora* has a chapel at Palazzo Gritti. Why is she coming to the basilica?"

"To show off her wealth..."

"Is her sister coming to Venice too?"

"The *señora* and her daughter are Portuguese *conversos*. Why aren't they being deported?"

"Doge Francesco Donato is afraid of a woman..." someone laughed bitterly.

"That's not it at all. The doge wants to avoid a war with the sultan."

The fear that our secret would be revealed shadowed me everywhere. I asked myself whether I should have waited until I had set foot on the soil of Constantinople before returning to Judaism, and took care to stay away from the Jewish neighborhood at Ghetto Nuevo.

I met maritime insurer Simone Scopio along with my agent Duarte Gomez and my representative in Venice, Marco de Mollino, at the offices of the insurers' guild, which were quieter than they had once been. I asked him for a quote for insuring my ships that would be sailing from the East to the Port of Ancona.

"I hope the House of Mendes ships will resume trading with Venice," Señor Simone Scopio said softly.

"Since the House of Mendes ships no longer dock at the port, the scope of trade has decreased, and the markets are almost empty of merchandise," said Marco de Mollino.

I wrapped the black hairnet tighter around my head. "Life leads us down winding roads. Many duchies are fighting over the right to trade with House of Mendes. The pope has offered me a discount on taxes and custom fees for boats docking at the Port of Ancona," I said.

The meeting lasted for quite a while. Señor Scopio was clever enough not to invite me to the literary salon at their home in Marco de Mollino's presence. I, in turn, took care not to ask after his lovely wife, or inquire about old Rabbi Lucato.

When I returned to the palazzo, a letter from Juan was waiting on my desk. It had been sent from Paris, and brought good news. He had contacted Henri the Second's mistress, Diane de Poitiers, and at her recommendation, the king issued a royal writ repealing the seizure of

House of Mendes's assets and merchandise. As a token of his gratitude, he was endowing her with a handsome sum.

Our agent Augustino Henricks managed to collect the funds that merchants and debtors who had taken advantage of the seizure order had failed to pay.

***

A cold sun was peeking through the clouds. Ana was sitting on the balcony overlooking the Grand Canal, embroidering her dreams onto a tablecloth she was preparing for her dowry. I wrapped a fur cloak around my shoulders and went out to the balcony to give her Juan's regards.

"When will he get here?" Ana suppressed a tiny smile. The needle embedded itself in her finger instead of in the tablecloth she was working on, and a red drop stained it.

I quickly wiped the blood off her finger. "Juan will be back soon."

A House of Mendes ship was making its way toward the port among the many vessels flying colorful banners.

"It's La Chica," Ana leapt up, waving hello enthusiastically.

La Chica, who was standing on deck, returned her greeting, but the ship sailed past Palazzo Gritti and kept going until it disappeared from our view.

"La Chica won't be living with us. Brianda has rented a palace for them not far from here, in Rio de Santa Caterina."

"How long will you fight? It's gone on long enough, concede to your sister." Ana hid her face in her hands.

"I, too, want to put an end to this ongoing saga, and to have the court rule in my favor. That's why I've hired a first-class Venetian solicitor to represent me at the hearing."

"Mama, I miss La Chica."

It began to drizzle, and we went into the living room.

"Ana, I'm sure we'll all be together soon. At the moment, despite the writs of patronage from the pope and Duke Ercole, I'm afraid that the authorities won't allow us to leave Venice, and so I've written a letter to Sultan Suleiman."

"Why? What did you write to him?" Ana asked.

"I thanked the sultan for his grace in sending his delegate, the *shawish*, two years ago to escort me to Istanbul. I apologized for being unable to leave Venice for his country due to several legal and commercial matters that detained me. I politely informed him of my wish to relocate to the grand Ottoman state and asked him to send the *shawish* to escort me to his country. Juan has also written to Efendi Moshe Hamon, the sultan's physician, and to the prince, Şehzade Saleem, and asked them to exert their influence over the sultan," I replied.

"Ana, pray with me that the sultan's ship, bearing the *shawish*, will be here before the hearings begin."

But the ship did not appear, and my days wavered between uncertainty and hope.

***

The sharp, ongoing toll of bell clappers on Sunday, November 8, 1551, startled the congregants who hurried out when the mass was concluded. Elegant ladies sauntering in their high heels, dandified noblemen milling about in Piazza San Marco, Republic Guard soldiers, the city's dignitaries, ambassadors, priests, merchants, children and peddlers—all of them streamed toward the port.

Among the vapors of mist rising from the canal, Sultan Suleiman's flag, embroidered with curly gold letters, was revealed before our eyes, waving in the wind, while the barrel of a cannon on the boat's deck was aimed at the city.

The ship's gangway was lowered, and a Turkish officer, his face the hue of *café au lait*, his black mustache curling down toward his mouth, wearing a brown coat and a turban upon his head, descended to shore, accompanied by three fair-skinned, blue-eyed janissaries in red uniforms, equipped with curving scimitars.

The crowd burst out in calls of alarm.

"The sultan's delegate... The *shawish* is here..."

"War!"

"The Muslims are threatening Venice!"

The head of the guard and his soldiers surrounded the sultan's delegate and blocked his path. The *shawish* handed the commander of the guard a royal missive, and the guard's commander passed it on to the doge's secretary, who had been urgently summoned to the port.

"The sultan's delegate requests an interview with His Majesty Doge Francesco Donato," said the commander of the guard.

The secretary produced a silk handkerchief and wiped the drops of perspiration dripping down his forehead. His eyes scurried between the warship, the Turkish *shawish* and the volatile crowd. Finally, he nodded.

The head of the guard whistled out a command, and the guard soldiers lined up in formation, escorting the sultan's delegate to Palazzo Ducale.

I made an effort to conceal the smile that lit up my face. "Ana, soon we'll be starting a new life. Come on, it's dangerous to stay here," I whispered, and we hurried back to Palazzo Gritti.

After a long, tense interval, my agent Duarte Gomez returned with the news that had spread throughout the city.

"The *shawish* gave the doge a letter from the sultan, informing him that the *shawish* is here on the sultan's behalf to escort the Mendes sisters and their families, along with their servants and property, to Turkey.

"The city's dignitaries are angry: two years ago, the *shawish* came to escort you to Turkey, but you wanted to stay in Venice. They're resentful toward the doge and the senate, which are fearful of the sultan and have allowed the *shawish* to stay in Venice until the hearing is concluded. They assigned him a palace on the island of Giudecca, with a view of San Marco, and placed guards, gondolas and an expense budget at his disposal," Duarte Gomez recounted.

"'Why does Venice need to fund the Turk?'

"'Because of the blood feud between the sisters, war is about to break out?'

"'It's better if we let the sisters leave, so that we don't enrage the sultan.'

"'We can't allow them to leave. They've taken advantage of our hospitality, gotten wealthy thanks to Venice, and now they want to leave!'

"'Why should Venice's ducats end up in the hands of our Ottoman enemies?'

"'Instead of thanking us, those rich sisters want to take off!'

"'To hell with them… Because of them, the sultan will declare war on Venice and send his terrifying navy to conquer La Serenissima!'

"'We should throw those Portuguese *conversos* sisters in prison again!'

"'Christianity can't surrender to these Muslim infidels.'

"'She's betraying the Religion of Truth!'

"'What about our children and families?' the people raged."

In my mind's eye, I envisioned the grueling days of arrest I had undergone two years ago at Palazzo Ducale. The guards who had held torches burning with red fire, illuminating the darkness of the prison's winding, damp and gray corridors. I felt their heavy hands, roughly grasping my arm, the rat that passed just a whisper away from me, the heavy door opening. I could smell the mold in the small room into which I had been tossed, and touch the slim ray of light filtering in through the window.

As if it was all taking place at this very moment, I could hear the heavy footfalls of the inquisitors, the shuffling of the prisoners, the terrible screams of the wretches tortured by the Inquisition in the musty cellars under the Grand Canal. The words "Esther" and "Sabbath," which I had managed to identify in the terrible cacophony of shouting, echoed in my ears.

I remembered my friend Amatus Lusitanus' consoling visit, thought of the *familiar* who had taken the risk of conveying Ana's painful letter to me, in which she told me of being sent to the convent, and about the chameleon, my only source of conversation in the cell.

The cold eyes of the head inquisitor, resembling the doge's greyhound, passed in front of my mind's eyes. I heard him barking out: "Does the accused wish to confess her sins?" "Has the accused lit candles on the eve of the Sabbath?" as well as the grave accusations of treason: "Did the accused make preparations to leave Venice and relocate to Turkey, an enemy country?"

Brianda's voice as she testified against me echoed in my ears once more: "My sister Beatrice de Luna has been living as… a Jew in secret."

"Forgive me," I heard her voice begging me when she was tossed into the prison cell.

I envisioned the sultan's warship, which had brought the *shawish* who had arrived to escort us to the Ottoman state, and was now threatening Venice. I thought of the letter of the sultan's Jewish physician, Efendi Moshe Hamon, to the doge, a letter that had put us in danger, in which he declared that Ana was going to marry his son in Constantinople. I also recalled my refusal to leave Venice, as well as Don Angelino's warning that the court was about to rule in favor of Brianda, and charge me with a heavy financial payment, and my decision to flee Venice under cover of night to the safe haven of Ferrara.

I listened to the raindrops and the sighs of the wind whipping at the shaking windows, and knew that my decision to return to the lion's den that was Venice had been the right one. The *shawish* had come to escort me to Turkey with the fortune I had earned using my wits during the fourteen years since I had left Lisbon as a young widow entrusted with the care of Ana, Brianda, Juan and Bernardo and up to the present day, when I was a businesswoman whose ventures encompassed the entire world, the owner of a fleet of ships, a bank and chests full of diamonds, precious stones and gold coins. Kings and dukes were begging me to settle in their countries.

I returned my gaze to Duarte Gomez, who was patiently waiting. "After the night, daylight will dawn. Let them talk. It's only words. The moments of difficulty in life make me stronger. Ultimately, I will achieve the goal I set for myself and move east, to the Ottoman state," I said.

***

Brianda stormed into my study, followed by an embarrassed La Chica.

"How impudent of you! Who allowed you to send that barbarian to the doge and inform him he's come to escort me to that terrible country?!" she burst out. "Have you seen their clothes? You want to live with the primitive barbarians?"

I gestured toward the armchair.

Brianda shrugged. "Who are you to decide what's right for me?" She turned her back to me and stormed out once more, with La Chica following her out.

The next day, rain washed over the city. The water in the Grand Canal nearly overflowed. The church bells rang eleven times. A black gondola stopped in front of my palace.

"Ahm... Ahm..." Major-domo Guillaume Fernandez, who had entered my office, cleared his throat and handed me a letter stamped with La Serenissima's orange lion seal.

The Republic of Venice
November 16, 1551
The Court of Foreign Affairs

For Señora Beatrice Mendes,

The hearing concerning the señora will take place tomorrow, at ten o'clock, in Palazzo Ducale.

Respectfully,
The Court Secretary

My good friend Don Angelino, who was among the few who came to visit me, removed tobacco leaves from a silver snuffbox and rolled them into a slim cylinder.

"Are things looking bad?" I asked.

Don Angelino placed the cylinder of tobacco against the table, striking it lightly to pack in the leaves.

"My darling, do you want to hear the truth?"

"Please. I've gone through a thing or two in my life."

Wrinkles etched his innocent face. "I've heard that the doge's crown nearly fell off his head when he looked out his window and saw the cannons of the sultan's warship turned toward his palace, and heard that the sultan had taken you under his patronage."

"I'm a Portuguese subject. It's my right to leave the island."

"I don't want to repeat the harsh expressions I heard from the doge and from the members of the Council of Ten. They haven't forgotten that you fled Venice, and are furious that you're not respecting the decision of the court, which favored you, to deposit one hundred and fifty thousand gold ducats intended for your niece La Chica."

I added a spoonful of cherry preserves to a glass of water and sipped a bit.

"Have they forgotten that they arrested me? How is demanding that I deposit a hundred and fifty thousand ducats favoring me?"

Don Angelino suppressed a hint of a smile. "Your sister demanded half of the assets of the House of Mendes, which totals three hundred thousand gold ducats, and the court reduced the sum by half."

"Things change. In Ferrara, we signed a conciliation agreement and decided that I would deposit a hundred thousand gold ducats."

Don Angelino lit the cylinder with a candle flame. The tobacco ignited with a red blaze.

"Have you deposited a hundred thousand ducats?"

"Not yet."

Angelino gazed at me through the smoke rings that floated around him. "Don't raise the winged lion of Venice from his rest."

The rage surged within me. "You have to understand. I have dedicated my life to increasing the fortunes of the House of Mendes. I can't bestow *a hundred thousand* ducats upon an eleven-year-old girl, so that my sister can burn through them, dispersing them like smoke in the wind."

Grayish smoke swirled around me. "Brianda's solicitor has informed the Council of Ten that she refuses to leave Venice," he said quietly.

I leaned back in my chair. "A family chooses to live joyfully or in melancholy. Sisters choose friendship or hostility."

Don Angelino extinguished the blaze in the ashtray.

"My advice is to hire the best solicitor in Venice for the hearing."

"Thank you—I've already done that. I believe I will win the trial. I will be appointed trustee of La Chica's inheritance, as I deserve, and will leave for Turkey with my treasure chests."

The Siege on Palazzo Gritti

I left Ferrara, and instead of sailing to Constantinople, in spite of the danger, I chose to return to Venice. I believed wholeheartedly that I would prevail in the trial and be appointed as trustee. But I preferred not to appear before the members of the senate in Palazzo Ducale, the palace that evoked bitter memories from the days when I had been imprisoned. I sent my esteemed solicitor to represent me at the hearing.

After the prolonged hearing, my solicitor arrived looking pale and breathing heavily, his assistant trailing in his wake with the heavy document case. The maid hastened to serve him some apple preserves and a cold glass of water. He sat down heavily and began to describe the latest developments in detail:

"The senate's representative, notary Paolo Leoncini, brandished his cape with a flourish and addressed the members of the senate with his ingratiating voice.

"'People of Venice, with your permission, the Senate of the Republic will today discuss whether to agree to the request of Sultan Suleiman the Magnificent to permit the sisters de Luna Mendes to leave La Serenissima.

"'Señora Beatrice Mendes has elected not to appear before the Venetian Senate, which had bestowed its grace and mercy upon her. Her solicitor is asked to present a statement on her behalf.' The courtroom grew silent.

"'Señora Beatrice Mendes accepts the sultan's invitation to depart for his country,' I informed the senate. 'Boo… Boo…' the calls echoed through the hall.

"Notary Paolo Leoncini raised his hand, silencing the court once more, and called Brianda to testify.

"'Gentlemen of the senate,' she began in a soft voice. 'My sister wishes to force my daughter and myself to relocate to the country of the Turk. I did not ask her to appeal to the sultan for a permit to move to his land.' Her voice grew sharper, her eyes lingering on the faces of the senate members. 'I want to stay in Venice, to live and die here as a true, faithful Christian.'

"'Bravo! Bravo!' the senators applauded her, rising to their feet and gazing at her in admiration.

"A heated argument, accompanied by loud exclamations, broke out between the senators who approved of granting an exit permit and those who opposed it.

"After a prolonged discussion, those senators fearful that the sultan would declare war upon the island and conquer Venice ultimately prevailed, and several decisions were reached.

"Paolo Leoncini huddled with the secretary writing down the minutes of the hearing. He brandished his cape once more and read out the summary.

"'The Senate of the Republic of Venice has decided to allow Señora Beatrice Mendes to leave Venice.'

"A young senator rose to his feet, calling out, 'You should be ashamed! She ought to be arrested!'

"Paolo Leoncini raised his hand, his eyes blazing in anger as he instructed him to sit down.

"'I don't want to be a part of this decision,' the senator said, storming out of the courtroom.

"Paolo Leoncini resumed reading: 'The *señora* shall immediately deposit one hundred thousand gold ducats in the treasury, the inheritance funds of Señorita Beatrice Mendes.'

"The senate decided to respect Brianda's wish to stay in Venice, and will send a letter to the sultan explaining that Madame Brianda would not be coming to his country, as the authorities of the Republic of Venice cannot compel anyone to leave the city against his or her will.

"Señor Ludovico Bacadelli, the papal envoy to Venice, began waving his arms and challenging the decisions agreed upon. He stationed himself across from the senate members.

"'Although I am the papal envoy, I cannot change the senate's outrageous decision.' He beat his chest with his hand. 'However, I must clear my conscience,' He raised his voice. 'I cannot help but cry out against this betrayal and slap upon the face of Christianity!'

"The envoy then produced a sheet of paper, and with a flushed face, read its contents. 'Before us stands a woman openly declaring that she wishes to travel to the land of the Muslim, apparently openly returning to practicing Judaism!' The veins in his neck protruded as if they were about to burst through his skin.

"'Why are the Venetians allowing the lady to leave, in order to live under a false religion? Why do you not punish her?' The papal envoy spat these words out at the senate members and stormed angrily out of the courtroom."

I smiled. I had won! I only had to deposit a hundred thousand ducats. I thanked my solicitor for his good work and asked when I could receive my confiscated chests from the treasury building.

"I'm sorry, due to the turmoil in the courthouse, the chests were not discussed. Señora, once you deposit the money, you may leave Venice," the solicitor said.

I requested that he inform the senate that I needed a few days' time in order to procure such a high sum. The solicitor apologized, saying he had to return to his office. His assistant picked up his case and the two of them departed.

***

A persistent knocking woke me from me sleep. I opened my eyes. Clara was standing in the doorway, a lit lantern in her hands. "*La Señora, pardon*, there are soldiers outside the house." The words tumbled from her throat like stones.

Teresa, pale and frightened, hurried in after her, helping me put on a morning gown with an embroidered hem and no collar. I peeked out through the curtains. Lit torches were illuminating the dark sky, and dozens of soldiers were surrounding Palazzo Gritti.

I descended quickly to the ground floor. Guillaume Fernandez's face was gray. "Señora, the city's senate has posted a guard around the palazzo," he said, opening the palace doors.

Gondolas bearing soldiers armed with axes and spears surrounded the palace. A notice had been affixed to the front door.

No one may enter or leave the house.

In addition, no possessions may be taken out of the house.

A broad-shouldered officer of the guard, wearing leather armor and a silvered helmet upon his head, disembarked from the gondola, drew out his long sword and blocked my way out.

"Commander of the guard Veniciano Raffaello hereby informs the *señora* that in accordance with the senate's decision, no one may leave or enter Palazzo Gritti until the *señora* carries out the court's decision and deposits the funds in the treasury house," he declared aggressively, closing the doors.

I climbed the stairs heavily. The assertive portrait of Pope Andrea Gritti, who had lived in the palazzo in the past, gazed down upon me. His mouth seemed to be gaped in amazement.

I sank down into an armchair. I possessed a certificate of transit from Pope Julius the Third, but now this authorization was a meaningless document, and Palazzo Gritti had turned into a gilded cage for me and my daughter.

"Mama, what happened?" Ana ran to me, her eyes frightened.

"The senate is worried that we'll flee Venice before I deposit the money in the treasury, and that we'll smuggle out gold and valuables."

"I'm afraid you'll be arrested and I'll be taken to the convent." Her entire body was trembling.

"They wouldn't dare!"

"Mama, they say you're the wealthiest woman in the world! Please, deposit the money."

"Under no circumstances! I have to carry out Diogo's will. When La Chica is fifteen, she'll receive her inheritance!"

I paced back and forth in my room, trying to soothe my boiling blood. Not only did the people here wear masks, but the city itself wore a mask as well. Under its dazzling beauty, it was a cruel place.

The thunder of mighty fists tore through the quiet. The servants peered curiously through the doors. Veniciano Raffaello, commander of the guard, accompanied by Guillaume Fernandez, stood at the entry to the library.

"The *shawish*, delegate of Sultan Suleiman the Magnificent, the only person who may enter and leave," he announced firmly, turned on his heels and exited the room.

The sultan's delegate stood before me in taut attention, his black eyes fixed upon me.

"Madame, at your service," he addressed me in French in an Eastern accent.

From a brown wool bag attached to his wide belt, he extracted a letter written in French:

Istanbul

For Señora Beatrice Mendes,

Madame, His Imminence Sultan Suleiman Han Hazretleri sends the shawish to do her honor's bidding.

Warm regards,
The sultan's physician
Efendi Moshe Hamon

"Señora, Sultan Suleiman will not be pleased to hear of your arrest in the city, or that the imminent sisters are not on their way to his country." The *shawish* ran his hand along his throat in a sharp gesture, signaling that the sultan would chop off his head if he did not carry out his mission.

"Please, let the sultan know that I await his swift intervention."

"Señora, at the senate's request, my deputy is returning to Istanbul to let Sultan Suleiman know that your arrest is not an attempt to insult the sultan, but merely to verify that the verdict is carried out." The *shawish* curled his mustache.

The sense of suffocation in my throat was gradually increasing. I had a hard time gathering my remaining strength in order to speak in a calm manner. I felt as if I was suspended between the mercies of the Venetian senate and those of the sultan.

"Please let the senate know that I will deposit the required sums after they remove the siege from Palazzo Gritti."

"Señora, I'm negotiating with the senate to get them to call off the siege. As the sultan's delegate, I suggest you convey a financial offer that will appease your sister Brianda and allow the removal of the guard."

Taking his advice was truly the last thing I needed.

"I'll think about it," I said.

The *shawish* bowed and left.

***

The next day, when the intense heat became oppressive, not only had the guard not dispersed, but twenty more soldiers were stationed near the entrance to the palazzo.

The panic within the house increased. Servants who needed to leave to tend to their own affairs could not do so. Marco de Mollino, who came to visit me, was not allowed to enter. Ana cried and begged to be allowed to leave and visit La Chica in her palace on a nearby street, but the guards stopped her. Teresa felt ill, but the commander of the guard would not allow the doctor to see her. I sat next to her bed, gave her my own concoctions and prayed she would get better.

The servants tiptoed around the house with glum faces, peering out occasionally through the curtains. We had a sufficient amount of sacks of flour and rice in the storehouse. Crates of fresh fruit and vegetables were placed at the entrance to the kitchen every morning. The cooks made risotto and pizza Margherita, and baked bread and cookies. My Ana could not taste the almond cookies she loved, and spent most of the day in her wide canopy bed. I tried to rally her spirit, along with those of the staff, asking them to have faith that the siege would be removed. "*Kon la esperansa, todo se alkansa*. Those who hope will attain their wishes."

Every morning, the *shawish* arrived at Palazzo Gritti, begging me to acquiesce to Brianda's financial demands, while she sat in her palace, pleased that I was under house arrest and that the senate was not demanding that she leave Venice.

The cold seeped into my bones and my joints hurt. Life became intolerable. House of Mendes's business had ground to a halt; I could not convey instructions, transfer money or manage the company. Any minute when I was not doing business spelled losses for the House of Mendes company.

Gold bars, lavish outfits, valuable jewelry—what use were they to me while I was held captive in my palace? After a week of house arrest, I decided not to tempt fate and asked the *shawish* to inform the senate that I was willing to once again sign the agreement I had reached with Brianda a year and a half ago in Ferrara.

The *shawish* returned, his face flushed and blotchy, and informed me that Brianda had many comments about the agreement signed in Ferrara, and she was demanding more and more money and was unwilling to sign.

White snowflakes fell, covering the gray stone tiles with a gleaming pallet.

The senate members, weary of the sisters' feud that had almost dragged them into a war with the sultan, and who had despaired of Brianda's demands as she delayed signing the agreement, informed her that if she did not sign it, she was free to leave Venice and sue her sister at her new place of residence.

The Republic Guard's gondolas and the soldiers laying siege to Palazzo Gritti disappeared from our view, and the light returned to Ana's eyes. She jumped for joy on my canopy bed.

The maids wiped the cold vapors off the windows, airing out the rooms.

However, Teresa, my beloved governess, who had been by my side my entire life, did not recuperate. A week after the siege was removed, her soul returned to her Maker.

The *shawish* disappeared and failed to return. From the news filtering into the palazzo, we found out that he had evoked anger with his coarse, impolite behavior. He demanded money from the senate and threatened to beat up the Venetian guards. The senate sent a strongly phrased complaint to the sultan regarding his improper behavior, and he was sent back to Istanbul. Rumors told of a long sword slashing his throat.

Christopher Manuel gave me some grim news about the bitter fate of our brethren fleeing Portugal. The ship *Sao Josepe*, under the command of Admiral Manuel de Sousa Sapolbade, carrying a cargo of cannonballs, gun powder, china, black pepper and gold coins, had been swept up in a storm and gone down opposite the coast of South Africa. Most of its passengers, Portuguese *conversos*, had drowned at sea. The only seven survivors, who had managed to escape and land on the shores of Mozambique, told a shocking take. Some of the survivors who had made it to shore died of hunger, while ten were eaten by natives of the Zulu tribe. I was overcome with fear; would this be the fate of some of my brothers, the hidden Jews?

Kamel Reis Pasha, Summer 1552

"The *shawish*, the sultan's new delegate, has arrived," Guillaume Fernandez informed me.

A Turkish officer of medium height, with a wide forehead, a thick mustache and an elongated face, entered my study. "Esteemed madam, Kamel Reis Pasha at your service," he addressed me in Italian. "Abu Daud is my Jewish name," he bowed his head.

"Welcome," I replied.

"Sultan Suleiman has sent me to escort the *señora* and her family to Constantinople, now named Istanbul, after the victory of Sultan Mehmed the Second over the Christian infidels."

"I hope you're more successful than the previous *shawish*," Guillaume Fernandez commented.

"We will be!" Abu Daud declared.

I liked his businesslike manner of speaking.

"My lady, I suggest the meetings alternate between *la señora*'s palace and Madame Brianda's palace in Rio de Santa Caterina. The first meeting will take place in your sister's home."

Negotiations conducted by the *shawish* took place over a week, once at my palace and once at Brianda's. The meetings took place in Italian, one of the six languages he spoke. He was quick witted and razor-sharp, delving into the roots of our disagreement.

"I understand that the problem began twenty-four years ago, in 1528. In the marriage agreement, Francisco promised half of his fortune to Señora Beatrice, and half to your future children. Contradicting the agreement, in his will, he bequeathed half of his fortune to his brother Diogo and half to your daughter Ana, who is currently seventeen." He raised his head, his eyes growing solemn.

I nodded.

Kamel Reis Pasha drummed his fingers on the table. "His brother Diogo married your sister Brianda, but disinherited her in his will. He divided his fortune between his daughter Beatrice La Chica and the *señora*, and appointed you as trustee over her inheritance funds." He leaned back in his chair. "I suggest that the *señora* go over the terms of her proposal to her sister once more, and attempt to improve upon them."

"In France, I lost thousands of gold ducats because of my sister, and she's trying to extort more and more funds from me," I said.

"Señora, an agreement must be reached. I am sure you will not regret your generosity."

***

Ana picked up a sheet of paper from the carved wooden box, dipped the quill in green ink and handed both to me. "Mama, add a handsome sum to your offer."

"Ana, you don't understand that soon, when you turn eighteen, you're supposed to receive your inheritance. I don't want you to lose a significant portion of it."

"Mama, we're rich enough. It would be a shame if you two continued to fight your whole lives."

Leave the feud behind you, clean up the murky residue, purify the pain, let light into your heart and start a new life, a voice whispered inside me.

I took the quill from her hand and wrote:

Agreement between Beatrice Mendes and Brianda Mendes.

I wrote, crossed out, added and subtracted sums. Finally, I sent Kamel Reis Pasha to inform Brianda that I wanted to conduct a private meeting with her at my palace.

When he returned, he hesitated briefly whether to hand me her answering missive. Finally, he gave it to me.

Beatrice, you know my address. If you wish to speak to me, although I don't believe you have anything new to say, I'll be at my palace tomorrow between ten and eleven in the morning. Brianda.

No one but her dared to refuse my requests.

The next day, I crossed the five-hundred meters separating the two of us on my own.

Jacob Morro, the dear accountant who had worked for me for many years and was now Brianda's business manager, greeted me warmly.

"Señora, there's a problem with the ship *Santa Helena*, docked at Ancona Port. It's loaded with bolts of wool, tins of oil and weapons. The authorities are not letting it undock and set sail."

"I'll try to help," I replied.

Jacob Morro invited me into the guest lounge. The atmosphere I found there was grim. The servants served me a pitcher of coffee and chocolate balls, which they placed on the table.

"Yes, what did you want?" Brianda asked, sitting on the edge of her chair.

"I want to put an end to this affair."

"I believe you enjoy torturing me."

I ignored her taunt. "I have a proposal for you."

"The only offer I'm willing to sign is La Chica receiving half of the sum of the inheritance and of House of Mendes's assets."

I produced the document I had prepared. "You could attain the standard of living of a noblewoman. But you should know I'm not willing to add another ducat to this offer."

"Stop your threats. Are you a queen who can't be contradicted? I'll listen and make up my mind."

I began to read the document out loud. "Doña Beatrice Mendes will continue to manage all House of Mendes business…"

"Well, that goes without saying. I didn't think you would delegate management to me."

"In addition, Señora Beatrice…"

"Would you stop referring to yourself in the third person?"

"It's a very generous offer. I'll deposit a hundred thousand gold ducats for La Chica in Venice's treasury. In three years, when she turns fifteen or when she gets married, she can redeem the money."

"Do you think I don't know how old my daughter is? And that I can't calculate in how many years she can get her money? Do you hear me?

Her money!"

"Brianda, that's enough. If you don't want to listen, I'm going," I said, folding the sheet of paper and rising to leave.

Brianda settled into her chair. "Talk. I'm listening."

"You'll receive a refund for La Chica's living expenses from the day she was born in 1540 and until she turned ten in 1550. She will receive a refund of fifteen hundred gold ducats a year, for a total of fifteen thousand gold ducats."

"That's it? You won't provide for my daughter until La Chica turns fifteen? You won't allow her to maintain an appropriate lifestyle? I thought you loved her." Brianda wrung her hands.

I looked out through the window. Reyna's words were echoing in my ears: *Mama, we're rich enough.*

"All right, I'll add fifteen hundred gold ducats a year for her until she turns fifteen."

"Just a moment, and what about living expenses for me? Do you want your sister to be a beggar?" she raised her voice.

"Be patient. You'll get fifteen thousand gold ducats from me."

"One might think that the money isn't from Diogo's inheritance, but from you."

"I'm willing to give you sixteen thousand gold ducats, a return on your dowry."

"How stingy of you. Do you think I could get along on such a ridiculous sum?" Her lips trembled.

"Don't talk to me that way. You should start to appreciate all that I do for you."

"'I do… I give…' Twenty thousand gold ducats, no less!"

"Brianda, we're not hagglers at the market."

"What are you saying? Do you want me to sign? So you can cleanse your conscience? So that everyone will say, 'You're so generous… taking care of your sister and her orphaned daughter.'"

"Eighteen," I said.

"Nineteen thousand. I've accumulated a debt a hundred twenty three and a half gold ducats for furniture, dresses and decorative objects," she said.

"18,123.50 gold ducats, so long as we put an end to this affair and you will not have any further requirements," I insisted.

Brianda sighed. "You're so harsh with me."

I corrected the sums in the contract.

"Read it over and decide."

"Give me a few days, I need to consult some people," Brianda said.

"Whom? Your advisors? Have you forgotten that their bad advice got both of us sent to jail? Make a decision on your own, and do it quickly, since the agreement has to be approved by the court."

"I want to think about it."

"Brianda, dark clouds are forming over our heads."

"So, what's new? Spring always follows winter."

"No, I'm sure you've heard of our brethren who fled Portugal and whose ship went down, and who ended up getting eaten by the natives?"

Brianda nodded.

"And if that wasn't enough," I added, "I've heard that due to some intense competition between two printing presses belonging to Old Christians in Venice over printing the Talmud, one of the competitors contacted the pope and lied that the other printer was publishing condemnations of Christianity. Due to the denouncement and the false accusations, the pope decided to convene an investigative committee."

"Rome is far away," Brianda replied.

"Don't be dismissive. I want you to come to Constantinople with us," I said.

"You want, you request, you demand, everything has to be dome in accordance with the will and whims of Princess Beatricci de Luna Mendes, Gracia Nasi. I'm staying in Venice."

"As a Christian?"

"You're not my mother. How is it your business how I live my life?"

"Brianda, stop it. I didn't come here to fight."

"Have you heard that the sultan commanded that the former *shawish*'s head be chopped off, because he returned home without the esteemed sisters?" Brianda said.

"I've heard. It will be hard for the girls to be apart."

"You're the one who chose to leave."

"As you wish. Juan and Bernardo are coming back to Venice soon to say goodbye to me. They'll stay on to handle selling the assets, so that I have money to pay you. One more thing: you can get assistance from House of Mendes agents Duarte Gomez and Augustino Henricks, who are staying in the city."

I signed the document and handed her the quill.

"Thank you," Brianda said, returning the quill to the inkwell.

"I'm leaving the agreement here for your signature," I said, departing from her palace.

***

In the heat of June, the palazzo was bustling with activity. The servants were sorting clothes and other possessions to be sold, donated to charity or packed. Christopher Manuel was constantly yelling at the maids, making sure no items were missing. Broad-shouldered porters loaded decorated dowry chests, loaded with immaculate linens, delicately embroidered with much dedication by the loving hands of dear women saved from the wrath of the Church; as well as rustling silk gowns, petticoats made from soft fabrics, pearls, gems, shoes, wallets, coats, silverware and gold tableware, linen and silk tablecloths, blankets, soft towel robes, delicate china dining sets, and many more possessions accumulated and meticulously packed in Ana's dowry chests.

I went over the company documents. Summaries, personal correspondence and business letters. How do you leave behind a whole world? What should I toss out? What should I take? I had to leave a clean slate behind me.

***

The senate's representative, notary Paolo Leoncini, demanded that Ana and La Chica take part in the last hearing, as the agreement involved their inheritance funds.

With Ana by my side, I entered the lavish court hall in Palazzo Ducale, where Brianda and La Chica were sitting.

Notary Paolo Leoncini and *shawish* Kamel Reis Pasha entered.

"Ladies and gentlemen, we have gathered here to sign the agreement between Beatrice Mendes and her sister Brianda Mendes, regarding the inheritance of their daughters. With your permission, I'll read the agreement out loud in Italian rather than Latin, so that the young girls can understand every word.

"I ask that everyone present, including the girls, confirm out loud that they understand the agreement and approve it."

"Yes, your honor," the girls replied.

The notary turned to gaze at La Chica. "Young Beatrice Mendes, are you aware of the fact that in three years, when you turn fifteen or upon your marriage, you will be entitled to receive your part of the inheritance?" he asked.

Brianda entwined her fingers with those of her daughter.

"Yes, your honor," La Chica replied.

"In accordance with the request of Señora Beatrice Mendes, and due to difficulties regarding liquidity, the moneys owed will be deposited in the Venetian Treasury after Señora Mendes receives the returns for selling her palaces, and no later than March 1553."

Notary Paola Leoncini opened the agreement on page 40 and placed it in front of Brianda. Our eyes met. Brianda picked up the quill and signed. The notary handed the agreement to La Chica, who signed her name in childish letters. The notary then passed the agreement on to me. I signed it, and after Ana did as well, the notary added his signature and *shawish* Kamel Reis Pasha twirled out his own signature in Arab and Latin print.

✳✳✳

"*La señora*, Don Juan Mickas requests to be received," Guillaume Fernandez smiled.

Juan entered my study with a vigorous stride, kissing my hand. "Aunt, I'm sorry for the suffering you've been through."

"Welcome back. Where's Bernardo?"

"He's gone to visit Brianda."

"Juan, I won. I signed the agreement with Brianda again."

"I hope you managed to obtain good terms."

"Instead of the three hundred thousand she wanted, and the hundred and fifty thousand that the senate initially decided upon, I only have to deposit a hundred thousand!"

"And you've decided to deposit the money?"

"I have no choice. I want to leave and release my funds from the treasury house."

"That's too bad," Juan blurted out.

"I want to leave, and I need cash. Start selling the House of Mendes's assets in Venice, and then in Lyon and Rome. But do it gradually, so we can sell them for full price."

"I need a list of all the assets."

"Christopher Manuel will give you one."

Ana entered the room. Her black hair was pulled back in a bun and entwined with pearls, and her blue dress complimented the tan skin of her face.

"Beautiful Ana, it's good to see you! It's been a long time since we met…" Juan did not take his eyes off her.

Ana lowered her gaze. "Hello, Don Juan," she said softly.

"I've missed you," Juan whispered.

I saw that she was yearning for him.

"Why don't you go out to the balcony? I'm sure you have many stories to share with each other."

Juan offered Ana his arm. "Shall we?"

"Yes…" she replied slowly, her cheeks flushed scarlet.

Through the windows, I saw Juan grasping both of Ana's hands, talking passionately.

I smiled. I had waited many years for this moment, ever since taking custody of Juan and Bernardo.

A short while later, Ana and Juan entered the room again, their faces illuminated with smiles.

"Aunt, I'm honored to ask for your daughter Reyna's hand in marriage."

I turned to look at my daughter, whose eyes glowed back at me.

"Congratulations! Congratulations!" I embraced Reyna. "You've made me very happy."

Juan opened the drinks cabinet and poured fine wine into goblets. "To us!"

"Mama, can we go to La Chica's palace and tell her?"

"Go, this is happy news!" I took out a handkerchief and wiped away my tears, which were flowing of their own accord.

I was deeply moved. My daughter was soon to be married. I was determined to conduct a Jewish marriage for them. Which meant we had to leave for the Ottoman state and that Juan had to return to Judaism openly and be circumcised. Another decision I reached was not to wait until March 1553 to deposit the coins. In September, after Rosh Hashanah, the Jewish New Year, I would deposit a large part of the sum in the Venetian Treasury.

Reyna and I would sail to Ragusa, from there to Thessaloniki, and finally to Constantinople.

Juan and Bernardo would leave for Rome, to authorize the delivery of a cargo of wine to Ragusa, and would return to Venice after Rosh Hashanah for the engagement party. They would stay behind in Venice to release my seized assets from the treasury, and then join us in Constantinople.

And perhaps, who knows, I might be lucky enough to get to Jerusalem.

Stacks

Pale morning light blurred my senses. The room spun around me and pain gripped my stomach and pinched it sharply. This was it, the time had come; I must prepare the ducats for deposit.

Brianda had not worked a single day in her life. She had never earned a single gold ducat, a gold florin, a ducatoni, even a single fiorini coin. Only accumulated debts upon debts.

But squandering money was her area of expertise. Wool coats from London; furs, hair accessories and decorative items from Antwerp; silk fabrics from Lyon; lace, high-heeled shoes, reticules, makeup and glassware from Venice; gowns and jewelry from Paris; custom-made furniture from Florence; gold dinnerware and silverware from Ferrara. She was world-renowned at shopping. My life's work, the fruits of my labor, would be dispersed like a cloud of dust.

My legs weak, accompanied by Juan, Augustino Henricks and Duarte Gomez, the House of Mendes agents, I went down to the safe room, outside of which the soldiers I had hired were standing guard. In addition to a sword and a dagger, they were also equipped with the latest invention: a lethal gun.

The officer called out a command and the soldiers assembled in two lines. I walked between them, and with a trembling hand, inserted the iron key in the lock. Juan tended to the second lock and turned the handle. We entered the treasury room, with its arches and decorations.

I took a deep breath and opened the doors of the wood escritoire I had received from the doge on the first Christmas we spent in the city.

Four beautiful iron chests, covered in leather, were lined up in front of me.

The men hefted two of the chests and placed them on the black, red-veined marble table. Juan produced two empty chests from the cabinet and placed them on an adjacent green marble table.

My broken heart fluttered within me. I inserted the key in the first lock. The lock opened with a small click.

Juan took out another key and opened the second lock.

With a trembling heart, I opened the third lock.

"Aunt, shall I stay with you?" Juan asked.

"I appreciate that, but I'm fine," I thanked them, closing the door behind them. I was left alone.

I lifted the lid of the chest.

Piles upon piles of shiny gold coins glittered at me.

Hello, our friend Señora Gracia, thank you for the honor of dwelling in your treasure chest.

My eye alighted upon one gold ducat that was winking at me. *Señora, por favor, choose me.* I picked up the shiny coin and placed it on the black marble of the desk. Sunlight fell upon the ducat.

I smiled to myself. This was the first ducat I had ever earned in my life, when I sold my assigned books in French, Latin and Italian to my friend Sophia. And those were the ten ducats I had received as a gift from my aunt when I turned twelve and the secret was revealed to me. Ahh, the secret that still needed to be kept.

A tear fell from my eyes and rolled onto the pendant. In my mind's eye, I pictured my poor fellow Jews, burned at the stake in autos-da-fé, and the holy letters burning in the Church's bonfires.

I rolled the coins between my fingers. A tear seemed to drip from the sapphire icicle, while the gems in the pendant cried with it. In ships secured by guards and spies I had hired, I had saved refugees fleeing from the terrors of the Inquisition. I had led them to countries of refuge, provided them with food, drink and hiding places. I bought their assets with promissory notes, so they would not lose all their money, so that they would not be penniless, forced to live off donations. Once they reached safety, my agents redeemed the promissory notes and gave them local currency.

Mother, with these ducats, I carried out your will. I saved the Children of

Israel 'belonging to the letter Yod.' The chain remains unbroken.

Sparks of light laughed to me from a small stack of ducats.

My dowry, silverware and china, cotton sheets. I breathed in the smell of the coins and remembered charming Francisco, walking with me, arm in arm, at our wedding.

The sun reached the summit of the sky, painting a steep hill of coins in shades of gold. My smile grew wider. My Ana was born.

Ana had lain on a lace pillow wrapped in an immaculate silk blanket, her tiny hands next to her head, her eyes closed and her sweet mouth curved in a peaceful smile. Priceless gold jewelry, gold chains, bracelets, earrings, gold and silver coins, all enveloped Ana, who still did not know what the future held in store.

I cradled a few ducats in my hand. *My Ana, these coins are intended for you.*

The crimson rays of sunlight rested upon a towering stack of coins. This was Francisco's inheritance. With these ducats, I left Portugal, a widow with her orphaned daughter, her sister and her two cousins.

And this mound was Diogo's inheritance. He had executed his brother's will. He knew that the fortune would only be preserved and grow if it was in my hands.

My eyes fixed upon the mountains of coins still filling the chest. I had earned all of those ducats with my own ten fingers, with my heart's blood, through long hours of negotiations, planning, bribery, and relinquishing my own private happiness. I had challenged kings and earls, fought Queen Mary and won.

I had bought groves of pepper, cardamom, cinnamon, cloves, and wheat. I had sold pearls, china, furs, gunpowder, guns, and cannons. I had loaned out money, funded the printing of the Ferrara Bible in Ladino, and distributed holy books.

I counted a ducat and another ducat, building a tall tower of coins. The sun had already begun to set, its light dimmed, the shine of the coins diminishing.

How many babies, children, mothers, fathers had been forcefully baptized into Christianity? My people, at whom the Inquisition brandished its claws, grabbing them by the back of their necks, tormenting their souls and burning their bodies in fire. Perhaps thousands of coins might buy and save their lives?

Such coins might pay for accommodations at an inn or a convent, purchase food and warm clothing, buy passage on ships to the sultan's land, pay agents to warn and sound out alerts to the presence of Inquisition spies, fund guides to help with border crossings.

These ducats could be snuck into the hands of priests and clerks, so that they would avert their eyes from the sight of the fleeing *conversos*.

A knock at the door woke me from my contemplation. I pushed back the chair. My hand bumped into the tower of coins, which leaned sideways, shuddered and collapsed. The gold coins fell, rolling and scattering with a sharp, discordant sound over the marble table, and from there, all over the room, under tables, shelves, chairs, cabinets and the sofa in the treasury room.

I dropped into the chair once more, covering my eyes with my hands.
"Blessed art Thou, O Lord Our God,
All my works have been done in His honor.
For Your grace, lend me strength, reach out Your hand to me,
Amen."

The loud knocking on the door continued. "Aunt, is everything all right? Please open the door," I heard Juan's voice.

Dizzy, I cracked the door open.

Juan entered with a tray bearing a plate with squares of Venetian bread and rings of mozzarella, garnished with basil leaves and olive oil, a bunch of grapes and a cup of warm water spiced with rosewater.

"Aunt, please, you haven't eaten a thing since morning. Please, eat." He placed the tray on the table.

"Thank you." I took one grape.

Juan bent down to the cold marble floor and began to gather the gold coins I had earned one by one, with my heart's blood, through battles and labor.

When the ducats ended up in Brianda's hands, they would be scattered to the four winds, like a passing cloud, a fleeting shadow.

Shadows filled the room. I placed the last ducat on top of the chest. "My friends," I addressed the coins, "I'm not saying goodbye to you. This is not the end of the story. You'll yet be returning to me." I lowered the lid of the chest and locked it.

At four in the morning, while Venice was still immersed in its beauty sleep, the guard unit, supervised by Juan, Augustino Henricks and Duarte Gomez, loaded the chests onto a gondola. In several minutes that seemed like an eternity to me, the gondola crossed the canal toward the cellars of Venice's treasury house.

Fiery Flames, September 1552

Rosh Hashanah came and went. The preparations for the arrival of Juan and Bernardo for an intimate engagement party, in which we would also bid them farewell, were at their height.

The comforting aroma of pastries, preserves and hot dishes emerging from the oven enveloped my heart with childhood memories.

Ana, now called Reyna, laid out the gowns the seamstress had brought and debated which of them she would wear to the engagement party: a purple one with a stiff collar, a green one with a square décolletage, or perhaps a brown one with embroidered leaves and puffed sleeves? Finally, she chose the purple one.

Juan and Bernardo returned from Rome looking gray-faced. Juan was loquacious by nature, and we expected him to be excited before his reunion with Reyna and the engagement party. However, he ensconced himself in silence.

Bernardo sipped the bitter coffee, took a deep breath, and told us the tale.

"On Saturday, the eve of Rosh Hashanah, we were in Rome, strolling with friends on Via Flora. On the way, we heard cheers of joy and curses against the heretics. At Campo de'Fiori Square, a crowd consisting of bishops, priests, monks, women, men and children was gathered around a giant bonfire, cheering on the soldiers of the Pope's Guard, who were tossing hundreds of Talmud books into the fire.

"Red fiery flames consumed the books. The pages were flying everywhere, and the sky filled with a heavy cloud of soot. The holy day had become a day of mourning."

The tolling of the cathedral bells interrupted him. Black smoke was rising over the palazzos of Venice. Bernardo, Juan and Reyna leaped from their seats.

"Reyna, stay away from the windows!"

"Close the blinds!"

"Please, don't go." I stationed myself at the doorway to the room.

But Juan and Bernardo went around me and ran down to the gondola in front of the palazzo.

***

They returned two hours later, their faces and clothes sooty and their eyes red.

Juan coughed, sipped a little water, sat down next to Reyna and began to describe what he had seen.

"We followed the enflamed crowd streaming toward Piazza San Marco. At the center of the piazza, near the well, a giant bonfire had been lit, into which Republic Guard soldiers were tossing hundreds of Talmud, Torah and *siddur* books, just like in Rome.

"The wind blew and swirled burned pages; letters swept through the air. Sparks scattered everywhere. The flames cast red shadows on the palaces and the jubilant crowd. The canal water was tinged in red."

I held the gold pendant against my heart and prayed that the airborne letters would make it to the Heavenly Throne.

"I've heard that tomorrow, in Castello Estense Square in Ferrara, the Talmud books forcefully collected from the homes of the city's Jews will be burned," Bernardo said.

Juan struck the table with his fist. "It's a shame that the Venetian Senate rejected my proposal to assign the *conversos* an island in the lagoon where they could live their lives."

"Why? Why?" Reyna covered her face with her hands.

"Where they burn books, they'll burn people," I said.

A shiver ran through me. I rose from my seat. "Who knows? Perhaps tomorrow, a new Muslim ruler will rise in Constantinople and strike at us like the Christians do? Perhaps it's time that we returned to the land of our forefathers?"

I knew that from now on, in my travels east, there was a new mission to my life.

PART SEVEN

Between East and West, 1552

Thessaloniki

The first officer laid the black pirate flag with a white skull at its center on the desk.

"Doña Gracia Nasi, the pirates are tied to the mast of the ship *Lisbona*," the officer said, his rigid face motionless.

"What did they rob from my ship?"

"Four chests of gold coins, three chests of jewelry and sacks of perfume," the officer scowled. "We fought, shots were fired, two guards were injured. One pirate was killed, and his body rolled off the deck into the sea. We managed to retrieve the treasure chests, and removed their flag from the head of the mast."

"Very good," I said.

"Señora, should we throw them into the depths of the sea or whip them?" he asked in his hoarse voice.

"What punishment does the ship's captain usually impose?" I asked.

The officer ran his bony hands over the deep scar slashing his cheek. "The captain puts the pirates in a sack weighed with stones, ties it firmly closed and throws them into the sea!"

The eyes of Abner Alperin, an agent of House of Mendes, scurried around in fright. "*La señora*, they say… they say that the pirates are Jewish," he stammered out in Ladino.

The calls of the muezzin and the toll of church bells mingled together.

"If that's the case, forty lashes, less one! No one will dare rob the ships of the House of Mendes!"

"At your command, *señora*!" the officer replied.

"Abner Alperin, set out for the boat. After the robbers are punished, hand them over to the governor of Thessaloniki," I said.

A dark-skinned servant with broad, sweeping trousers treaded softly to fill the mugs of the officer and Abner Alperin with dark beer.

The officer gulped down the mug of beer and signaled the cabin boy accompanying him to approach. The lad placed a small wooden chest on the table.

"Señora, I was requested by *il capitano* to give you the letters conveyed in ports where the ship has docked."

I placed a bundle of coins in the officer's hand. He tossed his braid over his shoulder, nodded his head and hurried out along with Abner Alperin.

Quiet engulfed the city of Thessaloniki. The shouting of porters at the harbor and the blaring of ship horns stilled; soon, the Sabbath would arrive. The murmur of water in the garden fountain was the only sound heard as I opened the letters arriving from the west I had left behind.

September 26, 1552
Venice

Ana, sister of my soul, how are you?

Fields of tears and an ocean of yearning separate us.

Life in Venice has changed without you. Palazzo Gritti, where we've moved, is quiet most of the time. During the day, I play music, draw, embroider, and stare at the lagoon, hoping you might return.

Ana, I'm not allowed to talk about it, but Mama told me the…! I'm sure you know what I mean.

Mama is tense. She is waiting for March, when Aunt Beatrice will deposit the remainder of the debt in the treasury, and promised she will hold a major celebration.

Ana, I think even though you were about to sail off to Ragusa, you should have held a larger engagement party. Can you imagine, the princesses and daughters of nobility cannot believe that Juan is engaged to you, and are fawning over him…

Although Juan is twenty-eight and younger than Mama by two years, he acts as if he is her and Bernardo's big brother. He objects to Mama meeting Michael, the doge's nephew who has been courting her, and wants us to join you in Thessaloniki.

I wish Mama would agree.
La Chica

***

October 1, 1552
Palazzo Gritti, Venice

For Doña Gracia Nasi,

The expenses of maintaining Palazzo Gritti are growing. The debtors are not paying their debts, and Christopher Manuel is negligent in collecting them.

Madame Brianda is very concerned about her financial situation.

Respectfully,
Jacob Morro
Accountant for Madame Brianda Mendes

***

October 12, 1552
Venice

Aunt,

As we agreed, House of Mendes agents Duarte Gomez and Augustino

Henricks and myself are making efforts to avoid depositing the dowry moneys, while releasing the seized property in the treasury house. We have made use of our connections in the senate, in the Council of Ten and with the duke. We've paid money, distributed important gifts, and I have promised loans under preferred terms, but the Venetians are stubborn.

I've managed to sell the merchandise storehouses at the port for an excellent price to the Venetian nobleman Barnabe. Duarte Gomez and Augustino Henricks have collected most of the debts from the merchants and noblemen.

I hope I can convince Aunt Brianda to move to Thessaloniki.

Please give my regards to my lovely fiancée Reyna,
Juan

✳✳✳

October 7, 1552
Ragusa

For La Señora Doña Gracia Nasi,

The Ragusa City Council thanks the esteemed lady who lived in our city and bestowed her kindness upon us. In her mercy, she saved the city's residents from hunger following the harsh drought we experienced, by importing sacks of grain for us.

In gratitude for her actions, the city council has decided to grant Doña Gracia Nasi a certificate of merit and to issue a writ of patronage to House of Mendes agents, extending to her property, her ships and merchandise including wool, spices and grains transported from the Port of Ragusa in the east to Venice and other areas of Italy.

In addition, the House of Mendes will receive a discount on sailing rights, storing merchandise at the port and insurance.

The payment for storing merchandise at the port shall be a mere five hundred gold ducats a year, and only four and a half gold ducats for every crate of wool fabrics, as well as one percent of the value of the merchandise.

Our esteemed lady may be certain that her graciousness shall be fondly remembered, and she will receive her due rewards one day.

May the Creator of the World protect and endow her with much wealth.

Ragusa City Council

***

October 12, 1552
Ragusa

For the exalted lady Doña Gracia Nasi,

The House of Mendes agents and their wives as well as the Jews of Ragusa thank our exalted lady for her many efforts with the Ragusa authorities.

Thanks to the accomplishments of our exalted lady, the authorities have exempted House of Mendes agents and their families from the requirement to live in the ghetto. Our wives have also been exempted from the requirement to pawn their jewelry as collateral for paying the housing fee.

The residents of Ragusa's Jewish ghetto thank Doña Gracia Nasi for her generous donation to the synagogue and to the community fund.

With heartfelt gratitude,
Señor Yitzhak Argas
House of Mendes agent in Ragusa

Escape

November 1, 1552
Palazzo Gritti, Venice

Ana, sister of my soul,

Have you forgotten me? Every day, I stroll to the port to see whether a ship is coming in from Ragusa, and whether there's a letter for me. I no longer enjoy the frolicking of the gulls over the water and the serenades of the gondoliers sailing their boats down the Grand Canal. When you read this letter, know that I have missed you and did everything I could to be with you, and may the Lord forgive me for my willingness to hurt my dear mother.

Juan and Bernardo are trying to convince Mama to let us join you. Juan says that the situation in Venice is dire for New Christians, and that we should flee. Mama doesn't agree, and insists we stay in Venice, especially now that she's meeting Michael, the doge's nephew, almost every day, and even escorted him to a sailing competition.

Mama says, pardon the harsh words, that her cruel, terrible sister left Juan and Bernardo as well as the main House of Mendes agents, Duarte Gomez and Augustino Henricks, behind her in Venice not so that they would tend to company business, but so that they would make sure we sailed to that "Levantine, barbaric" land.

Mama reminds me, as if I could forget, that in five months, when Aunt

Beatrice deposits the inheritance moneys Papa bequeathed to me in the treasury house, our financial situation will improve.

In the meantime, Mama is throwing parties, to which the artists she supports are invited, along with Venice's aristocracy, members of the oldest families that have been living here for hundreds of years (I'm sure you know what I mean).

I'm being courted by Giovanni di Pietro, a young man with mischievous eyes and a melting smile, whose father is a silk merchant and a member of the Council of Ten. Every morning, a messenger arrives with a bouquet of roses, a poem he has composed or a box of chocolates filled with wine.

I've heard my friends whispering among themselves that soon, I'll be the richest unmarried woman in Venice, and all the handsome, rich, successful princes will be courting me.

None of them know how lonely I am. You were my only true friend. Juan told me that he and Bernardo will be leaving Venice soon, and that if I want to keep my inheritance, I should travel to Thessaloniki with them, and from there, we'll continue to Constantinople. I don't know what to do.

With love,
La Chica

***

Palazzo Gritti, Venice
November 5, 1552

The city is engulfed in heavy fog; I can barely see. In a few minutes, Juan and Bernardo will come to fetch me.

Despite the fog and the cold, Mama's new friend, Michael, has sent a *gondola for her. Mama wore a lavish fur coat, a fur cap and deerskin gloves, and left for a game of cards at the doge's palace.*

I've packed a small bag with warm clothes, a box of cookies and a wallet with gold coins.

My heart is beating wildly. I'll stop writing now. I'm going to put on my new green wool coat. They'll be here to collect me any minute.

Yours,
La Chica

***

November 6, 1552

My cousin Ana Reyna,

Last night we left through the secret door in the cellar of the house and climbed the stairs going up to the street, with Bernardo keeping watch by my side to make sure I didn't stumble in the darkness covering the city. We strode quickly. The sound of the water in the canal increased, and Juan was afraid of the acqua alta, or high water; if the tide was high and water flooded the city, the boat would not be able to sail in the canal.

The boat was waiting for us in the lagoon. A yellow light signaled to show us where it was docked.

My legs trembled when I boarded the boat, but I also experienced a feeling of liberation: I was deciding where I wanted to live.

The stars disappeared in the black sky. I heard a whistle, and brief, rapid commands were whispered. The ship set sail and the sailors rowed quickly along the canal toward the sea.

My soul almost left my body when the boat crashed into a rock and nearly broke. My teeth were chattering, and I put my arms around myself in an attempt to suppress the constant trembling that had taken hold of me.

We reached shore toward morning. Isabella, Juan's friend, was waiting for us on the pier. I was soaked with saltwater and shaking from the cold. Isabella grabbed my hand and helped me disembark from the boat. "It's good to see you," she whispered to Juan, trying to talk over the whistling of the gulls flying over the sea. We rushed to board a carriage. Isabella covered me with a blanket. The carriage sped down side roads, among hills and vineyards. The screeching of animals and the wind blowing among the tall trees frightened me. I rested my head on Isabella's reddish cascade of curls. I thought about poor Mama returning home, and surely coming in to tuck me in and give me a good-night kiss. I imagined her screams when she discovered I had disappeared. Perhaps I shouldn't have run away from home?

Through the fog, I glimpsed the intimidating fortress of the town of Faenza.

Among the hills, between the trees and vineyards, hid Casa Bella, the Contini family's summerhouse, where we would be sleeping in the next few nights until a ship arrives to take us to Ancona, and from there to Ragusa, to Thessaloniki, and finally to Constantinople, Juan told me soothingly.

I'm giving this letter to Isabella. I hope it reaches you.

Kisses,
See you soon!
La Chica

***

Venice
November 28, 1552

Doña Gracia Nasi,

I am writing what I heard from Brianda's personal dresser:

"On a cold and foggy night, Brianda's screaming unsettled the house and woke me from my sleep. 'My daughter! Where's my daughter? Where is she? La Chica, where are you?'

"Brianda, who would go into La Chica's room every night, tuck her in and give her a good-night kiss, was appalled to see that the pink silk cover was spread tautly across the bed, her daughter had disappeared, and a letter was lying on the desk.

"She read the letter out loud, her voice choked with tears: 'Dear Mama, forgive me. I've left with Juan and Bernardo to see my cousin Ana. Love you very much, La Chica.'

"'My cruel sister has abducted my daughter! Juan and Bernardo wouldn't have dared do this. Beatrice, what do you want from me? You've stolen away my inheritance, and now you've also taken my very breath of life, my one and only daughter,' Brianda cried out. Suddenly, she clutched her heart and sank to the rug in a swoon.

"The maids laid her down on the bed, called the doctor, prepared water with cinnamon and honey for her, and summoned the police."

It's important to me that your ladyship receives the news first-hand. Please know, señora, that I am worried about Brianda.

Respectfully,
Augustino Henricks
House of Mendes agent

***

Venice
December 10, 1552

For Doña Gracia Nasi,

I am reporting to the señora on the continuation of events, as reported by Giovanni Battisti, head of the City Guard. Venice is in a state of great uproar. For three weeks, the city council's clerks interrogated the servants, searching the ports for anyone who could provide information. They questioned sea captains, sailors and fishermen. Warrants for Juan and Bernardo's arrest were posted in Piazza San Marco, on the stores in the Rialto Bridge and on the piers at the port, offering a reward of one thousand ducats for anyone who would turn them in and assist in bringing the kidnappers to justice. The prize offered would be taken from the kidnappers' seized property.

Brianda has appealed to the Vatican for help, and the pope sent his soldiers to take part in the search and return La Chica to her shattered mother.

Respectfully,
Augustino Henricks,
House of Mendes agent

***

The Contini family home in Faenza
January 1, 1553

Ana,

Forgive me for my illegible handwriting. Soon, they will come to take me to a ship that will return me to Mama.

For three weeks, we hid in Villa Bella Casa, waiting for a ship sailing to Ragusa, but it failed to arrive.

The quacking of geese, barking, loud calls and a powerful knocking on the villa doors put an end to my dream of seeing you.

Soldiers armed with spears and daggers burst into the library, grabbed Juan and Bernardo and pulled them out violently toward the horses in the yard. I was taken out of the room and placed on board a carriage.

Luckily for Isabella, she had gone out to pick artichokes for dinner and was not at the villa. The soldiers took us to Ravenna and locked us in a room at city hall in Piazza del Popolo.

The commander of the guard positioned himself across from Juan and Bernardo and made a slashing motion across his throat, saying the Venetian authorities had issued an arrest warrant against Juan and Bernardo, that they were facing a death sentence, and two gallows had been prepared for the two of them in Piazza San Marco. He informed me that I was being returned to Mama in Venice.

My legs collapsed under me. The room spun and grew dim around me. I dropped onto the sofa in the room and the letter fell from my hands. The Lord protect and save us; being hung in Piazza San Marco, like common criminals. Why? Why the death penalty? What had they actually done? This was a cruel Venetian revenge for the fact that I had left their city.

I sipped a little water, picked up the letter and continued to read La Chica's account

Bernardo fainted, and the guards grabbed him so he wouldn't fall and splashed water on his face to wake him. Juan grew pale when he heard the verdict, but managed to maintain his equanimity. As you'd expect, he was already searching for a way to get out of trouble.

When we were left alone, Juan whispered to me that if I want to save their lives, we had to get married. It was the only way to escape the gallows.

I was stunned. This was not the wedding I had been expecting. But what could I do? I nodded in agreement. It was a brilliant plan; I would never have thought of it. I blushed. It was odd that out of all the beautiful, wealthy women, my cousin was marrying me...

When the commander of the guard returned, Juan explained to him that there had been a misunderstanding, and that we had arrived in Ravenna in order to get married, and Bernardo and Isabella were our groomsman and maid of honor.

Juan begged him to allow us to get married, emphasizing that canceling the wedding and the sorrow Juan would be causing his beloved would be on his conscience.

The commander of the guard said he could not decide on his own, and called Isabella's father, Alberto Contini, a member of the city council.

Señor Contini heard Juan and declared that the three of us were under the protection of the city of Ravenna, that it was our right to get married, and that wedding preparations had already been completed at the Basilica of San Vitale. The cardinal was awaiting the couple, and we had to hurry. He demanded that Bernardo serve as groomsman.

"Love defeats destiny," Giovanni Battisti surrendered, allowing us to be married in a brief ceremony, with Bernardo serving as groomsman. Juan and Bernardo shook his hand and thanked him.

I couldn't stop my tears. I was besieged by doubts: had I done well to run away from home? Getting married without Mama! I had imagined getting married in a lavish wedding, with plenty of guests. Perhaps I shouldn't have agreed?

But what could I do? I hadn't imagined all the complications that had occurred when I ran away, resulting in a death sentence for Juan and Bernardo. If we didn't get married... I didn't even want to think about what might happen to them. Juan soothed me, saying it would all work out and when things calmed down, we would have a proper, opulent wedding.

Isabella was allowed to come meet us, and at her father's request, brought me a red brocade dress with delicate lace adorning the neckline and a silver silk shawl. She escorted me to a private room, where I put on the dress, wrapped the shawl around my shoulders and decorated my hair with a pearl broach.

Accompanied by a guard of soldiers, we quickly strode to the basilica.

"You look beautiful!" Bernardo's eyes gaped when he saw me.

"Lovely bride, congratulations!" the curious onlookers gathered in the street and the balconies called out, tossing flowers at us.

I heard two women whispering that they had heard of a couple in love who had fled Venice because the bride's mother was opposed to the wedding, and they had come to see us.

Juan, noble and impressive as always, stepped toward the cardinal, accompanied by the commander of the guard and Bernardo, turning his head to smile at the crowd gathered in the church.

To the sound of the organ, I walked down the aisle, escorted by Isabella's father. Under the dome of the basilica, decorated with a colorful mosaic, the cardinal quickly married us. The soldiers cheered and began singing and stamping their feet.

"Many waters cannot quench love, neither can the floods drown it."

Giovanni gave us two hours to celebrate the marriage in the Contini family's home. Servants served wine, chilled pomegranate granita and tiramisu cake. Albert Contini and his wife distributed goblets of red wine to the soldiers who were guarding the house.

When we were left on our own, Juan hugged me. "My beauty, take care of yourself. I'm fleeing to Rome, to receive confirmation from the pope that the marriage is valid."

He waited till the guards fell asleep and jumped out the window, followed by Bernardo, to the horses that Isabella had prepared for them. They galloped off. I did not see them again. After the wine I had drunk (at home, Mama won't allow me to drink wine; she claims I'm still a child), I was so tired that I immediately dropped into bed and fell asleep.

Giovanni Battisti was furious when he discovered that Juan and Bernardo had fled, and his soldiers are looking for them. Instead of a promotion, he's facing a court-martial.

It's hard to believe I'm almost thirteen and a married woman.

I'm giving this letter to Isabella, and hope my husband and Bernardo will manage to reach Rome safely.

Beatrice La Chica Mickas

The Gallows

My body began to shake and I was flooded with sweat. I envisioned Juan and Bernardo hanging in Piazza San Marco. *I hope the pope confirms the marriage and they'll be saved from the gallows*, I thought in terror. But Reyna couldn't find out. Perhaps the marriage between La Chica and Juan would be annulled? And if that was the case, perhaps he would marry Ana-Reyna as planned?

I fell asleep. I didn't notice Reyna come into the room and peek over my shoulder. "Mama, who's the letter from?" she woke me up with her question.

"Oh, some business matter," I stammered, dropping the pages on the sofa.

"Mama, that's La Chica's handwriting. Why are you reading my letters?" she said angrily, and promptly picked up the letter.

"Don't read it. It'll cause you sorrow."

She sat down on the sofa. "I'm eighteen years old!" she scowled while her eyes began to move across the lines of the letter. I noticed that her hand had begun to shake.

"Has Juan lost his mind? What were they thinking, kidnapping La Chica?" she raised her eyes to me. "Mama, were you a part of this abduction idea?"

"Heaven forbid. Do you really think I'd take part in such an outrageous idea? After all, you two are engaged."

"He's torn my heart to bits." She began to weep bitterly, curling up in my lap.

"La Chica Mendes, that traitor! How could she do this to me? She's married Juan!" She shook her head in disbelief, large tears rolling down her cheeks. I put my hand on her shoulder, but she shrugged it off.

"My daughter, Juan and Bernardo had good intentions, but there were complications. The Venetian authorities will claim that without Brianda's permission, the marriage is null and void, and the marriage certificate is a worthless piece of parchment."

"But La Chica was alone with him."

"They didn't consummate the marriage."

"How do you know?"

"La Chica wrote that immediately after the ceremony, when the soldiers got drunk, Juan and Bernardo fled to Rome."

"Ahhh…"

"Don't be afraid. The marriage is fictitious. The rabbis have decreed that the New Christians' wedding ceremonies are not valid unless they're immediately followed by a Jewish wedding.

"The important thing now is how to save Bernardo and Juan. They're in danger. If the soldiers of the Venetian Guard capture them…."

I took the pages from her hands and brought them to the candle's flame.

"Mama, what are you doing?" Ana tried to save the pages. The fire seared the paper, which shrunk and burned completely.

"People make mistakes; that's why they're human. Learn to forgive, forget what happened and never bring it up again. Juan is your fiancé. When he arrives in Constantinople, you'll get married."

"If he arrives."

***

The Holy See of Rome
February 1553

Esteemed Señora Beatrice Mendes,

I wish to inform the señora that the Vatican is doing all it can for her protégé, Don Juan Mickas.

His marriage to Señorita Beatrice Mickas, née Mendes, have been approved. The Vatican acknowledges Bernardo Mickas as a groomsman.

Don Juan and Don Bernardo Mickas are safely ensconced in one of the monasteries, and are awaiting Venice's response.

We hope the señora properly appreciates the efforts of the Holy See, which acted in contrast to the opinion of the Venice City Council.

Respectfully,
Father Sebastian

I made a note to myself to make a sizable contribution to the Holy See for saving Juan.

***

Venice
February 1553

Esteemed Señora Beatrice Mendes,

I wish to inform the señora that the authorities of Venice have issued a new warrant, according to which Don Juan Mickas is permanently banished from Venice,

If he returns to the city, he is guaranteed to be hung between the two gallows in Piazza San Marco, his head will be cut off, and will be displayed in the central square.

The sum of the reward for anyone turning in Don Juan Mickas has been increased: three thousand gold ducats for anyone who delivers him to Venice alive, and two thousand ducats for anyone who delivers his body. Two thousand ducats are promised to anyone who delivers Don Bernardo alive, and fifteen hundred to anyone who delivers his body.

I'm sure your honor is aware of the fact that according to Venetian law, the couple's marriage has no legal validity. The dowry chests shall remain in the city's treasury until Señorita Beatrice La Chica turns fifteen.

Respectfully,
Your friend, Venetian nobleman Barnabe

I sipped a glass of water. They must flee to Constantinople. The Venetians had declared a brutal revenge, and would search for them throughout Europe. I would pay any fortune in the world to save Bernardo and Juan from the gallows.

Venice
February 1553

Esteemed Señora Beatrice Mendes,

On behalf of Charles the Fifth, King of Spain, Emperor of the Holy Roman Empire, and his sister, Regent Mary Queen of the Lowlands, we convey our condolences to the señora for the calamity that has come upon her.

We were sorry to hear that our friend Sir Don Juan Mickas has been permanently banished from Venice and is facing the threat of the gallows.

We sincerely hope his young bride is doing well and that the couple can soon be united.

Here's hoping for better days.

Respectfully,
Augustino Leonardo
The emperor's ambassador in Venice

***

Rome
February 1553

Aunt,

I've found sanctuary, while Bernardo is on his way to Ragusa with friends.

I offered King Henri the Second a loan, in exchange for intervening on my behalf with the Venetian authorities. However, the king refused.

Juan

***

I quickly wrote a missive to Juan.

Thessaloniki
March 1, 1553

Juan,

I ask that you leave Rome immediately for Ragusa. The Venetian authorities have expanded the number of policemen searching for the two of you. Catch up with Bernardo; don't linger on European soil.

At my request, the sultan is sending a ship with armed janissaries to the Port of Ragusa. Board the ship that will take you to Constantinople.

Worried,
Your aunt Doña Gracia Nasi

***

A light knock was heard on the door.

"Doña Gracia Nasi, I'm sorry to interrupt, I see that the lady is busy," Kamel Reis Pasha said with a nod.

"Pasha, you're not interrupting."

He extracted a parchment scroll from a silver cylinder, undid the red ribbon and read the missive out loud.

June 1553
Istanbul
The Sublime Porte

For Doña Gracia Mendes Nasi,
At the Sultan's Command

A procession of the carriages of His Magnificence Sultan Suleiman and the effendis is on its way to Ragusa, to escort the señora. We expect her arrival at the beginning of spring.

At the sultan's command, the Sublime Porte has issued a royal decree granting Doña Gracia Nasi a firman—a concession allowing herself, her family members and her servants to conduct themselves as foreign subjects in Istanbul and wear Venetian clothes.

The Sublime Porte grants the señora a firman to mine the silver quarries and export the metals; to mine and deal in salt; and to manufacture gunpowder for cannons.

She is also granted a firman to sew uniforms for janissaries. The concession includes the right to raise flocks of cattle, harvest the wool, process it, and provide embroidery, buttons, ribbons and sewing.

Doña Gracia Nasi shall pay half her profits to the Sublime Porte.

Respectfully,
The Grand Vizier
Rostam Pasha

The most important *firman* I had received from the sultan was the one allowing me, my family and my servants to conduct ourselves as foreign subjects in Istanbul.

If Juan and Bernardo had been in Thessaloniki, I would have danced with joy. The *firman* had granted me, as a woman who was a foreign widow, as opposed to Turkish women, the right to come and go as I saw fit throughout the state and outside its borders. In addition, the sultan had allowed us to continue wearing Venetian fashions, as opposed to oriental dresses. I suppressed a smile. Things were coming along to my satisfaction.

"The furniture and chests were loaded on Sultan Suleiman Han Hazretleri's carriages. Another warship is on its way to Ragusa," said Kamel Reis Pasha.

"Pasha, I hope the sultan's ship arrives quickly to save Juan and Bernardo."

"*Inshallah.* Amen."

PART EIGHT

Constantinople
1553-1569

Sultan Suleiman Han Hazretleri, March 1553

I shifted aside the silk curtains on the lavish carriage and peeked outside. Kamel Reis Pasha, the sultan's *shawish*, raised his hand. The procession of escorts that had accompanied me from Thessaloniki, comprised of four large carriages seating Ottoman effendis, the members of my entourage and a guard of janissaries riding forty noble steeds, came to a stop.

Kamel Reis Pasha opened the carriage doors. I disembarked with Reyna onto the path, next to which stood a *sebil*—a small structure housing a public drinking fountain, decorated with blue Iznik tiles, with a sign upon its façade: "The construction of this blessed *sebil* is at the command of our master, the Honorary Sultan Suleiman, son of Sultan Saleem Han, may Allah perpetuate his kingdom." We were greeted by a fresh scent and the chirping of birds.

"Señora, soon we will bid farewell to the Via Egnatia, the beautiful Roman road on which we have traveled from Thessaloniki, and enter our lovely city of Istanbul through the gate in the city wall."

"Would the *señora* and her daughter like to freshen up at the *Han*, the inn?" Kamel Reis Pasha asked.

"Thank you, there's no need. We're only a bit thirsty."

Kamel Reis Pasha signaled to a dark-skinned Spanish maid, who hurried toward the *sebil*, quenching passersby with its pellucid waters.

The serving girl offered us two cups of waters. I sipped the chilly water and a coolness spread through me.

"Mama, why are your eyes tearing up?" Reyna asked.

I took her hand in mine and led her to the black carriage behind us.

Kamel Reis Pasha opened the carriage door, nodded to us and walked several steps away. Three small coffins, carved in wood, were lined up across from us on the woolen rug spread over the floor of the carriage.

"Reyna," I stroked her hand. "We must bid farewell to our loved ones," I said. "When we enter the city, the caskets of your father, Francisco, and my parents, may they rest in peace, will continue on their way to their final resting place, the Valley of Jehoshaphat on the Mount of Olives in Jerusalem."

Reyna laid her head on Francisco's casket. "Papa, I'm sorry I didn't get to know you."

"Your father loved you very much," I caressed her hair.

Kamel Reis Pasha approached us, stationing himself politely several steps away.

"Excuse me, señora, we must hurry to the reception."

***

I looked out through the window of the carriage, whose wheels were clattering over the paving stones.

The procession came to a stop. "Madame, Istanbul." Kamel Reis Pasha gestured at the hills of the city before us. "The esteemed ladies are invited to disembark briefly to witness the beauty of our city from the top of the hill."

The skyline displayed an abundance of castles, the glittering domes of mosques, and spiking up between them, turrets challenging the sky and the masts of ships at the faraway harbor. The calls to prayer of the imams from the heights of the minarets mingled with the cries of the gulls.

The sights left me dizzy. Thessaloniki and Ragusa were a combination of West and East, while Muslim Istanbul proudly displayed its Eastern architecture.

Kamel Reis Pasha pointed straight ahead. "The Topkapi Palace. Only those who are rare and exceptional are invited to enter its gates," his voice trembled.

"Over there, you can see the Süleymaniye—the opulent mosque that architect Sinan is building in honor of the sultan, and over there is the

Aya Sophia Mosque, once a byzantine church. The structure next to it is the Haseki Hürrem Complex, in honor of Roxelana Sultana, the sultan's wife."

The procession continued on its way and swiftly entered the gate in the city's stone wall.

Reyna glanced at the Venetian mirror and brushed her hair. "Mama, we're here." She put her hand in mine.

We approached the harbor, where tall gray waves crashed on the pier. Red flags with the yellow crescent at their center flew high upon the masts of the port's ships. The salty scent of the sea smelled sweet to me.

I held the pendant against my heart and closed my eyes. *I'm blessed,* I thought to myself. *This is it; there's no way back. I've thrown off the old world and arrived at a new world, foreign and different.*

"Please, Señora Gracia Nasi and daughter are invited to the reception." A smile reflected in the eyes of Kamel Rais Pasha, who opened the carriage door before us, inviting us to alight.

"The sultan's physician, Efendi Moshe Hamon," he introduced me to a distinguished-looking man with a broad, lined forehead, his eyes illuminated and his beard graying.

"Señora Gracia Nasi, Señorita Reyna Nasi, welcome." The man examined us curiously, bowing his head in greeting.

"Greetings, Efendi Moshe Hamon. Thank you for all your generous help."

"Señora Gracia Nasi, it is an honor for us to assist the *señora*. Legislator Sultan Suleiman hopes your cousins will escape the trouble in which they find themselves and reach the Ottoman state soon."

Reyna turned away, watching the ships sailing the sea.

"Amen," I said. If I had known a sharp sword would be laid against their necks, I would have relinquished my remaining property in Venice and insisted they accompany me, I thought to myself.

We began to stroll slowly, with Kamel Reis Pasha and Efendi Moshe Hamon by my side.

Men in a variety of colorful capes, turbans on their heads, and women in long dresses, with puffed harem pants peeking out beneath them, their hair covered with veils, made their way to the open space of the dock.

Gypsy children in colorful clothing ran down the pier toward us, cheering with joy, holding out their hands and calling, "*Baksish! Bakshish!* A little money!"

A crowd was huddling on the pier, surrounded by janissaries in their red uniforms, armed with curved swords. The sounds, the smells and the multicolored clothing made our head spin. The masses stared at us. Reyna held on to my arm.

"*La señora! La señora!*"

"Doña Gracia Hannah Nasi!"

"Doña Gracia, queen of the Jews!"

"Queen of the Jews!"

The calls repeated themselves among the crowd coming to welcome me.

"The Portuguese lady!"

"The Venetian!"

"The lady wears Venetian clothing!"

I waved to the throng.

"*Merci,*" I thanked them, distributing thousands of coins to the excited masses, who kissed the coins.

A drummer with a rotund belly paced among the two rows of the throng. Soldiers were securing a red carpet laid out all along the lines of people stretching out on both sides like an honor guard.

The drummer struck his drum and called out: "Make way! Make way! The Grand Padishah, Sultan Suleiman Han Hazretleri!"

The *shawish* swallowed emphatically. "Señora, you have been granted an extraordinary honor worthy of kings. Our master, Legislator Sultan Suleiman, called His Highness Suleiman the Magnificent in the West, has never come to welcome anyone, much less a woman."

"The sultan has come to welcome Doña Gracia Nasi," I replied.

"Make way! Make way! The magnificent sultan, Sultan Suleiman Han Hazretleri!" the drummer declared.

The crowd surged back. A heavy silence engulfed them.

The musicians in the military band, the *mehterân*, blew their trumpets, which were glittering in the sunshine, beat their drums and struck their percussion instruments.

"Glory to our Shah, Sultan Suleiman, Sultan Suleiman the Legislator, Commander of the Faithful, Shadow of God, Lord of the Lords of the World!" the commander of the janissaries declared.

"Glory to our Shah, the Grand Padishah Sultan Suleiman Han Hazretleri!" the dignitaries replied, while the members of the crowd fell on their knees upon the ground.

Proud and regal, Sultan Suleiman the Magnificent strode toward the lavish reception tent. He wore a silvery silk cloak embroidered in gold and a cape of glistening black mink fur. His nose was pointy, his short beard black, and on his head was an immaculate white turban adorned with a red ruby. Three handsome princes were by his side. "Those are his sons, from his wife Hürrem Sultana," Efendi Moshe Hamon whispered. "The blond one, Şehzade Saleem, made friends with Juan Migois when he came here to ask the sultan to intervene in your release from the prison in Venice. Next to him is Şehzade Bayezid and the handsome prince with the hunchback is Şehzade Cihangir."

"Make way! Make way!" the drummer struck his instrument fiercely.

"Make way for the esteemed *señora*, Doña Gracia Nasi!" he declared.

On a low red silk sofa, adorned with mother of pearl, Sultan Suleiman the Magnificent sat erect with regal elegance, his right hand resting on his left knee and his left hand on his left thigh, a curious spark reflected in his brown eyes.

Grand Vizier Rostam Pasha signaled me to approach the sultan.

I strode upon the silk carpet, with Ottoman dignitaries and ambassadors from many countries lined up on both sides.

The Venetian ambassador shifted uncomfortably in his place as I passed him. A tiny smile emerged at the corners of my mouth.

Rostam Pasha raised his hand, and I stopped some distance away from the sultan.

I curtsied.

"Welcome, Venetian Doña Gracia Nasi, to Istanbul," the sultan said, his voice confident.

"Sultan Suleiman Han Hazretleri, I'm honored to arrive in the magnificent, much-praised Ottoman Kingdom." I replied, presenting him with a book wrapped in blue velvet fabric and tied with a golden ribbon.

The sultan undid the silk ribbon and read the heading in Arabic: "*The Poetry of Rabbi Yehuda Halevi.*" He leafed through the book, his eye coming to rest on one of the poems, which he began to read out loud in a pleasant voice.

"Do the tears know the eyes that bear them
Do hearts know who has overturned them."

"Thank you, poetry is one of the loves of my life," the sultan smiled.

"To the honorable Sultan Suleiman Han Hazrelteri, a gift from Doña Gracia Nasi," the *shawish* declared. Three pairs of janissaries came in with their heads bowed, carrying silver chests embedded with precious stones.

Cries of amazement were heard when Rostam Pasha undid the chest's golden lock and, with both hands, presented the sultan with a rare dagger inlaid with rubies, emeralds and diamonds.

"Thank you." The sultan passed his right thumb, on which he wore a gold ring sporting a large ruby, over the sharp blade.

"A present for the sultan's wife, Hürrem Sultana, and for their daughter, Mihrimah Sultana, the wife of the grand vizier," said Kamel Reis Pasha.

The vizier opened the second chest, which contained jewelry, jars of perfume, beauty aids and rolls of Venetian silk fabrics.

The sultan smiled. "Hürrem Sultana and Mihrimah Sultana will enjoy your gift and be happy to meet you."

The vizier opened the third chest. Thousands of gold coins glinted in the sunlight. A murmur passed through the audience.

"Sultan Suleiman, I've heard word of the of the many acts of charity and instances of kindness carried out by the sultan and his wife Hürrem Sultana, directed at the people of your country as well as my own people in Jerusalem. As a token of gratitude, I present a contribution to the residents of the city."

After the moving ceremony was over, a procession of carriages set out, accompanied by a unit of janissaries in their red uniforms, mounted on tan steeds, escorting me and my large entourage to my new palace.

The procession drove slowly down the streets of Istanbul. Dozens of boys and girls ran after the coaches, stretching out their little hands and calling, "*Bakshish, bakshish!*"

"Mama, look." Reyna pointed at the crowded wooden house, whose balconies seemed close enough to reach out and pluck the laundry off the wires, the peddlers' stalls, the old women sitting in the houses' doorways, the men with their overgrown mustaches, rolling prayer beads in their hands, as the carriage drove among the steep, lovely alleys.

Wagons loaded with vegetables crossed the road. Farmers wearing *sharwals*, loose-fitting trousers that narrowed at the ankle, holding pitchforks in their hands while their donkeys, overloaded with sacks, walked in front of them, stopped at the side of the road to wave hello to us.

In every village and town we reached, I stopped the procession and handed out thousands of coins to the town's poor.

"Mama, you're handing out too many ducats," Reyna said.

"My daughter, the bible says '*that thy brother may live with thee.*'"

"Mama, these are not our people."

"Reyna, Constantinople has opened its gates to us. It's our duty to pay its people back."

The shores of Galata Bay, whose blue waters shimmered in the golden sunlight, the well-tended neighborhood of Galata, the villas, the pretty squares and the profusion of flowers all reminded Reyna of Venice and Ferrara. Finally, a smile appeared upon her face.

The carriage stopped in front of a beautiful villa, located on the beach of a blue-green bay. Small waves crashed on the golden sand, seeming to greet us.

"Belvedere Palace, designed by royal architect Sinan." The *shawish*'s eyes shone.

One gold ducat a day! The rent was excessive, but I had no choice; the sultan was not allowing me to purchase the palace, and price is always a matter of supply and demand.

"This is where I bid you farewell, Doña Gracia Nasi. It has been an honor to serve you, fare thee well!" Kamel Pesha turned his horse around and galloped away in the direction from which we had come.

The iron gates opened. A row of servants greeted us by bowing and curtseying deeply.

We strolled through the garden, admiring the beauty of the flowers, breathing in the intoxicating scent of jasmine and roses.

I ordered that the villa be furnished with the best Venetian furniture. The architect swore to me that Constantinople had unique handmade furniture, and so I allowed him to equip the repose lounge with Oriental furniture, but I was not willing to sit on cushions and dine at the low tables. At Belvedere, meals would take place at a Venetian table, with the diners sitting upon chairs. If I was displeased, I would replace the furniture.

It was painful to me that Brianda, who had fallen ill since the abduction, and La Chica had stayed far from us, beyond the sea, and worrying about Juan and Bernardo, who had still not managed to escape Europe, kept sleep from my eyes.

"Please write this down and send a runner to the House of Mendes ship sailing to Italy today," I told Victoria, my spinster, thirty-year-old secretary, the daughter of one of the sages of the Portuguese Torah study hall.

Constantinople
June 1553

Juan and Bernardo,

An Ottoman warship is on its way to you. Wait at the Port of Ragusa.

Doña Gracia Nasi

Reyna came in quietly, standing close to me. She peeked at the letter.

"If he hadn't kidnapped her and married her…"

"Never mention this affair again. It never took place. Do you understand?!"

"But it did…"

Şehzade Mustafa, Autumn 1553

Dark clouds obstructed the skies of Istanbul. Sultan Suleiman had embarked on a campaign of war against Persia, taking two of his sons with him. Şehzade Mustafa, his eldest son from his first wife, admired by the Turkish people and the janissaries due to his integrity and courage, stayed behind in the seat of his power.

My agents reported that the markets had emptied out, and the cafés where the city's residents and the janissaries once sipped bitter coffee, sweetened with *rahat lokoum*, also called Turkish delight, were now abandoned. Concerned merchants whose wares remained on the shelves unbought, waited for the return of the janissaries from their campaign with the spoils of war and bags full of coins.

Tension reigned throughout the city. Everyone was discussing the rumors that the Grand Vizier Rostam Pasha, and the sultan's wife Hürrem Sultana, whose adversaries referred to her as "the witch," had falsely accused Suleiman's eldest son, Şehzade Mustafa, of forging an alliance with the Persians to rebel against the sultan in order to inherit his throne.

✳✳✳

"*La señora*, Don Benardo and Don Juan Mickas," the major-domo informed me.

"Thank the Lord, you made it here safely!" I hugged them.

Juan, who looked like the son of royalty, kissed my hand.

"Dear aunt, thank you for helping Bernardo and me to escape."

"We were miraculously saved from the gallows at Piazza San Marco." Bernardo's voice shook; recent events had clearly left their mark on him.

He looked tired, and gray strands had woven themselves into his beard and hair.

"Bernardo, you mean that my diplomatic efforts and the bribe money I distributed were the miracle that saved you," I said.

"Aunt, I'll never forget your generosity," Bernardo said.

Juan looked out through the window at the Bosporus Strait. "When we got off the boat, we heard the sultan had summoned Şehzade Mustafa for an inquiry due to the rumors that he was planning a rebellion, and that Mustafa was on his way to Konya military camp in Antalya."

"Hello, Bernardo, welcome," Reyna said when she entered the room.

"Hello, Reyna," Juan's eyes scurried frantically.

Reyna clenched her hands, her almond eyes piercing him like a sharp sword.

"Why did you kidnap La Chica? How did you dare marry her when we're engaged?!"

"Reyna, I told you never to mention this incident…" I looked at her in anger.

"It's fine," Juan nodded. "If I hadn't married her, my head and Bernardo's would be hanging side by side in Piazza San Marco, and I wouldn't be standing before you today." He straightened his short coat.

"Yes… but you're married."

"The marriage is fictitious, invalid." His voice grew hoarse.

"You broke my heart." Reyna turned her back to him.

Juan approached her. "Reyna, please, look at me."

Reyna turned slowly, her eyes downcast. He placed his hand on her chin, raising her face to his. "I'm sorry, darling, if I hurt you. Please forgive me."

"I'm having a hard time doing that."

"Reyna, my queen, my lovely fiancée, please don't break my loving heart."

The shadow of a smile sparked in Renya's eyes.

"I'm Jewish. I'll only marry a Jew," she said.

"Juan and Bernardo, it's time you returned to Judaism. Tomorrow, you'll be circumcised!" I informed them.

"Tomorrow?" Juan flinched back. "We only arrived today. I don't need to be circumcised at my age."

Bernardo placed his hand gently on Juan's shoulder. "My brother, we've been waiting for this moment our entire lives."

"Everyone who is a part of the Mendes family is circumcised, including the clerks and our servants. Do it," Reyna said firmly.

"Reyna, my friend the writer Andrés Laguna begged me not to let your mother persuade me to return to Judaism. He swore the Inquisition would persecute me forever, and that I'd regret it my whole life," Juan said.

"That will never come to pass. I'll take care of him. I'll make sure he won't have even a single Turkish eshrefi coin," I said.

"Reyna is right. If we want to be part of the Nasi family, we must be circumcised," Bernardo said, winking at Reyna.

I produced a bottle of *raki*, an anise-flavored alcoholic drink. "Don't be afraid. Drink two glasses before the surgery, and it will help you overcome the pain."

Bernardo uncorked the bottle and poured its contents into goblets. "Well, at least we can enjoy the drink." He hefted the goblet, gulped down the beverage, and almost choked from the ensuing cough.

"You forgot to add water..." Reyna smiled.

"When I was in Constantinople, I made sure to send Saleem bottles of *raki* and special wine from Cypress, which I hid under a cargo of furs and salt, so that the palace clerks wouldn't discover them," Juan contributed.

"That's why they call him 'drunk Saleem.' After all, Muslims are forbidden from drinking wine," I said.

"I didn't know that you'd been in Constantinople before," Reyna said, surprised.

"I went on a covert mission to meet the sultan, his son Şehzade Saleem and his doctor, Moshe Hamon, so that they would take action to free Aunt Gracia and Brianda from prison, and you and La Chica from the convent. And as you know, I succeeded."

A fleeting smile appeared on Reyna's face.

Juan opened an oblong chest containing four of the newest type of guns. "A present for the sultan and the princes. I also brought three prime steeds for the sultan."

Reyna covered her mouth with her hand, concealing a tiny yawn.

The major-domo entered looking distraught. "*La señora*, it's a disaster! Şehzade Mustafa, the heir to the throne, is dead. Sultan Suleiman has murdered his son in his tent. He strangled him with his own two hands, using a bowstring, while his loyal followers stabbed Mustafa, who fought with all his might, with daggers."

"That's shocking. I can't believe it. Who said that?" Juan called out.

"Şehzade Mustafa's bodyguards, who fled from the military camp after the murder, saw his body tossed inside the tent. The janissaries and the entire Turkish people loved Mustafa." A tear shone in the eye of the major-domo.

"And that's not all. The kindhearted Şehzade Cihangir's grief over the death of his brother has caused him to become ill. He cries all day and refuses to eat."

I paced the room in a state of inner turmoil. If the educated, poetry-loving, rule-legislating sultan, builder of lavish structures and protector of the Jews, could murder his own son, who could guarantee that tomorrow, he would not turn his back on us?

***

Tall waves crashed on the beach. The ships in the Bosporus Strait were rocked by the storm. Gray clouds lurked above. Heavy rain was falling. Turkey donned black, mourning the death of the beloved Şehzade Mustafa. His coffin was placed in Aya Sophia Mosque, and from there, the funeral procession left for Bursa, where he was buried.

The sky over Istanbul grew dark, and a storm was about to break out at any minute. The janissaries blamed Grand Vizier Rostam Pasha and Hürrem Sultana, the sultan's wife, for poisoning the sultan against his son from his first marriage.

In an attempt to quell the rebellion the country was facing, Sultan Suleiman fired Grand Vizier Rostam Pasha.

But peace did not resume quickly. The kind hunchback Şehzade Cihangir died as a result of his depression and sorrow for being unable to save his brother's life. Those who hated Mustafa were not appeased by his death; several months later, his eldest son was murdered.

My thoughts tormented me, leaving me sleepless. Perhaps Sultan Suleiman would forget about the Jews' knowledge, their various crafts, the banking, the book publishers, the commerce, the medical skills and all the good and plenty we had bestowed upon the Ottoman state? And what if a new ruler rose and persecuted us?

Expulsions, book burning, our brothers being burned at the stake in auto-de-fé, waves of hatred threatening to drown our people.

"The Jews must have a plot of land of their own. We must return to the land of our forefathers," I told Reyna.

"Mama, you're dreaming. Who would allow the Jews to purchase ground in the Holy Land and manage it? The cruel sultan?" she asked.

"Dreams are meant to come true. The dreamer is victorious," I said.

Every Wise Woman Buildeth Her House

Within the Jewish Sephardic community, a nineteen-year-old unmarried woman was considered an old maid. The time had come to realize my plan and arrange Reyna's wedding. I summoned Juan and Bernardo, who had recuperated from the circumcision. I informed them that from now on, we would address them by the Hebrew names given to them by their parents, Samuel and Rosa Migois, when they were born.

"Juan, from now on your name is Joseph."

Bernardo bowed to his brother in an elaborate gesture. "Hello, Don Joseph Nasi."

Joseph, who was taller than most people, seemed to stretch out even more.

"I'm honored, my brother Bernardo; excuse me… Don Samuel Nasi." Joseph shook his hand firmly.

"Joseph, it's time for you to marry your fiancée Reyna."

Joseph leaned against the windowsill. "Why don't we wait a little? It's important to me to get married only once I have property of my own. Şehzade Saleem gave me a concession to plant an orchard and establish a vineyard. The good soil and the rainy weather will provide me with quality vines. Instead of exporting wine from France, I'll produce wine, and earn high profits."

Samuel apologized, saying he saw that the conversation was growing personal, and left the room.

I turned to look at Juan. "Some gossip reached my ears about you spending time with Rachel, one of the harem women, when you were in

Constantinople, and about one of the princes being called 'the Jew's son.' They say he's yours."

Juan placed his hand on his heart. "I swear that's a lie."

"Why would someone malign you with lies?"

"Aunt, Şehzade Saleem's enemies do not approve of my connection with him, and they would do anything to banish me from his court."

"I accept what you're saying, but be careful. You're about to marry my daughter. Stay away from the harem. I want you to respect Reyna's feelings, and for the two of you to get married soon."

Joseph walked around the room, examined the blue Iznik tiles and the adornments of the copper table, on which Turkish delight and quince preserves were laid out.

"Reyna is dear to me. We'll decide upon a time…"

Joseph examined his well-groomed fingernails. "We need to discuss the sum of the dowry."

I did not think Joseph would bring up the subject of the dowry so quickly.

"Don't worry. I won't deprive my daughter."

Joseph polished his nails against the back of his hand. "Aunt Gracia, what sum were you thinking of putting down?"

Ships going down the river blew their horns, warning a ship that had come too close.

"Seventy thousand gold ducats is a very handsome sum."

"Aunt, this is your beloved daughter Reyna," Joseph said quietly.

"Ninety thousand gold ducats."

Joseph cleared his throat, bowed his head, kissed my hand and brought it to his forehead. "Aunt, thank you for your generosity," he said, his voice choked.

I asked the maid to call my daughter and serve refreshments.

Reyna entered, her hair loose, looking fresh-faced and vibrant.

The maid served us chilled water, cherry preserves and semolina and almond cookies.

"Reyna," Joseph leaned in toward her. "You said it was important to you that I be circumcised, and now I stand before you, a proper Jew. We've waited enough. I ask that we become a family."

"I want to think about it. I want to talk to Mama."

Joseph smiled. "I'll await your answer patiently," he said, leaving us alone.

Reyna twirled the engagement ring on her finger. "My friends say that Joseph is older, and is only marrying me for my dowry and inheritance."

"My daughter, who are you listening to, your jealous friends or your mother? There's no one in the world who wants the best for you more than me. Joseph is family, a good man and a successful businessman. You'll have a good life with him. I have faith in him and believe in him. That's why I made him my right-hand man in the company."

Reyna clasped and unclasped the bracelet on her hand.

"My friends tell me that Joseph smuggles in wine for 'Drunk Saleem,' and at night, they cavort with the beauties of the harem."

"That's a vicious rumor spread by those who are jealous of him. Esther Kira, who purchases perfume and jewelry for the harem women from me, interrogated the woman in charge of the harem's inhabitants, and the rumor is entirely false. It's all a matter of politics.

"My daughter, Joseph's acquaintance with the kings and rulers of Europe, his nobility, his good manners, his wisdom and generosity and the important information conveyed to him by his agents in Christian lands grant him influence and high status in the sultan's court. He has been appointed as Şehzade Saleem's agent in the gem trade and is advising Saleem on the inheritance battle against his brother Şehzade Bayezid, who is jealous of him. If Saleem is appointed sultan, Joseph will receive the title of *muteferik*—a member of the sultan's entourage."

"I'm not interested in his title. I'm not..."

"Reyna, are you thinking of someone else?" I asked.

"No."

"My daughter, *la mujer sevia fragua la kaza*—the woman runs the home. In your wisdom, you will know how to establish a good household, and guide Joseph in any way you see fit."

Days of Light, 1554

In the opulent reception tent set up at Señora Synagogue, I sat along with Samuel, greeting the wedding guests: Grand Vizier Kara Ahmed Pasha, effendis, rabbis, ambassadors and friends from Thessaloniki, Ancona, France and Safed. I invited Brianda and La Chica to the wedding. Brianda sent a polite letter stating that unfortunately, they could not attend Reyna's day of joy, along with a gift of a ruby necklace and earrings for Reyna, and gold cufflinks for Joseph.

The servants milled among the guests with gold and silver trays offering *maamoul* cookies with nuts, crispy *kadaif* pastries made of filo dough, and baklawa drizzled with honey and rose blossoms.

Reyna, lovely and radiant, was wearing a purple velvet wedding dress with gold embroidery. Her hair was set in an elaborate braid woven with pearls. The sapphire necklace and earrings she wore provided a handsome frame for her round, tan, delicate face, emphasizing her almond-shaped eyes. She closed her eyes and prayed silently from the silvered *siddur* prayer book she had received as a gift from me.

"My beauty, I love you," Joseph's lips whispered as he approached her, tall and regal, covering her face with a veil embroidered with golden thread and adorned with pearls.

The women sang wedding songs and burst out in cries of joy. Reyna's friends beat the drums and the cymbals, dancing around her. I made sure that the envious friends who had tried to sway her against Joseph were not invited.

I was covered with gooseflesh as I escorted the beautiful, radiant Reyna from the bridal seat, entwined with orchids, to the *chuppah*, the ceremonial canopy. I was sad leading my daughter to the *chuppah* without

Francisco. I recalled my secret wedding and my father's death.

In my mind's eye, I envisioned Francisco's form, watching me with a hint of a smile on his face. I heard his deep voice telling me, *Gracia, congratulations, our daughter is getting married. I'm proud of you; you've raised her well. I'm with you, watching over our daughter from above.*

It had been a long time since I'd felt as happy as I did the moment we were standing under the *chuppah*, and I gave Reyna wine to sip from the *kiddush* glass.

For a month, I held parties and balls, distributed gifts to the city's poor and funded weddings for Jewish orphans.

When Reyna and Joseph returned from their honeymoon in Marmaris, a heavy weight descended upon my heart. I had hoped they would stay and live in the guest quarters of my palace, but she insisted that she wanted to live an independent life. They needed large stables for the horses, a hall for the collection of guns, bayonets, swords, helmets and armor Joseph had brought from Europe, and an extensive garden to host the dueling competitions he liked and at which he excelled. In addition, they needed to be able to keep a close watch on the vines growing in the immense vineyard Joseph had purchased, she claimed.

I tried to convince Reyna to stay and live in Belvedere Palace. I told her she would be alone during the day, as Joseph accompanied Şehzade Saleem on his hunting trips, but I did not manage to change her mind.

The young couple rented a palace on the other end of Galata, on the coast of the Bosporus Strait, which they renovated and furnished in a style similar to the one employed in Palazzo Gritti in Venice. Reyna informed me that she had decided to purchase a printing press and establish an independent publishing house.

"Why can't you print books at the printeries I own?" I asked, annoyed.

Reyna wrapped her flowery shawl tighter around her shoulders. "I want to print the books that Joseph wrote. The first, *The Interpretation of Dreams*, is about the dreams of the biblical Joseph. The second is *Thoughts on the Holiday of Sukkot*. In addition, I'm considering publishing an anthology of bible stories, and stories for children in Hebrew and Spanish," she said.

I leaned back. I did not know that Joseph was writing religious books.

However, it was also clear to me that Joseph was the one pulling the strings. Reyna would never have thought to establish her own publishing house. I hoped he would not squander all her money.

"My daughter, don't waste your dowry on adventures. Ninety thousand gold ducats is a vast fortune. Money should make money. You must increase the fortune and save the ducats for your children, as well."

"Don't you trust me? Don Joseph invests my money wisely. The principal has increased by ten thousand gold ducats." She stood her ground.

"That's good," I nodded.

"I preserve the principal, and dedicate a tithe of the profits to the charity funds I've founded. A trust to fund the studies at a school for orphaned boys and girls, and a charity fund to support sages and writers."

I kept my silence. *From now on, I'll be the lonely queen of Belvedere Palace.* I wept internally.

Little Hannah, 1555

Thunderstorms replaced the hot days.

On the Sabbath, the holiday of Sukkot, I gazed down from the women's section at my son-in-law, Don Joseph Nasi, who was sitting in the seat of honor, wrapped in a tallit, holding the ceremonial palm frond in his hands. Reyna, who was in the eighth month of her pregnancy, had stayed behind in the palace as her feet were swollen and she had a hard time walking to the synagogue.

Suddenly, I sensed my secretary Victoria leaning over me.

"*La señora*, your daughter is about to give birth. Matilda the midwife is with her."

I grew frightened. The expected date of the birth had not yet arrived. I left the synagogue and strode quickly along with Joseph and our escorts to their nearby palace. I whispered a prayer to the Creator that the premature birth would pass safely.

I entered Reyna's room.

"*La señora*, congratulations! It's a girl! Reyna was a true heroine," Matilda said.

I was flooded with happiness. After all the trouble and the wandering, I had been blessed with a granddaughter. I was a grandmother! However, pain pierced my heart due to the fact that Francisco was not with us. Grains of hot pepper and crystals of sugar: this was the texture of my life.

Reyna was lying on the bed, pale and exhausted. In her lap was a tiny baby, her head covered with brown fuzz, her eyes half-closed.

"Reyna!" I hugged her and kissed her forehead. "Congratulations, my daughter. You're a mother."

Reyna, who was utterly depleted, could only flutter her eyelashes.

I was afraid the baby would drop out of her weak hands. I picked her up and cradled her in my arms. "My granddaughter." I breathed in her pure scent and examined her delicate features. "Reyna, she looks like you," I said.

I glanced at my gold pendant. "My granddaughter, you belong to the People of Israel." I kissed her cheek and scattered pellucid sugar crystals around her.

Reyna caressed the tiny girl's pink cheeks. "Joseph wanted a boy..."

"*Amor de madre, la nieve no la va yelar.* Not even the snow can chill a mother's love," I said, laying my granddaughter down in her mother's arms.

"Congratulations, Joseph, we have a daughter!" Reyna said when Don Joseph entered the room, his tallit draped across his shoulders.

"Reyna, my pretty, this baby continues the family tradition of beautiful girls." He kissed the baby's forehead.

If my son-in-law Joseph was disappointed not to have a son, he took care to hide it well.

"Mama, we decided that if we had a daughter, we would name her after you, Hannah."

I believed everyone present could hear the beating of my excited heart.

***

Efendi Mouiz, my accountant, climbed the rungs of the ladder heavily and brought down the accounting ledger I had asked for. A cloud of dust struck my face when I opened the last page for the year 1542. My finger came to rest on the last line of numbers, underlined twice.

I was right: in the thirteen years since Diogo's death, I had single-handedly tripled the fortune of House of Mendes. And now I had to provide for my sweet granddaughter Hannah.

I closed the ledger and wrote a letter to Jacob Morro, Brianda's accountant. I asked him to do all he could to prevent Brianda from gaining possession of the chests of gold I had deposited in the Venetian Treasury.

It was inconceivable to me that La Chica would receive the fortune I had amassed, despite the signed agreement and the fact that she had turned fifteen.

About a month later, Victoria placed the reply on my escritoire. Jacob Morro had managed to do the impossible. The Venetian authorities had changed their policy in regard to Brianda, despite the signed agreement. The authorities had added an additional demand to the agreement: my solicitors and Brianda's had to confirm with their signatures that they agreed to the conveyance of the chests of gold I had deposited in the treasury to La Chica.

I poured myself a glass of cherry liqueur and drank it to celebrate my success.

Jacob Morro reported that a House of Mendes ship loaded with a cargo of fine Merino wool, set to sail from the Port of Ancona, in the pope's domain, to Venice had failed to arrive at its destination. The rumors claimed the authorities in Ancona had seized the ship and the merchandise it carried. He wrote that he was leaving on a brief journey to the Port of Ancona in order to release the ship and its cargo, before meeting up with his wife and sons, who had sailed for Thessaloniki.

I smiled in satisfaction. I knew I could count on Jacob Morro to bribe the court clerks in Ancona to change their decision, and that he would manage to release the House of Mendes ship from the Port of Ancona.

I finished sipping the liqueur. I wrote him a letter of thanks, informing him that I had increased the endowment I had promised him to thirty ducats.

A Letter from Venice

Reyna received a surprising bundle of letters from her cousin La Chica, which had been sent to Belvedere Palace.

Venice, Palazzo Gritti
June 4, 1555

To Reyna,

My cousin, a dark, deep sea separates us. My ocean of tears has dried up. Only the pain that cuts at my heart remains.

Mama was raging with fury when she received the demand that Aunt Beatricci's, pardon me, Gracia's solicitors signed the agreement granting me the chests. Mama suspects that Duarte Gomez, Augustino Henricks and Jacob Morro (who is no longer employed by Mama) were the ones to bribe the clerks of the Venetian Treasury in order to delay the conveyance of the funds. Otherwise, why would they suddenly add a new requirement? Why do my aunt's solicitors need to sign in order to release my funds?

It makes me sad to see Mama hurt, and I feel angry not to receive the chests I expected to receive. Mama thinks Aunt doesn't want to give me my part of the inheritance, is getting her revenge on Mama for refusing to come to Constantinople with you, and is hoping we will leave Venice, which will never happen.

Mama canceled the masquerade ball she had planned to throw in honor of my fifteenth birthday, even though the seamstress had sewn me a dress embroidered with blue butterflies, and the mask maker had designed a white mask with gold leaf decorations for me.

You wouldn't believe what an amazing surprise we've had lately. Mama almost fainted when her brother Leo, who had left Lisbon when she was a little girl, arrived in Venice on a business trip and knocked on the palace gates one day. He came to visit with his blonde-haired wife. He has returned to Judaism and his name is Arye de Luna. We see them quite frequently now. Mama says she's ecstatic to have found her long-lost brother, who is her only family.

I wish I were a butterfly; I'd cross the great sea and come to see you.

Send me a drawing of your daughter Hannah.

Beatrice La Chica

I was amazed. Where had my long-lost brother Leo been all those years? Why had he not contacted me? But there was no one to answer my questions. I opened another letter and read it.

Palazzo Gritti
June 30, 1555

To Reyna Benveniste,

Unfortunately, I have still not been granted permission by the Venetian authorities to receive the funds I am owed from the treasury.

Luciano de Costa, our major-domo, has been arrested. Duarte Gomez and Augustino Henricks, the House of Mendes agents, have informed the Bureau Against Heresy that Luciano de Costa has been living secretly as a Jew in our palace.

Mama is certain that the long arm of Aunt Beatricci, excuse me, Gracia, has been stirring all this up. She has been wanting to fire Duarte Gomez and Augustino Henricks for a long time now.

What happened was that Luciano de Costa, who was interrogated by the Bureau Against Heresy, broke down. At the age of fifty-eight, he is to stand trial before the Inquisition. He did not passively accept being informed upon, and reported that merchants Doctor Duarte Gomez and Augustino Henricks are also secretly Jews.

I find it odd that people working for Mama, all of whom are Portuguese conversos, are informing on one another, especially since they know each other and have been working together for many years. Sometimes I don't understand people. Aren't they afraid of the Inquisition? Of revenge? Of punishment from the Creator?

Mama suspects that your mother's Jewish agents turned in Luciano de Costa for being Jewish because they wanted to break her spirit and force her to move to the sultan's land.

Mother's financial situation is dire. She has many expenses and is truly not feeling well. Ever since Luciano de Costa was arrested, there is no one to manage the business. Mama has a cash problem, and has begun to borrow money. I worry about her. She is lethargic and gets headaches. If you know some good medicine, send it to me.

Yours,
Beatrice Le Chica

***

Venice
August 1555

For Reyna Benveniste,

Mama and I received an "invitation" to the Bureau Against Heresy, to testify at the trial; apparently, someone informed on Mama as well. And you can't refuse an "invitation" from the Inquisition.

My legs were trembling when we entered the Porte della Carta, the palace's ceremonial entrance, with the statue of the winged lion before which the doge kneels right above us. Mama held my hand tightly and whispered that I had to be brave, that it was all for the best, and asked that if I hear some things in her testimony that surprise me, to have faith in her.

When we climbed the Scala dei Giganti staircase, accompanied by the soldiers of the City Council Guard, I was afraid to stroke the white and pink marble columns. There's so much power in stone. I felt tiny facing the enormous statues of the land and sea gods, Mars and Neptune.

The breathtaking arced gold ceiling of the Scala d'Oro was reflecting in the marble floor. I silently prayed that Holy Queen Esther would watch over us.

The soldiers of the guard instructed me to stay in the waiting hall outside the Sala del Consiglio or conference room, instructing Mama to enter the royal hall of the Council of Ten.

The fear spread through me.

After he had been under arrest for three months, today I saw Luciano de Costa for the first time as he walked past me, led by the soldiers of the guard and dragging his feet.

His eyes looked extinguished, his gray beard had grown longer, and his disheveled clothes hung loosely on his body. What had happened to the energetic, impressive man who had imperiously managed our household? Had he undergone torture, like the whispered accounts I'd heard of people being hellishly tormented in the cellars?

Through the half-closed doors, left cracked open with the help of a few ducats I slipped into the hands of the guards, I could eavesdrop on the hearing.

I almost did not recognize Luciano de Costa's voice. His assertive manner of speaking had become frail. He recounted briefly that he had been born in Viana do Castelo in Portugal to the Habibi family. His voice shaking, he said that he had been forcefully baptized into Christianity in 1497. When he grew older, he got married in a church. His children had been baptized and lived with his wife in Thessaloniki. He said he had managed Mama's household in Ferrara, and moved to Venice along with us.

The interrogator asked him whether he practiced Jewish customs, and Luciano de Costa replied that he did not participate in Jewish prayers or use a Jewish name, and that he always wore the black hat customary among Christians.

The interrogator asked whether he attended church services. De Costa hesitated and finally quietly admitted he did not.

I felt relief when the judge decreed that de Costa would be permanently banished from Venice. It was a good thing he was not sentenced to be imprisoned; I don't believe he would have survived. Mama helped him and gave him money to live on.

Augustino Henricks testified that he had been born in Lisbon as a Christian and was forty-five years old. He had studied philosophy, theology and medicine, and was a lecturer at the university. His three older children lived in Venice, and the younger ones lived with their mother in Ferrara. He had portraits of the saints hanging in his home, and his connections with Jews were for purposes of commerce.

Duarte Gomez's legs almost collapsed under him as he climbed to the stand. He testified in a whisper that he went to confession and took the Eucharist. It was true that he owned Talmud books, but they were related to his theological studies, and he intended to donate them to the Church.

Much to my joy, both of them were cleared of any guilt.

Mama was then called to testify. As she walked slowly toward the witness stand, she noticed me standing beyond the door and nodded at me.

"Esteemed members of the council, Brianda Mendes stands before you with great humility. As a girl, I left my homeland of Portugal for Venice, the republic of freedom, which has a government with no king, and a ruler with no heir."

The interrogator drummed his fingers upon the table, and said the council had received testimony that Mama was living in her home as a Jew.

Mama's lips trembled, but she did not manage to make a sound.

The interrogator raised his index finger and asked firmly why Madame Brianda did not allow her daughter Beatrice to move to a convent and live as a devout Catholic.

Mama hesitated, and finally replied quietly that she had always obeyed the leadership, but her life was suffused with torment and suffering. She was persecuted by people who wished to harm her and had maligned her with lies before the priest, claiming her daughter wished to leave her and live in a convent.

"I believe that two years ago, your daughter left your home of her own free will," the interrogator commented mockingly.

Mama turned her head away and did not reply. I felt regret and much pain over the sorrow I'd caused her.

The interrogator was relentless, asking what Mama had meant when she said she had "always obeyed the leadership." Which leadership did Señora Brianda mean?

Mama looked directly at the members of the council and said, in a clear voice: "I am a New Christian, but in my heart, I am Jewish! That is the way I choose to live my brief life on earth."

I swooned when I heard Mama confessing that she was Jewish. The hall of the Council of Ten grew silent, after which turmoil broke out, with statements tossed from all directions.

"Brianda has stated that she is Jewish!"

"She's been dissembling her whole life."

"She'd claimed she was a faithful Catholic, that she aspired to live as a true Christian, and begged that we protect her."

"For years, we supported her in her feud against her sister."

The heavy doors opened and the members of the Council of Ten emerged from the hall, their faces gray and their capes whipping in anger.

Mama was led out of the hall, looking pale, and burst out in bitter tears. I ran to her, but the soldiers of the guard stopped me and demanded that Mama wait far away from me.

Frightened, I submerged into myself like a stone sinking to the bottom *of the lagoon, engulfed by a feeling of loneliness. Suddenly, I heard my name being called. The soldiers of the guard signaled me to approach and escorted me to the hall, with the frightening paintings of the Day of Judgement hanging on its walls.*

The head of the council addressed me in a soft, kind voice. "My child, what is it you want? Does the señorita wish to move to a convent, or live with her mother, Señora Brianda de Luna Mendes?"

I replied that I wished to live with my mother, in accordance with the lifestyle upon which my mother decided.

I was asked to go out and wait.

After a long interval of consultation, we were called in to hear the decision.

The head of the council scowled at Mama and informed her that the Council of Ten had decided to banish us from Venice immediately, and that Señorita Beatrice Mendes, who had turned fifteen, was permitted to receive the moneys deposited for her in the treasury.

I don't know how my mother found the courage to ask the council's permission to live in the Venice ghetto. Mama is a very smart woman; she planned everything in advance, and managed to outsmart the Council of Ten. Thanks to her confession, we received a certificate of transit allowing us to leave Venice; otherwise, we never would have left the republic.

Reyna, the winds of autumn are blowing, and my shoulders are already wrapped in a wool shawl.

Our lives, hopes, disappointments, sadness and joy are packed up in chests, including, oh happy day, the inheritance chests, secured with two locks: Mama holds one key and I hold the other.

In this lovely city, I leave behind my double life. Is there truly no more secret? Will it sink to the depths of the lagoon?

The synagogue's rabbi has declared us to be Jewish. We've been privileged with the right to take off the mask. Tomorrow we leave the Venice ghetto where we're living now, and sail off to the Duchy of Ferrara.

Duke Ercole the Second has granted us a writ of patronage and a transit certificate, and Mama has agreed to his request and granted two thousand gold ducats apiece to the duke's brother and to the cardinal.

Yours,
Beatrice La Chica

I placed the long letter on the desk. The interrogation of House of Mendes's agents left me sad. Neither did I feel particular joy over the fact that Brianda and La Chica had returned openly to Judaism and were on their way to Ferrara. I felt as if I had found a valuable piece of jewelry that I had lost: glad to find it, but in my heart, I had already been resigned to its loss.

Disaster

I opened the missive Jacob Morro had sent me from Ancona and my breath became labored.

Ancona
July 16, 1555

Esteemed Doña Gracia Nasi,

The clerks of the new pope, Paul the Fourth, have seized the ship Eleonora and all of the merchandise and crates of wool on board, claiming the ship belongs to Casa Mendes, owned by Señora Beatrice Mendes, a converso who has returned openly to Judaism in Constantinople.

The new pope has repealed the rights granted to the conversos by our benefactor, Pope Julius the Third. Paul the Fourth has issued a papal bull including harsh decrees. He has forbidden the Portuguese conversos to return openly to Judaism and hold assets. Paul has ordered the establishment of a ghetto in Rome, forced the Jews to wear the Jewish badge, a yellow cap for the men and a yellow kerchief on the women's heads, has prohibited them from owning houses and stores, employing Christians, trading in money or working in the field of medicine. He has permitted Jews to deal only in used wares. All synagogues in Rome, excluding one, shall become churches.

The pope demands that the priests give sermons attacking the Protestants, whom many of the annusim have joined.

Jacob Morro
House of Mendes Agent

Joseph's chin clenched in anger under his black beard, but before we could talk, the door opened.

"*La señora*, excuse me," the major-domo said. "A messenger has arrived from Ferrara, and he insists on coming in."

"I was asked to give the *señora* an urgent missive." The messenger thrust it toward me with both hands.

Port of Ancona, on deck
July 1555

Gracia,

Several days ago, Jacob Morro's assistant handed me a brief note and immediately ran off.

"Run! Inquisition! It's a hunt!"

I thought I had time to pack my research, but suddenly heard the maid yelling: "Inquisition! They're getting close!" followed by the thud of fists and boots on the doors.

I left behind the research on circulation on my desk, my medical books, gold coins and a silk robe with an important list in the pocket, and at the very last second, leapt from the window of the second floor.

I fell, but got up and started running. I hid in the doorways of houses, running to my brother's house in order to warn him, but the Inquisition's armed forces were already surrounding the house.

I hid in doorways, in a well and in stables. I saw a procession of dignified women and men bound in iron chains and dragged barefoot

along the sweltering road. Among them I saw the righteous Ja-
cob Morro, who had saved me, but unfortunately not himself, and
Yitzhak Argas, who had arrived from Ragusa to meet him. They
walked in a procession, their heads bowed. I hid all day until dark-
ness fell, drank a little water from a puddle and ate a slice of moldy
bread I found.

I gave the few gold coins in my pocket to a sea captain and boarded
a ship sailing to Ferrara, where my friend Michaela had moved.

A passenger on the ship who had managed to escape from his store
across from the offices of the House of Mendes told me that Jacob
Morro had managed to escape the building, but the Inquisition's
policemen had caught him and tossed him in jail.

The Inquisition has seized all of the property of the Portuguese
conversos *who were living openly as Jews in Ancona.*

Rumors claim that Duke Ercole de Este of Ferrara is granting refuge
to those fleeing. May the Lord in Heaven protect the wretches!

Amatus Lusitanus

"If they're accused of secretly practicing Judaism, their lives are in danger. The Inquisition might burn them at the stake," Joseph's voice thundered.

I struck the table with my fist. "The only chance of saving them is if Sultan Suleiman declares all those arrested to be under the patronage of the Ottoman Empire, and therefore, any harm done to them would be a personal insult against the sultan's honor. I intend to request a meeting with the sultan and his wife, Hürrem Sultana, and ask for their immediate intervention. Merchant Esther Kira has ordered perfume in the scent of passion flower, beauty products from China and jewelry from Venice from me for Hürrem Sultana. The delivery from India arrived yesterday, and Hürrem Sultana will be happy to receive them."

Twilight covered the sky.

"I've had enough! I'm not willing to have them strike at us while we take it silently. Something must be done! The Jews and *annusim* cannot be constantly persecuted, living in fear our entire lives," I raised my voice.

"I intend to lay an embargo on the Port of Ancona," I added.

"Doña Gracia Nasi wants to boycott the pope's city?" Joseph gaped at me.

***

The next few weeks were among the most turbulent of my life, and it's not as if my life had ever been placid.

We appealed to ambassadors and princes, asking them to intervene and act to free the Portuguese *conversos* who had been captured and imprisoned in Ancona, the pope's city.

I sent a special emissary to the pope's legate in Ancona, asking him to reapprove the certificates of the *conversos* arrested as New Christians who had returned to Judaism. I hoped that thanks to these new certificates, they would be released, and sent along a chest containing ten thousand gold ducats as ransom money for the Vatican.

But the pope remained determined and refused to renew the certificates.

I raised the sum of the ransom to twenty thousand gold ducats, but the Church demanded thirty thousand from the *converso* community in Ancona.

The community of Portuguese New Christians managed to recruit 17,500 gold ducats. I sent them the remainder of the sum, but by the time the messenger arrived in Ancona, the pope had had a change of heart. He prohibited releasing the prisoners in return for money, and annulled the charters of rights that some of the prisoners held. He insisted on prosecuting the poor wretches.

House of Mendes agents bribed priests, jailers, soldiers, and anyone with any connection to the jailhouse, in an attempt to smuggle the prisoners out.

A letter from Yitzhak Argas, who had been my agent in Ragusa, hit me hard. The guard had "forgotten" to lock the jailhouse door. Yitzhak

Argas managed to escape along with thirty other prisoners, and all of them arrived in the Duchy of Urbino. Yitzhak wrote that tragically, Rabbi Jacob Morro was held in the second floor of the prison, and had been unable to escape.

Yitzhak apologized for being forced to tell me about the torture he had undergone during the interrogation to force him to confess his Judaism. The entire world had to hear of the Inquisition's viciousness and cruelty.

I was hung naked on a post, heavy weights were tied to my feet, and I was freed abruptly to fall to the floor. My feet were placed in iron shoes with an iron spike in the heel, and I had to walk in them, and that's why I limp today. I was tied to a wheel and spun around, and every time I refused to answer a question, water was poured down my throat; I almost choked.

Doña Gracia, the cries of the tortured won't let go of me. Please do everything to save them. If they are found guilty, our brothers will be burned at the stake.

I vomited violently when I read about the extreme torture to which he had been subject. I had thought such dreadful torture was no longer taking place in Europe. The realization that it did was appalling to me.

Grand Vizier Rostam Pasha, who had been reinstated in his role, summoned the representatives of Ancona's embassy in Constantinople. He informed them that Sultan Suleiman firmly demanded that Doña Gracia Nasi's seized property be returned to her, and that the prisoners who were Levantine merchants under the patronage of the Ottoman Empire be released.

The pope opposed the request, and informed the grand vizier that the Church would not release the *conversos* suspected of practicing Judaism.

I was received for a meeting at Topkapi Palace with Sultan Suleiman and his blue-eyed, regal wife Hürrem Sultana. They listened in interest to what I told them, growing angry when they found out that esteemed Turkish merchants who had purchased merchandise from the Portuguese prisoners would lose their money. They agreed to my request to appeal to the pope in a request to release the prisoners. The sultan sent an urgent request to the pope.

The pope informed the sultan that only prisoners who had spent time in the Ottoman Empire in the past and were considered Levantines—subject to Ottoman patronage—would be freed. However, *conversos,* New Christians, who had never lived within the borders of the Ottoman Empire would not be pardoned.

The prisoners' trial came to an end and a death sentence was hanging over their heads. The New Christian communities throughout the cities of Europe were stricken with terror, shocked by the situation in Ancona and the mortal threat facing the wretched souls there. The fear that the Inquisition would expand its activity to additional cities increased, and emissaries were sent to me for consultations.

***

"Trouble in Ancona," my son-in-law Joseph sighed when he came to spend the Sabbath in my palace along with Reyna and my granddaughter.

"Excuse me, señora, I've been asked to give you a personal letter," I was approached by a tall man of forty or so, dressed in the Italian style, his eyes bloodshot.

"Thank you." I opened the envelope and my eyes sped through the page.

Pesaro
Señora Gracia Nasi,

We ask that the señora put her trust in the conveyor of this letter, Señor Yehuda Perach. The community of Portuguese conversos in Pesaro has appointed Señor Yehuda Perach, who has fled from Ancona, as their representative in Constantinople in order to tell the esteemed señora and the heads of the Jewish communities of the disaster in Ancona and ask for your help.

Always at her service,
Yitzhak Argas
House of Mendes Agent

"Disaster in Ancona!" I repeated the words that had caught my eye.

"Child, tell *la señora* what you saw," Yehuda Perach requested from a girl of twelve or so. The girl, terror reflecting in her brown eyes, stood close to Reyna.

"*La señora*," she said in a weak voice. "I was there and saw the horror with my own eyes. From the window of a building near Piazza della Mostra in Ancona..." Her voice grew choked. "I saw two men jump to their death. A moment before their bodies hit the stone ground, I heard them cry out: '*Moshe emet vetorato emet...! Moses is a true prophet and his Torah remains true!*'

"'*Shema Israel!* Hear, oh Israel' the men and women beside me called out.

"A member of the Inquisition's guard ran toward them. I heard him calling out, 'Jacob Morro!' But the poor man did not answer..."

I was appalled. Who knows what manner of torment, tortures of the body and the soul, my dear friend Jacob Morro had undergone in the cellars of the Inquisition until this strong man, who had supported and encouraged me my entire life, understood he would not be pardoned and chose, along with another *annus*, to sacrifice himself in the Lord's name. What a loss.

I grew dizzy and darkness engulfed my vision. I held on to the synagogue post and wept bitterly. For a long time, I could not quell the tears. Reyna hugged my shoulder and stroked my face.

Don Joseph read the letter and thrust his chin forward, his face flooded with anger. Once the prayer was over, he talked to Sephardic, Portuguese and Levantine rabbis as well as the community's dignitaries.

"We must discuss the situation and decide on a course of action," Joseph addressed the Ashkenazi Rabbi Tsontsin. Rabbi Tsontsin pursed his thin lips into a narrow line. "Blessed be the True Judge! Don Joseph Nasi, you can't conduct business on the Sabbath."

"This is a matter of life and death," Joseph said.

"My friend, they're in a better place now. There's nothing to be done at the moment," Rabbi Tsontsin said.

"Rabbi, you're invited tomorrow morning to an emergency conference with the heads and dignitaries of the community. We can't simply ignore this," I said.

"Esteemed Doña Gracia Nasi, I'm sorry, but I cannot attend. I teach an ongoing class on the Sabbath."

"I assume the class Rabbi Tsontsin teaches takes place in the Torah Study Hall for Young Men that I have founded in the memory of my husband Francisco-Zemach Benveniste, may he rest in peace. The lesson can be taught just this once by one of the regular participants. I expect to see you at my home."

"Doña Gracia Nasi, I'll try to make it. I don't want to disappoint the regular students who attend the class," Rabbi Tsontsin said, not daring to look at me directly.

Rabbi Yehoshua Tsontsin had arrived in Constantinople from *Ashkenaz*—Germany, only five months ago. I had heard that he was wise and fluent in the Torah, and had appointed him as the rabbi of the large synagogue. I funded his salary, as well as a stipend for those studying at the study hall and the extensive library, with my own money. Every day, he dined at my table along with eighty other guests, and he dared refuse me, in front of everyone, at the synagogue. Internally, I fumed.

"Rabbi Tsontsin, Doña Gracia Nasi has invited you to the meeting. I expect to see you there," Don Joseph Nasi said.

Rabbi Tsontsin seemed to shrink in his place, the furrow between his black brows deepening and his mouth twisting slightly.

"Doña Gracia Nasi, I suggest the meeting be held on Sunday."

Challenging the Pope, 1556

The meeting held in my palace on Sunday consisted of a gathering of the sages of the Constantinople community and delegates from the communities of the *annusim*: Rabbi Joseph Ben David Iben Lev, the head of the sages of Constantinople, who managed the yeshiva I had established; Yehuda Perach, the delegate from Pesaro; Rabbi Ephraim Feigi and Shlomo Sangi, the delegates of the Venetian community; Rabbi Moshe Almosnino, the delegate from the Thessaloniki community; Rabbi Meyer Katzenellenbogen, known as the Maharam of Padua; Rabbi Moshe Matarani, a member of the rabbinical court headed by Rabbi Jacob Berav in Safed; and Rabbi Yehoshua Tsontsin, who was the last to enter.

"Learned gentlemen, thank you for coming on such short notice. I now turn the meeting over to the esteemed *señora*, Doña Gracia Nasi," my son-in-law opened the meeting.

"Gentlemen, sages of Israel and delegates of the communities overseas, we've received the terrible news from Ancona, and therefore, I've asked you to attend this emergency meeting.

"Señor Yehuda Perach, who has managed to flee Ancona, and who arrived two days ago on a ship from Ferrara, please update us on the situation."

Señor Yehuda Perach rose slowly from his seat, wiping away a tear. "The Jews of Pesaro have asked me to come to the sultan's land, to meet *la señora* and tell all of you about the terrible events." His voice trembled. "I am a refugee from Ancona, and the sights I've seen haunt me like a nightmarish shadow.

"The city's secular authorities have required all residents of Ancona to show up at Piazza della Mostra on Sunday and watch the auto-de-fé procession.

"At the head of the procession marched the priests, bearing a flag with the ironic declaration 'Justice and Mercy.' After them trailed twenty-four prisoners condemned to death, including one woman, barefoot and bent, wearing an apron adorned with a drawing of flames, the outfit of the condemned. On each of their heads was a pointy hat with drawings of demons and flames upon it, and in their hands they held a large green candle.

"They were followed by the bearers of the 'weave and weft' and the Inquisition's police force, may their names be forever damned, bishops and two witnesses from among the city's citizens. At the end of this parade of horrors marched army soldiers.

"The head inquisitor and the city's governor sat on the stage across from the stake, on high chairs, with the 'weave and weft' displayed behind them. The inquisitor opened the proceedings by swearing in the witnesses:

"'Citizens of Ancona, you have taken it upon yourselves to aid the Inquisition. You must swear to do all that I command you to do.' He then turned to the condemned and began his sermon, of which I remember a few terrible sentences.

"'Oh, lowly remnants of Judaism! Reviled Catholics, despicable even among the Jews themselves, as you chose to convert to Christianity, and yet do not observe its rules. Your Jewish sons ungratefully turn away from You and refuse to acknowledge You as their messiah. Because you have resumed your sins, we excommunicate you from the Church and hand you over to be judged by the people.'"

A commotion broke out around the table, accompanied by cries of anger and disbelief.

"Please, let him finish," Don Joseph Nasi requested.

Yehuda Perach choked upon his tears. "The inquisitor addressed the condemned: 'Heretics, repent.'

"One by one, the poor wretches were brought up to the stage. 'Lost sons, repent your sins, return to the fold, confess and declare yourselves to be loyal Catholics.'"

Yehuda sighed, sipped some water and continued.

"Our brothers, the holy men of Ancona, refused to confess and atone for their sins. The inquisitor pointed his finger at them in accusation, turned their 'weave and weft' over, and thundered out: 'You are doomed to die! Burn them alive!'"

Yehuda Perach produced a handkerchief from his pocket and wiped away the tears falling from his eyes.

"'Light the fire!' the inquisitor ordered. A roar rose from the enflamed crowd gathered in the square, which cursed and called out: 'Add kindling to the bonfire! Make the fire stronger!'

"The priests burned incense and sang hymns. One by one, the holy souls of Ancona were brought onto the stake. It was a terrible sight; it was heartbreaking to see and hear the cries of desperation and pain of our brothers going up in flames. I hope their suffering was brief, as early in the morning, before the condemned arrived at the square, I gave the guards ten gold coins so that they would not add water to the kindling. If they had to die, I wanted the death to be quick, rather than tortuous. They'd suffered enough," Yehuda Perach sighed.

There was not a dry eye left around the table. "Blessed be the True Judge!" everyone said, wiping away tears.

A cry of pain burst from my throat. "The pope won't get away with this," I said.

"We have to avenge the blood of these holy souls!" my son-in-law rapped on the table.

"That's right," people echoed in assent.

"Doña Gracia Nasi wishes to speak before you," Joseph said.

I stood up, my hands gripping the table.

"Gentlemen, my brothers, you are the leaders of our people. There is no herd without a shepherd," I said.

"There is nothing worse than the burning of the *annusim* due to their faith. We've had enough of begging and groveling before kings, earls and the heads of the Church! Enough talking, enough distributing of bribes, enough of the sea of tears! It's time for action! The pope has blasphemed the name of heaven. The Jewish community must come together and react to this terrible act through direct, immediate political and financial action that will hurt him hard and quickly."

"How?"

"Leaders of the generation, my proposal to you is to boycott the Port of Ancona in the pope's domain!"

"Boycott?"

"But Ancona is the pope's land."

"That's very dangerous! It's a declaration of war!"

"It's time to fight! We can no longer bend our back and succumb to the blows," I replied.

"Fight?"

"Since when do Jews fight?"

"How?"

I listened patiently to the comments tossed into the room.

"Ancona is the only port city in the pope's kingdom. Therefore, we have to hit him where it hurts most. In the pocketbook." I looked around.

"Gentlemen, we must agree that all ships belonging to Jews and *annusim* will stop docking at the Port of Ancona. Instead, they'll start docking at the nearby Port of Pesaro. I promise to compensate the merchants who will be harmed by the embargo."

The room grew silent.

"Gentlemen, the boycott will directly impact the pope's income."

"Isn't the *señora* going too far?" I heard the thin voice of Rabbi Tsontsin.

Don Joseph Nasi rose from his seat: "Esteemed gentlemen, you've heard the proposal *la señora* and I have been thinking of since we first heard news of the disaster. Now we ask your honors to state your opinion in an orderly manner."

The startled glances that the attendees exchanged tore through the silence of the room. I knew Maran Joseph Karo, the greatest Jewish sage, among the Jews exiled from Spain who now lived in Safed, supported the idea of the boycott, and read his letter of support out loud. Rabbi Shlomo Sangi huddled for a long time with his friend Ephraim Feigi, exchanging whispers, then stood up.

"On behalf of myself and Rabbi Ephraim Feigi, we want to thank *la señora* for her brave speech, and for *la señora*'s daring proposition to boycott the pope and to stop dealing with the accursed city of Ancona.

I'm sure my father and teacher Rabbi Meir Iben Sangi, who made me swear before I embarked on this journey that if the verdict against our people's martyrs is indeed carried out..." Rabbi Shlomo Sangi sighed heavily, "...we must avenge their blood. My fellow sages, on behalf of the Venetian community, we support the proposal," he said, resuming his seat. Rabbi Ehpraim Feigi and the other attendees shook his hand.

"I have a comment to make. The Port of Pesaro is small. I think it will be hard for large commercial vessels to dock there. We have to give this some thought," said Rabbi Ephraim Feigi.

"Rabbi Moshe Almosnino, delegate of the Thessaloniki community," Joseph addressed him. "Please tell us what you think."

"*La señora* is a prominent, much admired woman. Señor Don Joseph Nasi, your reputation has spread far and wide. The community of Thessaloniki remembers Doña Gracia's visit to our city, and her contribution to the establishment of yeshivas, Torah study halls, hospitals and craftsman workshops. We will never forget she saved the hidden Jews.

"On behalf of the Thessaloniki community, I accept Doña Gracia Nasi's brave and admirable suggestion not to conduct commerce with the city of Ancona."

Good, I smiled to myself when Joseph walked over to shake his hand.

Rabbi Joseph Ben David Iben Lev, known as the Ribal, stood up. "The refugees of Ancona are right. We must stand united and act on behalf of the holy men burned in Ancona. I agree with the statements of my friends, that Jews should sever their ties of commerce with Ancona, as well as leave the city."

Rabbi Moshe ben Joseph Matarani, known as the Mebit, stood up.

"Gentlemen, the embargo on the Port of Ancona will cause financial damage to the city's Jewish merchants," he said. "If we decide that ships will dock in Pesaro, the Jewish merchants in Pesaro will grow rich. I think they should compensate the merchants of Ancona for their losses; otherwise, the merchants of Ancona will oppose the boycott."

"I recommend that the Jews of Ancona, who contribute significantly to the city's economy, leave Ancona and move to Pesaro," I said.

"*La señora*, I don't think the rich Jewish merchants will agree to leave Ancona. The Port of Pesaro is small, and is not suitable for ships to dock in. The vessels will have to dock far away, and convey the merchandise to the city in boats, which will cause a rise in prices," said Rabbi Ephraim Feigi.

"Rabbi Yehoshua Tsontsin, what's your opinion?" Joseph addressed him.

"Gentlemen, first, allow me to congratulate the beneficent lady, 'a crown of glory upon the forces of Israel, every wise woman buildeth her house in holiness and purity.' *La señora* and Don Joseph Nasi, these are difficult days for the people of Israel. I like your suggestion, but before I sign the letter of agreement, I want to think about it some more."

"Rabbi, what is there to think about?" Joseph grew angry.

"Gentlemen, the boycott is dangerous. The moment commerce in Ancona stops, the immense financial income of the pope's republic will suffer."

"The pope has blasphemed the name of heaven," said Rabbi Meyer Katzenellenbogen.

"The boycott is not a matter of necessity but of choice," Rabbi Yehoshua Tsontsin commented loudly.

I examined each of the attendees slowly.

"Our learned guests, Sultan Suleiman the Magnificent appreciates my opinion, as well as that of my son-in-law, Don Joseph Nasi, who, as you know, is the advisor to Saleem, the heir to the throne. Gentlemen, the sultan supports the boycott!" I said.

"Is Doña Gracia Nasi certain of that?" Rabbi Tsontsin asked.

"The sultan supports the boycott and sees it as an important tool against the hegemony of Christian infidels," Don Joseph Nasi replied.

"Gentlemen, leaders of our generation! Never, in all my actions, have I asked for agreement from the sages and rabbis of Israel. Even after I returned to Judaism. But this time, I'm afraid that throughout the Christian world, our brothers 'belonging to the letter Yod' will be accused of practicing Judaism and burned at the stake. I ascribe supreme importance to the consent of the sages of Israel. After all, we are all brothers, and our strength lies in our unity," I stated.

Murmurs of consent were heard.

"It's very important to take the initiative and carry out political and commercial action that will make it clear to the pope that we will not take the assault against the holy souls of Ancona lying down. I appeal to the Jewish heart within you and ask you to sign the letter of consent that will be sent to all Jewish communities within the sultan's lands and the Christian ones and ask them to take part in the boycott."

An intense argument took place around the table. Rabbi Yehoshua Tsontsin tried passionately to convince the sages that the boycott should not take place, raising many arguments against it.

"I'm afraid the Christians' revenge shall be bitter, and ultimately, all of the Jews and the *conversos* will be punished," he said.

In contrast, voices chiming out in support were also heard.

"Enough with the fear, we have to react!"

"We must punish the pope, so that the whole world knows and no one dares burn *annusim* at the stake ever again."

At the end of the day, after hours of discussion and conflict, a majority decision was reached to boycott the Republic of Ancona, and the rabbis composed a letter expressing their agreement to the boycott. Initially, the boycott would be temporary, for a period of eight months until Passover in the Jewish year 5318, or 1557.

"Be strengthened and blessed!" Don Joseph Nasi shook the hands of the meeting's attendees. I hoped the boycott would prove successful, and that we would be able to extend it.

After the meeting, Joseph sent urgent letters to all Jewish communities, accompanied by the letter of consent signed by the Jewish sages, and recruited our agents to make sure the embargo was indeed being carried out.

The Ancona Boycott

The news that Doña Gracia Nasi had challenged the pope and declared a boycott on Ancona, and that all the Jewish communities had joined this boycott, was received in amazement in the Christian world. Kings, princes, dukes and ambassadors could not believe that the Jews dared confront the Christian world, backed by the sultan, no less. The Jews, too, reacted to this daring act with wonder and admiration, mingled with fear and apprehension regarding acts of retaliation.

My agents in Italy reported that within a week from the moment when the ships of Jewish merchants stopped unloading and loading merchandise at the Port of Ancona, all financial and commercial activity in Ancona ground to a halt.

Ships laden with merchandise turned to Venice and Pesaro. Rabbi Ephraim Feigi was right. The Port of Pesaro was narrow, and large ships could not dock there. The merchants were forced to convey their cargo to the port using boats.

The global mayhem was significant. Merchants were leery about dealing with the merchants of Ancona. The prices of Turkish leather and metals escalated. Fabrics from Ancona intended for Turkey stayed in the warehouses, and many of Ancona's merchants lost their assets and their fortune, facing bankruptcy.

Ambassadors, consuls, high Church officials and wealthy merchants asked to meet me and my agents in order to understand how Doña Gracia Mendes Nasi, a widowed woman, a Spanish Jew, dared to do what was unbelievable and inconceivable—take on the Church and punish it with an embargo and financial isolation.

I explained to the stunned ambassadors that the blood of the *conversos* could not be spilled without consequence. It was our right to protect ourselves and our people so that we would no longer be persecuted, and the Church must stop the auto-de-fé, the burning of *annusim* at the stake.

However, I found out that my power was limited, and that opposition to the boycott and objections to upholding it were in fact rampant among the Jews, of all people.

The letter of agreement from the sages made no impression on the Jewish merchants in Ancona, who were harmed by the embargo. They raised their voices in protest, sending letters to all communities against the boycott, which was harming their livelihood.

I fumed when I found out that Rabbi Yehoshua Tsontsin, who lived on my financial support and who, without my help, would have stayed on in the Torah study hall without anyone being aware of his existence, was opposing me. Behind my back, he sent letters supporting the merchants of Ancona's request to return commerce to the city.

He claimed to be acting out of true concern toward the merchants of Ancona, based on his own views, but I knew that he and others could not see the big picture. The Jews could not be submissive and humiliated. This was how the Christians wanted us to live, but we had to protect our dignity and our right to live as Jews.

In my parents' home, I learned that the sages were worthy of respect. I did not wish to shame Ashkenazi Rabbi Tsontsin for opposing the agreement of the Sephardic rabbis and my own opinion. I decided to be the bigger person and allowed him to keep his position. However, I might have made a mistake.

I missed Amatus Lusitanus during that period. He would have given me drops to soothe my turbulent spirit and my aching stomach. However, he continued in his travels and moved to Thessaloniki.

Eight months later, when the temporary boycott came to an end, I sadly approached Sage Bashi.

"Sage Bashi, I did not manage to prevent the death of Jacob Morro or save the lives of the twenty-four holy souls of Ancona. I believed the boycott would be effective, but some of the ships of the *conversos* merchants have resumed docking at the Port of Ancona."

"*La señora* is a devout woman. All is determined by heaven."

"I was hoping the boycott would continue," I said.

"Doña Gracia Nasi resembles the valiant Deborah of the bible. The lady has brought honor to our people with her actions," Sage Bashi consoled me.

Death in Ferrara

"Excuse me, *la señora*."

I raised my eyes from the book I was reading.

"You've received a missive," my secretary said.

November 1556
Castello Estense, Ferrara

To Doña Gracia Nasi,

I'm sorry to inform you that Señora Brianda Mendes passed away unexpectedly at the age of thirty-five.

Brianda was buried in the Jewish cemetery. Her tombstone was inscribed with her Jewish name, Reyna Benveniste.

My wife Duchess Renée and I are sorry for your loss, and promise you we will take care of the orphan Beatrice La Chica Mendes.

The missive dropped from my hand. For a long time, I remained sitting, immobile, looking at the setting sun coloring the river water red. The old stomachache hit me with all its might.

I closed my eyes and remembered Brianda standing on the deck of the ship approaching Antwerp, her hair gleaming in the sunlight emerging from between the dark clouds. "Beatricci," she held on to my arm, "I'm glad you took me with you." She smiled at me.

Brianda, my sister, where are you now? Lying under the ground with your lovely long hair, which, many years ago, when we were still girls, I braided and tied in ribbons…

Francisco's voice echoed within me as he told Papa, "This beauty must be Brianda," along with her melodious laughter as she curtsied lightly before him.

I miss you, Brianda. If I had known that Venice would be our last meeting, I would have held you tight and told you that you were dear to me, and that I would always love you.

Tears began falling from my eyes. Brianda and I splashing each other with water from the fountain in the garden of our home in Lisbon, sneaking into the kitchen, taking warm cookies that had just come out of the oven and going out to the garden, laughing, sitting under the tree as I told her a story I'd made up. Brianda had always loved my stories about princesses and knights. *Brianda.*

I took the letter-opener and tore my dress in the traditional gesture of mourning.

"Blessed are You, the Lord our God, the True Judge," my lips whispered.

I picked up the missive and continued reading.

The Court of Ferrara has confirmed the request of young Beatrice Mendes and she has been declared as the general and exclusive heir to her mother Brianda Mendes.

I have appointed her uncle Leo de Luna as the orphan's guardian until she is married or reaches the age of eighteen.

Respectfully,
Duke Ercole de Este the Second

"The letter didn't mention Brianda leaving a will. Duke Ercole de Este, my brother Leo, his blonde wife and the debtors will all try to get their hands on her property. I'll ask Augustino Henricks to help the orphaned La Chica and keep an eye on what's going on," I told my secretary.

"If La Chica was married, her husband would manage the inheritance funds and prevent all those greedy people from stealing away her money," she said.

"My sister passed away at a young age. She didn't have time to arrange her daughter's marriage," I clutched my heart.

"*Kuando la persona va estar debasho de la tierra, entonses se savra su valor.* When a person is buried in the ground, he is missed," my secretary sighed.

***

"Let Don Samuel know that I'm waiting for him in the study. Ask Efendi Mouiz, the accountant, to bring the emergency coin chest from the safe room, and send the servant to call my daughter and son-in-law."

Darkness fell, and the maid lit the candles.

Autumn winds blew leaves hither and thither. The world was changing in front of my eyes. Charles the Fifth, Emperor of the Holy Roman Empire and King of Spain, had abdicated the throne. Along with his sister Mary, regent queen of Hungary, they had departed the Port of Antwerp as part of a royal flotilla, to live out the rest of their lives at St. Jeronimos Monastery. Prince Maximillian, Juan's friend, had been crowned emperor, and Charles's son Philip the Second was now king of Spain.

"*Eskrito en la palma lo ke va pasar la alma.* The palm reveals the soul's destiny," I remembered Mama's saying. What had happened could not be undone; the hollow gaping in my heart would never be filled.

The Gold Medallion, 1557
Ferrara

Dear Reyna,

My cousin Bernardo, Don Samuel Nasi, went down on bended knee and proposed to me.

Grief and sorrow are tearing at my heart. How can it be that Mama is not beside me, rejoicing along with me? I don't know if she would be happy about my marriage to Samuel, who is older than me by eighteen years. I hope she is looking down at me from heaven and sees I'm happy with him.

I think Mama would have liked the dress I sewed for the engagement. I wore a dress with a raised collar and puffed sleeves, along with earrings I had received from Mama. I didn't pull back my hair the way your mother likes, but allowed it to cascade over my shoulders, covering it with a shawl adorned with two lines of pearls.

My fiancé gave me a copper medallion engraved with my portrait as a gift. The Italian artisan de Pastorini, who moved from Sienna to Ferrara, designed it for me. It was hard to sit for hours, motionless and in profile, at his atelier and enable him to engrave my portrait. My back hurt, and the moment I moved, he began to wave his arms and shout that he couldn't take it anymore, and that I had to gaze directly into the horizon.

At Don Samuel's request, the craftsman engraved my name in Hebrew, Gracia Nasi, at the edge of the medal, along with my age, eighteen, in Roman numerals.

The wedding will take place in two months at the synagogue. The rabbi of Ferrara's Jewish community will conduct the chuppah. The Finzi-Contini family, who were friends of Mama's before the disaster, will throw the wedding party in the garden of their palace.

I dreamt that Mama was leading me to the chuppah. I can't believe my beloved mother will not be with me at my wedding.

Beatrice La Chica (soon Benveniste)

"Grandma!" I heard the cheerful voice of my granddaughter Hannah, who had come to visit along with my daughter and Joseph. The little one extended her hands to me and leapt down to me from her father's shoulders. I gathered her to me. "Sweetheart," I hugged her and breathed in her sweet scent. What a shame that Francisco had not gotten the chance to see his beautiful, almond-eyed granddaughter.

"I managed to use my connections. The grand vizier received a letter from Duke Ercole de Este that all Brianda's debts have been paid off. My brother Samuel and his fiancée La Chica have received a certificate of passage to leave Ferrara," Joseph said.

"Thank the Lord! The duke should have already given them a certificate of passage to reunite with us a long time ago."

"There is one problem." Joseph's expression grew solemn. "Samuel let me know that Augustino Henricks is refusing to return the money you loaned him. He claims he spent lots of money on helping La Chica attain the certificate of transit from Ferrara to Constantinople."

I was amazed. In his will, Diogo had asked me to put my trust in Augustino Henricks. I had gotten him into dealing in salt, wool, silk and weapons. He and his entire family had grown very wealthy thanks to me. Had he been betraying me all these years? Had he been the one to inform the authorities of my plans and actions? Perhaps he had been conducting business behind my back? Was it possible that he had not passed on all the funds that I was due?

"Grandma Gracia, can I have another candy?" my granddaughter asked.

I looked at her and thought that for the sake of my granddaughter and the other grandchildren I would have, there was no point in dwelling on quarrels and people who had betrayed me. It was time to move on to the ultimate task of my life—making sure that my grandchildren would live in a safe place. I had always dreamt about securing the future of my grandchildren and of the Jews as a whole.

The Vision of Returning to Zion, 1557

The flame of the candle commemorating the holy souls of Ancona flickered upon the missive sent by David Iben Arditi, my emissary to the Land of Israel:

> The pasha of the village of Jaffa, the entryway into the country of our forefathers, along with the Ishmaelites, prey upon the Jews... In the slopes of the mountains, along the narrow, winding road from Jaffa to Jerusalem, Bedouin and Arab highwaymen lie in wait behind the olive trees for the processions of pilgrims. Jerusalem is surrounded by the mighty walls built by Suleiman... The governor of Jerusalem is harassing the long-time settlers, the Jews who have never left the Land of Israel, charging them heavy fees...

> At the entrance to the Western Wall, entrance fees are charged by Turkish soldiers. I prayed at the Western Wall for la señora's welfare and for the success of my mission.

> About fifty Sephardic families are residing in the Jewish Quarter in Hebron, making their living from agriculture.... In the village of Gaza, on the way to Cairo, there is a large Jewish community... The sages of Israel dwell in the holy city of Safed, and about five thousand of our people live there...

> Tiberias is a desolate, ruined fishing village—a pile of black stones with the Sea of Galilee at its center. The soil there is good, and there are also hot springs, where visitors are obliged to pay an entry fee...

I knew that Sultan Suleiman had invested in the development of Jerusalem, building a wall around the city and renewing its water supply. His wife, Hürrem Sultana, had established the Haseki Sultan Almshouse in Jerusalem, to distribute food to the poor.

I decided to request a meeting with Sultan Suleiman the Magnificent in order to advance my plans.

My fingers fluttered against my gold pendant. The time had come to realize my vision of renewing the Jewish settlement in the land of our forefathers, the Land of Israel.

***

Accompanied by two janissaries, I paced slowly through the garden of Topkapi Palace, among the beds of breathtaking tulips, above which flocks of butterflies were fluttering, to the tent where Sultan Suleiman was sitting. His hair was sprinkled with white, and sadness dwelled in his eyes.

"Señora Mendes, welcome."

I curtsied lightly. "Bless the sultan."

"Señora Mendes, from your missive I understand that the *señora* seeks a *firman*, to lease the taxes of Tiberias and the villages around it."

"Honorary Sultan, the financial development of Tiberias will yield gold coins for the empire's treasury. The Jews who are being persecuted in Christian lands will settle in Tiberias, develop commerce, agriculture, fishing, the silk and wood industries and the hot springs, as well as grow sugar cane, resulting in increased revenue from taxes."

"What do you think?" the sultan addressed Grand Vizier Rostam Pasha.

"My ruler, pardon my irreverence. I'm afraid that Jewish settlement in the Safed region will undermine the area's stability. The governor of Damascus believes it is not a good idea to have the Jewish and Christian infidels settle among the Arabs."

The sultan looked at the grand vizier sharply. "Señora Mendes is promising to bring new life to Tiberias."

"I apologize, my ruler," Grand Vizier Rostam Pasha bowed his head.

"Tiberias shall be a Muslim religious trust," the sultan decreed.

"My ruler, the Sublime Porte requests that Señora Mendes increase her monetary offer."

"Honorary sultan, in return for the *firman*, I'll pay a thousand gold ducats a year, and in a decade, I'll multiply it tenfold."

The sultan stroked his beard. "Señora Mendes, the Sublime Porte will discuss your proposition and will inform you of my answer."

Tiberias

In the new, lavish Señora Synagogue attendees were packed in so tightly that the blue waters of Bosporus Strait were no longer visible through the arched windows.

People both young and old were standing shoulder-to-shoulder in the wide aisles. Youths in their best clothing were climbing the windowsills while children huddled around the stage.

The scents of perfume, both light and heavy, mingled to engulf the women's section. Ladies and young girls clad in the best of Constantinople's fashions crowded in and jostled against each other behind the wood partition, waiting expectantly.

Pretty girls, their hair tied back with white silk ribbons, passed by with baskets adorned in lace, handing out almond candy and Turkish delight wrapped in delicate fabric to the praying women.

Don Joseph Nasi raised his hand. The crowd grew silent. Two janissaries, displaying medals of commendation on their chests, stationed on either side of the tall wood doors, stood tensely at attention.

The audience parted, making way for me. The rustle of my silk Venetian dress was the only sound heard as I strode slowly toward the stage. The gold coins adorning the white silk shawl covering my hair glittered in the light of the waning day.

"Dear fellow Jews, brothers and sisters," I began. "I, Gracia Hannah Nasi, formerly Beatrice de Luna Mendes of the house of Benveniste, stand before you, deeply touched and awed. I thank the Creator of the World for the right to pray openly in our ancient language." I paused briefly.

"On behalf of the Jews who are residents of the Kingdom of Turkey, known as Turgema, allow me to thank Sultan Suleiman Han Hazretleri, his father Sultan Saleem the First, and his grandfather Sultan Bayezid the Second, for sending ships to Spain and to the Christian lands to bring our brother, expelled from Spain and forcefully converted in Portugal, to their kingdom. I want to thank the sultans, the rulers of the world, for allowing our persecuted brothers to settle on Turkish soil and return openly to Judaism."

Enthusiastic applause was heard in the synagogue.

My son-in-law, Don Joseph Nasi, handed me a parchment scroll. I undid the golden ribbon as my eyes scanned the large audience, lingering upon Reyna with a loving smile.

"Gentlemen, we have been blessed by the fact that Sultan Suleiman, the exalted legislator, known throughout our settlements as a ruler of generous sentiment, whose heart is full of compassion for our tormented, persecuted brothers, has responded to my appeal to him on the question of the fate of the Jews, and allowed us to hold this elevated occasion."

"What?"

"What does the *señora* mean?"

Joseph raised his hand, and the attendees grew silent.

My heart was beating wildly and my face was hot.

"Approximately one thousand, five hundred years ago, we were exiled from our city of Jerusalem, and scattered in all directions. Many of our people were banished to the Roman Empire, also known as the Kingdom of Edom. Over the years, our brothers were forced to convert to Christianity, persecuted by the Inquisition and burned at the stake. The Jews of Spain who did not convert to Christianity were exiled by the evil monarchs Ferdinand and Isabella, under the influence of our great foe, Torquemada. Some of them ended up in Portugal like my family, and were forced to give up their religion and convert.

"My holy, persecuted brothers, the question of the Jews' fate shall not disappear on its own. The time has come to take action!

"My fellow Jews, recently, we have been able to hold our head high. We dared to do what many generations of our persecuted brethren before us had not dared to do. We protected ourselves and boycotted the Pope's state!"

"Bravo!" the young people called out.

Don Joseph Nasi, who was standing beside me, smiled and raised his hand.

"My brothers, the time has come to take our fate into our own hands!" I declared, standing erect and proud. The crowd gradually calmed down.

"Dear fellow Jews, men and women, we must act for future generations and for the children who are here with us. The time has come to be a nation like other nations. We are no longer willing to be persecuted, and we will not allow ourselves to be burned at the stake. We must take action for the sake of the memory of the holy souls of Ancona and other tragically slain Jews who were persecuted, tortured and killed solely due to their faith."

The applause and the beating of fists upon tables created a deafening roar in the hall.

"We want our forefathers' land, a piece of land on which to rest our heads, to carry out our forefathers' customs and to defend ourselves.

"We are now taking another step; the time has come to gather our people. The exalted Sultan Suleiman the Magnificent has granted me a *firman*, a concession to lease and settle in Tiberias and the nearby settlements, to build houses there and plant vineyards, to deal in merchandise. God willing, after fifteen hundred years of exile since the destruction of the Second Temple, my people the Jews will return to Zion and settle in the Land of Israel, and the Lord will show us the way."

A massive commotion broke out in the hall. A thundering, noisy uproar of cries of joy mingled with exclamations of protest and fear.

"*Mon dieu.*"

"*Firman.*"

"Tiberias?"

"A Jewish state?"

"The heart of her people!"

"We cannot 'storm the wall' and forcefully reclaim the Land of Israel."

"You cannot bring on the End of Days."

"*La señora!*"

"Why not Jerusalem?"

"The courage of Deborah!"

***

On Friday, shortly before noon, the major-domo invited the guests to enter the gold room with the blue marble pillars, the gold-coated capitals and the crimson Persian rug, which resembled one of the halls of the Topkapi Palace.

I sat down at the head of the green Venetian glass table with its legs of gold.

My son-in-law Don Joseph sat down at my right.

"Greetings, bountiful lady Doña Gracia Nasi."

"Welcome."

"Greetings, your honor Don Joseph Nasi."

"Peace by with you," Joseph replied.

"Please help yourself and sit down," he gestured.

"Esteemed lady, Doña Gracia, please," Joseph turned to me.

I examined the guests. Our visitors from Safed, poet Shlomo Alkabetz and my friend Bat-Sheva Modina, who had been widowed two years ago and married fabric merchant Eliyahu Kordova; bankers Chaim Bachar and Ya'akov Amslem; merchants Aaron Iben Ezra and Yitzhak Ninio; Señora Esterika Kira; the representative of the Cori community, near Rome; and our emissary to Tiberias, Master David Iben Arditi

"Esteemed ladies and gentlemen, dear guests, thank you for coming. Thank you for consoling me in my mourning over my dear sister Brianda, who has passed away.

"'My daughter, the chain remains unbroken,' my mother once made me swear. The cries of our loved ones murdered in Ancona still echo in my ears. A decade ago, I dreamt of a place where our people might settle. My son-in-law Don Joseph Nasi proposed to the government of Venice to buy an island in the lagoon and settle Jews there, but his proposal was rejected. Perhaps it was for the best.

"Is there a place in the world where a Jew can live his life? It is time we had a place to live our lives peacefully and safely. Some of you were present at Señora Synagogue when I announced receiving the royal *firman* signed by Sultan Suleiman the Magnificent, granting me an eternal concession to lease the village of Tiberias and seven villages around it.

"Ladies and gentlemen, these dreams are coming true. Leasing Tiberias costs plenty of money. I have committed to pay the sultan a thousand gold ducats a year."

"An immense sum, which we will pay from our own funds," Joseph added.

"My guests, despite this, the money is not sufficient to support all the settlers. It's important to us that each and every one of you offers support and a financial donation to our brothers who will settle in Tiberias.

"At the moment, we're in the midst of a battle with Henri the Second, king of France, who refuses to repay his immense debt to the House of Mendes. As far as I'm concerned, these funds are designated for settling the Jewish refugees and developing the town and the villages surrounding it.

"Sultan Suleiman the Magnificent is following in the footsteps of his predecessors. King Cyrus issued the Edict of Cyrus, permitting our people to return to Jerusalem and build the Second Temple. Sultan Bayezid the Second sent ships to save our brothers who were exiled from Spain. The great Ebussuud, mufti of the Ottoman Empire, issued a *fatwa*—an advisory opinion acknowledging the rights of the people of Israel over the Land of Israel.

"The *firman* over Tiberias allows us to channel the refugees and the persecuted to the land of our forefathers. Tiberias will be a central region to all the villages in the area, and perhaps when the time is right, we will realize a long-standing dream and be permitted to settle in Jerusalem."

"Amen and amen," the attendees replied.

"Ladies and gentlemen, I've appointed my son-in-law Don Joseph Nasi to manage the program of settling Tiberias. His role focuses on foreign relations with the world's Jewish communities, collecting donations, and helping refugees and escapees to immigrate to the Holy Land. Don Joseph will present a general review on carrying out the plan," I concluded my speech and sat down. Loud applause was heard around the table.

"You are fortunate, dear, generous Señora Hannah Nasi, to have been blessed and to bless us with realizing our dream of returning to the land of our forefathers," Don Joseph congratulated me.

"Much to our joy, Sultan Suleiman and his heir Saleem support the settlement, and are providing us with modest financial support. Our delegate, Efendi David Iben Arditi, is receiving an endowment of sixty apsar per day as well as eight slaves, and will receive an endowment of five thousand francs if he completes the construction of the wall of Tiberias ahead of schedule.

"Ladies and gentlemen, these days I have distributed a letter of information to all Jewish communities, inviting them to settle in Tiberias. Happily, all of the Jewish residents of the Cori community, near Rome, headed by the rabbi and doctor, Malachi Angelo Gallico, have answered my call and boarded the ship we sent to collect them. Two weeks ago, they arrived in Tiberias. A representative of the community is here with us."

"Be strengthened and blessed!" the guests shook the hand of the Cori community's representative.

"Our delegate, Efendi David Iben Arditi, please give us a brief report on the settlement efforts, and succinctly summarize what has been done up to this point."

"Thank you, *la señora*, for the faith you've placed in me. The Rosh Hashanah tractate states, '*And Tiberias is the lowest-lying of them, and from there they are destined to be redeemed.*' At the request of *La Señora* Doña Gracia Nasi, we began planting mulberry trees for silkworms, in order to establish a glorious silk industry to rival the one in Venice, planting vineyards to manufacture wine, and establishing vegetable gardens to provide fresh vegetables.

"Don Joseph Nasi had exported a flock of Merino sheep from Spain, and two families are taking the herds to pasture.

"Among the immigrants from the city of Cori, two families are expert weavers, and have brought their looms with them.

"We have hired builders. Fifteen families have left Safed and the surrounding villages and have begun to renovate the ruins of houses in the area. Seven families have already settled in Tiberias.

"We've started constructing the wall around the town, but the Arabs are disrupting our work."

The attendees promised they would help in raising donations and encourage settlement of Tiberias.

The hour grew long; the sun was now at the apex of the sky.

"Rabbi Shlomo Alkabetz," Sage Bashi addressed him. "The liturgical song you composed is sung in all our synagogues."

Rabbi Shlomo Alkabetz smiled in embarrassment. "On Friday evenings in Safed, I go out to the field with Rabbi Joseph Karo and our students to welcome the Sabbath," he replied, and began to sing:

"Come, my friend, to meet the bride, let us welcome the Sabbath."

Don Joseph Nasi, Duke of Naxos, 1566

Turkey donned mourning garb and shed many tears. Sultan Suleiman the Magnificent, ruler of the world, passed away thirteen years after I arrived in his land and eight years after the death of Hürrem Sultana. Şehzade Saleem was crowned Sultan Saleem the Second.

"I didn't attend the lavish coronation ceremony," Don Joseph told me, "because on my way from the army camp in which Suleiman died to the capital city of Istanbul, an unbelievable gesture of respect was bestowed upon me: Sultan Saleem the Second appointed me as duke of the island of Naxos and the islands surrounding it, formerly ruled by the Republic of Venice. Most of the islands' residents are Christian. I immediately set sail for the island to my opulent appointment ceremony as Duke of Naxos. I have to pay the sultan an annual tax, but all of the Duchy of Naxos's tax revenue belongs to me. The sultan has granted me a title of nobility, and affectionately calls me 'a role model for the great figures of the Jewish nation.'" Joseph straightened in his place and thrust out his chest.

"Congratulations. This is an event that calls for a major celebration."

Don Joseph, who had been born a Christian, lived secretly as a Jew, had been persecuted by Christians and sentenced to death in Venice, had now been appointed as ruler of the Duchy of Naxos, which had once been ruled by the Doge of Venice. My daughter Reyna was now the Jewish Duchess of Naxos. I smiled internally.

Joseph produced a bottle of red wine and poured it for us. "It's a double celebration. I hope the sultan's request that Charles the Ninth, king of France, repay his debt of a hundred and fifty thousand ducats, is effective, and they do indeed repay the debt. If they don't, I've proposed to the sultan that he act firmly against France." Joseph struck the table with his fist, nearly breaking the glass.

"'Firmly' is a nice word, but what do you actually have in mind?" I asked.

"I suggested to the sultan that the Ottoman Empire boycott ships sailing under a French flag, and seize their merchandise for the purpose of repaying the debt."

"Joseph, do you want to lead Turkey into war with France? Remember that in 1535, France and Turkey signed an agreement guaranteeing the rights of French merchants sailing in the waters of the Ottoman state."

Joseph laid out a copy of the agreement on the table. His eyes quickly scanned it, pausing on one of the lines. "This item explicitly states that in case of a dispute between French merchants and the subjects of the sultan, the French are not subject to a trial under Turkish jurisdiction, but merchandise may be seized!"

A week later, Joseph placed a chest full of coins on my desk, and told me that the sultan had accepted his proposal and issued an order of requisition in regard to the merchandise on ships flying the French flag on behalf of House of Mendes. After the deduction of the pasha's handling fee, we received twenty six thousand gold ducats.

"We have to continue seizing merchandise. I don't think the king of France will want to initiate a battle against the Ottomans. All of Europe is quaking before them. The French ambassador contacted us and asked that we prepare a contract for the repayment of the debt. I've prepared a contract with the French in Hebrew."

"In Hebrew?" I raised an eyebrow.

Joseph produced the contract, written in clear Hebrew letters.

"Ever since Şehzade Saleem appointed me as a representative of the Ottoman nation in Europe, most of the foreign ambassadors in Istanbul call me the head of the Jewish nation. The time has come for the French to learn to respect Jewish subjects as well."

"Joseph, don't brag. Take care not to grow too arrogant. Falling from a great height is very painful," I said.

The Inheritance Trial

La Chica and her husband Don Samuel finally arrived from Ferrara. I hugged La Chica, whose eyes filled with tears.

"It's too bad that Mama did not get the chance to come with us," she said, proudly showing me her daughter. "This is Estherika. Look how much she resembles Mama."

Samuel placed his hand on her shoulder. "*Carida*, my dear, don't cry."

"Hello, sweetie," I stroked Estherika's cheek.

"Brianda is watching over you from heaven," Reyna consoled her.

"La Chica, you and Samuel filed a claim against me in court and demanded to receive the House of Mendes's assets in Ferrara," I addressed her in a businesslike manner.

"La Chica is requesting what she deserves of the inheritance of her father, Diogo Mendes, may he rest in peace," Samuel said.

"I've also appealed to the Duke of Ferrara," Joseph said.

"You've appealed to the Duke of Ferrara? What's your connection to La Chica's claim?" I asked in amazement.

"I've appealed to Duke Ercole de Este on Reyna's behalf and requested that my wife receive her part of her father's inheritance from House of Mendes's assets in Ferrara."

"Joseph, you're being impudent! Reyna, did you have any part in this?" I turned to my daughter.

But Reyna did not answer. She was busy chasing little Hannah, who was hiding under one of the tables.

"It is my duty to take care of my wife and to make sure Reyna gets what she deserves."

"Joseph, have you no shame? Aren't you ashamed to appeal to the

Duke of Ferrara and sue me?"

"I'm not suing you; I'm claiming my wife Reyna's inheritance."

Reyna curled up in the armchair with Hannah in her lap, her eyes fixed upon Joseph.

"Joseph, I raised you and your brother Samuel in my home. You were like sons to me, and what I get in return is ingratitude."

"It's my duty to look after my wife's rights. Don't be angry—the law is on our side."

"Don't hide behind your wife. The wedding presents and a dowry of ninety thousand ducats aren't enough for you? Reyna received her inheritance money a long time ago, in the immense bribes I had to pay to get her freed from the convent and in escaping the clutches of the Inquisition and its interrogators.

"All my loved ones are coming out against me! You ate from my spoon, you slept in my home, I tended to your every need, and in return I get a lawsuit. You've conspired against me, joining La Chica and Samuel's suit behind my back, and instigating a legal claim against me. Like vultures, you're grabbing at the fortune I earned with my own ten fingers."

"Mama died from sorrow and pain," La Chica burst out.

"I'm sorry that my sister died young," I said.

"It hurt Mama that guardianship over my inheritance was taken from her, and that you were Papa's heir."

"Do you know why your father Diogo bequeathed half of his property to me, and appointed me as trustee? He knew very well that I should have inherited Francisco's fortune, and was afraid that your mother would spend all his money."

"Mama said that you agreed to Francisco's will."

"The will was sealed and locked away, and I didn't know about it."

"My wife deserves her inheritance. Why are you depriving her?" Samuel asked.

"Are you aware of the vast sums I spread around the Church and various royal courts to bribe whoever needed to be bribed and free you and Reyna from the convent? Do you have any idea how many tens of thousands of ducats I had to pay to ensure my release from jail in Venice? And all because my sister Brianda informed on me.

"And you, Joseph and Samuel," I directed a chilling gaze at them. "Have you forgotten that I saved you from the Inquisition in Portugal, that I raised you, and that all your living expenses were paid by me? It was only recently that I saved you from the gallows in Venice! What did you think, that you were freed because of the doge's goodwill? I spent a fortune bribing anyone possible in order to save you."

"We appreciate your actions, but Reyna and La Chica are entitled to their inheritance funds," Joseph said.

I looked at him in amazement. "The fortune of the Mendes company, which I increased dozens of times over, belongs to me."

"The Mendes Brothers Company is my father's company!" Beatrice La Chica's eyes sparked in rage. "And all my money is being wasted on saving *annusim*."

The old pain gripped my stomach. How dare she talk to me in that tone and oppose the rescue campaign? "You dare question my actions?" I raised my voice at her.

"With all these expenses, soon there won't be any money left," La Chica spat out.

"Aunt, we returned to Judaism. According to Torah law and the laws of Turkey, sons are eligible to inherit, rather than the wife. We've filed a claim with the Jewish court," Joseph said quietly.

"What do you want? To steal away my life's work, cheat me of my entire fortune and leave me destitute?" I burst out. "Now I ask that you get out and leave me alone,"

Mama, don't be mad at me, Reyna's eyes begged me as she left.

Throughout the night, I debated how to save my fortune. As morning neared, I decided to address a letter to the sages of Israel and ask them to rule on the two couples' suit against me.

***

After about six months, I invited Reyna, Joseph, Beatrice La Chica and Samuel in order to convey the Jewish sages' replies to them.

Outside, a thunderstorm was raging, while the atmosphere in the reception hall was tense. Hannah and Estherika stared in fright at the ships rocking in the waters of the Bosporus Strait, which had turned black in their turmoil.

"Rabbi Moshe Matarani's reply was the first to arrive," I said, handing them the long, well-reasoned missive that the rabbi had sent me.

"The Mebit, as he's known, rejected your suit and confirmed my claim that Diogo was not Francisco's partner but an employee of the company. The Mebit ruled that the prenuptial agreement is binding: 'Therefore, his widow is entitled to half the money and her daughter Reyna to half,'" I read them the summary.

The faces of all four were pale.

"Maran Rabbi Joseph Karo did not accept my claims. He does not acknowledge Catholic marriage and ruled that Francisco's will is binding."

"Well ruled!" Samuel said.

"Excellent!" Beatrice La Chica's eyes lit up.

"We were right!" Don Joseph rubbed his hands together.

"Wait. Listen to all of the answers."

"I'm sorry, Aunt Gracia, you appointed the sages and the heads of yeshivas to whom you appealed to their positions, and they are supported by you," said Don Joseph.

"Joseph, you dare question the judgment of the sages of Israel?" I focused my gaze on him.

"No, Aunt, I was just noting an important fact pertaining to the matter."

I decided not to reply and produced the third missive.

"Rabbi Samuel de Medina arrived this morning on my new merchant ship, and sent me the missive by messenger."

"And what's his decree?" asked Don Samuel.

"Rabbi de Medina ruled in my favor, saying the prenuptial agreement is binding, and I'm entitled to half the assets and half of the company's profits."

"Samuel de Medina was appointed by you as head of a yeshiva and of the Livyat Chen Synagogue in Thessaloniki, named after your Hebrew name, Hannah." Joseph raised an eyebrow.

"Joseph, respect the ruling of the rabbis!"

"And what was the ruling of Rabbi Yehoshua Tsontsin? Who also receives very generous financial support from you?" Joseph asked.

"'Thanks and glory to Doña Gracia,'" I read them the opening statement, leaving the four of them very tense.

"Rabbi Tsontsin thinks that the marriage of *annusim* in a church is valid, as it takes place between a man and his wife, and why should we mind if it happens in the presence of a priest. The will of Francisco, may he rest in peace, is invalid. His widow is entitled to half the assets and the profits, and must bear the expenses of the trial in regard to the deceased Brianda's suit concerning Diogo's inheritance."

"Well, that's something…" Beatrice La Chica said.

"Rabbi Joseph Iben Lev also ruled in my favor: 'Doña Gracia is entitled to half the assets of Francisco Mendes, considering the immense sums she had to spend in order to preserve the company fortune, so that it would not fall into the hands of '*goyim*' and in order to mend the mishaps caused by Brianda turning her in.'"

The room grew quiet.

"I think the ruling by Maran Joseph Karo, the most respected of all the sages, is the deciding one," Joseph mumbled under his mustache.

"You are the family members closest to my heart. Your suit has broken my heart, but I didn't show you how much you hurt me. Now that most of the sages have ruled in my favor, I want to put the whole affair behind us. I've provided for you all my life, and will continue to do so."

My daughter was the first to embrace me.

"Aunt Gracia, I hope you don't bear a grudge against us," Beatrice La Chica said, gathering Estherika into her lap.

"You're my family. As far as I'm concerned, this is all behind me now."

The Story of My Life

The first letters sent to me by Efendi Arditi, my delegate in Tiberias, were optimistic.

I was pleased to hear that the construction was being carried out quickly, as I had requested. The building of one thousand and five hundred meters of the wall around the city had been completed. The gates of the city and the watchtowers had been constructed. A Torah book had been brought into the synagogue. Abandoned houses had been renovated and new houses were being built, along with workshops for wool and silk. Vines had been planted, as well as seedlings of fruit and strawberry trees to manufacture wool. The Merino sheep had arrived, and two families who came from Safed were raising them. Recently, the placement of the roof in the palace I had ordered built for me on the shore of the Sea of Galilee had been celebrated.

However the latest letters evoked concern and disappointment.

Efendi Arditi reported that following speeches of incitement claiming that the revival of Tiberias was harming Muslims, the Arabs had stopped respecting the sultan's instruction to assist in the building of the town. They refused to continue working on the construction, threw stones at the Jewish workers, destroyed houses, stole the sand intended for construction and uprooted seedlings. The Arabs sent letters of complaint to the pasha in Damascus, which resulted in the pasha issuing a decree to stop all work.

***

I was overcome with fatigue. My Jewish brothers who cheered me on, calling me "the heart of her people," and the rabbis who praised me as "the bountiful lady" and "a crown of glory upon the forces of Israel," the prominent sages of Israel and my fellow Jews studying and praying at the Torah study halls and synagogues I had founded, enjoying my financial support, were not standing in line to board my ships, waiting for them at the ports to bring them to Tiberias, as I had hoped. The donation boxes to support the settlement in Tiberias, which we handed out to the Jewish communities, were only being filled slowly.

A tear fell from my eye on the cover of the thick *Biblia*, swallowed by two sailboats fighting the stormy waves depicted on the cover. The voices of Yom Tov Atias and Avraham Osheki echoed in my memory.

When they had presented me with the Ferrara Bible, the first translation of the bible into Ladino, they had dedicated it with shaky voices to:

"Her majesty the exalted lady Doña Gracia Nasi,
the noblewoman who saved our persecuted brothers,
who deserves it due to her greatness,
her acts of mercy and heroism and her love for her native land."

I leafed through the bible and remembered their words about the love of my people for the exalted lady, and the blessings of longevity they had showered upon me.

My heart was in turmoil, seeking solace. I opened Samuel Osheki's book, *Solace of the Trials of Israel*, and my eyes skimmed the dedication to Doña Gracia Nasi:

As the heart is the dwelling place of emotions in the body,
so does Doña Gracia feel the pain of her people and come to their aid.
Like our foremother Rachel weeping for her children,
Gracia weeps for the travails of her tortured brothers.
Like the prophet Miriam, she loves her people.
Like the prophet Deborah, she leads her brothers.
Like Queen Esther, she has saved her people while risking her own life.

Another tear rolled down my cheek. Despite their love for me, my people did not leave the places where they dwelled. The voice of the sages of Israel calling them to ascend to the Land of Israel and settle in Tiberias did not echo from one end of the world to the other.

***

A ray of light breaking through the cloudy sky illuminated a sailboat crossing the Bosporus and the chambers of my heart. I came to a decision to sail to the Land of Israel and settle in Tiberias. I would witness the building of the settlement and my palace on the shore of the Sea of Galilee, inquire why the work was being delayed, and advance the city's development.

As I was afraid the climate in Turkey might change, and that although Don Joseph was Saleem the Second's advisor, the sultan might prevent me from leaving Constantinople, I did not tell anyone I was planning to travel to Tiberias.

I informed my family, the House of Mendes agents and the palace staff that after the holiday of Shavuot, I was planning to leave for a restorative vacation of three months in the hot springs of the village of Bursa.

***

A variety of colors and an intoxicating aroma engulfed the palace, which was decorated with jasmine flowers and green branches. Porters had come from the great bazaar, carrying upon their bent backs fish that had just been plucked from the water, purple eggplants, lemons, small zucchinis, and peaches and pears picked early that morning. From the kitchen came the scents of pilaf with pistachios and raisins, prepared in honor of Shavuot.

Reyna raised the lid of the bowl and took a tiny grape leaf filled with rice, drizzled yogurt from the pitcher upon it, and savored it.

"Grandma Gracia, what did they make for me?" Hannah asked.

"My sweet," I opened the jar and gave her a cookie sprinkled with powdered sugar. "An almond cookie, of the kind I loved when I was little."

"Really, Grandma, you were little once?" Hannah's eyes opened wide.

I heard the voice of Samuel, practicing reading the Book of Ruth, and Estherika's melodious laughter.

In the afternoon, my family arrived, a hundred and twenty guests and friends.

We raised a glass to the success of the Jewish settlement in Tiberias.

I took the pendant off my neck.

"Hannah, my beloved granddaughter, I received this gold pendant from my mother back in the days when we still lived secretly as Jews. The pendant guarded me and reminded me that I was part of the chain of generations of the People of Israel. Take good care of it." I kissed her forehead and clasped the pendant around her neck.

**

The next day, I wrote a letter to my friend Bat-Sheva, who lived in Safed:

Constantinople
Tuesday, Sivan 9, 5329
May 24, 1569

My dear Bat-Sheva

Excitement fills me as I write these words. The time has come, and in a few weeks I'll be blessed with treading upon the soil of the Land of Israel. I'll visit the graves of Francisco and my parents in Jerusalem, and from there I'll travel to Tiberias, to witness the progress of the construction and settlement of the city.

My cousin Samuel and his wife La Chica have informed me that they have decided to visit the Land of Israel at the end of summer. They'll stay in Safed and then go to Jerusalem.

Bat-Sheva my friend, in a few minutes I will hold the gold handle of the middle drawer in the pretty wood escritoire I received from the doge of

Venice, which has been wandering along with me among my various palaces in the world.

I will extract a small key from a hidden pocket in my gown, and open the secret drawer.

I will kiss the pages of the story of my life goodbye, place the diary in the drawer, lock the best years of my life behind me, and open a new chapter in my life.

See you soon,
Your friend Doña Gracia Nasi

***

Doña Gracia passed away in 1569 in Constantinople. The site of her burial remains unknown to this day.

Acknowledgments

Ever since my childhood, when my feet walked the alleys of Istanbul where Doña Gracia Nasi once walked, and my father told me of the 'Queen of the Jews' who saved the *annusim* from the clutches of the Inquisition, her character has captured my heart.

This historical novel about Doña Gracia was written out of deep respect for a woman much admired in the history of our people, and serves as a connecting link between the past and the present. The novel connects to the experiences of my life and moves between historical reality and my artistic freedom to create a world with my imagination; writing it required me to delve into the internal world of the characters and immerse myself in the pages of history, researching the sixteenth century in Eastern and Western countries.

***

I thank the Creator of the Universe for privileging me with writing the wondrous story of Doña Gracia Nasi.

Much gratitude to my husband Shmuel Regev, may he rest in peace, who supported my creativity and encouraged me to write, but did not live to see the book.

My gratitude also goes to my dear mother, Rachel, may she rest in peace, and my father, writer Ya'akov Sika Aharoni, a fascinating storyteller, from whom I learned the art of the story.

Much appreciation to my son Omer Regev, who accompanied me through the stages of editing and illuminated me with significant insights. I'm grateful to my sharp-eyed daughter Shira Frumer for her corrections to the manuscript. A special thanks to my daughter-in-law Oshrat Regev.

With gratitude to my partner Zvika Goldberger for his support during the research and the writing.

I thank my sons, Orel Yehuda and Daniel Regev, as well as my beloved grandchildren, who were by my side throughout the writing years.

Many thanks to my brother David and my sisters Dr. Sharona Goldenberg and Dr. Shlomit Leer for their good advice. Thanks also to Anat Atzil and Dr. Tova Yedidiah.

A bundle of thanks to historian Cecil Roth for his book, *The House of Nasi*. Thanks to historian Dr. Zvi Sechayek for his research regarding leader Doña Gracia Nasi. Thanks to Prof. Joseph Hacker, a historian specializing in the Jewish people, Prof. Aviad Hacohen, dean of the Sha'arei Mishpat Academic Center, Aharon Goldes for his legal expertise, as well as to Dr. Avner Peretz and Dr. Nivi Gomel for their knowledgeable advice.

I thank my friends Miriam and Elyakim Rubinstein, Dr. Hannah Schmerling, Inbal Hameiri, Hadara Goldes, Gideon Shamir and Debbie Toren.

Thanks to Orit Zemach, Elad Zagman, Shulamit Avrahami, Ofra Cohen,Francoise Coriat, the Museum of Italian Judaism and the Union of Italian Jewish Communities. I also thank translator Yael Schonfeld Abel for her dedicated work.

Thank you, dear readers, for choosing to read the novel and take part in the tale of Doña Gracia, the woman who changed the face of the world.

Made in the USA
Middletown, DE
16 May 2020